PRAISE FOR THE NOVELS OF *USA TODAY*
BESTSELLING AUTHOR EVA LEIGH

"A classic finessed by an expert . . . generously, unabashedly sexy."
—*NEW YORK TIMES* ON
HOW THE WALLFLOWER WAS WON

"*My Fake Rake* is a feast of female empowerment, positive friendships, feel-good moments, and social satire."
—NPR

"Eva Leigh is one of my favorite authors. Her books are pure romantic delight."
—TESSA DARE, *NEW YORK TIMES* BESTSELLING AUTHOR

"Smart and sizzling . . . This risqué romp will have readers hooked."
—*PUBLISHERS WEEKLY* (STARRED REVIEW)
ON *THE GOOD GIRL'S GUIDE TO RAKES*

"Many romances explore young women fighting against the patriarchal standards that dictate their lives. This story not only does that with aplomb, but also considers the intersection of gender and class . . . Delightful dirty talk and dazzling prose contribute to making this book a standout."
—*KIRKUS REVIEWS* (STARRED REVIEW) ON
THE GOOD GIRL'S GUIDE TO RAKES

"Leigh's heroines are complex, vivid characters who seem to have stepped out of an enviable time and place, and not just because of all the satisfying, sexy romance they get to have."
—SARAH MACLEAN, *WASHINGTON POST*,
ON *FROM DUKE TILL DAWN*

"Leigh consistently crafts whip-smart heroines and irresistible heroes delivered in packages bursting with wicked wit, feminist leanings, and sex positivity . . . For any who question whether historical romance is outdated or can be feminist, look no further than Eva Leigh's work . . . [S]he delivers intoxicating yarns that bulldoze tropes and flip gender expectations on their head."

—*ENTERTAINMENT WEEKLY*

THE SEA WITCH

ALSO BY EVA LEIGH

LAST CHANCE SCOUNDRELS
The Good Girl's Guide to Rakes
How the Wallflower Was Won
A Rogue's Rules for Seduction

UNION OF THE RAKES
My Fake Rake
Would I Lie to the Duke
Waiting for a Scot Like You

LONDON UNDERGROUND
From Duke Till Dawn
Counting on a Countess
Dare to Love a Duke

WICKED QUILLS OF LONDON
Forever Your Earl
Scandal Takes the Stage
Temptations of a Wallflower

THE
SEA
WITCH

EVA LEIGH

CANARY STREET PRESS

CANARY STREET PRESS™

Recycling programs for this product may not exist in your area.

ISBN-13: 978-1-335-14376-1

The Sea Witch

Copyright © 2025 by Ami Silber

All rights reserved. No part of this book may be used or reproduced in any manner whatsoever without written permission.

Without limiting the author's and publisher's exclusive rights, any unauthorized use of this publication to train generative artificial intelligence (AI) technologies is expressly prohibited.

This is a work of fiction. Names, characters, places, and incidents are either the product of the author's imagination or are used fictitiously. Any resemblance to actual persons, living or dead, businesses, companies, events or locales is entirely coincidental.

For questions and comments about the quality of this book, please contact us at CustomerService@Harlequin.com.

TM is a trademark of Harlequin Enterprises ULC.

Canary Street Press
22 Adelaide St. West, 41st Floor
Toronto, Ontario M5H 4E3, Canada
CanaryStPress.com

Printed in U.S.A.

To Zack, always sailing beside me through this wild adventure.
Love you forever.

CONTENT WARNING

*Please note this book contains descriptions
and depictions of enslavement.*

CHAPTER ONE

Massachusetts

1719

T HE COLD THICK shadows of midnight were her only safety. Alys Tanner galloped her stolen horse into the shelter of a stand of trees. Pulling sharply on the reins, she urged her mount to stop within the white oaks' sanctuary. The trees shifted and rustled with the wind, whispering sullenly to themselves, resenting her presence. These woods had protected Alys her whole life, given her a haven when she needed to hide. Yet now she wasn't welcome, a fugitive, even as she hoped the oaks' shadows hid her.

She closed her eyes and concentrated, reaching out to the night, drawing on its darkness. Though she was half a mile from the ocean, the water was near enough, strengthening the power within her so the night thickened into a briny scented cloak that hid her and her horse.

Beneath her, the anxious animal stepped sideways. It tossed its head, making the hardware of its bridle jingle. She leaned forward as best she could with her skirts wound around her legs to ride astride, and stroked the horse's damp neck in an attempt to soothe it.

The beast wasn't familiar with magic. In Norham, and small villages up and down the Colonies' coast, power such as Alys's was always ruthlessly stamped out the moment it appeared. Any boy who showed magical aptitude went to be educated at the academies and make his fortune in the larger towns. Any girl who failed to hide her supernatural ability was killed.

She tried to quiet the horse, yet there was no one to soothe her own rattling nerves.

Hoofbeats thundered on the road and the glow of torches streaked past.

She held her breath as the mounted group of pursuers drew to a halt. They gathered in a circle in the middle of the road, not thirty feet from her. Her mantle of magic-summoned shadows clung to her and her horse. For now.

A dozen men massed, all of them as known to her as her own blood kin. Some of them *were* her blood kin. They wore cloaks over their rough fishermen's clothing, the hoods pulled up and low, but she recognized them just the same.

"Her house is empty." The glow of torchlight shone on Lawrence Charles's face, his expression twisted by anger and the dancing flame.

"You should have waited," Constable John Vale protested.

"The dresser drawers were on the floor, clothes were scattered."

"How did she know we were coming for her?" Vale growled. "Her magic?"

"How would I know?"

"You could've warned her. Or maybe she *is* there, and you're lying."

"Alys may be my cousin," Lawrence threw back, "but there's as much love between us as two stones. 'Struth, I can well believe she's a witch in league with the devil. Since she was in leading strings, she had an uncanny way about her. The way she spoke to the sea, the fire in her eyes whenever the moon was full. And then when her husband died—"

"When she *murdered* him," Quinton Brown said grimly.

THE SEA WITCH

"Used her magic to strike him down upon the deck of his own boat so she could take the vessel for herself."

The men muttered prayers.

It wasn't true. Samuel Tanner had possessed a weak heart, which proved to be his doom. Yet if these men believed Alys had been the agent of his death, her fate was cast.

"It's in her blood," Vale grumbled. "That sister of hers, Ellen—"

"Keep that woman's name from your lips," Davy Smythe said quickly. "The sister may be dead, but witches can have power from beyond the grave. In Virginia, they burned one at the stake. With her last breath, she cursed her executioners, and three days later, those that brought her to the stake and lit the flames all died of putrid fevers. Speak no more of Alys Tanner's sister."

Hot tears burned Alys's eyes, and she blinked them back.

"The sooner Alys is at the end of a noose," Lawrence vowed, "the happier I'll be."

"The happier *any* of us will be," Quinton snapped. "The road to the east past the village is cut off to her."

"Dougan and the others have the roads out of Norham watched," Vale said, confident. "None of Alys Tanner's witches will get far."

"Unless they use their infernal magic to take to the skies," Quinton pointed out, and the men cast their fearful gazes up to the dark night above.

Despite her fear, Alys nearly laughed. How powerful did they think her to be? She was still learning the limits of her magic, so long suppressed. Flight was one art she'd yet to attempt.

"Head to the crossroads. We'll block her escape routes to the north and south." Lawrence kicked his horse, as did the others, and with the pounding of dozens of hooves, they were off on the hunt.

Alys's hands tightened on the reins.

Damn them all.

The glare of torchlight was swallowed by the trees along the road. Her eyes adjusted to the night, making sense once more out of shadows, before she urged her horse into a gallop. The world was huge and dark around her, sinister where once she'd been most alive and herself in the hours between midnight and dawn.

She headed back to the village from where the men had ridden. Alys slowed the horse as she neared a stone house at the edge of the settlement.

A man armed with a musket stood sentry outside the front door. He peered sharply into the shadows, eager to make his name as a hero.

Late autumn mists muffled sound, and she called upon their dampening ability to deaden the noise of her horse's hooves upon the ground. In muslin tatters, the fog silently crept forward. The guard outside the house shifted from foot to foot, looking nervously around as the fog slid over the terrain and surrounded the cottage, turning the world hazy and indistinct.

He remained at his post, but held his musket closer, as if more for comfort than protection.

The longer Alys waited, the more the noose tightened around her neck. Once again, she held her breath as she guided the animal around the back of the house. There was no one standing guard back here, and the windows were all dark.

She dismounted and loosely tied the horse's reins to a birch standing white and ghostly beside the house. The animal shifted restlessly and she rubbed its muzzle to calm it, but the beast was unused to being abroad at this hour, and with an unfamiliar rider.

Not merely any rider. A witch.

With arms grown strong from climbing masts and fastening rigging, Alys pulled herself up the tree, until she reached a second story window and peered through it.

THE SEA WITCH

Light from the moon slid into the chamber, revealing the rough-hewn wooden floor, a washstand, and two narrow beds.

Alys tapped on the glass. Faintly at first, and then a little louder. Two figures clad in pale nightgowns came to the window, which swung open with a squeak. Alys winced at the sound.

Cecily's and Polly Gower's astonished faces appeared. Both had plaited their hair for sleep, though Cecily's braid was flaxen and Polly's braid was black. In the moonlight, Cecily's fair cheeks glowed ghostly white, while Polly's bronze skin shone deeply.

Polly had been forcibly taken from her Pawtucket family as a small girl and "adopted" by Reverend and Mrs. Gower. The Reverend liked to claim he treated Polly as his own daughter, insisting she and Cecily were sisters in every capacity, but Cecily didn't have to scrub the chicken coop, or draw bucket after bucket of water for the household's baths, or a hundred other tasks Polly was made to do.

Before the women could speak, Alys whispered, "Whatever's most precious to you, grab that, and dress warmly. Quickly, now."

Cecily said, "What—"

"Talk softly," Alys hissed. "Henry Dales stands guard outside your front door, waiting for his comrades to join him and seize us." At the Gower girls' questioning looks, Alys explained, "You, me, Susannah, the others. I overheard men talking by the courthouse. We're to be arrested and charged with witchcraft."

The girls' eyes widened.

Alys drew in a shuddering breath. "They've made charges against you and me and the rest, and they're coming for us tonight."

"Will they—" Cecily's hand went to her neck.

"A trial is too much bother for them. We won't live past sunrise."

"We can take the southern road to Gloucester," Polly said.

Alys pressed her lips into a line. "The roads out of the village are watched."

"Then there's no way to freedom." Cecily's words were despairing.

"There's *always* a way to freedom." Voice firm with conviction, Alys instructed, "Dress quickly, take only what you must. The men are at the crossroads, there's no way out to the north and south. Sentinels are stationed at our houses. Use the forest and the fields and gather the others. I'll summon as many shadows as I can for you. Meet me at the docks in quarter of an hour. Come now, Ellen."

A pained silence fell.

Alys closed her eyes, but it never stopped the images from flooding through her mind, and she would never, *never* forget the sound of the tree limb creaking from the weight of her sister Ellen's lifeless form . . .

"Hurry, girls," she said.

The other women nodded.

"Good lasses," Alys said. "Spines stronger than any mainmast—that's what you've got."

Polly gave her a brief smile. "With you as our example."

"The sun will be up too soon. Grab Susannah and Jane and Josephine and Faith. I'll gather the others. Find me at the docks."

"Yes, Alys."

Cecily and Polly moved toward the clothes press, but Cecily stopped and moved back to the window. She grabbed Alys's wrist.

Pride swelled in Alys's chest to feel the tightness of Cecily's grip, power that was acquired from hauling ropes and manning the tiller. Only six months earlier, Cecily had possessed the soft hands that belonged to a reverend's daughter, but they were rougher now, callused and strong. Bright currents of magical energy coursed through her fingertips, traveling into Alys's skin, strengthening her own power. Surging through them both with life.

"I'm not sorry," Cecily said, fierce.

THE SEA WITCH

"Not for a moment," Polly added as she stuffed clothing into a satchel.

"Me, either," Alys answered.

She slipped free from Cecily's hold and climbed down the tree. Quickly, she mounted up before leading her horse back onto the road, careful to stay within the shadows and mists she'd fashioned so the sentry outside the reverend's house wouldn't notice her. When she was in the clear, she pressed on toward the east end of the village. Here, amongst the austere stone cottages with faces as dour as the people of Norham, more of the witches lived. Women whose power was nurtured and strengthened by the sea.

She could smell it here, the brine of the water, heavy in her lungs yet lifting her up.

Though she put no faith in Sunday sermons, Alys prayed to any listening deity that the women she'd taught had the courage to see this through to the end. It was only going to get harder from here.

TWELVE WOMEN WAITED in the shadows by the harbor. Not all of them possessed magic, but they each held power of one form or another. The women looked to Alys, fear in their faces, their postures tense but ready.

Closer to the sea, more magical power flowed into Alys. It lapped against the pilings with welcome murmurs, filling her with energy, like the rush of catching a gust of wind in the sails, and it pushed back against the terror that wanted to consume her.

Cecily and Polly were there. With them was Susannah, who was technically a freedwoman but treated as an unpaid servant by Josiah and Mary Lawford. Also amongst their band of escapees was Jane, the wife of the town bully, as well as eight more, women who had sought something for themselves alone.

Alys had trained them to sail, helped some to nurture their magic, but the next step was into the unknown.

In their hands, they held carpet bags, battered and worn satchels, or blankets hastily tied into bundles, holding the contents of their lives. Alys had left behind the cedar chest she had packed when she'd moved from her childhood home into Samuel's house, too heavy and clumsy to take with her in the heat of flight. Instead, she'd grabbed a quilt her mother had sewn and given to her when she'd first bled, and used it to hold only the most basic of needs. Shifts, stockings, a seashell that Ellen had given her, and a compass that had once been Samuel's, but she'd given to herself after his death.

Nothing else in his house held meaning or value for her. Everything else was tainted by shame and drudgery.

"There must be a plan." Without fail, Polly thought ahead, and Alys was grateful for her clear-eyed perspective.

"There's only one way out of here to safety," Alys answered. To muffle their voices, she summoned a mist, cool and damp.

She looked behind her, to the dock, where the tied fishing boats bobbed on the swells of the water, including her own boat. It was a small vessel, barely able to hold a crew more than four in number. A stab of pain lanced through her to think of leaving the boat behind. Humble though it was, the boat had given her the gift of the sea, and awakened the power that had simmered in her veins. It was more her parent than her mother or her father had ever been.

"Take a fishing boat?" Jane asked. "We can sail it down to Delaware or Maryland. Somewhere far away."

"I've a bigger prize in mind."

Alys pointed to a two-masted brigantine, its foremast square-sailed and its mainsail gaff-rigged, anchored at the end of the dock. Norham seldom saw ships of that size, since merchantmen usually sailed into Portsmouth or Boston, but as fortune had it, this brigantine had docked earlier in the day to unload its cargo of British pewter and furniture to be sold around the Cape.

THE SEA WITCH 9

Some fanciful boatwright had carved and gilded leaves around the bow and at the railing of the quarterdeck. The figurehead was a buxom woman in flowing robes, her hair streaming across her shoulders.

"The biggest vessel we've sailed is a trawler," Cecily said.

"We'll learn the way of it," Alys answered. "Slow and cautious earns us nooses around our necks."

Anxious murmurs rose up from the women.

"They'll soon discover all of us gone," Alys continued. "We have to get aboard and set sail now."

Susannah exclaimed, "They won't simply *let* us take the ship. Not without at least raising the alarm and bringing the whole town down on us."

Everyone turned to regard the brigantine, where a lantern drifted back and forth across the upper deck, and another figure stood at the head of the lowered gangplank.

"Two men," Jane said acidly. "A trusting lot, to keep so few on watch."

"This isn't Boston or Charleston." Alys studied the ship. "Not much fear of piracy here in Norham. Yet we'll need surprise and silence—and I've got a plan to give us both. Gather close and listen."

There were gasps and more uneasy murmurs as she explained her scheme, yet Polly and Cecily nodded as Alys detailed what would be required. Slowly, the other women added their own nods.

"We're in agreement, then?" Alys looked at each of them in turn, making certain she took everyone's opinion into consideration. "No going back after this. Either we succeed, or this is the end of our freedom—and our lives."

A moment's silence fell, followed by a whispered chorus of "Aye."

"We trust you, Alys," Cecily said, pinning up her hair.

10   EVA LEIGH

Alys breathed in sharply. "That might not be wise. You trusted me when you asked me to teach you to sail, and behold, we're about to become fugitives."

"Better fugitives than anyone's forced peon." Polly's mouth twisted. "They tell us it's for our own good, but they say it with their boots on our necks."

"Or their fists in our faces." Jane touched her jaw.

Red glittering sparks curled out from Polly's and Jane's chests. Sparking magic rose up in the other women, sharp and fiery-hued from their anger, casting long dancing shadows against the walls of the dock's warehouses.

"Time for our fury later," Alys said tersely. "Right now, we've got to dim our light. Keep unwanted eyes off us."

The magic faded, leaving them in the darkness of the wharf.

"We won't be dim for much longer," Alys assured them. "Those swimming with me, our skirts have to come off."

A moment later, the group broke apart. Without long skirts hampering their movements, Alys and five others slunk to the dock's edge before slipping into the water. The cold stole her breath, but the welcome embrace of the sea gave it back. It was a homecoming after the fear and sharp edges of fleeing the village.

She gave one quick wave to those remaining in the shadows ashore.

Alys and her allies softly paddled around the ship's hull. Her movements were hindered by the coil of rope she'd draped around her arm and concentrating on not dropping the knife held between her teeth. Yet, she'd started swimming when she was a small girl splashing in quiet marshy inlets, pretending to be a mermaid. Even then, being near the water had gathered currents of gleaming energy around her legs—until her mother had slapped her face, saying that no one could ever, *ever* see Alys in the water, if that kind of magic happened when she swam.

THE SEA WITCH 11

But the warning wasn't enough. Tonight, Alys was condemned as a witch. Anger kept her from being paralyzed by fear as she swam as quietly as possible.

Moving through the water, more and more power surged into her body, brought forward by seawater and all the living beings that dwelled in its depths. Just as they had when she'd been a girl, glimmers formed around her body as she swam, currents of stars within the water. She swam faster, and kept to the far side of the ship away from the night watch.

The brigantine creaked and groaned as it slept at anchor. It was a beauty of a vessel, well-maintained and, from the looks of things, recently careened so that all the barnacles and seaweed had been cleaned from the ship's bottom. She would be a lovely thing to command and take far across the sea, to places Alys had only dreamt of.

If Alys lived. Now, she set her mind and muscles to climbing up the ship's starboard side, which was hidden in darkness. Like spiders, she and the others scaled upward, finding handholds where they could to haul themselves higher and higher, until they all reached the gunwale at the top of the hull.

Holding tightly as her heart pounded in her ears, careful to keep from being spotted by the watch, she peered over the rail. She pulled more magic from the night to swath her and the other women in darkness, hiding them.

A man in the loose clothing of a merchant seaman slowly paced the length of the upper deck, holding aloft a horn lantern, while a second watch stood at the top of the gangplank. Though their faces were indifferent, ignoring the sentries' threat would be a fatal mistake.

"Avast," the one stationed by the gangplank said as steps sounded on the wooden board. "Who goes there?"

"Only a concerned villager," Cecily answered, coming up the ramp. Light from the horn lantern gleamed on her freckled pretty face as she climbed the gangplank. She smiled winningly as she nodded toward the covered basket on her arm. "A long and hungry night you have of it, lads, so I've brought you bread and cheese from my own larder."

As she spoke, the other sentry neared her, his expression both cautious and curious.

"Cap'n wouldn't like us having grub when we should be keeping watch," the first man said.

Cecily laughed with the same laugh Alys had heard her use when accompanying her father on visits around the parish. "As if there's harm in taking a small bite. I'd wager you'll be sharper with a morsel of food in your bellies. Come, I've good cheddar and bread made with the whitest and finest of flours."

While Cecily chattered, Alys and the other women noiselessly pulled themselves over the gunwale and onto the upper deck. They slunk toward the watchmen, whose backs were turned and were far too absorbed in a winsome local girl to notice half a dozen wet, anxious, but angry women creeping toward them, leaving gleaming wet footprints upon the planks.

"Here," Cecily said brightly. She opened the basket. "Have a look for yourself."

The two men peered into the wicker container.

"We can't eat ladies' shoes and underwear," one of the men complained.

Alys moved. She pressed herself tight to the sentry's back as she held her knife to his throat. Beside her, Jane did the same to the other watchman. Both men stiffened.

"Not a sound," Alys hissed. "Or I'll give you a new way to sing."

My God—was she truly saying such a thing? Threatening a man's *life*? He didn't know that spilling his blood was the very last thing she'd ever do, but the more he believed it, the better her and the others' chances were of making it out of Norham alive.

"How many else on this ship?" Alys demanded.

THE SEA WITCH

"Just me an' Bleeker," the sentry stammered. "The rest went ashore."

"Then there's none to notice if you doze." She pulled the dark blue energy of a tranquil summer night, and swirled it around the men. It spun and eddied like ink in water. The sentries' eyes rolled back before they slumped to the deck—asleep.

"Stifle and bind them," Alys ordered. "Douse their lanterns."

Immediately, the other women took the ropes she and Jane had brought and trussed up the two unconscious men. The months of learning how to tie knots served them well now as they bound the sentries. While they were being tied, gags were stuffed into the men's mouths, and their lanterns were extinguished to plunge the deck of the ship into darkness.

As soon as the men were bound, the rest of the women in their group hefted the sleeping sentries and carried them down the gangplank and onto the dock, stowing them behind a stack of empty lobster traps.

The watchmen wouldn't be discovered until Alys and everyone else were long gone—hopefully.

She hissed, "Away aloft," and gave the other women instructions as they readied the ship to sail. It was hasty, fumbling work. With so few in their number compared to what likely had to be a crew of forty, there was much to do. Yet no one complained and no one questioned their orders.

Pausing in the middle of climbing the rigging, Alys looked toward the dock, and beyond it, the village, gray, stiff shouldered, and somber. A throb resounded in her chest, but it was too light and winging to be sorrow.

She'd married Samuel Tanner after a short courtship, which hadn't been her choice.

Samuel hadn't liked her spending time with Ellen.

"*It's my love for you,*" Samuel had often said. "*It makes me clamor for all your time. I want every piece of your attention, my wife.*"

14   EVA LEIGH

"*Surely, I can see Ellen,*" Alys would protest.

"*My love's so consuming,*" he'd answer, always gripping her tightly like he'd squeeze the very breath from her body. "*It's an agony to share you with anyone. Besides, it's your safety I fear for. That . . . that magic you and your sister use, it'll get you both killed. Especially if anyone sees you.*"

So, the moments between visits with her sister had been too few. And Alys had barely learned the limits and potential of her magical power. All for love.

Ellen was gone now, ripped away from this life by brutal hands, and Alys would leave no one behind in Norham.

She turned her face toward the harbor, and the open sea that stretched into forever. It smelled of salt and wind and freedom and *magic*, all the things she'd been refused, first as Alys Cabot, later as Mrs. Tanner.

If Alys hadn't gone to sea on her own, fishing the steel-hued waters beyond Cape Ann in the boat Samuel had left her, she would've had nothing for herself. There was a handful of cousins, but beyond that, Alys had no family of her own. Not anymore.

Everyone had expected her to sell the boat, move into Samuel's parents' cramped house, and become a drudge to those sour-faced and bitter-tempered pair of haddocks who'd always hated her and spoke loudly about the evil of witches.

She'd rather drown in brimstone than let the Tanners force her to hide her gift, as their son had done. There was only so long a person could permit themselves to be throttled before they had to pry the fingers from their throat.

The sea carried the scent of all the things denied to the women of Norham. Men were so afraid of the females and their power, they were willing to kill them.

"Alys." Susannah pointed toward the village. Light from torches appeared, weaving through the buildings as they headed toward the docks. The arresting party had discovered that the witches were gone and watching the roads would yield no captures.

THE SEA WITCH   15

Fire burned in her gut and seethed through her limbs as she slid down from the rigging to stand on the deck.

"Everything been made ready?" she asked, as the women gathered around her.

"Aye," they answered.

Alys gazed at the twelve of them, her sailors. "There *are* thirteen of us. A true coven." After the women nodded grimly, she said, "Susannah, loosen the rope from the bollard, and get back aboard quick as you can, before we pull out too far from the dock."

"Aye, captain," Susannah said.

Alys started. "I'm no captain. Any one of us could answer to that title."

"There's no leader in all this but you," Polly pointed out. "Teaching us to sail. Proving our magic was nothing to hide or fear. Those in favor of Alys as captain, show of hands."

Twelve hands went into the air.

Alys took a deep breath. All she could do was her best—but would it be enough?

"Now," she said, humility and duty pulsing through her, "we shove off."

A whispered chorus of "Aye" followed. The rope tying them to the quay was undone.

With the foresails now billowing with the wind, ripe with promise, the ship moved away from the dock. Away from the village, and the only life Alys had ever known. A confining life, one that clipped her and the other women's wings. She choked, remembering every sneer, every critical glare, every suspicious glance.

And Ellen, beautiful, dreamy Ellen, who refused to hide the fact that she could speak with birds and whispered incantations to the forest. Taken from Alys, stolen from the world.

The horizon paled with the approach of dawn. Faintly, the sound of men's angry voices rose up and grew louder. At the far end of the quay, a line of torches appeared. Faces twisted with fury glowed in the firelight. These were the true faces of the men of Norham, incensed and righteous and fearful.

Men clambered into their boats in pursuit. They carried muskets and sharp loading hooks.

"It's death if they reach us," Alys said tightly.

Jane looked toward one of the guns mounted at the gunwale.

"No time to learn its ways," Alys answered. "We use the very thing they want to destroy."

Swallowing down her uncertainty, Alys raised her hands. She'd no idea where to begin, but recalled the punishing hurricanes that slammed into the village late in the summer. Sea magic swirled around her fingers, alive and surging with strength.

Wordlessly, the women with magic collected at the gunwale, their own power gathering. Summoning the energy of the seething sea.

"Now or never, witches," Alys commanded. "The sea serves as our warrior."

The women pushed their hands toward the water. Alys held her breath and then—

Waves exploded with force. They rose upward into a wall that towered twenty feet high before rushing toward the pier.

The water slammed through the largest boat, smashing into the quay itself. Sounds of splintering wood and men's screams filled the early morning as waves crashed against the harbor.

Alys's crew stood in mute shock as they saw what they'd done. The dock was badly damaged, listing and staggering like a drunkard, while the vessels had become heaps of driftwood bobbing on the churning waves. Those men that had tried to sail after them were being dragged back onto dry land by other villagers.

Norham's wharf was left in ruins.

The only boat undamaged was Samuel's vessel. Instinct had Alys reach for the line fastening it to the remainder of the pier.

THE SEA WITCH   17

A streak of lightning shot from her hand, severing the rope. The line burned and frayed, and the boat bobbed away from the dock, until it sailed on its own, without a crew, off to seek an unknown horizon.

She stared down at her hand. Never before had she been able to harness lightning. She curled her fingers into her palm, cradling this new power.

The pier grew smaller with the tide in their favor, and the brigantine sailed out to sea, putting the harbor and all it held behind them. Alys's legs shook beneath her, and it appeared that her friends with magical ability were just as drained after they'd summoned the water.

There were limits, it seemed, to their powers.

A few of the women gave unsteady smiles, while the witches sagged against the gunwale, drained.

"I ask one more thing of you, my lasses, and that's to rally," Alys said, as much for herself as her crew. "We've much open sea ahead of us."

Even as she spoke, the women were already in action, well-taught by their previous instruction.

"Where to, Cap'n?" Polly asked.

"What's next?" Susannah added.

Only after Samuel's death did she learn what it was like to make a choice for herself. And now, these women asked her to make the most monumental choice of all their lives.

She'd led them this far, and they'd survived. Now they were sailing to freedom, because *she* had led them.

The world was a big place, far bigger than she could ever fully know. But there was one place she'd heard sailors speak of in eager and excited voices.

"It's said that witches aren't hunted in the Caribbean," Alys suggested. "They say it's a place of limitless freedom, where anyone can make themselves into someone entirely new. What say you, ladies?"

"The Caribbean," came the response from her crew.

Alys took the wheel and pointed them south.

Samuel's boat continued to move out to open water, heading on its own adventures. They were parting company, her and the boat. Old lives exchanged for new ones.

Finally, she lost sight of the small vessel.

Alys turned toward the horizon. It was as wide as dreams, and terrifying.

CHAPTER TWO

Isle of St. Gertrude
One year later

"I<small>F YE BE</small> hearin' this," the silver-haired, one-eyed man read as he stood atop a table, "it do mean that I, Little George Partridge, be dead."

Mutters and murmurs filled the taproom of the Wig and Merkin, teeming with pirates from every corner of the Caribbean that had gathered by specific request to hear the final message of one of the sea's most notorious buccaneers.

Alys eased her way into the crowded room, slipping between benches and tables, with countless suspicious eyes fastened on her.

It was a ramshackle tavern crouched in the center of town. The walls of the pub's central taproom were streaked with smoke from thousands of pipes. A spray of rust-colored droplets near the bar was the result of John Clay ill-advisedly starting a fight with the notorious mage Luca Pasquale. They said it took three whole weeks before the smell disappeared, but even then, the stench was mostly covered up by new aromas.

Scarred wooden tables were scattered through the room, though the prized seats were the settles shoved against the walls. The tall-backed benches ensured that no one could come up behind you and slit your throat or cast a blood seeping curse without you being able to throw a shielding spell. Tonight, though, every seat in the Wig and Merkin was full, men jostling for position so they could take part in the evening's . . . well, *party* wasn't quite the right word, but wakes weren't often held in the tavern. Death was a part of life in the Caribbean, as much as heat or hurricanes or red-streaked sunsets.

"What are *you* doing here, Tanner?" A weather-beaten man looked at Alys with distrust. Fontaine was missing most of his left ear, but his right ear was adorned with a golden ring.

"*Captain* Tanner. And you weren't the only one to be summoned here tonight."

Fontaine grumbled, "Only been a year since your ship and your infernal witch magic appeared in these waters. Not long enough to say you're pirates."

"We've made use of that year. No need to be idle when there's so much plunder to be grabbed—and if my company and I raid ships for loot, that qualifies us as pirates."

"Witches as buccaneers, instead of brewing love potions," he muttered to the mustached man sitting next to him. "I wouldn't believe such a yarn if someone told it."

"You'd be surprised what witches can do," Alys threw in, "given the same chances as mages."

A bald man dressed in crimson from head to toe moved through the tavern. Like all mages, he wore an embroidered black sash, indicating that he'd been educated and trained at an academy. He waved his hands over candles and lamps scattered atop tables. With each flick of his fingers, the wicks glowed to life, flames appearing to bring further light to the taproom. The candles staked onto the overhead wheel-shaped wooden chandelier blazed, and the already hot taproom turned sweltering.

No one blinked or looked skeptically at the mage. But they *did* glare in Alys's direction.

A sandy-haired, bearded man glowered at her. "Shouldn't even *be* here," the pirate grumbled. "Witches an' ships be bad luck."

"We're in a tavern, Culver," Alys pointed out mildly.

THE SEA WITCH

He scowled. "You an' that brigantine full o' witches, doin' things only men and mages should do. They talk about ye from Maracaibo to St. Augustine. Ain't right."

"We signed articles like every other pirate ship." She glanced toward a buccaneer seated at one of the tables, and the shaggy man immediately scuttled away, leaving her to sit at the now empty table. "Even with our magic, we obey the rules of the sea. Unlike you, Culver, we don't double-cross anyone."

Culver's hand went to the handle of his cutlass. Alys didn't touch her own weapon. Instead, she snapped her fingers.

All at once, every light in the tavern went out. Curses and swears rose up from the assembled pirates.

They fell silent when a single flame wreathed Alys's fingertip. All eyes were on her as she touched the fire to the wick of a candle at her table. Smoke curled up from the wick, and she blew on it. The smoke formed into a sea serpent. At another gust of air from Alys's lips, the creature writhed and dove about the room, until it exited through an open window.

Stasia, her second in command, would've rolled her eyes at Alys's theatrics. Yet a point had to be made, and, judging by the silence that now ruled over the tavern, Alys had done just that.

Just in case, she kept her other hand loose and ready near her cutlass. It had seen her through some rough and vicious fights. For a woman who, one year ago, never so much as touched a blade longer than four inches to clean and gut fish, she'd quickly taken to the curved and deadly sword. Now it was her trusted companion, as much as her brace of pistols. And the spells that danced at her fingertips, glittering with potential.

When it comes to those that take their living from the sea, her second in command had instructed Alys and her company, *trust nothing and no one. Stay armed and alert—with steel,* and *with sorcery.*

A moment passed, and then the red-clad mage moved through the tavern once more, relighting the candles and lamps and chandelier that Alys had extinguished.

22   EVA LEIGH

"'Tis a solemn occasion," Culver mumbled. "Little George wouldn't want a fight."

"Of *course*, Little George would want a fight," Alys said. "And I'll be happy to give him, or anyone, a brawl."

"Ain't fair for a witch to use magic in a fight," Culver muttered. "'Tis only fit for mages."

"By all means, let's soothe your worries." Alys held up her hand, where a flame still danced on the tip of her finger. With a wave, the fire winked out. "I'll still beat you from Bermuda to the Bay of Honduras, even without my magic." She cupped the pommel of her cutlass.

Culver glanced from her hand on her sword, and then to the steely determination in her eyes. Slowly, his own scarred hand moved from his weapon.

"Ay, that's the way of it."

Alys turned toward Rodrigo Flores, sitting nearby. The pirate gave her a smile, revealing several golden teeth.

Flores continued, "If you, Culver, a man with the brainpower of driftwood, have a right to be here, then so does Capitana Tanner, who's vastly more intelligent, and twice the swordsman you'll ever be."

Culver muttered but didn't argue.

Alys sent Flores a quick nod of gratitude. Though most pirates tended toward suspicion, there were a handful who welcomed her into their ranks.

She turned to face the front of the room, where Little George's final letter was being read. She kept her awareness on Culver, in case he decided to slip a dagger between her ribs. Or if he might give the mage a nod, and she'd be suffocated with a smothering spell. Here in the lawless Caribbean, anything was possible, and she had learned to stay nimble as a wheeling gull to keep herself and her company safe.

The fact that now over half her crew was comprised of witches made them even more hunted by militias and the Royal

THE SEA WITCH

Navy. She and her company had come to the Caribbean to find freedom, and they had. To a point. There was nowhere safe.

Nowhere, except on the deck of the now named *Sea Witch* surrounded by her crew.

"If I be lucky," the one-eyed seaman continued to read from the creased letter in his hand, "I'll go to me Maker as I lay in the arms of a sweet and willing lass, but 'tis most likely that foul murder has sent me speedin' to Hell, as I justly deserve."

No one could argue that Little George Partridge had earned his reputation through acts of unequaled violence—though he always showed exceptional kindness toward animals, particularly cats. Alys had crossed paths with Little George only a handful of times, but when she received word that she was summoned to this tavern on this lawless island to hold a wake for the departed pirate, she made sail for St. Gertrude.

Little George wouldn't request a simple wake. There had to be more to this gathering than that.

"For now," the one-eyed man went on, reading aloud, hefting a sack of coins, "I command all ye gathered to drink a toast to me memory, paid for by none other than Little George Partridge."

A resounding cheer went up in the tavern as the coin was thrown to the landlord, who began filling tankards as fast as he could, which were handed out by a trio of harried barmaids.

As she sipped spiced rum from a dented pewter mug, Alys took measure of who else she was drinking with. Every wanted pirate captain that sailed the blue waters of the Caribbean was in the Wig and Merkin. She recognized the majority of the men that filled the smoke-stained taproom. These were the most feared sailors known, infamous buccaneers, some missing body parts and most completely lacking morals. They were men who had come to these waters from every corner of the globe to seize a fortune in blood-soaked gold and treasure. Young men barely able to shave, craggy-faced veterans, and everything in between. Mages, too, flocked to the Caribbean, harnessing their academy-trained magical abilities to grab their share of wealth when it was well known that the Royal Navy and merchants paid far less for enchantments, curses, and spells.

A wicked collection of men, like an iron coffer filled with rotten meat. Here in the tavern, they carefully kept from meeting Alys's gaze, and others glared with mistrust.

Some, though, were like Flores. Not precisely moral nor law-abiding, but they had a form of honor, and were willing to share the seas with a ship crewed entirely by women. They gave her a polite nod. Even these small gestures showed her more respect than any of the men back in Norham.

She didn't finish her rum. Unlike the other pirates, she hadn't the luxury of indulging in drink here. A witch pirate surrounded by hostile buccaneers couldn't be at ease. Still, better a wary pirate with magic than a soul-crushed fisherman's wife forced to keep her power hidden.

Pretending to drink more of her rum, she stood and ambled around the smoke-filled tavern, purposefully making her steps seem aimless when they were far from that.

Why did Little George want his wake to be held here, on this island, in this tavern? His viciousness was only matched by his cunning, so there had to be a reason that the old barnacle had picked the Wig and Merkin.

Something was here, something that Little George had hidden.

"I've another letter," the one-eyed pirate said, getting back up onto a table. He waved a square of wax-sealed paper over his head. "Supposed to read it once the first round is drunk."

"Is it extra coin for more rum?" someone shouted, followed by raucous laughter.

"Down to the depths with ye, Van der Meer," the one-eyed man yelled back.

Alys listened to the sniping as she continued her reconnaissance of the tavern. The Wig and Merkin was a two-story structure, with a staircase leading up to a catwalk, and branching off the

THE SEA WITCH

25

catwalk were rooms, likely where seafarers would take their pleasure with lovers for hire. It was much like any tavern at any number of lawless pirate-infested towns scattered across the Caribbean. Nothing special about it.

At the top of the stairs, though, was a window. Candlelight glinted on the glass.

She straightened and, as discreetly as possible, began to climb the staircase. Windows in and of themselves weren't so out of the ordinary. They were needed to let in breezes that might cool down the tropical atmosphere that collected heavily indoors, yet the fact that this window held expensive *glass* was unusual. Especially considering that all the other windows were simply open to the elements.

As she eased her way up each step, the one-eyed man continued to read.

"Before the Brethren of the Coast," he said, "I make my full confession to unburden me heavy heart. I been colludin' with Admiral Strickland of the British Navy, using me own secret abilities as a mage. 'Twas I who helped him create the magic to bind a leviathan to the navy's will, to help him build up the Crown's power here in the Caribbean. Power used to fight and destroy pirates."

Alys paused in her climb as the gathered crowd muttered in angry shock. Little George had been cunning to the last. Not only was he actually a mage, but he'd worked with the enemy to use magic against his own buccaneer comrades.

Every pirate lived in terror of the navy's leviathan. It accompanied the naval flagship, and was unbeatable in combat. Dozens of pirate ships had been destroyed by the beast. Alys and the *Sea Witch* had fortunately never encountered the British man-o'-war and the leviathan. Thank the tides for that. But no thanks to Little George for creating the problem in the first place. It was only a matter of time before she and her crew found themselves facing the naval flagship and the creature they had enslaved, and when that happened, may all the goddesses of the sea protect her and the *Sea Witch*.

Damn Little George.

Yet, it was impossible to be disappointed in someone who had been a devious and underhanded bastard to all who knew him. There wasn't a man in the tavern who hadn't in some way been deceived by Little George.

When Alys had met him, he'd stared at her as if conniving some way to slip poison into her rum. Considering that he was also secretly a mage, it was a damned shock that he hadn't snuck a potion into her drink that could've turned her into a crab. Either she'd been beneath his regard, or—and this was what she suspected—he had some hidden plan for her. One that brought her here tonight, amongst pirates who had sailed these waters for far longer than she had.

"If I be dead," the letter went on, "know ye that me murderers serve the king, and I be surely double-crossed. But I see the blade comin' for me throat, and so I've made a fail-safe to be used against me betrayers. This fail-safe do sever the magic that tethers the leviathan to the navy, freein' the beast."

More growls sounded from the crowd, but even as Alys continued up the stairs, she kept careful attention on the letter still being read.

"The fail-safe be hidden," it went on to say, "to keep it from fallin' into the Royal Navy's hands. But I trust in me fellow pirates to find it, for it can only be discovered by those who know these waters as well as I—your most ever lovin' and deadly Little George Partridge."

While the buccaneers muttered amongst themselves about what all of this meant, Alys reached the landing at the top of the stairs. A corridor stretched ahead of her, lined with doors that led to the prostitutes' rooms, but her interest lay elsewhere. After making certain no one was looking in her direction, she peered closely at the window.

THE SEA WITCH

27

"Holy hell," she murmured under her breath.

A message had been etched into one of the panes of glass.

"Weigh anchor!" somebody shouted below. "'Tis the Navy!"

THIS WAS BENJAMIN Priestley's chance. His hand upon the pommel of his cutlass faintly shook. The metal rattled until he released his grip.

"You're a sailing master, Priestley." Lieutenant Oliver folded his arms across the wide breadth of his chest, broadened from the exercise of personally administering the many floggings their commanding officer was so fond of bestowing. "Your duties are with the ship, not mucking up our opportunity to finally capture scores of pirates. What do you even know of close combat?"

"I defeat you," Ben answered, "each time we spar."

"You can't win a ruthless war on a battlefield because you beat your opponent at chess in the drawing room," the first mate said.

Ben fought for calm as he faced his admiral in the HMS *Jupiter*'s great cabin. The admiral's quarters ran the length of the back of the ship, as excruciatingly tidy as one might expect from a commanding officer who ran his ship with the same ruthless efficiency. All the charts were carefully rolled up, the books upon the built-in shelves smartly arranged by subject matter as well as height, and the bedlinens on the berth appeared lacquered on. No pictures of a spouse or lover, but then, Admiral Strickland always said that anything other than his ship was a mewling distraction hardly worth the trouble.

"Our ship's navigation falls to *me*," Ben said to his admiral, "and *I* have been the one responsible for tracking down every lead on capturing pirates, getting us to the proper locations to intercept them. The more time we spend here in counterproductive argument, the greater the likelihood that all of the buccaneers gathering in St. Gertrude will slip through our grasp."

28   EVA LEIGH

Oliver opened his mouth, but their commanding officer spoke first.

"Avast," Admiral Strickland clipped. His expression remained as icy as it always did, even when disciplining seamen for insubordination.

Ben swallowed around the coral lodged in his throat.

"We'll have to move with all haste," he replied. "I know the layout of the town, and I *need* to be part of this mission. With all due respect, sir," he added when Strickland narrowed his eyes warningly.

"Five years ago, I accepted your request to transfer to the *Jupiter* because no one is more dedicated to eradicating pirates than you, Mr. Priestley," the admiral said. "But that doesn't mean I tolerate disobedience, no matter how many buccaneers you've helped us locate and capture."

Ben inclined his head. "No, sir."

"*I* was there on this very ship when we found the smoking ruins of your father's vessel," Strickland added. "*I* saw the bloody effect of the pirates' greed when they stole the ship's cargo, and the lives they took, including Captain Priestley's."

Guilt cut through Ben, as it always did, whenever his father's death was mentioned. Ben should have been there that day . . . He could've helped . . . Done *something*.

But he hadn't been on his father's ship.

"This gathering of pirates at St. Gertrude's," Ben said. "The most infamous buccaneers will be there. I've narrowed the possible suspects to four men, and surely one amongst them will be in attendance. I can question them—"

"You interrogate maps, not suspects." Oliver rolled his eyes. "Leave such dangerous matters to me and the trained marines."

Ben tightened his jaw. "You *must* let me go, Admiral."

"Do not lecture me on my duty, Mr. Priestley," Strickland retorted. "As sailing master, you're a considerable asset aboard

THE SEA WITCH

the *Jupiter*, and I must weigh your value to this ship over your sense of personal justice."

"Sir." Ben took a step forward. "I . . . I appreciate the gravity of what I'm asking. Sailing masters are stationed on the quarter-deck during combat. We do not fight. If I could just . . . If you would permit me to accompany Lieutenant Oliver, I will stay out of his way. I won't interfere or be one more responsibility for him to shoulder. Only . . ." He hauled in a breath. "*Please*, sir. I need to be there."

There was a long pause, and then Strickland snapped, "Go ashore with Mr. Oliver. And Mr. Warne."

Ben's gaze flicked toward Warne, standing at the admiral's left side. The mage had a full head of white hair, even though the man himself was only a few years older than Ben, and he flouted regulations by wearing it loose rather than in a queue, as if mages didn't have to adhere to the code of conduct that kept the navy orderly and just. He did, however, sport the black sash around his waist that all naval mages wore.

"But mind, Mr. Priestley," the admiral continued, "you are not to engage unless absolutely necessary. I want your sharp eyes, not your sharp sword. I'll need a full report of everything you see and hear, most particularly whatever relates to Little George Partridge. That pirate was a thorn in the navy's hide, and there's no telling what sort of malice he has perpetuated from beyond his waterlogged grave."

"Aye, sir." Ben saluted.

The first mate also saluted, but not before glaring at Ben. Warne followed, silent yet ominous in his shadow-colored coat embroidered with twisted vines.

"Dismissed," said Captain Grey, standing on Strickland's right side.

Easy to forget that Grey was aboard, when Strickland ran nearly every aspect of the *Jupiter*.

30   EVA LEIGH

They quit the admiral's quarters to walk the narrow passageways. Sailors went briskly about their duties. The ship teemed with over seven hundred men crammed together on a first-rate man-o'-war. It reeked of sweat, seawater, and soup.

Ben, Oliver, and Warne took the companionway to the upper deck. A group of red-coated marines armed with muskets snapped to attention, their eyes fixed into the martial middle distance. The landing party waited as their longboat was lowered. Ben's heart pulsed in his throat as the small vessel reached the surface of the water, and when it came time for him to climb down into the boat, his hands trembled on the rope ladder.

No one spoke as they began rowing toward an inlet close to the island's town. When the boat was a dozen yards away from the *Jupiter*, water roiled and swirled, glinting off serpentine iridescent scales the size of dinner plates.

Lifting its massive head, the leviathan regarded them with pale green eyes, and Ben's breath caught, as it always did, to be so near such a gigantic beast. It stayed beneath the water, but he could still make out the shape of its long twisting body and the talons that tipped its grasping claws. Powerful musculature shifted under its scales. The creature could destroy them with a single flick of its tail.

For a moment, its eyes darkened, pupils widening from slits to the size of a man's hand, as if spotting prey. Ben made his limbs loose and ready, in case he was thrown into the water and had to swim for safety.

On the other side of the longboat, Warne muttered incantations as they rowed past the creature. Vacancy suddenly clouded the leviathan's gaze, its pupils turning back to slits before it dove back beneath the waves. It kept close to the *Jupiter*. Not close enough to harm the ship or its crew, but near enough that should its might be needed in battle, it could be summoned at once to do the navy's violent bidding.

THE SEA WITCH

31

He'd seen it happen, the creature unleashed upon whoever was foolish enough to challenge the *Jupiter*. Hulls were crushed beneath its coils, men devoured whole by its gaping, serrated mouth, leaving limbs and smears of blood upon the surface of the water and screams of agony and terror in its wake. He hadn't slept for a week after the first time he'd witnessed the leviathan attack. The only way to live with the memory was to place it in a strongbox and let it sink to the bottom of the sea, never to be unlocked.

Ben exhaled. "We've enough manpower of our own not to press that creature into service with unnatural magic."

Warne's smile was thin. "You say that now, but when we're set upon by an armada of buccaneers, you'll bless me for leashing it to my will."

Ben would sooner kiss a pirate.

"You'll have to choke down your distaste for the navy using monsters," Warne continued. "Wiser minds than yours have taken my counsel into consideration. There will soon be more beasts added to our arsenal."

Ben wiped his face clean of expression, even though this was the first he'd heard of this scheme. How much could he trust what Warne said? But if the mage spoke the truth . . . God help whoever crossed the navy's path. And God help the poor beasts that were forced to kill on command.

The longboat rowed on, the goal to put in at a small distance from the St. Gertrude harbor with a complement of marines. This would give them an element of surprise as they entered the town. Admiral Strickland had ordered that the *Jupiter* would sail around the island and position itself near the low cliffs that edged the island's only town once the ambush on land had been executed.

Though Ben made certain to keep his expression stoic, his pulse was a hurricane. Soon he'd be in the largest gathering of

32   EVA LEIGH

pirates since New Providence in the Bahamas had restored law and order.

"Playing nursemaid to a sailing master." Oliver shot Ben a scowl. "Look at you, shaking like a virgin on her wedding night." He leveled his finger at Ben. "Mind what you said to the admiral, Priestley. You stay in the back and you don't get underfoot. Or killed."

"I can assure you on the former," Ben said with as much calm as he could summon, "and will do my best on the latter."

Oliver looked away, muttering under his breath.

Ben checked his pistols. Both were primed and loaded. He partially unsheathed his cutlass, and then his dagger.

"First combat?" one of the marines asked, not unkindly. At Ben's quick nod, the marine said, "Staying in one place'll get you a boucan knife to the belly or a truncheon to the back of the head. Guts and brains a-spattered everywhere."

"I've seen the effects of close fighting." Still, Ben gingerly touched the back of his head, then his fingers drummed across his churning stomach.

"From a distance. Ain't the same when you're in it. Be quick on your feet, and no lingering. That's how you survive the skirmish."

Ben gave the marine another nod, even as coldness spread throughout his limbs.

"I heard that the witch pirate Captain Alys Tanner might be there," one of the rowers noted. "They say she's a withered crone with dried dugs down to her knees."

"I heard she's got a face like an eel and files her teeth so she's got a shark mouth," another seaman ventured. "An' she cuts off men's bollocks an' swallows 'em down like oysters as part of her magic spells."

"Quiet," snapped Oliver, "and put your backs into your oars or I'll give you all thirty lashes."

The men silenced, and Warne smirked.

THE SEA WITCH

Ben pressed his lips tight. Strickland insisted flogging was the best way to maintain discipline. Though punishment was typically done by the boatswain's mate on other ships, on the *Jupiter*, Oliver himself carried out the admiral's orders. The first mate wore a vicious little smile whenever he cut bloody stripes across the men's backs with a cat-o'-nine-tails. Warne gathered up the spilled drops of blood for use in potions.

The longboat neared the inlet, and once they were close enough, several of the seamen jumped out and dragged the boat onto the beach. Oliver, Ben, Warne, and the marines clambered out of the small vessel.

Ben staggered as he waded toward the beach. Not long now until he'd be actually facing off against pirates.

Water foamed around his ankles, trying to pull him back into the sea. He struggled against the tug of the water.

"Look lively, Priestley," Oliver snapped.

Ben pushed onto the sand and joined the others as they scrambled up a sloping hill. A fringe of spiny palm trees stood in whispering sentry, but there were no villagers to witness their ascent.

A pale thin shape flickered at the edge of the trees. Ben whirled, cutlass out. Only palms swayed in the slight breeze, their fronds taunting as they bent in the wind.

The marines chuckled as Ben sheepishly sheathed his blade.

"Be chary, Priestley." Oliver shook his head. "You'll gut one of our own men before even clapping eyes on a pirate."

"Aye," Ben said, then added at the lieutenant's hard stare, "sir."

They emerged on the edge of the town, where the dilapidated timbered buildings were more scattered apart. At once, people nearby spotted them and hastened away or darted into structures, slamming doors behind them. Though St. Gertrude was known as a pirate haven, where law had little weight, no one wanted to be caught in any potential crossfire.

"Word is that pirate captains are all gathered at someplace called the Wig and Merkin," Ben said to Oliver and Warne.

The officers strode in the direction of the tavern, and Ben quickly followed. They passed cluttered shops filled with stolen merchandise, and shabby doss-houses where those that didn't run away lolled on porches or catcalled from open windows.

"We ought to approach it from the side," Ben said to Oliver's back. "Not through the front door."

"We'll go straight in." Oliver spoke over his shoulder without breaking stride. "Any attack will be met head-on, with the full confidence and conviction of the British navy."

"And here's my contribution," Warne added, his hands forming patterns in the air. As he did, fiery energy collected around his fingers. He tapped each of the marine's cutlasses and the bayonets of their muskets. Power seeped from his fingers into the steel, making the metal glow.

Grinning, one of the marines swiped his blade through a thick wooden column. The wood split apart as if it was only a twig. The roof it supported slanted and, groaning, collapsed. A man in a stained waistcoat yelled in indignation, but no one paid attention.

When Warne reached for Ben's cutlass, Ben pulled back.

"I'll do this on my own," Ben answered.

The mage shrugged. "Matters little to me what you do, Priestley."

Ben said nothing as he kept pace with the landing party, striding over the uneven and rutted dirt road leading to the center of town. His gaze was never still, moving from building to building, alley to alley. Faces appeared and retreated into the shadows cast by oily torchlight. The smell of unwashed human bodies, rum, and roasting meat clung to the lanes that wove through the settlement.

Even at this late hour of the night, a thick and heavy heat lay upon the streets. Perspiration made Ben's shirt cling to

THE SEA WITCH

35

his back. A shame that officers couldn't wear the lightweight loose shirts and billowing pants favored by sailors and citizens, but appearances had to be kept up, and so he was dressed in a full-skirted dark blue coat over a long gray waistcoat, his gray breeches tucked into tall leather boots. At the least he was properly armed.

"Ahead." Ben pointed toward the two-story building on a corner. As they neared, many raucous voices tumbled out. The tavern was full to bursting with buccaneers.

Ben's skin went hot and tight.

Oliver and the marines pushed forward, striding quickly toward the tavern. Ben hurried to come abreast of the lieutenant.

"I strongly suggest we go in through the side," Ben said to Oliver's stern profile. "Otherwise, they'll flee ahead of our entry."

"A sleeping incantation could subdue some of their numbers before we even set foot inside," Warne offered.

"Silence, both of you," Oliver snapped. "We attack through the front—now!"

The lieutenant charged through the tavern's open doorway. Marines surged in behind him. Ben stood in the street, then took a breath.

He stepped into the tavern. At the same time, someone inside cried out, "Weigh anchor! 'Tis the navy!"

A cascade of pirates tried to push through the front door. Ben shouldered into them. Unlike the orderly appearance of the navy, the pirates were a collection of men both garish and ragged. Some wore coats with embroidered cuffs and gaudy buttons, with gold glinting from their ears and gemstones on their fingers. Others were grimy and unkempt, threadbare clothing stained, and their hair caked with God knew what. Yet from the ostentatious to the shabby, they all had the same greed and viciousness in their gazes. None of them valued human life over treasure and plunder.

Chaos was everywhere as the armed marines clashed with the buccaneers. The marines' magic-charged cutlasses slashed through tables and bucklers as though the heavy wood and metal shields were made of paper.

Ben struggled to grab a blond pirate by the sleeve.

"Where is Jacob Van Der Meer?" he bellowed at the struggling man. "Louis Dupont? Diego Sanchez?"

"Piss off, navy man." The pirate shoved at Ben. Buffeted by a human tide of fleeing buccaneers, Ben staggered. His grip slipped and the pirate disappeared into the throng.

A jet of fire shot toward Ben, flung by a pirate mage. Ben ducked. Heat from the spell sizzled along his back.

Hell. He'd never had magic used against him.

Ben straightened and elbowed the mage in the face. The magic user fell to the ground, and fleeing pirates stepped on and over his prone body.

Jostling against the escaping buccaneers, he fought to grab another pirate, a man with half a nose. There was too much pandemonium, and he couldn't get a decent grip before the ruffian was borne away on a human tide.

Ben's chance to capture and interrogate the pirates was slipping through his fingers. The rough plaster walls of the building shook, and any second the melee would bring the roof down on everyone's heads.

A blast of hot, crackling magic detonated behind him, throwing him onto a quaking staircase that led to a second floor.

He leapt to his feet, struggling for balance as the stairs shuddered beneath him. The lower half of the staircase crumbled. There was no choice but to go up.

A glimpse of someone with long red hair caught Ben's attention. A barmaid, no doubt, caught up in the turmoil, trapped at the top of the stairway and in need of aid.

Ben took the remaining stairs two at a time, until he reached the landing.

THE SEA WITCH

37

"Miss, you must come with me," he said. "I'll get you to safety."

"Just the same," the woman answered in the flat accent of a Colonial, "your help isn't wanted."

Only then did Ben realize that the *barmaid* was wearing a full billowing shirt, leather tunic, and snug breeches with boots that climbed up to her thighs. With her own brace of pistols, her cutlass, and the dagger poking up over the top of her boot, he'd never seen any woman so well armed. Hair the color of the burning sky at sunset trailed in a braid down her back, and though it wasn't possible to tell the hue of her eyes in the candlelight, they gleamed with intelligence and determination.

In her hand, she held a shield made of glowing energy, carrying it with the confidence of one who was well-familiar with wielding magic.

She was no tavern wench. She was Alys Tanner, the captain of the pirate vessel the *Sea Witch*.

And a witch herself.

Her attention ricocheted between him and the window she stood before. The glow of her magical shield revealed what appeared to be writing on the glass.

Before he could make out what the inscription said, Alys Tanner threw her energy shield through the window, shattering the glass. She gave him a tiny ironic salute before diving through the open pane.

Ben hesitated. And then he leapt after the pirate witch into the darkness.

CHAPTER THREE

A LYS TUCKED HERSELF into a ball. She surrounded herself with a cocoon of protective energy, hit the ground, and rolled. Even with the shield of her magic, the impact jolted the breath from her body.

She leapt to her feet and took off at a full run, down the road and toward her ship. The rutted dirt path threatened to trip her, but she fought to stay upright and moving forward. She ran straight through puddles of unknown origin, splashing herself and anyone who happened to be unluckily nearby, ignoring their cries of outrage.

She risked a glance over her shoulder.

"Fuck." The naval officer chased after her, and it was a damn shame that he was so well-conditioned, because he wasn't more than a dozen yards behind. His long legs were far too quick.

She leapt over a cart holding jugs of wine, then paused long enough to summon energy to knock over the heavy cart. Clay shattered and wine spilled everywhere, filling the air with the sharp smell of cheap alcohol.

Taking off again, she chanced a quick look back, to see the naval officer vaulting over the mayhem before continuing in his pursuit.

The town was a maze, winding and snaking in confusing disorder, leading to dead ends. Yet no matter how many twists

THE SEA WITCH 39

she took, he stayed close on her tail. There wasn't time or focus to summon a spell to hide her from his sight. If she paused long enough to call forth a shadow, he'd be upon her.

She couldn't veer into the woods. They were full of jumbies—spirits of the dead—and drunken pirates who wandered into the forest were often never heard from again.

She had to get to her ship, and the fastest way there was a tricky one, but she'd no choice.

Instead of making for the quay, she sped along a slick, uneven cobbled path toward the cliffs at the very edge of town. Buildings thinned out as she neared the village's perimeter. She dodged the few drunkards and surly dockworkers that staggered along the lane. Moments later, she reached the bluffs.

She gulped. The bluffs soared above the water. A fall from them meant shattering your body on the pointed rocks below, where waves hammered against stone.

The naval man drew closer, leaving her no choice.

She reached her hands toward the crashing water below, stirring it higher and higher. The breeze rose up from the now towering waves. The wind transformed—from gusts of air into powerful swells of energy so strong they buffeted Alys as she stood upon the rock.

She took a breath, and then stepped out into nothingness.

A terrifying moment passed as she fell through space. Her stomach pitched into her throat in the freefall.

Half a second later, the gusts lifted her, as if she was sea-foam spinning upon the breeze. She half tumbled, half danced atop the air, high above the water. A startled laugh leapt from her. This wasn't exactly flight, but it was damned close, and it was wondrous.

Hell. Her elation crashed as she spotted a naval ship. It hadn't been there when the *Sea Witch* had dropped anchor. Cannons bristled from its decks, and the man-o'-war was nearly twice the size of her own vessel. It lay between her and the *Sea Witch*.

40   EVA LEIGH

Worse, it was the *Jupiter*. The navy's flagship.

Teeming with guns and armed seamen, the flagship struck terror into the hearts of every pirate, and, seeing it for the first time, she was no exception. If she'd thought she'd left the danger behind on land, she was dead wrong.

Sea air magic couldn't carry her far enough to the *Sea Witch*, anchored hundreds of feet away. Beside the Royal Navy ship, the horrifying, slithering shape of a leviathan shadowed beneath the water.

Ice flooded her. Never before had she caught a glimpse of the leviathan. The beast was as long as the *Jupiter*, and glassy emerald scales covered its shifting muscles. Teeth the size of a human's forearm glinted in its maw. Landing in the water meant those teeth would be waiting for her to stain the sea with her blood.

Using the wind, she flew toward the *Jupiter*'s foremast before dropping onto the yardarm. The wood was heavy and solid beneath her feet. She gripped the yardarm until she was secure enough to scramble toward the mast. Confused sailors ran back and forth across the upper deck thirty feet below, pointing up at her. Only one marine had enough presence of mind to aim a musket in her direction. She ducked just as the weapon fired with a loud crack.

The bullet slammed into the mast, narrowly missing her shoulder.

In the silence that followed the musket firing, a creaking noise caught her attention. The crane upon the bluffs turned in her direction.

The pursuing naval officer clung to a rope at the end of the crane as the loading device rotated its full reach toward the *Jupiter*. He swung on the rope, the skirt of his coat billowing behind him, his hair pulling loose from its queue.

He leapt onto the foremast yardarm, and the wood shuddered as he landed.

THE SEA WITCH   41

"Oh, hell," she muttered. Was there any man so cursedly persistent?

She slid down the mast, leaping the rest of the way to hit the upper deck. Yet before she could break for the gunwale, and the longboat hanging from a davit on the ship's stern, the naval officer landed mere feet away from her, blocking her path to escape.

Marines massed around him. Hopefully, the naval mage she'd spotted at the tavern was still ashore and couldn't use his powers against her. For now, though, she was hindered by ordinary yet still challenging manpower.

Summoning the ocean air to give her flight had drained some of her magic. She had enough strength to muster the force of a horse's kick to knock several of the marines to the deck with a wave of her hand.

Even with the men lying stunned on their backs, there was only one route open to her: belowdecks.

Alys half fell down the companionway that led to the passageway, landing in an ungraceful heap. She struggled to her feet before rushing down the narrow corridor, lanterns illuminating the smooth wooden floor and rows of closed doors. Her gaze darted this way and that in search of something to provide a distraction or slow the chasing officer. His footfalls thundered behind her.

Sailors tried to block her path, their faces set but uncertain. She shoved them and threw punches to clear her way. The hallway was cramped, and when a quartet of sailors armed with clubs appeared at the other end, she ducked through the first open door.

A table laden with maps, weighted down with a variety of brass and wooden navigational instruments, gave her pause. There were waggoners, too, books of bound maps. The chart room. As valuable as any chest of doubloons, her company could surely use the maps, but now wasn't the moment to gather them up. A distraction was needed.

She cupped her hands and whispered between her palms. Though she had little magic left, she called upon the heat of a lightning-fed wildfire. Blazing energy formed in the bowl of her hands, red and shining, and she lifted it high above her head.

"No," came a voice behind her.

She spun to see the pursuing officer standing at the entrance to the chart room. His eyes were wide.

"My maps," he exclaimed.

Grunting, she threw the fiery energy at the table holding the charts.

He lunged, but there was nothing he could do. The ball of flame hit the maps with a snap. In moments, crackling fire spread across the scrolls of paper and books as thick smoke filled the room. The destruction of so much knowledge twisted in her belly, yet she gained time as he stopped his pursuit. He grabbed a bucket of water to douse the blaze.

The porthole was too narrow for her to wriggle out, so she pushed past the frantic officer, and was once more out in the passageway. She kicked at the chest of an advancing sailor, a man twice her size, channeling all her force into her boot. He toppled back. Like dominoes, the seamen behind him fell, crying out in astonishment and confusion. She didn't hesitate to step on them as she ran to the companionway and climbed to the upper deck.

More armed marines met her, carrying bayonet-topped muskets in their callused hands. Her cutlass hissed as she drew it, and several of the marines stepped back in alarm. She launched into an attack, holding the men back with slashes of her blade. Three marines held short swords, and she parried their strikes, the sounds of metal against metal ringing in the air. All the while she edged toward a longboat hanging off the side of the hull. She drew her pistol.

Drawing a deep breath, she summoned a final sputtering burst of power to pour flickering magic down the barrel of her

THE SEA WITCH 43

firearm. She pointed her weapon at a cask of gunpowder on the deck and kept her arm steady as she fired.

Wooden planks splintered and the advancing sailors fell back from the explosion.

She had barely enough time to jump into the longboat and cut the gripes holding it.

As it plunged to the sea, she clung to the small boat's sides. She shook when the vessel hit the water, but she collected herself to grab the oars. They were thick in her hands, worn from use, and she gripped them tightly as she rowed as quickly as she could toward the waiting *Sea Witch*. Her ship had already raised anchor and was sailing to intercept her, thank the stars. Still, her arms burned as she put as much distance between herself and the naval ship.

She almost pitied the resolute sailing master who had pursued her through the town and onto the ship, since she'd destroyed his charts and waggoners, but she'd had no choice. There was no way to stop him from coming after her. The determination in his gaze left little doubt of that.

Cannons booming rent the air apart. She ducked. But no whizzing sounded overhead. The *Jupiter* wasn't firing on her. It aimed its weapons toward a ship now sailing around the island—the *Diabolique*, René Fontaine's vessel.

The *Diabolique* attempted to skirt past the British ship. Only a few cannons fired, a result of the man-o'-war being damaged from the explosion Alys had caused. Fontaine and his crew might make it to freedom.

A huge form glided beneath the water. The leviathan reared up from under the waves, and wrapped its long sinuous body around the *Diabolique*. The buccaneer sloop resembled a collection of fragile twigs as the huge beast surrounded the hull with broad scaly coils. Screams echoed from the *Diabolique*. Pirates leapt from the top deck, only to be gulped up by the leviathan's cavernous mouth.

There was a long loud groan, followed by the cracking of thick timbers. The sloop snapped into thousands of pieces. Its masts and decks sank beneath the water. The terrified shrieks of men attempting to swim to safety disappeared as they were swallowed whole.

Wooden splinters bobbing on the waves were all that remained of Fontaine's vessel.

Three minutes. An entire ship and its crew, destroyed in less time than it took to drink a tankard of ale.

The leviathan swam toward the *Jupiter.*

Closing her eyes, Alys urged the water to push her along. Almost no magic rose up within her, wrung dry from all the energy she'd used. Yet she gathered enough power from even the tiniest filaments of her body to give her a small amount of help as she rowed.

She neared the *Sea Witch*. It had undergone changes in the year since they'd stolen her from the dock in Norham, with more guns, more crew, a new name, and it was home now.

The company gathered at the gunwale. A rope was thrown over rail, and with her limbs trembling from physical exertion and magic use, she climbed it, leaving the longboat bobbing on the waves. Many hands reached down to assist her up.

She climbed onto the deck of the *Sea Witch* to see many familiar faces, and others who had become part of their pirate company over the course of the year. Whatever roles they were forced to play on land, on this ship, they could be whomever they wanted, and they dressed accordingly. Some wore loose trousers and shirts, others favored a mixture of bodices and breeches, a handful wore skirts, and all of them were armed with weapons of every variety. Cutlasses, clubs, knives, pistols, and potions. A few had cut their hair short, and others wore their locks long and loose.

Her crew was comprised of many colors and sizes and ages and countries of origin, and they each had voted her into the role of captain.

THE SEA WITCH

"The *Diabolique*," Alys gasped.

"We saw it," Stasia, her second-in-command, said grimly. Black-haired, sharp dark eyes lined with kohl, she was dressed in an embroidered bodice and the loose vraka pantaloons of her Aegean homeland. "Looked like a roaring party ashore."

"That was *before* the British Navy showed up." Alys curled and uncurled her hands, which had cramped on the oars. Though her body was weakened from using so much magic, she was still standing. "Little George gave many gifts at his wake, including a clue to—"

"Who the hell is *that*?" Susannah pointed toward the gunwale behind Alys.

Spinning, Alys gaped as a pair of man's hands gripped the railing. She darted to pry them loose from the gunwale, but she was too late.

Sodden, gasping, the naval sailing master hauled himself over the railing to stare at her with triumph in his eyes.

"Got you," he panted.

NO SOONER HAD the words left Ben's mouth than he found himself at the point of a dozen cutlasses, with nearly as many pistols aimed at his head and heart. Glowing, jewel-hued spells appeared above the fingers of many of the crew and the air held the mineral scent of magic.

Oh, hell.

As if awaiting inspection, he straightened his dripping coat.

"Hold." Narrowing her eyes, Alys Tanner slowly approached him. Her cheeks were pale, her features drawn, making her freckles stand out like drops of blood. "Don't kill him. Yet."

"Appreciate your forbearance." He fought to calm his ragged breathing.

"I said *yet*." She stopped and tilted her head. "Only a dolphin could swim to my ship so quickly. Unless you have magic of your own."

"I clung to the side of the longboat—you rowed us both here."

A tiny smile tipped the corner of her lips. "Whoever you are, navy man, you're fucking persistent."

Such foul language shouldn't have been shocking. He'd been at sea for most of his life and had encountered every sort of person of all genders in his naval service, especially those who didn't adhere to society's rules. But he jolted to hear Alys Tanner curse.

"Benjamin Priestley." He bowed. "Sailing master for the HMS *Jupiter.*"

"The *Jupiter* is now nearly a mile behind us, and too impaired to pursue." She gazed over his shoulder, and he followed her attention to see the dark smudge of the British naval ship growing smaller by the moment. "A far distance between you and a friendly face, Sailing Master Priestley."

Damn. The leviathan couldn't give chase, either, since the spell that kept it imprisoned to the navy's bidding meant it could not attack without a Royal Navy ship—and mage—nearby.

"Throw him overboard," someone shouted.

"Shoot him and *then* throw him overboard," another female voice chimed in.

Anyone who claimed women were less bloodthirsty than men needed to spend ten seconds aboard the *Sea Witch.*

He darted forward and snatched a pistol from one of the crew's hands. Shouts rose up, outraged female voices, but before any of them could act, he raised the pistol.

And fired it into the air.

He grunted as a trio of women launched themselves at him, throwing him to the deck. His head hit the planks with a thud, and his hands were quickly pinned down. A band of glowing red energy pressed against his throat. Strangled noises escaped from him as he fought for air.

THE SEA WITCH   47

"Impossible to state how hugely stupid that was, Sailing Master." Alys Tanner loomed over him, her hands on her hips as she shook her head. "The deck could be splattered with your blood right now, and for what? You signaled your ship so they know you're here, but they're busy mopping up the remains of the *Diabolique*. Even if the ship hadn't unleashed their leviathan, they're too damaged to be of any assistance to you."

"Damaged thanks to you," he managed to rasp.

"I don't regret what I've done."

"Neither do I." He pressed his lips together to stop himself from blurting anything more. Provoking her wasn't going to keep him alive.

She clicked her tongue, as if *disappointed* in him. Then she stood back. "Let him up but hold him fast."

The energy around his throat vanished but many strong hands gripped him tightly as he struggled to his feet and faced over a score of hostile faces. Damn, he *was* alone on this pirate ship. Alys Tanner could have him flayed and disemboweled, then thrown overboard, and no one would ever find his remains.

She frowned as she stared at him, her attention lingering on the backs of his hands, and then moving to the part of his neck that wasn't covered by his neckcloth.

He couldn't tug his cuffs down, or pull the linen at his throat up higher. She'd seen his markings now, and there wasn't anything he could do about them until the seawater on his skin dried. Then, and only then, would the ink-dark patterns on his skin fade.

At the question in her gaze, Ben tipped up his chin. He didn't owe this pirate an explanation.

She narrowed her eyes. "What do you know of Little George Partridge? Answer quick," she added, curling and uncurling her fingers around the glittering beginnings of a spell, "or I'll find new means of loosening your tongue."

"Why would I know anything of Partridge?"

"On account of the fact that you serve aboard the *Jupiter*, which is Admiral Strickland's ship, and Little George was colluding with Strickland in creating the magic used to force the leviathan into serving the navy."

Ben jolted. "*What?*"

Alys Tanner smirked. "This act of innocence doesn't become you, Sailing Master." When Ben remained silent, she continued, "A letter was read at the tavern on St. Gertrude, a letter from Partridge himself, asserting that he and Strickland had worked together to fashion the magic that binds the sea creature."

"Doubtless, the captain knew what he was doing. A leviathan is one more weapon in the arsenal."

There was no need to tell her about his revulsion at enslaving the sea creature. It was a weakness she could exploit.

"Yet Little George wasn't entirely a fool," the witch continued. "He knew the Royal Navy would stick a knife in his back. Little George made provisions for that. A fail-safe to break the spell holding the leviathan captive. And it's hidden somewhere in these waters."

Ben kept his expression impassive even as astonishment rocked through him.

"Tell me what you know, navy man," she demanded. When he hesitated, she drew her cutlass and pressed its point into his chest.

"I'm as ignorant as a piece of flotsam," he answered.

"He is not," said one of the pirate crew, a woman with a Mediterranean accent and dark- lined eyes. "I have heard him spoken of, this Benjamin Priestley. Born and raised in the Caribbean, and he knows this territory, land and sea, better than anyone. They say he is the best navigator in the Royal Navy."

"I have a reputation?"

The Mediterranean woman snorted. "You will develop one for false modesty."

"We've need of you, Sailing Master," Alys Tanner said.

THE SEA WITCH   49

"You sail the Caribbean, too," he answered. "And you possess your own navigator."

"We do," the captain said. The tip of her blade dug into his waistcoat, through his shirt, and nicked his skin beneath. "You're ensuring we don't have need of you. Which makes it hard for me to stay my hand."

The paleness in her cheeks had lessened. This close, he could see that the color of her freckles had shifted. They had been blood red, but now they were tawny.

He straightened. "I cannot and will not help you."

Her eyes—the irises contained a mixture of green and light brown—widened.

"Do it, navy man," one of the buccaneers holding him snarled, giving him a shake. Despite his size, he still rattled from her force. The woman was strong, stronger than many men.

"Thank you, but no," he answered.

Idly, Alys Tanner noted, "Torturing you to tell us whatever you know is an option."

"Except," he said as evenly as he could, "the accounts given by people who've lived through your pirate attacks say that you're no enthusiast of torture."

"These aren't typical circumstances."

"Cut off one of his bollocks," someone in the crew shouted. "That'll make him sing like a siren."

If Ben's hands had been free, he would have used them to cover his groin. As though reading his thoughts, the captain snickered.

"Kill him now," the Mediterranean woman urged. "Use the spell of extinguishing."

"No spell needed when steel will do." Captain Tanner moved her cutlass up and pressed the blade against his neck. He tried not to swallow hard, lest he accidentally slit his own throat.

She stared at him for a long time. This might be his last moments alive, his final sight the face of the witch pirate captain as she studied him the way he would study a navigational chart. He could change his mind and plead for his life. But he would never help a pirate. If he *was* to leave this earthly existence, he'd do so with as much pride as he could muster. Father died courageously, and Ben would sail the same course.

"Take him to the brig," she finally said.

He stared at her. She stared back.

Their gazes broke apart when the members of the company that held him dragged him away, while others kept their swords and guns pointed at him. Another pirate kept a spell dancing on her fingers, ready to be deployed. Right before he ducked to climb down the companionway, he looked back to see Alys Tanner standing at the gunwale, gripping the handle of her cutlass, looking toward the black horizon.

There was no comfort in the captain's reputation for leaving people alive. His life was hers now, to command or extinguish, and he had little faith that she saved any of her mercy for him.

CHAPTER FOUR

"I DO NOT LIKE it," Stasia muttered, pacing in Alys's quarters. She paused long enough to stroke the throat of Eris, her magpie familiar perched on her shoulder. The bird made a pleased, muted sound as it rubbed its beak in Stasia's thick dark hair, gently nibbling on her curls. "I do not like *him*. He is too handsome to be kept alive."

Alys poured two tankards of rum and handed one to her quartermaster. The tall mugs were of English silver, covered in elaborate scrolls that could only come from a skilled craftsman. These had been taken from a British merchantman.

She wrapped a square of silk around her head. The scarf had been seized from a Spanish galleon headed for Hispaniola. Its deep green color had been too delicious for her to resist, especially after the coarsely woven gray woolens she'd been forced to wear back home were an abrasive memory against her skin. Even so, she only wore plain gold hoops in her ears, rather than the pearls and gemstones other members of her crew favored.

"Staying a step ahead of him kept me too busy to notice whether or not he was handsome," Alys answered.

"He has pretty blue eyes and a face too gorgeous for the good of anyone." After setting Eris on top of a table, Stasia drained her tankard and threw herself into the seat in front of the large window that ran the length of the ship's aft. "I want to finish the job you started and cut his throat."

Alys supposed that Sailing Master Benjamin Priestley of His Majesty's Navy was good looking, in a tidy way, with a hewn jaw and sharp nose, and instead of a wig, he wore his dark brown hair in a queue. He filled out his fine clothes well, too, and she had ample evidence he was in good physical condition.

She eyed her friend. "It isn't his handsomeness you fear."

"While he is on the *Sea Witch*, he is a danger to everyone aboard."

Alys drank from her tankard, yet bleakness flattened her words. "What happened to Fontaine and the *Diabolique* . . ." She shuddered.

"I hope to never witness such a horror again." Stasia muttered an incantation in Greek.

"So long as the Royal Navy has the leviathan in its power, we're all a moment away from annihilation. There's no fighting it. No way to escape it. All the witches aboard our ship, using every ounce of our power . . . even together, we couldn't stop that creature."

Both she and Stasia fell silent, considering this ominous fate.

"Little George's fail-safe is our sole hope of eluding certain death," Alys concluded. "Priestley may yet change his mind, and if it means outwitting the navy, I'd be a fool to snuff out our most promising lead of reaching that fail-safe."

"But what *is* it, this fail-safe?"

Alys could only shrug. "Little George said nothing on that front. It could be anything."

"The sailing master brings more peril than promise of finding it."

"He might be just what we need." When Stasia opened her mouth to speak, Alys held up a hand. "You think I'm unaware of the threat he presents? Forty-five women have now elected me their captain. They follow me on raids and into battle. Their

THE SEA WITCH   53

lives are *my* responsibility. And to protect them, I've got to find that fail-safe. If that means keeping the sailing master alive for a little longer, then . . ." She inhaled raggedly. "I accept that risk."

Stasia gazed at her, and then gave a quick nod.

Alys poured herself another drink. She had met Stasia Angelidis shortly after the *Sea Witch* had first docked in Tortuga, a year ago. Stasia had been a corsair in the Mediterranean, but no pirate companies in the Caribbean were willing to take on a female crew member, and certainly not one who was a witch.

When Alys had first encountered Stasia, the Greek woman had pinned a buccaneer to the wall of a tavern, magical vines keeping the pirate restrained as Stasia calmly finished a mug of ale. To ensure that the buccaneer didn't move, Stasia had enchanted a knife to rest against his throat. It turned out that the pirate had tried to intimidate Stasia with the threat that all men deploy against women. Stasia's crime: daring to seek a place aboard a ship as a crew member.

That pirate's poor judgment had been to Alys's benefit. She'd gained not only a quartermaster, but a stalwart friend and counselor.

They'd spent many nights together, studying pilfered tomes about magic. Those books had been remarkably short on details about how, exactly, one wielded supernatural power, hoarding that knowledge for the magic academies that only admitted male students. The volumes that Alys and Stasia did find were quick to condemn women who claimed magic for themselves.

Many of those late nights with Stasia had been occupied with testing their magic, experimenting with what they could and could not do, and writing down everything they learned so that future generations of witches wouldn't be raised in ignorance, as both Alys and her quartermaster had. Barred entrance to education, witches had to rely on rumor and word of mouth to gain any knowledge about how to use their powers.

When there were lulls in the ship's duties, Alys and Stasia would gather the ship's witches to pass along everything they'd learned from the books. Their knowledge would be a flame, lighting one candle, and then another, and another, until someday, the whole world would be brightened by witches' magic.

It was Stasia that Alys spoke with first thing each morning, and Stasia who Alys said good-night to at the conclusion of every day.

A plate of stewed chicken now waited for Alys, and her stomach rumbled with interest. She hadn't eaten since noon.

"You aren't joining me?" Alys asked.

"I dined while you were attending the festivities ashore."

Sitting down to eat, Alys said, "Make sure some food is brought to our guest in the brig."

"His comfort should not be at the uppermost of our minds."

Alys shook her head. "*Men* treat their prisoners poorly."

Stasia pushed up from the window seat and opened the door of the cabin. To an unseen member of the crew, she issued commands, and then went to stand at the window.

"We would not serve the king so kindly," the quartermaster grumbled.

"The king happily makes war to line his coffers. He's an eager enslaver, too." Alys prodded her stew with the tip of her knife. "This sailing master is, right now, merely a mechanism I intend to use. A mechanism you say is handsome." She exhaled. "Having men on our ship makes my skin crawl. They're so . . . messy. Yet I'll learn what Priestley knows. He pled ignorance about his captain's involvement with Little George. Might be a ruse, might not."

"He hates pirates. You can see it in every part of his body. He is a warrant officer in the navy. It makes sense he holds no love for buccaneers. He seems uncomfortable in the presence of

THE SEA WITCH   55

magic, so a ship of witches is not a place he cares for. Butchering him would be wisest."

"Killing in the heat of battle has a different flavor than murder committed in cold blood. A flavor I can't swallow."

Stasia clapped her hand across her forehead. "The twists and turns of your heart have always been baffling."

"I'm equally baffled by myself." Alys took a bite of chicken. "But sending him to hell sits poorly with me. The *Sea Witch* and its company sail differently from other ships."

"There *are* exceptions," Stasia noted.

"And I make them, without question."

No one who commanded or crewed on a ship transporting kidnapped Africans was ever spared. Once the people trapped in abominable conditions in the hold were freed and brought onto the *Sea Witch* for medicine, fresh food, and proper clothing, Alys and her company locked the captain and crew in the cramped space where they'd held their captives. She always ignored the sailors' pleas for mercy when the enslaver ships were set ablaze.

"I'll kill him *if* I deem it necessary," Alys said.

"It is a wonder we have any reputation at all," the quartermaster groused. "Fine, fine," she added when Alys shot her a pointed look, "he lives, but when he is no longer of use to us . . ." She drew her thumb across her throat.

Eris chattered in agreement.

Satisfied, Alys finished her supper, and drained a mug of rum to chase it all down. She wiped her arm across her mouth.

"Where's your modesty?"

Samuel's once-constant demand came back to her in a rush. There'd been a day when she had spoken to Quinton Brown before the other man had addressed her first. Samuel had quickly dragged her home, sat her at the table, and lectured her for a full hour about her wrongdoing.

56   EVA LEIGH

"*I'd only asked him to thank his wife for her gift of elderberry jam,*" Alys had protested.

"*Your eyes weren't downcast, either. You looked around as if you were the mayor and the reverend and the governor all mixed into one boastful, lewd woman.*"

"*I knew the road, and didn't need to look down.*"

He'd sat down and clasped her hands in his. "*I love you too much to let you attract any censure. What if someone gets ideas and follows you and sees you . . .*" He'd shuddered. "*Using magic.*"

"*They won't—I'm careful.*"

His face darkened, and only then had she realized her mistake.

"Before my recollection of it grows blurred," she said to Stasia, banishing the memory, "we need to figure out what Little George's clue on the window glass leading to the fail-safe meant."

"Speak, Oracle." Stasia waved her hand.

"A golden, holy key you seek to open the gates,
But first, you must be penitent.
Bow at the feet of the Weeping Princess
And behind her vale of tears, you will find your way."

After this recital, both Alys and Stasia fell silent, considering what the riddle could possibly mean.

"Within the Caribbean, is there anything known as the Weeping Princess?" Alys asked.

Stasia looked baffled. "I have been in these waters for only a year longer than you."

"Damn." Alys pulled out several charts and spread them open on a table—a mahogany table, Alys was pleased to note, that she had actually *paid* for at a port of call, rather than seized from a captured ship.

She and Stasia studied the charts thoroughly, reviewing the maps that had been painstakingly rendered by cartographers from around the globe, with territories and towns all carefully inscribed,

THE SEA WITCH

just as the creatures and supernatural beasts that dwelled in the waters and forests were depicted in all their powerful splendor. Yet there were no indicators of anywhere that bore the name the Weeping Princess. "Perhaps it's a nickname for some church or tower."

"Hell, if I know." Stasia folded her arms across her chest as she scowled at the stack of useless maps.

"Perhaps this'll do." Alys spoke the riddle again as she summoned a spell from a thick honey-scented candle, calling upon the knowledge bees possessed when finding their way from hive to flower and back again. She focused her attention on her words, bringing to mind the bees' flight, and cast the spell over the maps. It shimmered for a moment, and she held her breath, hopeful that the enchantment would alight somewhere on the chart that might show them where they needed to go.

Yet the glittering spell turned to flakes of useless ash that scattered across the map.

"Fuck," she muttered. She dropped her head. "A disaster of a captain I am, and an even bigger failure as a witch, if I can't lead us toward the one thing that might turn the tide in our favor."

"Alys," Stasia said firmly. "You *can* do this."

"I'm glad one of us has confidence in me, if not my choices."

Alys exhaled roughly. Her stomach knotted when faced with the immensity of her situation. She had to find the fail-safe, and she'd kept the naval sailing master alive for that very purpose. But was that the right decision?

She looked down at the charts. "If our powers fail us, then surely there is someone in our company who will have the answer."

For the next half an hour, every single member of the crew was brought into Alys's cabin, and heard Little George's riddle, making certain to include Luna, who served as their navigator. Yet, for all their varied experience with the Caribbean, not a one could hazard a guess as to what or where the Weeping Princess might be.

58   EVA LEIGH

"Damn." Alys planted her hands on her hips as the last of the company left her cabin. "We've one option left."

"No," Stasia said at once.

"Fetch our guest from the brig."

HIS WRISTS AND ankles in manacles and shackles, Ben sat on a narrow cot in a narrow space bound on three sides with iron bars that glowed with pale green light. A wooden bowl of untouched stewed chicken had been placed on the floor.

What the hell had he been thinking, chasing Alys Tanner all the way to her own ship? What had he expected to accomplish?

No one had ever accused him of being reckless.

"*Your logbook is remarkably precise and detailed, Mr. Priestley,*" Admiral Strickland had often told him, reviewing his account of the day. "*Fastidious, one might say.*"

"*Pry that ramrod out of your arse, Priestley,*" Lieutenant Vickers had frequently snapped at him whenever Ben took an additional ten minutes to make up his berth. "*You make my bollocks shrivel.*"

The lone time Ben had been impulsive, he'd wound up here.

Escape wouldn't be possible. The ship was in the middle of the sea and the likelihood of commandeering one of the *Sea Witch*'s jolly boats was slim. There were also suspicious eyes all around, watching. More than a few of them were witches, who had God only knew what kind of power at their disposal to painfully dispatch him.

One of the crew guarded him now, a lean West Indian woman dressed in a loose linen shirt and flowing culottes. The bright blue of her headscarf contrasted with the burnished copper of her skin. She kept her hand on the pistol tucked into her sash, and maintained a healthy distance between Ben and herself, as if she expected him to lash out at any moment.

"Have you served on this ship for long?" he asked her.

THE SEA WITCH

She said nothing, but her hand tightened on the butt of her flintlock. The handle of the pistol was worn and smooth from much use.

He'd never set foot on a pirate ship. When the navy fought and then captured buccaneers, he wasn't involved in rounding up prisoners or seeing to their captivity, but he had been present when the outlaws were brought aboard the ship.

Ben had been the object of those men's hostile glares before. Yet they didn't possess the personal element that he received from the company of the *Sea Witch*. No one aboard this vessel liked him. There was far more safety within the confines of the brig than anywhere else on the ship.

Even so, to be on this ship, alone, *surrounded* by pirates . . . and *witches* . . . He knew something of the first, and far less of the second.

Tentatively, he touched the shimmering bars of his cage, then pulled back when hot sharp pain shot up his arm. The brig was enchanted. He'd have no way out.

If he stayed alive long enough, perhaps he might be able to get some word to Admiral Strickland and the *Jupiter*. He could lead the navy to the *Sea Witch*. And see every last one of the ship's crew arrested.

"Tanner must be a good captain," he tried again, "to inspire such loyalty this crew shows her."

More silence from his guard.

"Though she seems impetuous," Ben said.

The guard's eyes flashed, yet she remained mute.

"Raiding nearly fifty ships in the course of a single year," Ben continued. "An impressive reputation for any pirate company. And to do so without resorting to the depths of vicious bloodshed so many other buccaneers revel in, well, that's not without merit."

The guard's expression remained impassive.

60   EVA LEIGH

"Yet you kill when met with resistance," Ben went on. "The crews of slave ships face the worst of your brutality. Other pirate ships sell the enslaved for profit, but I've heard you never keep the human cargo. It's said this ship takes the freed people to a safe haven."

The woman standing sentry revealed nothing, not even a look of pride.

There *was* allegiance here amongst this ship of women. Unlike on naval ships, where the captain was assigned by the admiralty, by custom, pirate companies elected their captains, and another vote could see a buccaneer captain replaced by someone else. When captured by pirates, many prisoners opted to sign the articles and become part of the crew. On a ship such as this, they had an actual say in who commanded them.

Almost commendable, except for the fact that they were thieves, taking what did not belong to them.

The ship and her captain were paradoxes and enigmas—two things that had no place in this world with space only for right and wrong, certainties and truths.

How was it possible that Strickland had actually worked *with* a pirate? No one dealt as harshly with buccaneers as the admiral. Few of the pirates he captured ever made it to Port Royal for trial. In the five years Ben had served on the *Jupiter*, he'd witnessed the execution of scores of buccaneers, all at Strickland's orders.

Many others had been killed by the leviathan. The destruction of the *Diabolique* wasn't the first time Ben had witnessed the beast's deadly power, but that didn't stop a shudder from working its way along his spine as the terrified pirates' screams echoed through his mind. There was no honor in ridding the world of buccaneers, not that way.

Strickland had swallowed his ethos long enough to collaborate with an infamous pirate. Yet it was to create a weapon *against* pirates.

THE SEA WITCH
61

Ben winced as contradictions battered against the inside of his skull.

Steps sounded in the passageway, and the woman with the Mediterranean accent appeared at the entrance to the brig. She had a profile as noble and strong as any ship of the line. A black-and-white magpie perched on her shoulder, chirping lowly. The woman shot Ben a glower before turning to the guard.

"Captain wants to see him, Dayanna. Has he been giving you trouble?"

"Trying to worm intelligence from me." Dayanna handed the Greek woman a ring of keys that glowed with magic. "But that tree bears no fruit."

"That is why we trust you with the keys," the other woman said with a small smile. She inserted a key into the lock, and the glow vanished from the bars.

He could try to flee now—but he wouldn't get far.

The bird on the woman's shoulder flapped its wings. Once the door to the brig swung open, she snapped her fingers at Ben. "Up, malákas."

Whatever that word meant, it wasn't good.

Standing whilst bound at the wrists and ankles wasn't easily managed. Yet he struggled to his feet and shuffled after the Greek woman as she led him through a passageway, which was neat and orderly, up a well-maintained companionway—even more difficult with the shackles at his ankles—and then down another corridor, until she stopped outside a door and knocked.

"I have brought the pútsos," she said when a voice within bid her to enter.

"It's Sailing Master Priestley or Mr. Priestley," he reminded the Greek woman.

She leveled him with an indifferent look before shoving him inside.

Between the hard push and the bindings around his ankles, he stumbled forward, landing uncomfortably on his knees.

"That's how a man is supposed to approach a woman," came a wry feminine voice.

His gaze landed on the toes of a pair of boots, and then went higher, roaming up the thigh-high boots, along feminine thighs and hips encased in snug breeches, up over a leather tunic secured with a wide belt, going higher still until he beheld Alys Tanner's face, looking down at him with a mixture of contempt and amusement. She'd taken a kerchief of bright green silk and wrapped it around her head, and the color was striking against the red hue of her unbound hair.

"Speaking boldly to someone who's bound isn't an indicator of courage," he answered as best he could with a dry mouth.

She tipped back her head and laughed. It was a husky, plush sound, resonating with far more maturity than someone of her young years usually held.

"Provoking me into freeing you is a strategy that might work with a less secure person." She placed her fingertip beneath his chin and lifted it, so that their gazes met. "I've nothing to prove—to you or anyone."

"A woman in command of her own ship has much to prove."

"Men think women need to show how much they deserve something." Her finger stroked back and forth along his jaw. "When they themselves take whatever they want without considering whether or not they merit it. Most of the time, they don't."

Their gazes held, and a peculiar shiver moved through him, hot and cold at the same time. It must be some kind of enchantment she'd tried to place on him.

She leaned down, her warm rum-scented breath feathering over him, before she grabbed his manacles and hauled him up to standing. "Time to earn your keep, Sailing Master. Tell me about Little George."

"All I know of George Partridge is what's found in any broadsheet." He tried to follow as best he could as she pulled

THE SEA WITCH

him toward a table laden with charts. "As a fellow pirate, surely you have a better familiarity with him than I."

He glanced around the cabin. It wasn't as large as Admiral Strickland's quarters on the *Jupiter*, but it was sizeable enough to hold a carved dresser of walnut, a rosewood desk inlaid with mother of pearl that had surely been taken off a captured ship, a mahogany table laden with charts, and a narrow berth that was covered with gold-and-blue-patterned silk. There was a slight dent in the pillow, where Alys Tanner laid her head every night.

He ripped his gaze away from the bed to stare at the table full of maps.

"I'm giving you an opportunity," she said, "which men seldom deserve. Otherwise, we'll see how well you swim in irons."

Ben kept silent.

She tipped her head toward a chart that showed the whole of the known Caribbean. "The Weeping Princess."

He widened his eyes before checking his response and putting an impassive mask in place. Hardly anyone knew about the Weeping Princess. It was seldom spoken of anymore. Alys Tanner had been in the Caribbean for only a year, and if she spoke the name of it now, she'd learned of it, somehow.

Whatever she wanted, he wouldn't give her.

"A fanciful name," he said. "Whatever could it mean?"

She grabbed the front of his neckcloth firmly. Her face was tight with anger. "None of your hedging, Sailing Master, or I won't waste time with the brig. My cutlass can carve a neat path that'll spill your innards all over the deck."

"Messy."

"Call my bluff, handsome."

He blinked. "You think me handsome?"

Her lips curled into a smirk. "That's male perspective for you." Still staring at him, she said over her shoulder to the Greek corsair, "I'm threatening him with ripping out his guts, yet his attention snags on whether or not I've taken a liking to his face."

"Be done with it and split him open," the other woman growled. The magpie on her shoulder made a noise that sounded suspiciously like agreement.

"In time, Stasia." Softly, Alys Tanner asked him, "Will you tell me more about the Weeping Princess, or shall I satisfy my quartermaster's desire to see your intestines?"

"I couldn't answer that question," he replied. "Not without more information."

Her brow furrowed and she appeared torn. Then, after a moment, she released her grip on him.

He reached up and did his best to straighten the folds of his neckcloth. Without the free use of his hands, though, or benefit of a looking glass, it was a futile attempt to repair his appearance. At the least, his markings on his skin had disappeared.

"All you need to know is that I'm in search of it."

He studied her. "This has something to do with whatever was written on that glass in the tavern window. A riddle of some kind."

Her expression went opaque.

"So, I've the right of it," he surmised. "You saw something on the window, and then destroyed it to leave no trace behind for anyone else to follow. Something that has to do with that fail-safe George Partridge created, the one that severs the tie with the leviathan. The Weeping Princess might be the location of that fail-safe."

"I don't know that," she answered at once.

"But you suspect it."

When she said nothing, he knew he had his answer.

He raised his brows. "Surely your magic can tell you what you want to know."

Captain Tanner took a step back, crossing her arms over her chest. Which had the unfortunate result in drawing his attention to her breasts, the upper curves just visible above the low neckline of her shirt.

THE SEA WITCH

His last actual shore leave had been some time ago, along with the feminine company that could be found there. Clearly, it had been a long while, if he was contemplating the physical charms of someone he wanted to see clapped in irons.

She cleared her throat, and he dragged his gaze back to hers. Fortunately, the sun had deeply bronzed his face, or else he was certain she'd see his cheeks redden.

"I want the information from *you*," she said levelly.

"It appears there are limits to the scope of your magical power."

Her brow lowered. So, he was right. She did possess supernatural ability, but it wasn't as developed as he'd initially believed, if she couldn't suss out the whereabouts of the Weeping Princess with it.

"If the Weeping Princess is a location," she pressed, "you'll tell our sailing master where to find it."

"And have my throat cut for my service, while leading you exactly to the place where you could eliminate the Royal Navy's advantage over you." He would say nothing about Warne's intimations that more sea creatures might soon be added to the navy's arsenal. Giving her any information would only fuel her desire to find the fail-safe, and she could easily spread the knowledge amongst the Brethren of the Coast, undercutting the Royal Navy's advantage. "There's no upshot to this scenario."

"It'll mean preserving your life for a little longer." She studied him thoroughly, as if he could be read like the waves or the stars. "Are you so proud, Sailing Master, that you won't try to stay alive for as long as you can?"

He held up his manacled wrists. "I'm your captive, but my pride belongs to me alone."

Something like respect shone in her hazel eyes when he said nothing more. "Very well, Sailing Master. I'll spare you tonight. But by morning, I may change my mind and heave you overboard for the reef sharks."

"I am not reassured."

She stepped forward to weave her fingers into the hair at the back of his head. It was almost, almost like a lover's embrace.

"I don't care if you are or not," she murmured, tightening her grip so that tingling pain crept down his neck and along his shoulders. "Have faith when I tell you that I won't hesitate to end your life the *moment* you endanger me or my company. Understand that. Understand *me*."

In the whole of his life, he'd never met a woman with as much lethal confidence, as much *power*, as Captain Alys Tanner. A thrill of something ran the length of his spine, and it wasn't entirely fear or disgust or anger.

"Understood," he replied.

She didn't let go of him right away. Her grip on him lingered, and the narrow space between them seemed to grow vibrant and alive. Was she beautiful? All he knew was that he was profoundly *aware* of her, from the freckles scattered across her cheeks and the bridge of her nose to the unexpectedly rosy hue of her lips and the hollow of her throat, where a few pearls of sweat collected.

Her gaze dipped to his mouth.

"Alys," the quartermaster said loudly. The magpie also twittered.

The captain released him so abruptly that he had to fight to regain his footing. She took a jagged breath.

"Tell Faith to bring me a hammock," she finally said to Stasia.

"Your berth seems fine enough," the quartermaster replied.

"It's not for me," Captain Tanner answered. "It's for him."

Ben started. "Me?"

She regarded him with a smile that could only be called predatory. "You may yet prove useful to us, Sailing Master. I'm keeping you close. You aren't to set foot outside my cabin."

"I'm unarmed," he answered. "Manacled, shackled. Without magic, when many of your company are witches. Surely you can trust me with your crew."

THE SEA WITCH

"This is for *your* protection more than theirs. If you're in the brig, it'd be an easy enough thing for a member of my company to slip into your cage and slide a dagger between your ribs or cast a spell to turn you inside out." One of her brows arched up. "The safest place for you is beside me."

He stared at her. Trapped inside the captain's quarters . . . with the captain herself.

Safe? Hardly. Not with uncertainty and menace thick about him, like sharks circling bleeding prey.

CHAPTER FIVE

"Of your many good ideas, this is not one of them." Stasia spoke lowly to Alys, as two of the crew set up a hammock at one end of Alys's great cabin. It was a typical canvas hammock, no different from the other ones used by the rest of the crew. Neither a punishment nor a reward. Or so Alys told herself.

"I've run through several scenarios," Alys answered, "and this is the best option. He knows the Caribbean, better than any of us. Assets as valuable as him don't simply get caught in our trawling net. If I do this, I'll need him here, and safe."

"What about *your* safety?"

"The sailing master is shackled, manacled, and unarmed." She glanced toward the man in question, who stood near the large window and gazed around her quarters with a keen and interested eye.

If he was looking for telltale details that might give him more insight into her, he'd not have much luck searching the great cabin. There was the usual assortment of furnishings taken from plundered ships, including a French tapestry and a collection of gilded Spanish bowls that were nothing like the plain wooden ones she'd eaten out of back home. Alys still couldn't bring herself to eat from the gilded bowls, though, so they sat unused on her shelves.

THE SEA WITCH

When Alys had fled Norham, she'd taken the barest of essentials. Nothing from home held sentimental value, save for a compass, and the seashell Ellen had given her long ago, which now resided in a locked drawer in Alys's desk.

His sharp gaze fell on one of her few personal possessions that held any true meaning: between books on seamanship and navigation, there was a small painting of a woman reading by the light of a single candle, rendered in the Dutch style. The woman resembled Ellen, not so much in appearance, but in thoughtful, absorbed disposition. Yet he couldn't know this, and nothing in and of itself in the painting gave anything about her away. Even so, merely seeing him have this tiny glimpse into her made the impossible happen: she blushed.

"I can't sleep through a mosquito sneezing," she added. "With those irons on him, he won't scratch his bollocks without me hearing. Any attempted attack during the night will be met by a spell that summons the energy of a bear snapping saplings to break every bone in his hands."

"Physical attacks are not of much concern to me," Stasia noted dryly. "Even Blind Yannis from my village would be aware of how the sailing master looks at you."

"The navy man is afraid and uncertain."

"There is more than fear in his eyes."

Alys glanced in Benjamin Priestley's direction. His own gaze darted away, but not before she felt his regard on her, warm honey upon her skin. It wasn't quite the way a captive contemplated their captor.

He was a warrant officer of His Majesty's Navy. If he'd been so determined to chase her from the tavern through St. Gertrude and then onto the naval ship *Jupiter*, and *then* cling to the side of a longboat as she made her escape . . . she'd be a damned fool to think he wouldn't seize any opportunity to reverse their situation and see *her* in irons. And, unlike her general policy of not killing those she captured, if she fell into the hands of the navy, she'd be summarily tried and hanged at Gallows Point in Port Royal, with her rotting body displayed in a cage as a warning to others who might follow in her footsteps.

They would love to see not just a pirate but a witch executed for the crime of existing.

"He serves one purpose. Warming my berth is not it."

"You have another aim in mind. If it is what I believe you intend, I consider it a prodigiously bad idea."

"What choice do I have?" Alys demanded lowly. "He won't speak of what he knows, but there's another way to get him to reveal his secrets."

Stasia's lips thinned. "Dreamwalking is a dangerous tactic."

"What happens in dreams isn't real."

"Not in the dream itself, but," the quartermaster added in a whisper, "what happens *after*. I have heard that dreamwalking binds you to someone. It is impossible to step through someone's dreams without having a part of you interwoven with some part of them. There is no going back from taking that leap into their mind."

Dreamwalking was something Stasia had told her about, a legendary practice that witches and mages of the Mediterranean and Levantine Sea dared to employ whenever they needed to go deep within someone's mind to unlock hidden mysteries. It was seldom done, though, risky as it was for both the witch and the dreamer.

"How've you gained this knowledge?" Alys asked. "You've never done it before."

"Neither have you."

Despite the unease in her belly from the danger that loomed, Alys clipped, "I've little choice in the matter. His dreams will give us what we need, and the task's too important not to try. Consider what it'd mean if we used Little George's fail-safe. We'd have far less to fear from the threat of the *Jupiter* if it didn't have the leviathan. If that means taking this risk, I'll do it."

THE SEA WITCH

Stasia drew closer, and said in a whisper, "It is not something you can *force* upon another. If one party is unwilling, the dream-walking cannot happen."

"'You and me, we're enemies to the bone, but do you mind if I enter your dreams?'" Alys exhaled. "He'd never agree."

"I would not wish someone to do it to me. The mistakes I have made in my life have been my own—and even then, I paid for them."

Though Alys was tempted to press Stasia for more details, she held her tongue. They had grown close over the past year, but even so, the details behind Stasia's reasons for putting the Mediterranean behind her remained hazy. The few hints Alys had been able to figure out had been enough to reveal that a broken heart and betrayal lay at the core of the trouble, and when it came to matters of shattered love, it was best to leave that wreck at the bottom of the sea.

"I will leave his dreams alone," Alys finally said. "I'll find some other means of learning what he knows."

"There is no need to keep him this close. The brig should be where he sleeps."

"He'll be less of a mind to help us if his view is spoiled by bars. Staying in more comfortable quarters could sway him."

"Are you thinking of his comfort, or a view of his fine thighs?"

"I'm captain of this ship," Alys fired back, "and more concerned with the fate of my crew than the navigator's thighs." She forced herself not to look at Priestley, or the long taut length of his legs shifting beneath the tight fabric of his breeches.

"Apologies, I must be thinking of another redheaded captain who stares at him like he is the fresh beef after months of hardtack."

Alys sent her friend a rude hand gesture.

"Back to your duties," she said to the crew once they had finished hanging the hammock from two hooks. It swayed with the motion of the ship, as though being rocked by an unseen mother.

The crew saluted her before quitting her quarters.

"That includes you, quartermaster," Alys added for Stasia's ears only. "We'll break our fast at four bells. Josephine might be flattered into making coddled eggs and toasted cheese."

"Yet no one on this ship can make coffee worth a damn. Sleep as soundly as you can tonight."

"I sleep no other way."

"Mind, do not think of beef." After shooting her a wry glance, Stasia quitted the great cabin. Leaving Alys alone with the sailing master.

They glanced at each other before looking away. A strained and uncomfortable silence fell. Her body was curiously awkward, her tongue and gaze oddly shy. She snorted in self-disgust. She'd taken to the sea to never again have to adhere to social niceties or custom. Especially in the presence of men.

"Your quartermaster should be disciplined for being so familiar with you," he said.

"I rely on her familiarity. It helps me keep this ship sailing smoothly."

"Without regulation and order, and hierarchy, a ship falls apart."

"Everyone knows their duties on the *Sea Witch*, and we take pride in keeping her shipshape, but none of us are better than any other."

He shook his head. "The customs of pirates are inexplicable."

"Only to those passing judgment on us. We're all exiles aboard this ship, in one fashion or another. But not you. This sea is your home. You know it better than anyone."

She crossed the cabin to where the map of the Caribbean lay spread across the table. For over a year, she'd studied charts such as this one, learning islands and inlets and keys and archipelagos, and all the secrets that drew so many to this part of the world. It was beautiful and treacherous, a place of mystery and

THE SEA WITCH

azure water, beyond the scope of anyone ever fully grasping the complexity of such a vast place.

"A year isn't enough to understand this sea," she murmured.

"Lifetimes aren't enough." He clinked his way to stand beside her, and they both regarded the chart and its painstakingly rendered collection of atolls, peninsulas, and straits, islands both large and barely the size of a grain of sand. "Though I was born here, many of us will always be outsiders, so we cling to our maps to show us places and things we can't ever fully understand."

Her hands clenched and unclenched at her sides. "It hurt me, too, to set fire to your chart room."

"No one impelled your hand to throw that spell." His voice was flat.

"By chasing me, that's exactly what you did."

"A neat rationalization."

"You don't have the protection of the king here, Sailing Master. On this ship, in this cabin, we're simply people trying our best."

"I fail to see how making a living through theft and murder is *trying your best*." He set his hand on the table, and the chain stretching between his wrists rattled like metal bones.

Alys didn't tell him that she and the women of Norham had first come to the Caribbean in search of something else other than plunder. Freedom. Becoming pirates hadn't been part of anyone's agenda. Yet in order to fund their liberty, they'd turned to the only practical means available to them: piracy.

Having tasted the luxury of freedom piracy had provided, she wouldn't go back. Too long had she been denied the right to be whomever she desired. He'd no notion of that, no concept that it wasn't the plunder that brought her and her crew to these waters, but a treasure far beyond monetary value.

Why should the sailing master know any of this? It wouldn't change his opinion of her or her crew. His beliefs about them didn't matter.

"The difference between you and me," she said, "is that you pretend your theft and murder is a patriotic act."

"There's nothing of me that you understand."

She planted her hands on her hips as she turned to him. "I understand that men go to sea because they are forced to, or because they're searching for themselves. Impressed sailors of low birth don't usually rise high enough to become warrant officers and sailing masters, and they don't speak as you do, with words taken from expensive books."

His mouth tightened.

"Which all makes me believe you joined the navy to carve out your place in the world. In search of glory, maybe, when none was available to you on land."

There was a long silence, before he said quietly, "To follow the path of glory he wanted for me."

"He."

The sailing master spoke softly, almost to himself. "Yet I hadn't the ability to captain my own ship, as he did, and I took better to reading charts and stars and finding elusive longitude and guiding the ship safely to wherever it needed to go. There's . . . utility in that. Despite what he said. I found my purpose."

Her regard skimmed over the clean lines of the sailing master's face, how his jaw tightened as Priestley spoke of this *he.* Whoever that man was to him, the shadow *he* cast over his life was long, and darkened the sailing master's path to this day.

There was something in his words, the finality that came from grief and loss. She'd known it herself when her parents had been felled by scarlet fever, leaving her to the care of indifferent relatives, when she'd learned from her marriage that the love of songs and dreams wasn't the same as the love a husband used to fetter his wife and crush her spirit. She'd known grief, too, when her own sister had been killed by a mob.

THE SEA WITCH

"I *am* sorry," she said softly. "For burning your maps."

He gave a slight frown. Still, he must've heard the sincerity in her voice, because he answered, "You don't have my forgiveness, but you do have my understanding."

They were quiet together, each taking the measure of the other. All around them were the sounds of a ship at sea: creaking timbers, waves slapping against the hull, voices of the company gossiping and telling tales as they took the late watch. She'd grown used to these noises over the past year, comforted by them, far more than the wind rattling the bare tree branches in the depths of a Massachusetts winter or the yells of men bringing their fishing boats into the dock. Those noises only heightened her loneliness, and reminded her she was powerless.

The sea was her home now. It strengthened her resolve and gave her magic life. No one would take that from her. Including this sailing master.

He held the key to finding the fail-safe, but she'd have to find some different means of learning it other than dreamwalking. Best not to meddle in magic that she'd little understanding of, power that held consequences neither she nor Stasia grasped, and so it had to be set aside.

"Sleep now." Alys nodded toward the hammock, slightly swaying as the *Sea Witch* rose and fell upon the waves. "However they run ships in the navy, here we start early."

"Four bells," he said. On land that time would be six in the morning.

Sitting on her berth, she pulled off her boots and let them fall to the planks with a thud. She undid the large buckle of her wide belt, but set her flintlock on her pillow, before pulling off her leather tunic. Her hands hesitated at the hem of her linen shirt.

"Funny," she said softly.

"This scenario is about as far from amusing as we are from Shanghai." He'd clambered into the hammock, though it had taken a small amount of fumbling due to his bound hands and feet. Still, he'd managed to be as agile as anyone could be, given the circumstances.

"You won't hear any laughter from me." Her fingers plucked at the hem of her billowing shirt. "It's only . . . most nights I sleep nude."

There was a long silence, and then his voice came low and deep on the other side of the cabin.

"As do I."

His answer ran like a rough hot palm across her flesh. She ignored the shiver dancing over her skin, and the images his reply had stoked in her mind. She could only guess at the body that was covered by his clothing, but she'd no doubt he wasn't one of those soft gentlemen who didn't do a lick of work to keep a ship running. He *had* kept pace with her through the streets of St. Gertrude.

She pressed the heels of her palms into her eyes. As soon as the *Sea Witch* docked next, she'd find herself a warm and eager body to enjoy until she was thoroughly spent and ready to resume her solitary life.

As much as she told Stasia that she'd stay alert and armed for the duration of the night, Alys wouldn't be too foolish and strip completely while sharing her quarters with a man she'd met a handful of hours ago. A man who was in every capacity her enemy. Yet maidenly behavior wasn't her way, not any longer. Those embarrassed and chaste years were behind her.

She worked off her snug buckskin breeches and threw them beside her boots.

"Jesus."

His oath was low and barely audible.

She smirked to herself. Without pride she could claim that her legs were fine ones. Not a lady's legs—they were too muscled for that—but they were sleek, and she never felt unsteady on them. Clad only in her long loose shirt, she climbed into her berth, though she *was* careful not to give him an eyeful of her bare arse as she did so. A nice arse, to be sure, and he was entirely unworthy of seeing it.

As for the muslin binding around her breasts, which she kept secure for ease of movement in combat, that she'd leave on. It wasn't especially comfortable. She always looked forward to that time at the end of the day when she could unwrap the length of cloth from around her chest. Not tonight. He definitely didn't deserve seeing her teats, even with her linen shirt covering them.

She doused the horn lantern beside her berth by taking the fire back into herself, letting its spark become part of memories of midwinter bonfires. Lying back, she touched her hand to her trusty flintlock on the pillow beside her head. The weapon was already primed and loaded, and she held tightly to her dagger, which had been a gift from the crew after their first successful raid against a British merchantman and was as much a treasured possession as it was a weapon.

Thanks to the irons binding him, she did indeed hear his every shift and movement.

"Keep that clinking and clanking down, damn you," she growled into the darkness.

"Freeing me is the solution to that," he answered.

"I'm no cribbage peg to be moved around the board, Sailing Master."

"Stale mate, then."

"The other option is you could settle the fuck down and go to sleep," she retorted. "God—you had better not be one of those types who leap up and down all night like a flying fish."

"My duties aboard the *Jupiter* keep me busy from four bells to eight bells," he replied, his voice deep in the shifting shadows of her quarters. "The moment I lay down, I'm asleep."

"Chasing me all around St. Gertrude, onto your ship, onto *my* ship, getting captured. That qualifies as a full day."

"My current circumstances aren't calming."

"Manacled and shackled," she agreed. "A prisoner aboard a witch's pirate ship."

"That, and . . ." He cleared his throat. "Sharing close quarters with a woman . . . It's not something I have much familiarity with."

She lifted onto her elbow and regarded him as he lay in his hammock. The cabin was dim, save for the gleam of moonlight casting diamond-paned shadows through the long window. In the darkness, her quarters became as small as a pair of cupped hands, warm and close.

"Priestley by name as well as behavior. Or . . . you prefer men."

"Neither are true."

"A wife? A sweetheart?"

"Neither, again." There was a moment's silence before he spoke once more. "Most of the crew at sea go in search of company once they get shore leave. The same for me, when given the opportunity."

"Women aren't models of chastity, either, despite what preachers insist."

"Yourself included?" He turned enough so that the pale light shining into the cabin revealed the gleam of his eyes as he gazed at her. His fingers were interlaced across his flat abdomen, but there was tension in them, the veins on the back of his hands standing out.

"This furnace burns hot." She could scarce believe she told him such things, but there was a strange intimacy about speaking with him in the darkness, as if the words themselves drifted from her like so much weightless flotsam. Including telling him about the fact that she could barely go a day without some release.

Damn, with him in her quarters, she'd have no means of giving herself a climax. *That* would prove a problem.

"Mine as well," he answered, barely audible.

THE SEA WITCH

They stared at each other, the air thickening and heating more than the tropical climate surrounding them. He swallowed, and then returned his attention to the deckhead above.

"Then you're a liar," she said at last.

"The hell I am," he fired back.

"You *do* share a room with a woman."

"A bed for a few hours," he allowed, "but I never stay the night."

She continued to stare at the sharp line of his profile. "A few pumps and then you weigh anchor."

"Well," he said after a moment, "isn't that what's supposed to happen?"

"By the tides, you have been sorely led astray by many misguided voices."

"They enjoy it," he answered. "My lovers. They tell me so."

"Tell me, Sailing Master, do your lovers make *this* sound?" She let out a long moan. "Or do they say this, *Yes, yes, yes!*"

He said nothing.

Alys snorted. "Paying for your pleasure doesn't ensure your lover's." She lay back and stared at the beams overhead. "Your ship has the lines of a sloop but in truth you're a barge. I've nothing but pity for the women you take to your berth."

"Fortunate, then, that you'll never be in their place."

"I count myself blessed, indeed."

They both fell silent then.

He had better be worth the risk of having him aboard her ship. Hopefully soon she'd know what he knew. Not through his dreams, but she'd find another way.

Her breath slowed. Sleep crept in on foggy fingers. It *had* been a long day, fraught with danger and discovery. She welcomed oblivion.

Sinking into slumber, she heard his sigh. Even from across the cabin, it wafted across her skin, warm and intimate. Drifting through the layers between waking and sleep, she grew light as air and thin as a forlorn hope. And then she was asleep.

80 EVA LEIGH

The room was spare, institutional. A table held stacks of leather-bound books in tidy towers. Outside came the cries of harbor life, and above that, seagulls diving at the fishing boats' catches, though the sounds were distorted, as if through thick layers of glassy time. Priestley stood beside a window, his brow creased deeply as he ignored the harbor scene outside. Instead, he stared at a man who looked very much like him, same blue eyes, same pristine coastline of a profile, dressed in the bright coat of a naval captain. Gold braid trimmed his collar and cuffs. The spotless garments sat upon him well, as he stood comfortable in his authority.

Alys was there, in that room with them both, but not there, as if a specter. Yet she *felt* the frustration and confusion within Priestley as the older man regarded him with unyielding detachment.

"I will not be swayed in this, Ben," the older man said. "As master's mate, the compiling of the logbooks falls to you."

"I can do it aboard the *Valiant*, Father," Ben pled.

"You'll do it ashore, and here you'll remain until the ship returns."

"But—"

"Insubordination from my own son? A grim day, indeed. Now I'm certain you must remain behind for this operation. I cannot have anyone disobeying my orders, especially not you."

"Please—"

The room was empty, only the noises from the port town heard in the stillness, sea air thick in the chamber.

Father was gone, and Ben was alone with the stacks of logbooks.

Alys's vaporous hand rose up, yet suddenly Ben was smaller, just barely out of childhood, and a tide pool surrounded him. It was crystal blue, dotted with coral and tiny fish darting through the water. He played, waving a wooden sword as he commanded a fleet of leaves that he'd placed upon the water. And then, there

THE SEA WITCH 81

were tentacles . . . the flash of an animal's body undulating . . . and a terrible pain as ink spread through the water . . . ink choking him as it seeped into his skin. The pounding sea roared around him. There was fiery pain and harrowing fear and a loneliness that made him feel impossibly young as no one came to help. Was he being punished? Ben cried out, falling to the rocks, cutting his hands. Streaks of blood uncoiled in the stinging seawater.

This changed, too. She was in the shelter of the woods west of Norham, the slim birch trees rustling like dancers. Ellen was there. Her curls were the gloss of red-tipped wheat, a paler hue to Alys's own fiery hair. A tiny chickadee nestled in Ellen's cupped hands, and gazed up at her with black currant eyes. The bird chirped at Ellen, who answered in a low murmur, and she smiled encouragingly.

"He says he can lead us to bushes full of wild blueberries," Ellen said to Alys. "We can fill baskets enough to make a season's worth of preserves."

"But if someone asks us how we found so many berries," Alys protested, "what are we to say? The bird *told* us?"

"It's the truth, isn't it?" Ellen's moss green eyes were wide and guileless.

"Tell no one about this," Alys urged. "Being pilloried will be the least of our problems."

Ellen waved her freckled hand. "Who does it harm, if I speak to creatures like this chickadee? I should think the village would welcome the birds' wisdom "

Desperation scrabbled up Alys's throat. How could she make her sister understand the danger she put herself in, being so open, hiding nothing?

Yet Ellen dissipated like a mist, and the trees became a towering waterfall, pounding against rocks far below. It was surrounded by lush trees of every shade of green, the sky blue and fathomless above, and nothing else was nearby, not a village or a town or any other sign of human habitation. It was alone, solitary and splendid and terrifying. No one had been here, not for many years, and even its legend had faded with each passing generation.

The Weeping Princess.

"Where is this place?" Alys asked.

Ben was there, turning to her. "Alys?"

Within the dream, she and Ben were together on a curving white beach, a storm-riddled sky over them, the sand soft beneath them as they curled together. Their limbs were intertwined, their damp clothing forming the thinnest of barriers between their straining bodies. His hair fell damply around his face. His hands were on her cheeks and neck, in her hair, and he looked down at her with such desire and tenderness, she could hardly breathe. Her own hands moved over his shoulders as she pulled him down to her.

"Alys," he murmured, low and husky, "I've waited and wanted you for so long."

"No more waiting," she urged.

Any moment now, his mouth would meet hers, and she would have his kiss, the kiss she desperately needed. Against his bottom lip gleamed a bead of water.

A half-animal, half-human sound echoed. Something roared across the water and the sand. She reached out, desperate to stop whatever was coming.

Ben was torn apart into shreds—his blood spattered across her face. A nightmare creature towered above her, a mix of man and sea beast, ten feet tall and rippling with muscle, covered in scales. Its maw bristled with teeth, and black claws topped its huge hands. Raw horror froze her in place as it lunged for her.

She gasped as she tumbled onto the floor of her cabin. Her body shook and her legs trembled. Her hands pressed into the rough wooden planks. Sweat coated her skin, and she shivered with its cold.

THE SEA WITCH 83

Cold, yes. It was cold and real and she was awake. The dreams were only that. Just dreams. They were his dreams. And hers.

There was the rattle of chains as someone awkwardly shuffled closer. A pair of boots appeared before her, bound by iron shackles, and then a hand reached down to wrap around her wrist, bruising in its power. It hauled her up so that she was on her knees, facing Ben as he stood beside her bed.

"What the hell," he rasped, "was *that?*"

They stared at each other, eyes wide. Waves of confusion and anger swirled within her, leaving her adrift and isolated. And yet, though these emotions spun inside her, they belonged to someone else.

In his stunned face, she knew the devastating truth.

They were linked, woven together. A twin self beside her own, like another heartbeat. Fierce and pounding and close, so very close.

She was part of him now. Just as he was part of her.

And there was no going back.

CHAPTER SIX

Hot and cold danced over Ben's skin. His mouth was sand dry, and an incessant throbbing pounded behind his eyes as he stared at Alys Tanner, his hand wrapped around her strong, sinewy wrist. Beneath his fingers, her pulse hammered.

Despite the manacles binding him, he didn't relinquish his hold of her, pulling her up from where she knelt.

She allowed herself to be hauled to her feet. Whatever had just transpired between them, she had to be affected by it in no small measure, else she would have resisted him far more. There was fight and fire in the pirate captain. As it was, she was unsteady, and in the dimness of her cabin, her face was carved of pale marble.

"What have you done?" His words abraded his throat.

"I didn't mean to," she answered.

"You were . . ." He tried to run his free hand down his face, to ground himself with the textures of his own skin, but the chain stretching between his manacles was too short for him to hold her and touch his cheek. There was nothing to anchor him. "I dreamt. And you were *there*. And you're . . ." He was able to press his hand against his chest. "You're *here*."

Uncertainty cut through him, but it was *her* doubt he felt, *her* uneasiness and uncertainty and volleys of questions that buf-

THE SEA WITCH

feted him as much as they tormented her. The flame of her energy blazed within him, singeing him from the inside out.

His arms throbbed with the echo of her, a reverberation from his dream. The dreaming remembrance of her sleek and taut limbs pressed against his vibrated through his flesh. Even as the dreams faded, the resonance of her continued. He could still feel the sand beneath them, holding the impression of their bodies on an unknown beach, and feel the shadows of passing storm clouds.

"What *was* that?" he pressed.

"Dreamwalking. I'd planned to," she confessed, "to learn about the Weeping Princess. But . . . it's not supposed to happen . . . not unless both people involved seek it."

"I didn't *seek* that."

"Something . . . something made it transpire. Something in me sought you out. Something in you . . . came to me." Her look was unsure.

He tightened his grip, her flesh damp and hot within the cage of his fingers. Numbness ebbed, revealing a jagged, rocky shore of anger.

"I would never come to you," he insisted. "Not in the waking world, and certainly not in the world of dreams."

Her gaze met his. "Yet you did. I was in your dreams."

He grimaced. "And I was in yours."

There had been a gentle young woman, her hands careful as she had cradled a bird. And Alys's fear for this girl.

"The Weeping Princess is a waterfall, perhaps where we'll find the fail-safe," Alys said after a moment, "but the precise where of it, that I don't know."

"There are corners of my mind that you haven't plundered?"

"It wasn't intentional," she fired back. "And dreams are . . . the past, the present, history, and omens of things that may or may not come to pass."

"The beach. That thing on the beach."

A shudder coursed through her. "Meaningless images. But there was more, and still, that didn't give me . . . everything."

"Good."

"There's something between us now. A . . . bond."

He reared back as if she'd elbowed him in the face. "No."

"Neither of us have a choice, Sailing Master."

He tossed her wrist away from him, burned by her skin against his. Yet that did nothing to ease the sensation of her, fierce and alive and determined, inside of him.

"It's Sailing Master Priestley, or Mr. Priestley," he answered. "If you're going to thrust yourself into my mind, my dreams, have the courtesy to call me by my name."

"Ben."

"Only my family and those I call friend may call me that."

She paced away from him, her feet making soft padding noises upon the wooden planks of the floor. Her legs were still bare, the high firm shape of her buttocks evident beneath the long hem of her linen shirt. He refused to make himself look away.

She took a long drink straight from a bottle pulled from a cabinet. Then another. The column of her throat worked as she swallowed, and a single bead of liquid traced from her lower lip to settle in the hollow between her collarbones.

When she held the bottle out to him, he hesitated. Then strode to her to snatch it from her hands. He paused a moment before putting his lips where her lips had been. Niceties were long gone, drowned in an undersea cavern.

"French brandy," he said after taking a sizeable drink. "Stolen, doubtless."

"I'd never pay the doubloons such fine swill demands. The best we could hope for in Norham was cider from Uriah Nash's apples, or small beer."

"That's your accent. I'd figured you for a colonial. No deference for authority."

THE SEA WITCH

Her lips twisted. "Deference was the coin of the realm back home. A woman couldn't exist without the proper amount of fawning over the men of that fucking place."

"Unsurprising that you live there no longer."

He shook his head. It didn't matter where she came from. All that signified was what she'd done.

At the least, the brandy had pushed back memories of her in his dreams. Dreams of people and places he'd no desire to share with her—or anyone. Ever.

Yet he'd been in her dreams, felt her love for the young woman. And terror at what lay ahead.

She took another swallow of brandy, then handed it back to him. He drank. It was excellent quality, tasting of apples and vanilla and wood, far better than a warrant officer could afford for himself.

Bound to her. She would find her way into his mind, whether or not either of them desired it. His secrets were not his own. Not any longer.

"You won't find the Weeping Princess on a white man's map," he said after a moment. He gestured with his free hand toward the table covered with charts, the manacles clinking heavily. "Scarce people are alive who remember it, and they hold tight to the knowledge."

"They're few in number?" she asked.

"Disease has reduced their ranks to next to nothing," he said, grim. "A legacy of the Spanish."

"The English, too, I'd wager."

He fell silent, unable to refute this.

"The rest of it," she continued. "If you please."

"There is a small island, off the westernmost coast of Hispaniola. It's lush, abundant with flora and fauna. Legend has it that a princess fled there with her lover, a man her family had determined was unworthy of her. The princess and her lover thought they were safe, but her family gave chase and found them. He

88   EVA LEIGH

attempted to protect her, yet her kinsmen attacked and killed him, and he fell dead at her feet. Her tears were so copious, so eternal, that the nature spirits took pity on her and transformed her. Into a waterfall."

She was quiet, and then nodded. "Tell our navigator where to locate this island."

"And have my throat cut for my service." He shook his head. "I'll guide us there, step by step."

"You aren't in control here, navy man—Mr. Priestley."

He stepped closer to her, into the halo of invisible energy that surrounded her. The nearer he came, the more it resonated in his own body. There was courage in her.

And doubt.

He started.

This brazen buccaneer . . . uncertain? Yet she was. Beneath the hard carapace of her identity as a witch, and a pirate captain, it was there.

There was sadness in her, too. The bleak reverberations of loss.

She drew in a sharp breath, and he felt it then, the resonance of himself within *her*. All the parts of himself that he kept tightly locked away, they'd seeped into her. Desires and fears and hopes and sorrows. A thirst for things he dared not name, not even to himself. But now he'd become part of her, just as she had become part of him.

God *damn* it.

"We're neither of us in control," he growled. "Not anymore."

THE NAVIGATOR FOR the *Sea Witch* was summoned, a woman named Luna. The lone lantern cast wan light on her fair but tanned skin. She appeared at the door to Alys Tanner's cabin. Luna's long sandy hair lay in sleep tangles around her shoulders and her gray eyes were drowsy but keen, yet she was alert and eager to listen to Ben's directions on how to reach the island of the Weeping Princess.

THE SEA WITCH

89

She and Ben consulted as the captain looked on, nursing a tankard of rum. Fortunately for his sanity, Alys Tanner had put her breeches on. If he'd had to look at her bare legs a moment longer, with the dream memory of them wrapped around his body . . . The limits of his self-control could be tested for just so long, even if he still reeled at the way the sanctity of his dreams had been shattered.

He rubbed at the center of his chest. She'd said only one who desired the connection could make it happen. The last thing he wanted was to be linked to her. And yet he'd done it, anyway.

The task of guiding the ship's navigator to the island made for a welcome distraction.

"For years, I've sailed these waters," Luna admitted, her hands braced on the table as she studied the chart, her Scottish accent round and rolling, "and I never knew of this island or its whereabouts."

"It likes to keep itself hidden," he answered.

The navigator nodded. "All places have their own will, their own minds. I felt it in the Hebrides, where I was born, and strongly here, in the Caribbean."

"Is it not safer for you at home in the Hebrides? Aboard a ship such as this one, your life cannot last long." Unexpectedly, he liked Luna. Ghastly to think of her at the end of a noose, or splayed dead upon the top deck.

A corner of Luna's mouth turned up. "Where I'm from, they gave me the wrong name, the wrong clothes. It was only when I sailed away and found my true home on the *Sea Witch* that I could be who I was always meant to be. There's no safety in that, and the life I led there . . . it was hardly the one I wanted for myself."

Ben gazed at her, and then at Alys Tanner, who looked at him with a challenge in her eyes. He was filled with her protectiveness for Luna. For all her crew.

He returned his attention to the chart on the table.

"We should reach the island two days after tomorrow," he explained. "I'll give you further coordinates as we get closer."

"Those coordinates would be most useful *now*," the captain returned. "*All* of them."

"Leverage, Captain."

Luna made notes in her log, her quill scratching across the paper the only sound in the cabin. "I'll be back at four bells for more."

"Four bells, then," he said.

"Back to your berth, Luna," Alys Tanner directed. "Can't have you yawning over your charts all day tomorrow, or we might wind up accidentally sailing to Curaçao."

The navigator gave Alys a salute and a slight bow to Ben before hurrying out.

"I cannot speak to the rest of your crew, but you found yourself a fine navigator, Captain Tanner," Ben said, in the silence. He shook his head. "Odd, addressing you by so formal a name, when—" he swallowed "—you've been in my dreams. And I in yours."

Like a bell that had rung out across a silent valley, she continued to resound within him, even though they now stood at opposite ends of her quarters.

"Calling you *Sailing Master* or Mr. Priestley seems . . ." She gave an exhalation. "There aren't terms for what we are to each other."

"Not friends." Though weariness weighted his body, he stayed away from his hammock. Sleep was dangerous now. "Not allies."

"Not quite enemies, either." With a flick of her fingers, she summoned a flame and lit another lantern, which she carried to her desk. She sat down heavily in her chair, bracing her elbows on the crimson baize covering the wooden top.

"You're a pirate. And a witch." He remained standing, though the span of distance between them seemed to stretch more taut the farther away she was. "I'm a sailing master for the Royal

THE SEA WITCH

Navy. *Enemies* seems the right word to define our . . ." he cleared his throat " . . . relationship."

"On account of the fact that you won't hesitate to throw me and my company in irons, if given the opportunity. We all know where imprisonment for pirates leads, and the fate for captured witches is no better. Worse." Despite the brightness from the lamps, a shadow crossed over her face, carving the hollows in her cheeks even deeper. The whisper of past loss shivered.

"No one forced you to choose a life of piracy," he pointed out. "Or to be so open with your magic."

"I've learned they'll always find a way to come for witches," she continued, "no matter how much we subdue and refuse to acknowledge our power. It just takes a look, a whispered word, a grudge against a woman who rejects a man's advances, or the insistence that we bow our heads to any man—and then we're swaying at the end of a rope like so much dried fish. If I'm to be condemned to death one way or the other, then I'll do so using my magic as openly as I please."

"You chose to be pirates," he said again. "You can choose whether or not to use your magic, to let others see it."

She pushed up from her desk and stalked toward him. "I used to believe that. But I think differently now. Why should we hide our power? No one makes the same demands of mages, and they get velvet robes at their academies, roles of esteem in rulers' cabinets, well-paying jobs and black sashes as they sail on merchantmen and naval vessels and pirate ships. A mage is respected, revered."

There was fury in her eyes and though she spoke steadily, her body faintly vibrated. She could explode like so much gunpowder, if given the right charge.

And there had been that woman in her dream, the one she'd warned not to reveal her magic to others. Who was she? What had become of her?

Before he could ask, she went on in a tight voice,

"The same can't be said for a woman who shows the slightest leaning toward magic. Yet their powers are the same. The only difference is, when they are children, one's given a poppet and the other a wooden sword. And *that* decides if they're to be hunted or honored."

He stared at her, each of her words landing like a blow that took his breath.

"You're angry that we've walked in each other's dreams," she went on, "and angry that I picked a life of freedom upon the seas, where I can be exactly who I'm supposed to be. Judge me how you please, but I don't give a damn if I have your approval. I'll hold tight to all of the gifts I can claim. The other choice for myself, and for so many others, is misery and death. Understand that, *Ben*."

Rage emanated from her. Her anger thrummed, his own body shaking with its force.

"It would have been better," he said after a moment, "if we'd met under different circumstances."

A few grains of the fury in her eyes sifted away, and the barest hint of a smile wryly touched her lips. "No one asked either of us to write prophecies for what's to come. Like fools, we can only blunder in the darkness and pray we don't hurt ourselves as we stumble forward."

The lantern hanging on the wall cast shadows that swung back and forth with the movement of the ship. There was always a remarkable profundity about being on ship at sea, such a small and fragile wooden thing in the midst of the vastness of the ocean. And yet in Alys's tropic-warm cabin, with her body close to his, her gaze holding his, and the continued sonorous presence of her within him—nothing could be more intimate.

Three bells rang out. At this hour of the night, that meant it was half past one in the morning.

He and Alys blinked, stepping away from each other. Despite the distance they put between them, the air continued to

THE SEA WITCH

pulsate, even as she busied herself at her desk, flipping through pages in a leather-bound book that lay flat on her desk.

"Luna will be back in four and a half hours," Alys said gruffly, not looking at him. "Sleep while you've got the opportunity."

"I've little interest in having you tramp through my dreams again. Or to stumble my way through yours."

She looked up briefly before returning her attention to her book. "Perhaps if we both fight it, the dreamwalking won't happen."

"I'm not much comforted by your hopes and suppositions."

Still studying her tome, she muttered, "What you do with yourself bears little weight with me. Sleep, dance, frig yourself. I hardly care."

"All three of those things require privacy that I don't possess." Yet his jaw ached with the force of holding back a yawn. Much as he didn't want to return to his dreams, if he didn't sleep, he'd barely be able to function. And he needed all his faculties to survive the calculable future.

He went to his hammock and lowered himself back into it. Immediately, the rocking motion made his eyelids heavy. Through his lowering lids, he caught glimpses of her studying the book in her hands. Her head kept dropping, but she snapped it up and glared at the pages she turned as if whatever was written there had insulted her choice in firearms.

He closed his eyes. A hard, dead slumber dragged him down. But she was also afraid. She would resist sleep as long as she could. Staying awake would preserve the distance between them.

Yet it was already too late.

The game might not be entirely hers to play. She'd take what she wanted . . . and so could he. Make himself indispensable to her, insinuate himself. He had abilities and knowledge she needed, and with them, he'd lead her to the prize.

Together, they would find the fail-safe. And then, he would destroy it.

CHAPTER SEVEN

"SUNRISES UP NORTH weren't the riot of color they are here in the Caribbean," Alys murmured to Stasia, her hands on the wheel as she steered the ship eastward, into the apricot glow of the sun. Though the sky was clear, it still held a multitude of hues, from deep indigo to marigold, the shades saturated and profound.

"Gray and heavy as the village itself," Alys went on. "Every morning, I'd crack my eyes open and say, 'Oh, fuck, another goddamn day in *this* place.' Well," she amended wryly, "I'd *think* it, because if Sam or anyone ever heard me use such language, the best I could hope for was being pilloried. Olive Miller had very good aim when it came to throwing rotten cabbage."

"Today, you are eager to receive rosy-fingered dawn."

Standing beside her on the quarterdeck, her second-in-command sipped at a tiny cup of coffee. Upon rising, Stasia always made herself coffee with all the ceremony of an ancient priestess. She'd once admitted that the possessions she'd brought with her from Greece had been few, but the dented copper briki pot was absolutely essential. She'd also shown Alys her minimal other belongings that accompanied her from the Mediterranean, including a set of throwing knives, a brace of pistols, and her mother's coral komboloi beads, which she still carried and ran through her fingers when there was a rare moment of leisure.

THE SEA WITCH   95

Eris, perched on Stasia's shoulder, moved to dip her beak into the cup, but Stasia held it away from her familiar. The few times in the past that the magpie had managed to take some sips, it dove and swooped all over the ship and terrorized the company with its manic twittering.

"Impossible to stay in my berth when there's this to greet me." Alys gestured to the wide, gleaming horizon.

"It is only eagerness to see the morning," Stasia said dryly, "and not the fact that the navy man shares your quarters. Perhaps he snores as loud as a hurricane and you cannot sleep. Or is it," she added with narrowed eyes, "that you do not want to sleep now that you have shared your dreams."

"You drink too much of this stuff and it's given you wild imaginings." Alys snatched the cup from her quartermaster's hand and took a deep drink of what coffee remained, though she was careful not to get a mouthful of the thick sludgy grounds at the bottom.

The remainder of Alys's night had been spent sitting up at her desk, forcing herself to pore over magic tomes rather than sleep. None of the books had covered dreamwalking or, more urgently, how to undo the aftereffects of being part of such perilous magic. "Besides, I didn't do it on purpose. It simply . . . happened."

"Perhaps your mind did it without your permission because you wanted the dreamwalking to happen." Stasia took the cup back and eyed the grounds at the bottom for auguries.

"Being in his dreams . . . and him in mine . . . I didn't like it. He was in every part of me. And I was in him. I've never . . . I've never been so . . . so close to anyone." She closed her eyes against the rush of remembrance, all the parts of Ben nestling within her as though they fit together like dovetailed walnut, locking tight. "Nothing within me wanted that."

Alys nodded to the crew who were coming up from below-decks, having broken their fasts and now ready to face their tasks for the day.

"If there's any benefit," she went on, "it's that we now know where to find the Weeping Princess. We can't risk someone else finding the Weeping Princess and the fail-safe. Gods and goddesses know what they'd do should it fall into their hands. Little George colluded with the navy, and it's a safe enough assumption to think that any of the Brethren of the Coast would sell it to the Crown for enough ducats and doubloons. They wouldn't care if the leviathan kills other buccaneers. Few are as untrustworthy as pirates."

"We are, rather," Stasia said with a hint of pride. "Some consider this trait charming rather than a detriment."

"It's less charming when there's a noose around your neck or a spell that makes your innards boil like so much soup. Or makes you flee the sea you once called home."

Stasia inclined her head in acknowledgment. "You will have to sleep some time."

"There are other ways to find rest." Alys stepped aside when Hua came forward to take her usual position at the helm.

Moving to the railing, Alys leaned on the wood and surveyed her company, smoothly and efficiently carrying out their duties. Cora, Dorothea, and Dayanna began the strenuous process of swabbing the decks. Meanwhile, Susannah made fluid hand movements to summon swirling winds. The breezes gently lifted her up the mainmast, enabling her to take her place in the crow's nest.

"Aloft with you, too," Stasia murmured to Eris. The magpie crooned before flapping her wings, taking off to keep watch from the skies. "Poor leadership is all that can result from refusing to sleep."

"I will. At some point." Hopefully, the effects of the dreamwalking would fade over time. Weaving herself into Ben's mind and heart—and his into hers—carried too many dangers.

She sensed him now, fainter that there was some physical distance between them, yet his tension and restlessness coursed through her blood, pushing her own concern to greater heights.

THE SEA WITCH

If he ever crept back into her dreams, learning her own secrets, delving even deeper . . .

"In the meanwhile," Stasia said with a lift of her eyebrow, "I shall brew more kafés for you."

"If you've any kindness, you'll brew three more cups." Worry and fatigue made for a long and uneasy day, and, as her quartermaster had pointed out, Alys was the captain of this ship. Decisions, judgment, mediation—it all flowed through her, and the added burden of the sailing master pushed her into new doubt.

She couldn't fail her company.

If she made a poor choice with Benjamin Priestley, everyone aboard this ship would pay the price.

SHE TOOK HER midday meal. Stayed above decks all afternoon. After eating, she kept herself busy for several hours by cleaning muskets and pistols, carefully avoiding her cabin and the man that currently dwelled there. Even so, his unrest and determination mingled with doubt still hummed through her. He was an ember smoldering in the hold that only she could feel the heat from.

Anything to keep from going to her quarters, and facing him.

No one could fault her hospitality. Food and good ale were brought to him on a regular basis, entertainment in the form of books were provided, she even had a pitcher of fresh water and a cake of soap brought to him so he could clean his face.

None of that had soothed him. If anything, she was aware of his growing edginess, a knife being sharpened for too long until it cut the bladesmith.

There was curiosity, too. About *what*, though, she couldn't tell.

He hid something from her, too. But she'd once anchored the *Sea Witch* for eight days in a cay, waiting out a Portuguese ship that had hoped she would lose interest in the gold and silver stowed in its hold. She didn't lose interest. She knew something of patience.

"How fares our guest?" Standing in the prow, she spoke to Inés, who had brought him the water and soap.

The other woman rolled her ink-dark eyes. "Ricocheting off the bulkheads like he was fired from a musket. I wager he's not the sort used to doing nothing."

Six bells rang out. Ashore, it would be three in the afternoon. He'd been alone in her cabin for the duration of the morning, and a few hours after the midday meal.

"He'll have to accustom himself to the practice," Alys said. "He should be grateful he's not confined to the brig."

"*Grateful* isn't the word I would use to describe him," Inés answered. Her long tawny fingers picked at a thread that had come loose from her embroidered tunic, which was tucked into breeches that buttoned up the side. "I have seen more placid racehorses at the starting gate. I would bet on him, too. Snorting and stamping like a prized stud."

"That stud's not for breeding."

Inés chuckled. "As though Susannah would look kindly on me sharing my charms with anyone but her. Besides, our navy man will soon turn his spyglass to another star." She gave Alys a meaningful look.

"This ship's run with too liberal a hand," Alys answered gruffly, even as her cheeks heated. "Get to your duties."

"Aye, Cap'n." Inés saluted before climbing down the companionway.

After an hour spent practicing levitation spells with several members of the crew, Alys whittled and watched Cora challenge Polly to see who could make the heaviest object on deck move the farthest. It was a draw after they both managed to float a cannonball from the ship's bell on the foremast to the capstan. All the bets that were placed sadly had no outcome, and the crew adjourned, grumbling good-naturedly.

THE SEA WITCH   99

Soon after, Luna reported that she had consulted with the sailing master several times to double-check their heading as they sailed toward the island of the Weeping Princess. Stasia sent Eris ahead to scout any possible traps, and everyone on watch had kept careful attention, in case the navy man led them into an ambush. Nothing was found.

Alys didn't ask after him. They needed distance between each other.

It was late afternoon when Dorothea came to her, moving her square body with purposeful haste.

"Cap'n, we're not alone," she announced. "I been in the crow's nest and just before my watch was done, I caught sight of a ship trailing us. About a league south by southeast."

Alys looked meaningfully at Stasia, standing nearby. Together, they went to the railing and looked in the direction Dorothea had indicated. As Stasia sent her magpie familiar skyward, Alys pulled out her spyglass, and summoned the sight of a hunting hawk into the device. When the spyglass glowed with tawny light, she aimed it south by southeast. The enchanted lens immediately found the ship, a sleek schooner flying a black flag adorned with a skeleton in a tricorn, the ship's crew moving quickly around the vessel as it pursued the *Sea Witch*. A mage had positioned himself in the foredeck, his hands outspread as he summoned winds to push the ship forward, his black sash flapping in the breeze.

The captain of the tailing ship stood on the quarterdeck, clad in a skirted green coat with wide cuffs, the jade plume of his hat dancing in the wind. Alys's spyglass was so powerful she could make out the emerald adorning the captain's ear.

"Jacob Van der Meer," Alys muttered.

"Craftiest pirate this side of Santo Domingo," Stasia added grimly.

"He was at the Wig and Merkin, when Little George's letters were read. I kept well away from him."

"Old lovers can be such irritations."

"And he knows about the fail-safe. But not where to find it. Reckon he believes we know. Which," Alys went on, "we do. But we're keeping that to ourselves."

"Orders, Captain?" Stasia asked.

"Get Luna up here," Alys said to Dorothea. "We need her guidance. Go with haste," she added, though the crewwoman was already hurrying to fetch their navigator.

Luna arrived moments later, a chart tucked under her arm.

"We can try to outrun Van der Meer and the *Edelsteen*," Alys said without preamble. "But it solves nothing. A persistent bastard. He'll dog us from one end of the Caribbean to the other, burning valuable time."

"A fight?" Eagerness gleamed in Stasia's eyes. She curved her palm over the pommel of her blade.

Alys covered Stasia's hand. "Our aims can be met without a single drop of blood staining anyone's decks. Cheer up," she added when Stasia looked downcast, "if all our strategies fall short, I give you permission to be the first in the fray. Spells or steel—it'll be up to you."

Stasia looked slightly cheered. "Give us your strategies, then."

A quick consult with Luna followed, and Alys outlined her plan. As she spoke, her quartermaster and navigator nodded. When everything had been determined, Stasia strode about the ship, issuing orders to the company. Three of their witches were assigned to summon winds to give them speed, but others possessing magic were instructed not to use their power until Alys gave the command. Limited as their untrained magic was, they needed to hold some back in reserve, or the plan wouldn't come to fruition.

Tension grew as the *Edelsteen* kept a close pursuit, the distance between their ships holding steady, but it was only a matter of time until the larger vessel caught up.

THE SEA WITCH   101

What Van der Meer had planned for them remained unknown, but hard lessons had taught Alys that buccaneers remained ever capricious. Early in her career as a pirate, other captains had offered her alliances, only to have them decide after raids that they wanted all of the plunder for themselves. Murder or harmony—either were possible.

It didn't change matters that she'd spent a few weeks in Mérida sharing a bed with Van der Meer. If anything, their time together made him even more unreliable.

"How long until we reach our destination?" she asked Hua at the wheel.

"Quarter of an hour," the helmswoman answered, absently brushing at strands of straight black hair that had pulled free from her two thick braids. She adjusted the brim of her round cap. "You see it there, just off the port bow."

A thin finger of land emerged on the horizon, one of countless tiny islands that were scattered all across the Caribbean. Hua expertly steered the *Sea Witch* toward the island as the sky overhead deepened to sapphire with the coming night.

Alys stood on the quarterdeck, anxiety and excitement mingling in her belly like a potion. Life up north had been a constant series of identical days, with chance moments of fear from storms that battered the coast—and the constant threat of having her magic discovered. Her only glimpses of a life beyond that airless existence came after Samuel's death.

But even then, life had always come slamming down like the top of a pillory, locking her into place, whenever she'd had to sail Samuel's boat back home and resume her workaday life. It was only after they stole their ship and escaped Norham for good that Alys gave herself and the women who followed her the freedom she'd always hungered for.

For all the uncertainty and treachery and risk of sailing the Caribbean as a buccaneer, there was an untamed, reckless joy in it. Alys would rather meet death at the end of Van der Meer's cutlass than return to the drudgery of a fisherman's wife.

The sky darkened further, long streaks of gold piercing through the indigo, as the *Sea Witch* approached the tiny island.

Summoning the soft murmur of a late spring breeze, Alys whispered into her hands. The spell made sure that her words would be heard by her whole crew, but no one beyond the decks of the *Sea Witch* would hear even a sigh.

"We know what to do, my friends," she quietly informed the company. "Wait until I give the signal, and then we give them a display to rival any man-o'-war."

"Aye, Cap'n," came the whispered replies.

At the helm, Hua guided the *Sea Witch* into the inlet. It formed a cup, lined with tall rocky cliffs, and a narrow white sand beach meeting the water at the farthest end of the cove. Beyond the beach stood a fringe of mangrove trees, turning black as the night progressed.

Hua positioned the ship close to the base of one of the cliffs at the mouth of the cove. It was tricky work, ensuring that the vessel didn't get caught and founder on any of the rocks that lurked beneath the water, and that the masts didn't smash against the face of the cliff. Hua was one of the best at the helm, hailing from the East China Sea, where she had piloted her uncle's cargo ship, and now here, in the Caribbean.

Once the *Sea Witch* was in position, Alys whispered to her crew, "Witches, gather on quiet feet at the mainmast."

Those of the crew that possessed magic collected at the base of the mainmast, Alys and Stasia included. Eris perched on the yard, keeping close to her mistress, but she kept her usual trills to herself when, at Alys's nod, the witches held hands.

Everyone exchanged concerned looks. Twice had they attempted something similar, and only one of those efforts had been successful. When they had failed, they'd barely escaped with their lives.

THE SEA WITCH 103

"Stone and rock and sea and surf," Alys murmured, "veil us, hide us from those we don't trust."

Everyone softly but urgently repeated her words.

"Think of the cliffs, my girls," Alys urged, "and the water below. Let them form a cloak to hide us."

Intense concentration filled each of the crew's faces as they summoned a glamour to shroud the ship. At the center of their circle, a mist collected, faintly at first, then with growing thickness. It smelled of rain pattering onto rock. The mist deepened and condensed, collecting around the deck and then rising up the masts and spilling over the sides.

"That's it, beauties," Alys pressed. "They say women are tricky and hide their true selves. If that's what they believe, we'll give it to them. And reap the benefits."

The haze continued to grow, enveloping the ship. As it did, Alys kept wary attention to the mouth of the inlet, waiting for Van der Meer's ship to take the bait. Hopefully, her crew's magical ruse would work.

Moments later, Van der Meer's vessel appeared at the entrance to the cove. Everyone aboard the *Sea Witch* went silent, collectively holding their breath, as they watched the pirate schooner sail into the inlet.

Alys's heart climbed into her throat. If it came to a fight, she and her crew would give Van der Meer and his company a brawl. But, stars above, she prayed to avoid it.

The prow of the *Edelsteen* turned into the quay, the rest of the ship following. It sailed farther into the inlet, its progress marked by the lamps and torches gleaming on its top deck and glowing from the portholes.

Alys put one hand on the handle of her cutlass, the other on the butt of her pistol. She balanced on the balls of her feet, ready in case she might be called into action, a cry of command to attack already forming on her lips.

And then . . .

104   EVA LEIGH

Van der Meer's ship sailed right past the *Sea Witch*. The captain himself stood on the forecastle, gaze aimed straight ahead, looking for his target. The *Edelsteen* cruised forward.

Alys bit back a cry of exultation. It had worked. Neither Van der Meer nor anyone aboard his ship had spotted Alys's vessel, hidden as it was by the glamour conjured by the *Sea Witch*'s company.

"Now, Captain?" Stasia whispered eagerly.

"Not yet."

The *Edelsteen* sailed farther into the inlet.

"Now?" Stasia pressed.

"Hold a moment longer . . . only a breath . . ."

The *Edelsteen* sailed forward in slow degrees.

"Now," Alys said.

At Alys's command, her crew leapt into action. The company armed their cannon as Hua steered the ship away from the cliff. The helmswoman positioned the *Sea Witch* between Van der Meer's vessel and the mouth of the cove, blocking the *Edelsteen*'s only means of flight, and trapping it in place where its crew's only option was to abandon ship and flee onto the island.

Once they were in position, Alys ordered, "Drop the veil, beauties!"

As if burned away by a blazing sun, the mist surrounding the *Sea Witch* immediately disappeared. Alys raised her pistol into the air and fired. The sound echoed off the cliffs and into the depths of the dark blue night.

The crew aboard the *Edelsteen* rushed to rails and collected on the aft deck. They gaped as the *Sea Witch* appeared seemingly from nowhere.

Alys smirked at Van der Meer, who stared along with his crew. Beside him, his mage was just as immobilized by shock. The two men stood at the rail of the quarterdeck, gawking like greenhorns on market day, not seasoned buccaneers. The pirate

THE SEA WITCH

captain collected himself enough to scowl, and with his reputation for cleverness, it was no wonder. Falling victim to a ship full of witches' glamour wouldn't enhance his standing.

"Impolite," Alys called across the expanse of water that separated the *Sea Witch* from the *Edelsteen*. "Paying a call without properly announcing yourself. It makes a woman wonder at your motivations. Surely, they can't be nefarious, can they, Jacob?"

Van der Meer's features creased as he made himself smile widely. "So many guns pointed in this direction," he shouted. "Such displays of aggression are unbecoming in old friends."

"*Are* we friends, Van der Meer?" Alys wondered. "My memory recalls you attempting to swindle me out of my share of the gold in Île-à-Vache."

"That was a misunderstanding only, liefje."

"It's Captain Tanner. I'm *not* your sweetheart." *Not anymore.* "Explain what you mean by chasing after my ship, with no friendly flag flying."

"I—"

Alys held up a hand. "We parley on the beach. Then *you're* going to give me a thorough report of your actions and plans. If, for any reason, I don't like your explanation, over a dozen witches aboard my ship will use their collective powers to summon a hundred whirlpools to sink your ship. There won't be anything left, not even a length of cordage floating on the water, to show that you or the *Edelsteen* ever existed."

"Can we *do* that?" Stasia hissed in Alys's ear.

Alys answered lowly, "Van der Meer doesn't know what we are and aren't capable of. Let him believe we can mobilize all the fiery beasts of hell, if it means we keep him in fear. Answer quick, Jacob," she called to the other captain, "or things may start to spin for you."

To punctuate this, Alys made a swirling motion with her fingers.

Van der Meer nervously held up his hands. "We shall meet you on the beach at once." He turned to speak to a man who was likely his second-in-command.

Alys was already striding toward the jolly boat. "Stasia, you're with me. I want Jane, Susannah, Dayanna, and Inés. Polly," she said to the woman as she strode forward, "you have command of the ship until we return. And if *anything* looks dubious, if any one of his crew so much as farts suspiciously, open up every gun and summon lightning to strike his ship."

Though Polly had only actually accomplished the purposeful summoning of lightning a handful of times, she saluted. "Aye, Cap'n."

The jolly boat was lowered, and the requested crew climbed down the rope ladder to take up their positions in the small vessel. Alys moved to climb down, as well, but before she took a step, Polly asked, "What about the navy man?"

Alys paused for a moment. It had been almost a relief, having Van der Meer chase the *Sea Witch*, giving her a much-desired distraction from sensing Ben's presence both aboard the ship and within Alys's own mind. Yet merely hearing his name brought her perception of the sailing master back to the forefront of her awareness. Unrest drummed through the invisible fibers weaving between him and her, adding to her own unease. Something greatly troubled him.

She made herself shrug.

"This is pirate business, and as he's made clear, he wants no part of pirate business. He stays locked in my quarters." Alys continued descending the ladder to the jolly boat, forcing away thoughts of Ben. All her focus was needed for this parley with Van der Meer, and determining just what, exactly, the other pirate captain intended.

Whatever Van der Meer planned, she had to be ready for it.

CHAPTER EIGHT

Torchlight revealed only wary glances and suspicious glares. It lit the crescent of glittering sand beneath everyone's boots as both captains and crew faced off on the beach. Hands hovered close to weapons. Van der Meer's mage stood at the buccaneer captain's side, his fingers curved in preparation to deploy a spell, but then again, Stasia and Susannah also had glints of reddish magic dancing over their hands, ready to be called into use at the barest hint of treachery. Tension strung taut between the two parties.

Her hand resting on the pommel of her cutlass, Alys kept her attention fixed on Van der Meer. The torchlight rendered him even more striking than he appeared in daylight, cutting in the sharp planes of his face, making his teeth flash white in his sable beard, but she wouldn't be swayed by his handsome face again. Nor anything else he offered her. Deceit often lurked behind the most beautiful of facades.

Samuel had been widely considered the most fine-looking man in Norham.

"Hostility has no place here," Van der Meer said in his honeyed voice. "We're all of us friends, aren't we?"

"Friends don't chase each other from St. Gertrude to here." She gestured to the beach.

"We *could* be quite friendly once more, if you only say the word."

Stasia snorted.

"That port's no longer open. Besides, I don't expect you're tailing my ship just for a sentimental fuck."

The warmth in his dark eyes cooled. "You won't share what you know about Little George, and this fail-safe of his? We all saw what happened to Fontaine and the *Diabolique*. None of us want to suffer a similar fate."

"I'm a simple woman, Jacob. I keep to my ship, run my raids, and not much else." Alys was careful to keep her expression shuttered—but she had a lifetime of practice hiding what she thought and believed. Especially from men.

Van der Meer shook his head. "Ignorant people don't have naval officers pursue them from the tavern. Nor do they sail with such purpose as you have been since leaving St. Gertrude."

"I'm to believe you won't find the fail-safe, and then turn around to sell it to the Royal Navy. Stow your protests, Jacob, and don't pretend like I've insulted you," she said when he placed a hand on the center of his chest, as if personally wounded. "After what passed between us in Mérida and then Île-à-Vache, and your considerable record of betrayal, even Jesus Christ wouldn't have faith in you."

The other captain shrugged. "It's possible I have only been searching for someone that *I* can believe in."

"That wasn't me?" Alys feigned a sad frown.

"We needn't be enemies or competitors," he wheedled. "Why not search for the fail-safe together? Ridding ourselves of that leviathan would benefit every pirate. It would be an advantage, combining my knowledge of these waters with your ship's abundance of magical ability. After all, it has been merely a year since you came to the Caribbean, and there are gaps in your knowledge I would be happy to fill." He punctuated this statement with a roguish grin.

THE SEA WITCH 109

Alys exhaled. "Flirtation's a poor negotiating tactic when one party has no further interest in the goods being tendered. Besides," she added, "I recall at Île-à-Vache that you referred to me and my crew as *that seafaring pack of magical bitches*. So, much as I appreciate your offer, I decline."

"Liefje—"

"And if you follow me again," Alys continued, "I'll make good on my vow to send your ship to the bottom of the seafloor. There are nearly two dozen witches aboard my vessel, whereas you have only *one* mage."

She flicked a contemptuous glance at the man in question, who quailed beneath her regard. The mage shrank even more when Susannah and Stasia encouraged the magic around their hands to glow brighter, red light flitting demonically over their faces.

"I favor our odds," Alys noted. "Now, this parley's concluded. Good night, Jacob, and fair winds."

Van der Meer bowed, ever gallant, but he didn't look particularly pleased by the way negotiations had fared. He muttered angrily under his breath, little knowing that Alys knew Dutch and was well aware of the variety of insults he hissed at her.

"You're perfectly welcome to go fuck yourself," she said in cheerful Dutch.

He scowled but said nothing more.

With one eye on the other pirate captain, Alys turned to head back to their beached jolly boat. Her crew pushed the small boat back into the water and they all climbed aboard. As Dayanna and Inés took up the oars to row them back to the *Sea Witch*, Alys kept her attention on the beach while Van der Meer and his crew clambered into their jolly boat. The captain moved stiffly, his posture rigid. He wasn't happy, taking out his frustration by yelling at his men, who slouched over their oars.

"Will he shadow us?" Stasia also watched the other pirates.

110   EVA LEIGH

"Jacob's a cunning man, but not especially courageous. I reckon our *seafaring pack of magical bitches* is enough to keep him cowering and licking his own bollocks."

"There may be others," Stasia pointed out. "From what you said, that tavern was full of greedy buccaneers looking for any means of advancing their own causes."

"Jacob was skilled with his tongue," Alys said. "He also can't hold it. Word will get out that we're not to be trifled with, or consequences will be inflicted. Besides, half the Brethren of the Coast shits themselves in fear when our name is mentioned. I take comfort in that."

"We may want to reserve our concern for what is happening on our own ship," Stasia said, looking toward the *Sea Witch* with a frown. "It appears that our naval guest is trying to escape."

BEN'S FINGERS ITCHED for his rosewood and brass backstaff so he might measure the altitude of the sun, but all the tools of his navigational art remained behind on the *Jupiter*. Trapped as he was in Alys Tanner's quarters, he couldn't stand upon the deck to gauge the sun's shadow. The cabin held the heat of the day, yet without the warmth of the sun upon his back, a chill skimmed along his skin.

The sun and the horizon—beautiful eternal entities that only responded to a skilled hand coaxing the mysteries of location in the vast, vast world.

He had no polar stars to find his position.

Instead, his compass had been replaced by the captain. He'd sensed her throughout the day. She'd been solidly confident, but something troubled her. Unbalanced, as if she tried without success to steady herself with the horizon.

His own balance reeled. Without his tools, his work, nothing gave him equilibrium. Not the familiar texture of the brass buttons on his coat, not the tendons flexing in his hands, not the sounds of the gulls crying to each other.

THE SEA WITCH

He'd jolted with the realization that *he* was what unsettled Alys Tanner. It was mutual, then. Yet he took no comfort from this shared restiveness.

Restlessness made him rabid, desperate for anything to occupy his thoughts. He'd moodily stared out the window that ran the length of the cabin, watching the clouds, the water, the birds that wheeled above the waves, the dolphins cavorting below them—whatever might hold his attention.

Late in the afternoon, a speck of another ship appeared on the horizon.

Alys had left behind a spyglass on her desk, and Ben trained it on the dark fleck that grew larger as it attempted to close the distance between the two ships.

God, let it be a member of the Royal Navy's Caribbean fleet. Finally—he could end this nightmare of being trapped aboard a ship brimming with pirate witches, and sever whatever it was that wove his consciousness with hers. In every capacity, he pulsed with awareness of her.

His gut sank when, instead of the Union Jack, the ship flew a black flag emblazoned with a skeleton wearing a hat.

"Hell."

Jacob Van der Meer. A slippery eel of a buccaneer who was as known for his cunning as well as his duplicity. Only last month, Van der Meer had fired a pistol into the back of Enrique Ocampo when the other pirate captain had been foolish enough to partner with him on a series of raids along the Honduran coast.

Van der Meer was one of four other pirate captains spotted in the vicinity of his father's ship on the day of the murder. The Dutchman or a member of his crew could be the killer.

And if his ship, the *Edelsteen*, was following the *Sea Witch*, chances were high he possessed malicious intentions.

Ben raced to the door of the cabin. He'd raise an alarm so they might evade whoever was in pursuit. But then his hand hovered over the door, pausing before he could pound on the wood.

If Alys's ship evaded Van der Meer, Ben would lose a crucial, desperately needed opportunity. The closer Van der Meer's ship got, the more Ben could discover . . . He wasn't certain *what*, exactly, he might be able to find, but *something* was better than nothing. There could be a hint, a clue, *anything*.

He went back to the window, watching through the spyglass as the *Edelsteen* grew closer. His gut clenched and his muscles jumped with the need to move, but there was nothing to do except wait.

At some point, the *Sea Witch* became aware they were being followed, because the ship took up a very specific course. A tiny island was close at hand, reachable just before sunset, and it seemed it was their destination. But why would they pick that location, when it had a small inlet and rocky cliffs and not much else of note?

Ben kept his spyglass trained on the *Edelsteen* as night started to fall. The *Sea Witch* sailed right into the island's inlet, effectively cornering themselves.

It made no sense. Alys Tanner had proven herself a skilled captain. Only a novice would entrap herself and her crew.

He imagined her on the deck, gilded in the day's last light as she gave commands to her crew. What did she feel, as Van der Meer's ship drew closer, and her own ship cornered itself?

Guarded but determined. Not the emotions of a panic-gripped captain.

After the ship took up position beside the cliff at the entrance to the cove, a strange, potent energy enveloped the vessel, shrouding it in mist. *Magic.* It pulsed beneath Ben's skin, surging in his blood.

A small crimson chamber deep within him throbbed, awakened. An unknown core buried in the fibers of his self that blinked and roused, stretching itself, becoming aware.

THE SEA WITCH   113

Ben shook himself violently. Yet the sensation didn't go away. It strengthened, blocking out nearly everything.

The *Edelsteen* sailed past the *Sea Witch*, right into the inlet.

Some kind of glamour had been deployed by the witches of this ship. It worked, too, because Van der Meer had trapped himself, stuck between the beach and the *Sea Witch*.

Gasping, Ben sank to the floor when the glamour suddenly dropped. It was as though he had been released from a choke-hold, and he gulped down air.

He collected himself enough to stand. Van der Meer and his crew were close. If he could reach the ship, even merely spy from a better position, he could learn something.

Ben strode back and forth, but the window running the width of the captain's quarters hemmed in his view. All he could see was the mouth of the cove, and the dark waters stretching behind it.

He paced the breadth of the cabin, his teeth clenched in frustration, his muscles tight and vibrating. Locked in these quarters, with no means of getting a decent vantage of the *Edelsteen*. Maddening.

He tucked the spyglass into his boot, then strode to the diamond-paned window and pushed it open. A startled laugh escaped him. It wasn't locked. No one suspected he might attempt to slip free from his imprisonment this way. All he would be able to do was fall into the ocean and drown.

That was a very real possibility now, but there was no other alternative.

He clambered out the window to cling to the back of the ship—and slipped. Gripping the window sill, the muscles in his arms ached as he held on tightly. His feet dangled high above the water, and while the fall might not kill him if he managed to avoid slamming into the rudder, the weight of the manacles and having his hands and feet bound when sinking to the sea-floor certainly would.

114   EVA LEIGH

Gritting his teeth, he pulled himself up. Sweat slicked down his back as he managed to drag himself to perch on the window sill. On shaking legs, he rose to standing, then gripped the carved wooden ornaments that ran the length of the ship's aft hull. The captain's cabin was just below the quarterdeck, and he used all of the strength of his upper body to pull himself up to the quarterdeck's rear balustrade.

Ben peered over the edge of the railing. One of the crew had her back to him, her attention fixed toward the beach. He wouldn't be able to see much of the *Edelsteen* from the quarterdeck. He'd have to go higher.

Summoning another burst of strength, he hauled himself up to balance on the quarterdeck railing. He grabbed the main boom, sticking out from the mainmast, and pulled himself onto it. Surely the metallic clanking of his bindings would attract the crew woman's notice. Yet whatever was happening on the beach had her full attention, with the tides against the ship's hull hiding his sound. Beyond the ship's bow, torches gathered on the sand.

Carefully, he edged himself along the boom, until he reached the mainmast itself. With years of experience climbing masts, he began to ascend. The ship's deck beneath him grew smaller the higher he climbed, the stars above him shining down pitilessly as his whole body throbbed with the exertion of scaling the mainmast with his ankles and wrists fettered.

Finally, he reached the main top yard. With one more effort, he hauled himself onto the beam from which the sail hung. The deck of the ship was far below him, yet he was used to such dizzying heights. Instead, he focused on the other ship, swaying up and down on the cove's tide. From his boot, he pulled out the spyglass, unfurled it, and brought it to his eye.

Through the thick lens, the lamps that lit the *Edelsteen*'s upper deck were bright flickers. Much of the crew stood at the railing that faced the beach.

THE SEA WITCH   115

Ben choked around his own pulse as his gaze raked over the pirate company. They were a grizzled lot, many bearing scars and wearing clothing that was a jumble of the rough and the refined, which was obviously stolen, though even the most lavish garments were frayed and stained from use. All of them bore the hardened expressions of men who seldom thought of consequences or compassion.

His attention bounced from buccaneer to buccaneer. Surely *one* of them had an object in their possession that placed them at his father's murder—a trophy from the ship, like the engraved cutlass that Father had carried but was never recovered, or the ship's bell, or, hell, *anything* at all. He just needed *something*.

Ben turned toward the beach in search of Van der Meer. Flame red hair snared his attention. Some of the *Sea Witch*'s crew surrounded Alys, but even with a spyglass he couldn't make out their expressions.

She faced Van der Meer. A parley. Reaching an understanding about the fail-safe? Would they find it together, and use it as leverage against the navy?

Faint noises sounded below him. Shouts and yells. Commands. He paid them little attention as he watched the conference on the shore.

"Come down at once," someone called up to him, "or we'll use force get you down."

The words were as meaningless as a fly's buzz. Mentally, he swatted them away. He peered closer at the Dutchman. There had to be some sign on the pirate that marked him as his father's murderer.

"What the hell?"

His body went rigid. A net of humming energy closed around him, binding his arms to his sides and making it impossible to move his legs. The spyglass slipped from his immobilized fingers to shatter against the upper deck. Ben struggled against his bonds, to no avail. Trapped. Without the proper use of his feet to maintain balance, he lurched off the yard, pitching into the open air.

He squeezed his eyes shut, waiting for the sickening vacuum of freefall and the inevitable impact of his body on the wooden planks. He'd seen men plunge from the rigging and crow's nest before. Some survived the fall with broken arms or legs. Others broke their necks and never climbed again.

Ben braced his body for the crash. Then opened his eyes when it didn't come. Instead, he lowered slowly down from the mainmast's height, held by unseen hands.

Finally, he reached the upper deck. It wasn't the most graceful landing—set down abruptly in an ungainly heap of limbs, like a marionette with its strings cut. The buzzing energy of the spell dropped away enough for him to get to his feet.

Only to find himself surrounded by a score of crew members, all of them pointing pistols and cutlasses at him. Three of the crew that didn't have weapons trained on him had gold and purple magic dancing on their fingertips. All of them appeared ready to unleash the full power of their arsenal, both mundane and magic, on him.

An Indigenous woman stood at the fore, clearly the one in charge. Long-limbed but solid in stature, she held herself with authority. Her onyx eyes flashed with anger in her sun-kissed copper face.

"There's no escape, navy man," she said tightly.

Frustration clenched his muscles even more than the magic that bound him. The broken spyglass lay nearby, its metal body dented and its lens shattered.

"Give me another spyglass," he said to the woman currently in command.

Her eyes widened.

"Hurry," he snapped.

"Prisoners who attempt escape don't have the luxury of making demands," Alys said, climbing over the gunwale. The rest

THE SEA WITCH   117

of her crew followed to join her on the upper deck, but Ben's only focus at that moment was the *Edelsteen*, currently hoisting its anchor.

"Give me—"

"A spyglass, so you've said." She moved closer, glancing around at her crew that still had their weapons and magic aimed at him. Her gaze landed on the remains of the spyglass. "You've destroyed *mine* in a bid to escape, so I'm not going to put another one into your hands. Or give you anything at all that you want."

He hardly heard her. Van der Meer's ship had raised its anchor and was currently, cautiously, sailing past the *Sea Witch*. The other crew of pirates sped through their duties, and though they were too far away for Ben to see the expressions on the company's faces, they moved furtively, anxiously. Almost as though they were afraid of the *Sea Witch*. In a few minutes they would be beyond the cove, and heading into open waters.

"*Please*," Ben gritted to Alys as his gaze was fixed on the *Edelsteen*. "I have to see—have to know—"

"To the brig with him." Her words were clipped and cold. "Escape attempts aren't rewarded with staying in the captain's quarters."

"You don't understand—"

But four members of the *Sea Witch*'s crew laid hands on him and forcibly dragged him toward the companionway. He strained and fought against them, frantically trying to reach the railing so he could get a final look at the other ship before it disappeared into the night. Yet before he could reach the gunwale, another weblike spell encircled him, making it impossible to move. His feet lifted a few inches up from the decking. He *floated* across the upper deck, down several companionways. Until he found himself back in the brig.

He was thrown unceremoniously into the stockade, landing roughly on the floor. The bars clanged shut, and one of the crew murmured under her breath. Once again, the bars of the brig glowed with green energy.

"I have to get out!" he insisted. "Have to see—" Ben heaved to his feet and grabbed the bars of the stockade. He was thrown backward into the wooden bench that stood against the bulkhead behind him. The seat of the bench rammed into his spine, and he groaned in pain as he fell to the floor. Yet nothing compared to the agony of knowing that his chance to learn more about his father's murderer was, at that very moment, sailing away.

All of the crew left him, save for one woman who sat in a chair opposite the stockade, her pistol pointed at him, her face completely vacant of sympathy.

Ben sank to the ground, his head in his hands. Everything he'd done, all the risk and danger and hope. It had all been for nothing.

CHAPTER NINE

Alys strode down the passageway, her boot heels sharp on the planks beneath them. A bedeviling red-edged sensation gnawed at her.

She wasn't hurt. Anyone in the sailing master's position would have tried to escape. Alys would have done the same, and it was almost *more* admirable that he'd attempted to flee rather than sit meekly and pray that fate saw to his welfare.

And yet instead of going to her quarters to rinse off the sweat of the nerve-inducing day and have a hot meal, she found herself standing at the entrance to the brig. Inés served as guard, her pistol pointed into the stockade, her face wearing the same terrifyingly blank look she would use when playing cards. That expression had cost Alys more than a few doubloons.

Inés did, however, wink at Alys when she stepped into the brig. It was a brief wink, barely noticeable, but Alys saw it. Ben, however, didn't, since he was hunched on the floor of the stockade, his head in his hands.

His desolation was a palpable thing, in his posture. And within her, his fathomless sorrow and fury was harrowing.

Her heart squeezed, but it was a stupid and foolish piece of meat that only ever caused her problems.

"Is the ship gone?" he rasped from behind the cage of his fingers cradling his head.

"I've given Van der Meer ample time to lose himself and his ship," she answered. "By now, they should be en route to Havana, or wherever the hell he can peddle his unique flavor of charming treachery."

"Fuck," Ben said on a long growl.

She blinked to hear him curse. Sailors were infamous for their crude language, but not *him*.

With his hands and ankles manacled, any kind of escape attempt was rather impressive. Somehow, he'd gotten out of her cabin . . .

Hell. She hadn't locked the windows. Damned remarkable of him to climb out that way, and wind up on the upper deck. The physical strength and determination needed was beyond human.

She pictured him falling, sinking through the blue water, being pinned to the seafloor as the last of his air bubbled up from his lips, and then the bubbles stopping.

"Fucking *stupid*," she snapped with more heat than she'd intended. "If you were hoping to swim to the island, *that* wouldn't have been possible, and even if you did make it, you'd be bound *and* marooned. Not a winning formula for survival."

"I wasn't trying to get to the island."

She barked out a laugh. "Jacob would ransom you back to the Royal Navy, and deliver you to Port Royal with your throat cut. Difficult as it may be for you to believe, you're safer on my ship than you are on his."

"Escaping to Van der Meer wasn't part of my plan, either."

"Then what in the name of Christ's arsehole did you think you were doing?"

"Learning the truth," he answered

"What truth? We have everything there is to understand about the fail-safe, and there isn't a single buccaneer, pirate, privateer, or sea dog who knows any better."

THE SEA WITCH

Ben shot to his feet and lunged for the bars. She watched a magical shock course the length of his body.

Alys barely managed to keep from stepping back in alarm. He'd never lost command of his self-control.

Ben's angular face was hard with fury, his blue eyes fiery and sharp as blades fresh from the forge. And his anger resonated within her in hot waves.

"*Him*," he said through gritted teeth. "*Who* murdered *him*?"

Her lips opened yet no sound came out. *Him*. The older naval officer from Ben's dream.

"Your father," she whispered.

Ben's jaw clenched and his hands flexed into fists at his sides.

"Leave us, Inés," Alys said over her shoulder.

"Aye, Cap'n." The crew woman slipped out of the brig, and Alys was alone with Ben, who shook and shuddered. Frustration and rage and sorrow all drummed through her. She sailed through this storm every day, but the tempest she felt now was his.

Slowly, Alys approached the stockade. Behind the glowing bars, Ben appeared a specimen in an enchanted zoo: Vengeful Male.

"You served on your father's ship," she murmured, attempting to calm a feral beast. "And you didn't accompany him on one mission."

"I should have been there." His words were heavy with self-recrimination. "He gave me orders that morning: stay behind. Some useless task that only I could accomplish. Well, you saw," he added bitterly. "Compiling logbooks, as though that was a chore anyone asked for. No one cared. But no, he gave the order, and I had to obey. From the window, I watched the *Valiant* sail away. Off on a mission to patrol the waters off the north coast of Jamaica."

She kept silent.

"I wasn't necessary," he muttered. "I never had been. Not to him. And I wasn't there when the pirates attacked and killed him. But maybe . . . maybe . . ." He swallowed hard. "I could've helped. Defended the ship. Kept him alive."

"Master's mates aren't trained to fight."

"I wasn't then. I have more skill now."

"I—" Words formed and dissolved before she could speak them because, truly, what was there to say? Condolences were such puny and laughable things in the face of violent death. Even the few offered to her after Ellen's execution were worse than silence, devastating and pitiful and so unbearably useless.

"Admiral Strickland and the *Jupiter* found him and his ship." His tone flattened. "There were survivors, men too terrified to give much of an accounting of what had happened when they were brought back to Port Royal. I was never given permission to read the official record, scant as it was. I've collected rumors. Who was sighted off the north coast of Jamaica."

"Including Van der Meer and his ship."

Ben dragged his hands through his tangled hair and the chains between his wrists rattled like bones.

"Immediately after, I asked to be transferred to the *Jupiter*. I had to get back out onto the water as soon as possible, had to find—"

He broke off, and the column of his throat worked.

"So, you search," Alys said quietly. "The tavern at St. Gertrude. Climbing the rigging of my ship to get a look at Van der Meer and the *Edelsteen*. How long has it been, since he died?"

"He didn't *die*. He was *murdered*. You *die* peacefully in your sleep, in your own bed. You're *murdered* on the deck of your ship. Shot in the chest. Point-blank."

She was silent. Ellen had had her breath stolen, a rough hempen noose around her neck wringing away her life, and too many times Alys had imagined what it had been like for her

THE SEA WITCH

sister, slowly, slowly choking to the sounds of a crowd cheering on her death.

"Five years," Ben said after a moment. "Six days after my twenty-first birthday."

"A long time to carry the burden of vengeance."

"I'll bear that weight until the day I die."

"What'll you do, when you find whoever was responsible?"

"I . . ." He cupped his forehead. "I haven't thought that far ahead. Another way I've failed my father."

"You didn't fail him." She stepped closer to the bars. "What happened wasn't in your control."

"I should have been there."

"Sometimes, we can't be there for the people who need us most. And we have to live with that."

Her hands came up to reach through the bars and touch him, offer some measure of solace or comfort, paltry as it might be. But she forced them back down to her sides.

"Did you learn anything from looking at the *Edelsteen*?" she asked.

"Evidence was in short supply, but even if the killer *was* on that ship," he added, "peering at him through a spyglass from over a hundred feet away isn't the ideal way to gather intelligence. For all I know, he's on Van der Meer's ship. Hell, he could *be* Van der Meer, but being trapped here means I'll never get the truth."

"Van der Meer is all bluster. And a coward. Trickery is how he plays the game. He'd never look a man in the eye with the muzzle of a flintlock pressed into his target's chest. A dagger between the shoulder blades is his favored way, but even that's too messy for his liking."

"He has a reputation for guile, but he *might*—"

"Jacob wouldn't kill an officer in the Royal Navy. He'd rather fuck and cheat at cards than attack a naval ship."

"You sound confident in your assessment of *Jacob's* character."

124 EVA LEIGH

Her level gaze met his. "Want me to say it? We were lovers."

"*Were.*"

"Everyone makes mistakes. One of mine happens to be a handsome Dutchman who can eat cunt like a god but is as trustworthy as an adder."

After a long silence, Ben said, "That leaves Diego Sanchez, Louis Dupont, and Edward Best. The other pirates seen near my father's ship." He exhaled. "I'm trying to be Orestes, but I'm as useful as one of Medusa's victims, turned to stone."

She'd met some of those men he'd mentioned, yet they were no friends of hers and she knew little about their histories. After a moment, she snapped her fingers and the glow around the cage's bars disappeared. She took a key from her belt and used it to unlock the cage before stepping back.

"It's late and my crew's exhausted." She folded her arms across her chest. "Tomorrow, you'll get the chance to talk to each of them to learn if any of them know anything about your father's murder."

Motionless, he stared at her.

"We'll take you back to my quarters," she continued when he didn't move, "and through the forenoon watch, the company will come down one at a time and tell you what they know. Women aren't looked upon favorably on pirate ships, so they wouldn't have served with Sanchez, Dupont, or Best, and wouldn't have been present at the crime. Even so, it's always possible someone heard something, news or a rumor or anything that might give you more information."

Still, he stayed rooted to the spot. She felt his disbelief, a heavy weight dragging him down.

Alys gripped the bars of the cage's door and pulled it open. She waved her arm wide in invitation. "This isn't a trap, Ben. It's not freedom, either. I still need you, but I won't punish you for doing exactly what I would have done, had I been in your boots. For the record, I was a seventeen-year-old girl trapped in a grim Cape Ann fishing village five years ago. And I never knew anything about your father's murder until this very night. Believe me. Or don't. That's your choice."

His chains jangled as he took one step, and then another. He paused on the threshold of the brig, turning his head so his gaze met hers directly.

"I believe you," he said lowly.

His words sank all the way through her, landing deep in her belly with a peculiar shiver.

She motioned for him to precede her. As he clanked his way past her, their gazes held. An unnerving tremor moved through her.

By the tides, if only she hadn't dreamwalked with him. Yet she'd had no choice. Now they were tied to one another. And she had no idea when, or if, that connection could be severed.

The more she learned of him, the more tangled they became in each other. Such tethers could drag them both down into the depths, sinking together into the profound deep.

CHAPTER TEN

Ben started into wakefulness. The manacles on his wrists and irons on his ankles jangled with the movement and rubbed against his skin.

He was still Alys Tanner's captive.

Immediately, he turned toward her berth. Perhaps she'd still be asleep. Maybe he'd be fortunate or cursed enough to watch her dress.

She was gone. The berth was neatly made, as it had been the day before. Surprising that she would take the time to be so fastidious to tuck in her blankets, though a dent remained in her pillow.

Three bells rang out. Early in the morning.

She'd quitted her cabin without a word to him. A peculiar heaviness settled in his chest—doubtless because he was still sleeping poorly in an unfamiliar place and had strayed from his routine. He always woke at four bells, washed, brushed his clothes to ensure they were neat and trim as befitting a sailing master. Once he was satisfied with his appearance, he broke his fast with the other warrant officers, and immediately went topside to take readings and chart the ship's course. He spent his days going up and down the rigging to ensure his readings were accurate. Dinner at eight bells, including his single drink

THE SEA WITCH

of rum. Then reviewing charts, reading a few pages of edifying works of literature, and finally to his berth.

Now, all of that had been thrown off.

A pitcher and basin waited for him on a slim spare table. Thank God. He went to them and splashed water on his face, his manacles jangling. Well, he wouldn't trust himself, either.

She'd no idea his intentions toward the fail-safe.

The door to the cabin swung open and an angular, narrow-shouldered member of the crew came in, bearing a bowl and a mug.

It would take a very long time for him to get used to the sight of a woman in trousers, including the wide-legged ones worn by this particular female. At the least, they were much looser than the tight leather breeches worn by Alys, which left little to his admittedly detailed imagination. It didn't help that he no longer had to rely on imagination to picture the captain's bare legs.

The crew member set the mug and bowl down on the table. In a brusque colonial accent she clipped, "The cap'n says I'm to answer your questions."

"What's your name?"

She glanced at him suspiciously, then said, "Jane."

"Did you meet Captain Tanner here in the Caribbean?"

"She and I came from Norham," Jane answered. "Our village in Massachusetts."

"You were friends?"

"One of my few." Jane's mouth twisted. "I had no need for friends, or so my husband believed. He had strong opinions when he saw me talking to anyone he didn't approve of. He didn't approve of many."

She gently pressed a hand to the side of her pale freckled face, as if touching a bruise even though her skin was unmarked.

A leaden weight formed in Ben's gut.

128   EVA LEIGH

Jane shook herself, then cocked her head, her brow furrowing. "She said you'd ask me about something that happened five years ago, here, in these waters. Not about life in that piece of shit village."

"Yes. Right. Do you know of any pirate's involvement in the murder of Captain Daniel Priestley? I know you've only been in the Caribbean for a year, but perhaps you've heard something, perhaps a piece of gossip or rumor, or someone said something in your presence that might indicate they had a hand in it. Or perhaps they knew someone who did."

Jane exhaled. "I keep to myself whenever I go ashore. Hard to break the habit, I suppose."

"So, you've heard nothing."

"I have my haunts, and the sort of people who frequent them don't trade in that kind of information."

"What about Louis Dupont, Edward Best, or Diego Sanchez? Know anything about them? What they might have been doing five years ago?"

"I don't want to know what they do a quarter of an hour ago," she answered, folding her arms across her chest. "Men like them bring nothing but strife."

"I see."

"Apologies I couldn't be of more help," Jane said with surprising kindness. "Forty-five people crew the *Sea Witch*. Someone's got to be useful to you." She nodded toward the bowl and mug. "Josephine made hasty pudding. We're always happy on hasty pudding days."

With that, Jane left the cabin. The unmistakable sound of a key turning in a lock followed.

He sat at the table and ate. The porridge was flavorful and well-cooked, made with ground maize cooked in milk, and studded with dried fruit and a swirl of honey. Moments later, his spoon scraped the bottom of his now empty bowl. It was a far cry from most of the rations in the Royal Navy. As a

THE SEA WITCH   129

warrant officer, his food was slightly better than what the rest of the crew ate, but that still didn't make it particularly palatable.

Soon after he finished his meal, there came a knock at the door. Why even bother knocking when he was, for all intents, a prisoner? Yet he wouldn't begrudge them the courtesy.

"May I come in, sir? Cap'n bid me come and talk with ye."

"You may."

The door was unlocked, and a woman with curly brown hair and a cautious smile poked her head in. "Now a good time, sir? I can come back if you're, em, occupied."

"Your company is welcome." He stood. "I only have a few questions to ask you. Who do I have the honor of addressing?"

She flushed pink but didn't look away. "I'll do my best to answer 'em. Oh, I'm Cora."

"Cora, have you heard anything relating to the murder of Captain Daniel Priestley of the Royal Navy . . ."

And so it went for the duration of the morning. One after another, the crew of the *Sea Witch* came to speak with him. Some were shy, like Cora, others were suspicious, or contemptuous. The quartermaster looked ready to disembowel him with barely a lift of her eyebrow. Fewer of the crew were actually friendly, but they all answered with honesty. At least, they *seemed* to be speaking the truth.

Each of the *Sea Witch*'s crew members met his gaze. None of them fidgeted or touched their mouths or repeated his words back to him or offered too many details.

By the time the last of the company left the cabin, three hours had passed.

"Thank you for your time," he said to the final crew member, a Frenchwoman named Thérèse with tattoos on her hands and encircling her wrists. The sides of her head were close-cropped, leaving her amber hair longer on top and the back. Everyone aboard the *Sea Witch* seemed inclined

130   EVA LEIGH

to adapt their appearance to whatever pleased them, rather than adhere to prevailing beauty customs.

"De rien," she answered with a shrug. "And now I am to take you above deck, to see Madame Capitaine."

Ben straightened, tugging on his waistcoat and smoothing his hair. The chain between his manacles bumped against his nose.

He stopped when he caught Thérèse smirking at him.

"Come with me," she said, "and try nothing or I will make use of this." She plucked a trio of metal nails from her pocket, then spun her fingers through the air. The nails transformed into a glowing spiked sphere that hovered above her palm. "It attaches to the skin like a burr but it hurts much more than a burr. Much, much more."

"Your warning has been taken into consideration."

He hurried toward the door. He *tried* to hurry, but even after climbing the mainmast in his chains, he hadn't mastered the art of walking whilst manacled, and the shackles made him exceptionally slow and clumsy. Thérèse rolled her eyes at him, but said nothing as she pushed him along the passageway, the enchanted burr at her fingertips ready to be deployed.

As he wended his way through the ship, Alys's presence was an invisible sun. She burned through all the decks and bulkheads that lay between them, heating him from a distance. Even if Thérèse wasn't there to guide him, he'd know where to find the captain. His feet automatically went up the companionway steps that led above deck.

Dazzled, disoriented, he shielded his eyes against the glare of the actual sun in the sky. The smell of seawater filled his nostrils. Yet he heard nothing except the creaking of the sheets and canvas sails, and waves lapping against the ship. No voices, no commands.

Everyone was silent.

Slowly, his vision came back to him. Dozens of female faces

THE SEA WITCH 131

stared at him. He had met all of them, spoken to each, and some still looked at him with distrust and curiosity.

A collection of animals, including several cats, various birds, rodents, lizards, two dogs, and a small pig all curled together, napping in the sun. So many different beasts cohabitated peacefully together. Witches' familiars.

"No idling, navy man." Thérèse brandished the glowing burr for emphasis.

Staying ahead of her, he clanked his way up the quarterdeck. He followed the ember of Alys's presence. Her face was turned toward the horizon as she stood at the wheel, steering the vessel. A fist closed around his heart, squeezing, welcoming and painful.

The Greek woman, her quartermaster, leaned against the rail and watched Ben through narrowed eyes.

"I have him, Thérèse," Alys said. "You can return to your duties."

Thérèse brought her fingers together, and the spiked ball turned back into three metal nails. After pocketing them, she turned to go, but not before shooting Ben a warning glare.

"Anyone who says women are the gentler sex hasn't been aboard a pirate ship entirely crewed by females," he said to the captain.

"There's a whole flotilla of us?" she asked archly, though she didn't gaze in his direction.

"The *Sea Witch* might be the only one of its kind."

"We are," she answered, still not looking at him, "in all ways extraordinary."

"Anyone who argues otherwise is a fool."

"And you're no fool, Sailing Master."

Her hands turned the handles of the wheel with a loose yet capable grip.

"Even more extraordinary, no helmsman, but a captain at the wheel," he added.

"Hua's our coxswain, but every now and again I like to take the helm. Get the feel of the ship beneath me and the wind in her sails."

"Joy," he blurted. When she frowned at him, he explained, "Sailing a ship. It gives you joy."

Her expression shuttered. Wariness rose up like a wall of red-brick.

"I don't suppose you'd give me a razor?" he asked to break the strained silence. He tried running a hand down his face, cautiously avoiding the chain between his manacles. Stubble abraded his fingers. His beard always came in at an alarming rate.

"Not even a comb to neaten your mane."

He exhaled. "I probably resemble a man who's been marooned."

"The village sot whose spent the night sleeping under a hedge."

"I shudder at the dressing down I'd get from my superior officers." He shook his head.

A corner of her mouth lifted. "What've you learned this morning?"

He glanced toward the quartermaster, who scowled at him as she cleaned her fingernails with a wicked-looking knife. He had learned from this morning's interviews that her name was Stasia Angelidis, but she'd had no information about his father's murder. The magpie on her shoulder fixed Ben with a dark and calculating eye.

"For your ears alone, Captain," he answered.

Stasia jutted her jaw forward, but at Alys's look, she pushed from the rail and went down the companionway to join the rest of the crew. As she walked away, the magpie looked back at him.

"That bird is scowling at me," he murmured.

"Eris has no liking for men."

"Like many of the people who crew this ship." Cold glares from the company continued to singe his back with frost.

"Go ahead and explain to them *why* men don't deserve suspicion."

"That is a challenge I believe I shall decline."

"You can't win it." She adjusted the wheel and the ship moved effortlessly beneath her guidance. "Other than their well-earned

THE SEA WITCH   133

dislike of men, you've got something from speaking with my crew?"

After making certain he and Alys had a relative amount of privacy, Ben finally allowed himself to exhale. Only years of naval discipline kept his shoulders from slumping.

"I've learned exactly nothing," he said grimly. "None of your crew knows anything about my father's murder, not even scraps of anecdotes or tales told thirdhand. Nothing of Best, Dupont, or Sanchez. I'm no closer to knowing who's responsible than I was the day it happened."

"Ah, damn." She shook her head. "I'd hoped . . ."

Her words trailed away, and in that silence, he heard something he hadn't anticipated: genuine regret.

"My thanks." His words came out gruff.

She lifted one shoulder. "I only gave you more sources of frustration."

"It was helpful. In a way," he added when she snorted in disbelief. "It's as much about learning the dead ends as it is discovering the right way forward."

A skeptical look crossed her face.

"Before," he explained, "I had everyone in the whole of the Caribbean to question. In thanks to you and your company, my search has slightly narrowed. And *slightly* is better than nothing at all."

"Sometimes," she said lowly, "all we have is nothing."

The weight of her grief pressed down, crushing the breath from him.

"There's something I can do, though," he said, "to show my gratitude for your assistance."

She held his gaze and, in that moment when she looked into his eyes, something hot and living uncoiled low in his belly.

His heart beat thickly, and then she turned her attention back to the horizon.

"I'm curious what your gratitude looks like, Sailing Master."

He drew himself up as tension continued to snap between them. "You've never been to the island where we'll find the Weeping Princess."

"But you have?"

"There's only one safe anchorage where we can put in," he stated, "and finding and negotiating it is difficult—for those who've never done so."

"A sailing master, truly, to steer the ship that holds you captive."

He followed the contours of her profile. There was the smallest dip beneath her lower lip, unexpectedly delicate. Where else might she be delicate?

The mystery of her . . . He couldn't loosen its bond around him. Trying to extricate himself from it only made the strands wrap tighter around them.

"When we reach the island tomorrow morn," he went on, "I can take the helm to navigate the anchorage."

"Or you *tell* my helmswoman how to pilot us through."

"The safest option is for me to take the wheel."

"How, exactly, does this show your gratitude?"

"Keeping us alive and your ship intact seems a fair means of expressing appreciation."

After a moment, she gave a clipped nod. "Your place will be at the helm. Just for navigating the anchorage. Don't expect or suggest more control over my ship. Until my company and *only* my company decides otherwise, the *Sea Witch* is mine to command."

Her tone assured him that there would be no further discussion on this matter. "I know when to yield."

"If you did, you wouldn't be captive on my ship."

He shifted enough to make his chains rattle, evidence that she was entirely correct. "Persistent Priestley. That's what they call me behind my back."

"Not Pigheaded Priestley?"

THE SEA WITCH 135

"That has less of a poetic ring to it."

"Fortunate that I'm not earning my bread and rum as a poet."

Damn it, now he knew she had dimples.

"Hold fast to your dreams," he said. "If you aspire to iambic pentameter, it can be yours."

"I don't know what the fuck iambic pentameter is. Before this, I was a fisherman's wife, and there aren't many uses for poetry when you're gutting striped bass."

He hadn't known she had been married. Was the man back home, waiting for his wayward wife to return? Did that faceless husband understand her better than Ben did? Hard to imagine so, since Alys Tanner was here, sailing a pirate ship in the Caribbean, and not standing on some colonial dock as her husband's fishing boat returned with the day's catch.

"I can think of a few words that rhyme with *bass*," Ben said.

"Is that so?" She glanced at him, an alert heat in her eyes, her tongue darting out to wet her bottom lip.

You couldn't lie down to sleep beside a fox and then rise in the morning to hunt it. And who was the fox? Who was the hunter?

His silence lasted too long, and he couldn't suppress the wavering contradictions. Contradictions she surely felt.

"Below deck for you, Sailing Master." Her voice was wintry. "When we've need of you tomorrow, you'll be made useful."

She snapped her fingers, and Thérèse must have been standing ready, because she appeared instantly on the quarterdeck.

"Hold a moment." Ben stretched out his hand. "I could be useful now. Give me something to do. Anything."

Alys regarded him warily, with good reason. Surely, she felt his mercurial moods. They confused him as much as they did her. Long ago, as a lad, he'd gained his sea legs, but now on this ship, with this woman, his balance was gone and he didn't know how to regain it.

The pirate captain's long red hair streamed behind her like a streak of sunset pulled from the sky. Beneath his feet, the deck tilted even more, and the poles reversed, taking with them his sense of direction.

Yet if he was shoved into her quarters once again, he might do something truly foolish, like lie in her berth and imagine her in it with him, and try to convince himself she was different from other pirates, and he wasn't betraying himself or his blood to wish it so.

"Madame Capitaine?" Thérèse asked.

After a long moment, Alys said, "Some sails need mending."

"I can do that." He didn't like the eagerness in his voice.

"Take him to Fresia," the captain said to Thérèse. "They'll set him to his task. Mind they keep watchful over the needle in his hand."

"Oui, Madame Capitaine."

Alys didn't look in his direction as Thérèse led him down the companionway and across the deck to a member of the company.

"I'm Fresia, the sailmaker." They studied him from beneath a close-cropped mop of salt-and-pepper tresses, their deeply tanned face creased from life on the sea. "You know how to repair sails?"

"Yes, ma'am."

"Just Fresia will do, Sailing Master." They cautiously handed him a thick needle, though their hand never strayed far from the dagger in their belt.

Ben sat and began the slow process of repairing rends in the heavy canvas. The regard of all the women staring at him prickled. And all the while, Alys's heat continued to blaze over his skin and within him.

CHAPTER ELEVEN

Even with the sailing master quietly going about the work Alys had made him do, her gaze kept returning to him like following the North Star.

Going to her quarters was one option. But, having been above deck for most of the morning, finally heading below would look as if she was avoiding him. He'd notice it, too. Little escaped his attention.

A dangerous combination, looks and intelligence. It meant he was clever, and the only thing more dangerous than a stupid man was a cunning one.

As the morning had gone on and he'd been interviewing her crew about his father, his growing frustration had been a palpable thing within her. It was tied around her belly in a knot. She hadn't truly needed to ask him how his questioning had gone—she already knew, because she knew *him*.

"Is he trustworthy here, above deck?" Stasia asked, stepping onto the quarterdeck.

"I trust his sense of keeping his hide intact. He won't do anything stupid. And *I'm* not doing anything stupid," she added before her second-in-command could make a remark. "He has a value, but it's a temporary one. I'm counting the bells until that value is gone, and then he will be, too."

"Hua is worried you will not give her the helm back." There was warm humor in Stasia's voice.

"She's got nothing to fear. The wheel will be hers again. Before I came to the Caribbean, I'd only used a tiller to steer a boat."

"When I met you, you had already taken to the wheel well enough."

"Sailing down here from Massachusetts, that was my schoolroom. And a terrifying one at that. We'd set sail full of so much anger, and still half afraid that they'd come for us. Even so, none of us knew how little we knew. When I tried to cast a spell to bring strong breezes to speed us on our way, I stranded us in the doldrums for three days. Only pure luck had me stumbling across the right spell to set us moving again."

From a pouch hanging from her belt, Stasia produced an orange, which she deftly peeled. She handed Alys a segment. "By the time we crossed paths in Tortuga, I saw no outward signs of your fear."

"But you knew." Alys popped the piece of orange into her mouth and savored the tart and sweet taste.

"You are not afraid any longer. Not of sailing or captaining a ship, at any rate." Stasia glanced toward where Ben bent over the sail, making neat stitches in the canvas.

"He's one man, and a shackled and manacled one at that."

"The dreamwalking left its mark."

"The effects'll lessen with time. Won't they?"

Stasia spread her hands. "My understanding of the spell is not much more than what you know. Will it last a few days, a month, or the rest of your lives? Only our foremothers know, and if they wrote down that lore, it has vanished."

"Or been destroyed." Even as Alys spoke with Stasia on the quarterdeck, Ben's energy thrummed through her. There was a warm and soft kind of contentment in him now, as he repaired sails. To him, idleness was torture.

THE SEA WITCH

She nodded toward the deck, where a number of the company had enchanted scrubbing brushes to swab the wooden planks. The brushes moved of their own accord, spreading suds across the deck, but they required supervision, and so the crew kept a close eye on the proceedings.

"Enough chatter," Alys said. "They always sing when they work, and yet they're silent." Louder, to her crew, she called, "I've a mind to hear a good tune."

"Aye, Cap'n," came their answer.

As the three women charged with washing the deck watched over the brushes moving rhythmically back and forth across the wood, they joined their voices into a well-loved song.

"Come all you gallant seamen bold,
All you that march to drum,
Let's go and look for Captain Ward,
Far on the sea he roams.
He is the biggest robber
That ever you did hear,
There's not been such a robber found
For above this hundred year."

Alys hummed along, tapping her foot on the quarterdeck planks as the crew sang. Others on the deck who were whittling or simply enjoying the afternoon joined their voices. Susannah created a swirling cloud of energy that showed them an illuminated moving image of the legendary Captain Ward on his ship, sailing back and forth across the deck as he committed miniature acts of piracy—much to the delight of the familiars. The black cat and the orange cat, as well as Eris and a long-tailed, long-fingered lizard chased the illusion.

Unfortunately, the animals all scrabbled across the freshly-washed deck, to the annoyance of the crew charged with cleaning it. Yet no one seemed to begrudge a bit of play for the familiars.

140   EVA LEIGH

As the crew continued on to the next verse, a new tone sounded in the harmony, far deeper than the women's voices.

The illusion of Captain Ward faded and, one by one, the crew stopped singing. Until one voice remained.

Ben's.

Concentrating on his work of mending sails, he continued on with the tune.

> *"A ship was sailing from the east*
> *And going to the west,*
> *Loaded with silks and satins*
> *And velvets of the best;*
> *But meeting there with Captain Ward,*
> *It was a bad meeting;*
> *He robbed them of all their wealth,*
> *And bid them tell their king."*

His voice was a little rough, not in perfect tune. Yet it strummed along Alys's skin and through her, both unsettling and soothing in equal measure.

She'd always heard that sirens were female.

He glanced up, and seemed suddenly aware that he was the only person singing. Even from her place on the quarterdeck, she could see the redness that filled his cheeks, and how his hands hovered over the canvas sail spread across his lap.

Yet he kept on singing. It was almost a dare, to continue, when everyone gaped at him and his was the lone voice being lifted up.

Stasia looked at her with curiosity, and that curiosity turned to astonishment when Alys sang.

> *"O then the King proved a ship of noble fame,*
> *She's call'd the* Royal Rainbow
> *If you would have her name;*

THE SEA WITCH

She was as well provided for
As any ship can be,
Full thirteen hundred men on board
To bear her company."

Ben's gaze shot to her. The rest of the company stared, as well, but Alys didn't stop. She went right on singing.

Slowly, members of the crew joined in. One and then another and yet more, until everyone above deck sang—even Stasia. Susannah resumed her moving illusion, showing the pirate captain's ship in combat with the *Royal Rainbow.*

They reached the rousing conclusion:

"Go home, go home, says Captain Ward
And tell your king for me,
If he reigns king on all the land,
Ward will reign king on the sea."

The last few words were shouted, less of a song and more of a battle cry bellowed by many women and one lone man. Susannah's illusion ended in a tiny burst of celebratory fireworks.

When the final echo died down, the illusion fading away, Alys's ship went back to its business, the decks being swabbed, the sails mended, and crew up in the rigging.

Ben's attention pinned to her. The blue heat of his gaze danced over her like St. Elmo's fire.

He nodded at her, a brief, clipped movement that was still respectful and appreciative.

She returned the nod before giving her attention back once more to the horizon, steering her ship.

"HERE I THOUGHT men of the Royal Navy wouldn't know how to sing 'Ward the Pirate.'" Alys reached across the table in

142   EVA LEIGH

her cabin to break off a sizable chunk of bread, then dunked it
into her mutton stew. "Either I've misjudged the navy—or you."

"It's a common enough song." Ben dipped his spoon into
his bowl, yet he didn't hunch over his food, the way she did,
and kept his elbows off the table. When he'd helped himself
to bread, he'd used only the tips of his fingers and spilled a
minimum of crumbs. All his movements were economical but
graceful, belying the fact that breakfast had been served many
hours ago, and he was likely just as hungry as she was.

Alys started to straighten her posture, then planted her elbows
firmly on either side of her bowl and made a show of tearing another piece of bread and scattering crumbs across the table.

Yet there wasn't any distaste or displeasure in his crystal blue
eyes. If her table manners offended him, he hid it behind a
bright and interested gaze.

"A pirate king defeating the English monarch's ship seems
an unlikely subject for a British naval warrant officer to know
by heart." She took a deep drink of ale and dragged her sleeve
across her mouth like a proper pirate.

He still wore a faint smile as he looked at her.

"When you've been at sea for as long as I have," he replied,
"it serves you admirably to listen well." He was silent for a moment, then, "My thanks . . . I'm grateful you sang with me."

"My voice is passable." She shrugged. "Hardly worth praise."

"You've a fine alto." His gaze held hers and she stilled.

Perhaps she should have taken her supper with Stasia and the
others, rather than be alone with him in her quarters. Yet his
loneliness had been a tangible thing within her.

She gave another small shrug. "You'd have looked damned
foolish, bellowing on your own."

"I would've thought you'd relish any opportunity to make
me appear the fool," he said gruffly. "Even small victories are
victories."

"My best triumphs are at the end of my cutlass or from a

THE SEA WITCH 143

broadside—or summoning a blinding smoke that stuns and weakens my enemies. And the sound of a lone voice chafes against my hearing." Her fingers were suddenly restless, making her reach for more bread.

His broad hand covered hers.

Against her own, his skin was warm and callused. Her heart leapt like a dolphin. At that moment, there was nothing in the whole of the realm of the ocean that could make her pull away from his touch.

"Accepting gratitude for your decency isn't a weakness," he said lowly.

For a moment, she simply looked into his eyes and let him touch her. It was astonishing, how blue his eyes were, like the waters lapping in the bay of a Caribbean island, and just now they were as warm as the waters, too.

She dragged her hand back and curled it into a fist. At the same time, she returned her attention to her meal, as if she hadn't seen Josephine's version of mutton stewed with potatoes, carrots, and island peppers hundreds of times.

"It can be, if you're a pirate," she said. "Even more so if you're a witch."

He resumed eating, his manacles making dull metallic sounds as he moved. Perhaps they were rubbing against the skin of his wrists, but if they caused him pain, he made no mention of it. "I vow not to thank you again."

"See that you don't. There's no value to me from *your* high regard."

"I have a usefulness. For now. And nothing beyond that."

She appreciated that there wasn't any hurt in his words. "This," she noted, gesturing to the space between them as they sat at the table, "is brief-lived, and exists only because you've got knowledge my crew doesn't."

"It won't end well for you," he said softly. "For pirates, it never does."

"Have some imagination." She poured herself another mug of ale before silently offering to refresh his own mug. At his nod, she poured a healthy amount of ale. "Some buccaneers die in bed, surrounded by wealth and luxury. Or become governor, such as Woodes Rogers."

"Fortune doesn't smile upon exceptions. It's merely proof that anyone, even a murderous scoundrel, can exploit the world to their advantage."

She was silent, and then said quietly, "Even if you find the pirate responsible for your father's death, you'll have to sail forward. Say you get your vengeance, in whatever form it takes, it changes nothing about the past."

His jaw set. "That's a concern I'll face when I get there. Until then, it's the course I know."

She stood from the table and walked to the window that ran the length of the stern, giving her cabin a view of the sea churning behind the ship. The *Sea Witch* wasn't the largest brigantine, and she cut a clean line through the water, so she had a narrow wake.

"What's at the end of *your* voyage, Sailing Master? If you locate and punish whoever's responsible, *if* you get off my ship, then what? More esteemed service to His Majesty? A pension and a quiet life in a seaside villa when gray threads your hair? I hear tending roses is a favorite thing to do, when you're no longer at sea."

"You've no idea what I hope for."

Her lips twisted, wry. "Many sailors turn buccaneer when they learn the terms of pirate articles. Good pay, decent working conditions, and extra coin if they're hurt or maimed and can no longer serve on the ship. In one year, I've had only two occasions to flog members of my company. Once for hiding a share of booty for themselves without reporting it."

"The second?"

THE SEA WITCH

She turned to face him, and he was watching her carefully, his attention sharp and purposeful.

"Torturing a captive." She tilted her head. "That's a look of astonishment if ever I've seen one. You believe we're a lawless band of vicious thieves."

"Pirates *are* vicious thieves. There isn't a single one free from that charge."

"Painting with a broad stroke, when you're blind to the details. A handful of days ago, you hadn't even met a female pirate."

He pushed back from the table and walked slowly toward her, giving her fair chance to move away and place distance between them. Yet she stayed where she was, allowing him to cross the breadth of the cabin until he stood in front of her. She was within striking distance—they both were. It would be simple enough for him to lash out, perhaps wrap the length of chain between his manacles across her throat and pull hard enough to steal her words and her life.

She had a dagger in her sash. She could have the blade in her hand and through his windpipe before he could blink. She could force the air from his body, suffocating him.

A current of fire ran through her body. It intoxicated her to test this possibility, and press against the danger that vibrated between them.

"There's no reason to do it," he said lowly. "To take up a profession rife with men who are, in your words, a lawless band of vicious thieves."

"In *your* words, murderous scoundrels. My company is entirely composed of women."

"By design."

"Ask anyone aboard the *Sea Witch* the same question: what have men ever done for you? You'll get the same answer: nothing good."

For the remainder of her days, she'd see Ellen's lifeless form swaying gently in the late fall breeze, or how the line of torches had made their way toward the harbor.

"*Curb your tongue*," Samuel used to hiss when they were amongst the other villagers.

Other voices echoed: the upstanding men of Norham, coming to arrest her, kill her.

To her surprise, Ben didn't scoff. Instead, he rubbed at his chin, considering what she'd said. "To become *pirates*."

"As opposed to what?" She set her hands on her hips as she stared up at him. "Meek wives. Doting daughters. Spinster sisters dependent on someone to clothe and feed them, and give them a place to lay their heads each night. Robbed of the magical gifts we were born with. Forced to be ordinary, to be *safe* to men and their pride. Hunted and killed if we refuse to comply. Aboard the *Sea Witch*, we answer to ourselves alone. The only boundary is the endless limit of the horizon."

"Pursuing such a choice can only result in your death."

"Death is the result for everyone, not just pirates," she returned. "Whether we are sainted Madonnas or fallen whores, we all die. And if you're a witch, it's almost certain your life's cut short. This way, no man tells us who to be or how to live. I doubt you can say the same."

He jabbed his finger toward her. "The law is master over *all* of us, including you and your renegade band of women."

"Laws that benefit some but harm more are no laws to me. If that means sailing to the fiery gates of hell sooner rather than later, I know the better option. Where I was from, there were laws against witches, but simply because a law exists doesn't make it just."

His jaw tightened, and his chest rose and fell.

"Everythin' all right in there, Cap'n?" a crew member asked on the other side of the door. "There was shoutin' fit to make us think the ship was afire."

Alys forced herself to take long, even breaths. Hell. She hadn't

THE SEA WITCH 147

realized she was yelling until that moment—and she *never* raised her voice except in the heat of battle.

"Everything is fine, Cora," Alys answered, her gaze never leaving Ben's. "A friendly chat."

"Bit loud for *friendly*," Cora noted.

A corner of Ben's lips quirked. Low enough so that only she could hear him, he said, "Herein lies the fault in such a democratic approach to seafaring."

"I'd rather a crew member with a bit of sass than a cat-o'-nine-tails on my back, or a husband's ring on my finger or a noose around my neck." Louder for Cora, she added, "Back to your supper, Cora. There's nothing here I can't handle."

"As you like, Cap'n." Footsteps retreated in the passageway.

Alys and Ben continued to regard each other. Thank the trade winds she'd gotten back some of her poise. Fortunately, so had he. Pushed to the edge of his composure, he held an edge, a sharp gleam of possibility. What else might get him to unravel more? What would he look like . . . what would he do . . . when he did lose control?

"You're confident that you can *handle* me," he noted.

"I've done a fine job of it so far." She pushed past him, though he barely budged when she tried to jostle him out of the way. The contact of his solid shoulder with hers thrummed through her.

"Having me in irons hardly seems a fair assessment of how well you'd do against me in a one-on-one fight, cutlass against cutlass."

"Trying to nettle me into freeing you, just for the sake of my vanity." She shook her head.

"Men are vain. It stands to reason women are, too."

At her desk, she took the key that hung from a cord around her neck and used it to unlock a drawer. Taking her logbook out, she set it atop her desk and also removed a quill and pot of ink, but then paused, debating.

148   EVA LEIGH

"You claim you can wield a cutlass," she said after a moment. "What's your skill in wielding a pen?"

"I keep my own log that the captain and admiral review," he answered. "And write correspondence for seamen that don't know their letters."

"Then you're used to it, writing down what someone tells to you."

He took a step toward her, his expression carefully neutral. "If there's something you'd like me to transcribe for you, I can."

"Stasia—she can speak English better than I can, but she wants to improve her ability to read and write it. To help her, it's become our habit that I speak my captain's log, and she writes it down." Gruffly, Alys added, "I'm used to it now. Haven't written my own log in close to a year. Nothing personal in it, but . . ."

Without speaking, he pulled a stool away from the table and set it in front of the desk. He flicked the full skirt of his coat out before sitting, then picked up the quill. It was surprising, how fluidly he could move, even with the shackles and manacles.

Ben hovered its nib over the waiting inkpot.

She drew in a breath, then opened the book to the next blank page, before sliding it toward him.

He dipped the nib into the ink and looked up at her expectantly.

"The Eighteenth of May," she began, "1720."

The nib scratched across the paper as he wrote with an exceptional hand, bold but elegant.

Once the date was inscribed, he glanced up at her again, waiting without judgment. Yet she wouldn't unlock his manacles. Aboard this ship, he was still a prisoner. Still the enemy.

She couldn't allow herself to forget that.

CHAPTER TWELVE

"Luff sails," the sailing master called out.
"Luffing sails," several members of the crew answered, hurrying to follow his command.

As they did this, the sails slackened, slowing the ship's speed. Canvas shook in the wind.

Alys noted Ben's hands on the wheel were secure and certain, turning the *Sea Witch* into the wind to ensure a careful and steady approach into the island's treacherous anchorage. Land had been spotted early that morning, and, with Alys's leave, Ben had taken his place on the quarterdeck to serve as helmsman, navigating the brigantine through the dangerous shoals.

She'd witnessed many people steering a ship. Hell, she'd grown so used to the sight of Samuel at the tiller of his fishing boat, it was as familiar as her own fingernails. There was nothing remarkable in observing anybody piloting a ship.

Alys had even braced herself for being annoyed to see the Royal Navy man at the helm of her ship. It was *hers*, after all, and she'd hand-selected the crew that made the *Sea Witch* run as smoothly, as efficiently as it did.

Except watching Benjamin Priestley take sure and confident control of the ship's helm stirred a hunger in her.

It wasn't possible for him to turn the wheel with his hands manacled, so the irons around his wrists had been removed. Even so, Stasia stood nearby with her pistol trained on him, ready to fire should he do anything that could be considered suspicious, such as deliberately scuttle the ship. He hadn't objected to the fact that the quartermaster was poised to shoot him, and he calmly went about his business as if his life wasn't constantly in peril.

Now he feathered the ship, quickly turning the helm from one side to the other as he continued to reduce the *Sea Witch*'s speed. The ship immediately slowed—she could feel it was losing too much velocity to successfully negotiate the narrow passage into the island's anchorage.

"Sheet in on the main," he shouted.

The crew quickly obeyed, tightening the mainsail to gain a little more speed while the ship cut between two coral reefs that formed a natural protective barrier to the island's inlet.

Once they'd breached the bay, he guided the ship through the reefs before he called, "Back the mainsail."

When the crew followed his directive, the *Sea Witch* slowed to an almost complete stop.

"Drop anchor," Ben called.

Finally, they were in the bay at the far end of the island of the Weeping Princess. Where they would—hopefully—find Little George's fail-safe.

And then she would be free of Benjamin Priestley.

A stone formed in her gut. Clearly, missing breakfast in her eagerness to catch sight of the island had been a mistake. She was a woman of appetites—fasting never sat well with her. After they concluded their business ashore, she'd return to the ship and sup heartily.

"Admirably done, Sailing Master," she said as the jolly boat was made ready to bring them to the shore.

Lines briefly fanned in the corners of his eyes, then he gave her a clipped nod. Even so, there was pleasure in him. Like her, he enjoyed executing his tasks well. Deep within, he was glad he'd performed well in front of her.

THE SEA WITCH   151

Stasia moved to put the manacles back around his wrists, and he stepped back.

"I'll need my hands free when we're traversing the island," he said by way of explanation.

"That's supposing you come with us," Alys answered.

"No one else has been here. You'll have need of me once you're ashore."

She exhaled as she shared a look with Stasia. Unfortunately, he was correct, and so Alys silently told her quartermaster to keep the manacles off him.

"Leg irons, too," he had the nerve to insist.

Stasia glanced at her again, and Alys nodded. Her second-in-command muttered Greek curses as she unlocked his shackles. For his benefit, she added, "My pistol is going to be pointed at your back, navy man. If you scratch your arse suspiciously, there will be consequences."

"I don't do anything that crass in front of a lady."

Alys laughed, and Stasia and several other women joined her.

"This ship is crewed by women," Alys said, "but not a single lady amongst us."

She, Ben, and Stasia were joined in the jolly boat by Susannah, while Cora and Thérèse took the oars. Eris perched on Stasia's shoulder, already twittering with excitement at the prospect of exploration ahead.

Each of them was supplied with a skin full of water, and Susannah carried a pack with some bread and salted meat. Hopefully, they'd be back before dark, but it was best to be provisioned in case anything went awry.

While they rowed toward the shore, Alys studied the island. From what she'd been able to assess, it wasn't more than three miles from one end to the other. Just beyond the shallow white sand beach, the land was heavily forested with thick-trunked trees and swathed in green shadow. Past the forest, the land rose up in a sharp volcanic peak, but there were no ominous rumblings

152   EVA LEIGH

or columns of smoke to indicate that an eruption might happen anytime soon.

"Will we stomp through anyone's settlement?" she asked Ben.

"It's been decades since anyone lived here," he answered.

At last, they reached the beach, where waves the color of Ben's eyes crested and crashed.

Remembrance flickered. Yet this beach wasn't the same as the one they'd visited in their dream. Just the same, he also scanned the shore, searching for a hint of what might be.

Everyone disembarked to drag the jolly boat up the sand. It was agreed upon that Cora and Thérèse would stay with the small vessel while Alys, Ben, Stasia, and Susannah sought the waterfall.

"Lead us to it, Sailing Master," Alys commanded him.

He gave a rueful smile. "We'll learn its whereabouts together."

She glowered at him. "No time for fibbing and games. Take us to the Weeping Princess."

"The one time I came to this island, I was in search of pirates, not legendary waterfalls."

Stasia let out a long string of curses.

"You said we'd have need of you once we were ashore," Alys snapped. "That supposedly *you knew* where we were going."

"I can make myself useful on an expedition," he answered, "even if I don't know where we're headed."

Alys stepped closer to him, and demanded in a low hiss, "Then how did we see it in your dream, if you've never actually been there or clapped eyes on it yourself?"

"That, I cannot say. When I came here before, we had a sailor with us, Burgos, descended from the people who once lived here. He told me of the waterfall, but we never ventured inland to find it."

"Yet you and I, we *saw* it in our dream."

"Perhaps . . ." Ben's brow furrowed. "Perhaps something in it *calls out* to be found."

THE SEA WITCH

153

She rubbed her chin. "If the fail-safe uses magic, it might link with the dreamwalking somehow. There's still so much of magic I—" She stopped herself. Telling him how little she knew of the ways of magical power gave *him* too much power.

"Tracking is one of my skills," he said.

"God*damn* it," Alys growled. "I should make you wait with the jolly boat."

"But it's safer to have more of us in our party," he pointed out. "In case anyone gets into trouble."

"*You're* trouble." Yet what he said made sense. Besides, she could more easily keep an eye on him if he was with her.

Finally, she snarled, "*Anything* suspicious—"

"Your second-in-command is quite eager to shoot me."

Alys planted her hands on her hips and looked toward the thick steaming jungle, where, God willing, the fail-safe was hidden.

"Move out," she said decisively. "And if you *do* try anything, Sailing Master, it'll be *my* flintlock that tears through that body of yours."

"THE TERRAIN OFF the beach is too rugged and rocky to make passage possible," Ben explained to the group. "The lone means of going forward is ascending the gradual slope of the volcanic peak."

"Scout for us, my lovely girl," the quartermaster said to her magpie. The bird twittered and then flew off. She caught Ben staring at her and snarled, "What?"

"You talk to that bird with more warmth than you use with humans," he answered.

"Humans have far less wit than Eris."

"Don't you take offense to that?" Ben asked Alys, even though she wasn't affronted.

She only shrugged. "I'm seldom witty without a mug of rum in me. Enough chattering. Now, we walk."

154   EVA LEIGH

Alys took the lead, using a long wide blade to cut a path through the thickly wooded terrain. Ben followed her, and behind him was the quartermaster, doubtless ready with her pistol to send him to blazes. Another member of the crew, a Black woman introduced to him as Susannah, brought up the rear. She had pulled her many small braids back, out of her round umber face.

All four of them marched onward, the jungle dense and tall surrounding them. He moved in short quick steps. Then caught himself—he wasn't shackled anymore. He could move as freely as he pleased. And by God, did it please him. His whole body pulsed with energy finally released.

Ben tilted his head, listening.

"Something's out there." He peered into the shadows within the trees. "Many things."

"The people have gone," Alys answered. "But that doesn't mean no one lives here."

"Creatures," the second-in-command said. "Human eyes have not seen them in centuries, and they keep themselves hidden now. They are . . . shy."

"Should we fear them?" Ben searched for a weapon.

"Only if we rile them," the Greek woman replied.

"That doesn't console me."

The second-in-command shrugged, clearly unconcerned whether or not Ben was consoled.

Alys motioned for everyone to keep walking. As they did, Ben continued to glance around, wary. Yet whatever dwelt on this island seemed just as guarded and reluctant to engage.

"Best way to find a waterfall is to find its source," Ben said to Alys's back. Or rather, he *tried* to address his comments to her back, but as she moved, twisting this way and that, the skirts of her long coat kept shifting, giving him all too clear a view of the breeches snugly clinging to her arse.

"As you said, where there's water, a waterfall's sure to be

THE SEA WITCH

nearby." She glanced at him, and her lips curled into a knowing smirk when she caught him ogling her aforementioned arse.

Heavy moist heat pressed down on him, held close by the surrounding branches and vines. He'd grown up in the Caribbean, knew jungle islands like this one well, but this particular island kept its thick heat, held tighter by the dense foliage around him. Sweat slicked his skin. He sipped from the skin of water he carried.

Alys paused. "There's a speedier way to find water than stumbling through the jungle like a fool."

She used the toe of her boot to clear bracken from the earth at her feet, then dug the tip of her blade into the dark loamy soil. Her steel drew wavy lines in the dirt.

He frowned with confusion as she knelt beside the waves she'd drawn. She bent down, putting her face close to the inscription. Her lips formed inaudible words.

As she spoke, noises emerged from the jungle, the low sound of several voices in conversation. He couldn't make out the words they said, but some of them chuckled as if secretly amused.

Alarm shot down his back. "Give me your blade."

"The hell she will," the quartermaster snapped.

"The creatures," he growled.

When no one took up a defensive position, Ben glanced around sharply. He snapped a thick branch off a tree and brandished it like a club.

"Be at ease, Sailing Master," Alys said as she got to her feet. "Nothing's coming for us."

"I hear them," he snarled. "Can't you?"

There was no alarm in her, no fear. It was damned foolish when they were obviously outnumbered.

"It's the water," she explained with forced patience. "The spell I cast amplifies its voices."

He shook his head. "Water doesn't possess a voice."

She laughed, and the sound joined the chuckling that tumbled out of the forest. "Of course, water has a voice. Everything in nature has a voice. Trees, earth, sky. It speaks all the time. You only have to listen."

Susannah clicked her tongue. "No surprise he doesn't think so. Men stomp around and speak so loudly they drown out everything else but themselves."

"You've been at sea most of your life," Alys said to him, "and yet you've never heard it speak?"

Slowly, he lowered his club. "With fair winds and clear skies, the waves . . . murmur."

"And when there's a storm?"

"It shouts."

She held up her hand, the answer obvious.

"I didn't truly know," he said. "Not until now."

"To think that a naval man can actually be taught something," the second-in-command said tartly. "What a miraculous day this has turned out to be."

"He doesn't know what he doesn't know," Alys answered, wry.

"He's also standing here and sees no need for you to speak of him in the third person." Ben pointed with his club. "The voices sound as though they're coming from that direction."

Alys took up the lead again. The group continued onward, up a long gradual incline that made the muscles of his legs burn satisfyingly after several days of idleness. Thick vines drooped from tree branches, whose roots were as wide as a man's torso, as if bodies were only partially buried. Sunlight pierced the canopy here and there, casting verdant light onto the pirate captain's hair and glittering on her shoulders. She glowed like a ruby in the midst of a sea of emeralds.

Animal cries and songs stilled as they walked and remained quiet. Doubtless everything here was unused to the noises made by humans. Even a quartet of people attempting to move lightly

THE SEA WITCH   157

through the forest must seem like a jarring cacophony compared to the peace this island had known for a long time.

A low branch caught on Ben's coat, snagging a button and sending it flying into the dense underbrush. There would be no finding it amongst the thick foliage. Perhaps back on the ship, he'd find a spare button to replace it. He had some skill with a needle, and could ask Fresia if they had one he could borrow.

Perhaps they'd be in a generous mood if the landing party returned to the ship in triumph, having found the fail-safe?

But if he located the fail-safe here, he'd destroy it.

He wouldn't make it back to the *Sea Witch* alive.

Straightening his shoulders, he pressed forward, following Alys. She chopped away the dense vegetation and they continued on.

She came to a stop, and held out her arm in warning. "Come to where I'm standing, but go slowly."

Following her instructions, Ben stood beside her, with the quartermaster and Susannah also lining up next to her. The second-in-command let out a low whistle.

They stood at the edge of a deep rugged crevasse. It had been created when an ancient flow of lava had collapsed. It yawned below them, easily a dozen yards across and thirty feet deep, lined with rocks and tenacious ferns. A dank green smell emanated from the chasm. Far at the bottom, jagged stones poked up like teeth. Dense jungle continued on the other side of the ravine with thick vines hanging from the tree branches.

"Jumping the distance is impossible," Ben said lowly.

"Can't climb up and then down," Alys noted. "The rocks don't offer good handholds, and if we slip, it's a painful fall and sure death."

"How do we cross it?" the quartermaster asked, impatient.

"We find another way to the water." Alys turned on her heel and headed in a different direction.

158   EVA LEIGH

A shriek sounded, and the leaves exploded as something shot from the foliage.

Ben immediately darted forward, shoving Alys behind him as he raised his makeshift club.

"Hold," she barked as he lifted it high to strike whatever attacked them. "It's only Eris."

The magpie circled before settling on the quartermaster's shoulder. She stroked the bird's throat, and Ben fought against feeling like ten varieties of foolishness. Merely a bird, and a tame one at that.

He looked back at Alys.

"No need to serve as my guardian, Sailing Master," she said sardonically.

"I didn't—" He cleared his throat. If anything happened to her, he'd lose his only advocate aboard the ship. Naturally, he'd protected her.

"Eris says we are not to go that way," the quartermaster said as her magpie twittered into her ear.

"The creatures?" Susannah asked with a worried frown.

"Their den, with young ones."

"There's no choice," Ben pointed out. "If we take the other route, we're up against the crevasse."

"We make our own choices, Sailing Master," Alys answered.

She turned back to the ravine. Once again, everyone gathered at the edge, yet it looked just as impassable as before.

"That can be our bridge." Ben nodded to a fallen tree, now velvety with moss. "I could attempt to rig some vines into pulleys, but I'll have to find some means of getting *them* across the crevasse, and then angling the trunk so that it will lie in just the right place. If I had pen and paper, I could calculate the angles and make a diagram—"

Alys pointed at the vines hanging from the trees on the other side of the ravine. "We'll use those. Weave a bridge from them to get across."

THE SEA WITCH

"How?" the quartermaster asked.

"Think of them like . . ." Alys rubbed her chin. "Like strands of kelp, weaving together as they sway in the current. Can you do that?"

There was a hesitant pause, and then both the second-in-command and Susannah nodded.

"We should join hands." Alys held hers out, but when Ben moved to take it, she said, "Unless you've suddenly developed a gift for magic, Sailing Master, this is for witches only."

"Right." Abashed, Ben stepped back.

The quartermaster grasped Alys's hand, and Susannah took hers. The three women faced the crevasse.

"Think of that kelp," Alys murmured to the other witches. "How strong it is, how it plaits with the other strands, growing even stronger."

The other two women also wore intense looks of absorption as they directed their attention toward the vines. Ben glanced back and forth between the trio of pirates and the objects of their attention.

"Nothing's—"

"Shh," Alys hissed.

A glow appeared around the vines, like will-o'-the-wisps. Faintly, at first. And then it gathered and grew, hovering around the vines. Until dozens of them were bathed in light.

Ben bit back an exclamation of shock when they rustled. They moved slightly, then subsided, settling back into place.

The quartermaster cursed and Susannah frowned in disappointment.

"Keep at it, my beauties," Alys urged.

The women continued to fix their attention on the vines, and the glow surrounding them intensified. They slithered like snakes, shifting, sliding.

Ben held his breath as the vines moved, serpentine. They glided across the chasm. As they did so, they wove together as though invisible hands braided them. At first, they were slow. Yet as Alys and the other witches fixed their attention on them, the woody vines moved with more speed.

He glanced at Alys and the other witches. Sweat glossed their skin and their linked hands shook. All this time, he'd believed magic came swiftly and easily to them, as it did with the naval mages he'd encountered, but the effort to create this spell taxed the trio of women.

At last, the vines formed a bridge. It stretched across the ravine. Each end glowed, anchored by magic.

Yet it shuddered. A few pebbles shook loose, tumbling down the crevasse. They bounced from rock to rock before slamming into the ground below.

The women let go of each other's hands, exhaling shakily. Alys dragged her sleeve across her forehead. Her strain was tactile, pulling on him. Yet there was satisfaction, too.

"It's not going to hold for long," she said, nodding at the bridge they had created. "Across, quickly."

He almost suggested that he take the lead, in case the bridge didn't hold, but Alys shot him a cautioning glance.

Without hesitation, she climbed onto the bridge. His breath came shallowly as he watched her walk across. She darted from one end of the vine bridge to the other.

A moment later, she was on the far side. Only when the quartermaster looked at him sharply did he realize that he'd let out a rough, loud exhale.

"Move fast and light," Alys called across the crevasse. "Don't give the bridge a chance to throw you off."

Ben took a step toward the vines, but the second-in-command elbowed him back. Her face was drawn and tight, but she gamely climbed onto the bridge. She cursed her way across. When she reached the other side, she crouched down on her haunches and brought a handful of dirt to her lips.

THE SEA WITCH   161

"The bridge is growing less balanced the more people cross it," Ben said to Susannah. "You go while it's still stable."

The woman nodded, and mounted the bridge. It rocked beneath her, and she gripped a vine for balance. Then, before the bridge could collapse beneath her, she ran its length, and arrived at the other side. Susannah leaned against Alys for a moment, catching her breath.

It was Ben's turn.

He strode to the bridge, and as he stepped onto it, it shivered and trembled. The witches on the other side of the ravine were pale and shone with sweat from the effort of keeping the bridge intact and anchored.

God knew if it would hold him. Far below, the stones at the bottom of the ravine jutted up from green darkness.

It was no different from climbing a mast in a storm. Or so he told himself as he took a step and then another, pulling himself along by clutching a loose vine. The bridge quaked under him. His boots slipped. He fought to remain standing, even as the bridge shuddered.

The vines groaned. All three women let out a cry. The glow abruptly disappeared from the anchor point on the near side of the crevasse.

Ben had just enough time to grab the vine before the bridge swung free, gripping it. As he swung toward the far wall of the ravine, he braced for impact against the pointed rocks.

Vines knitted around him. They formed a cage, sheltering him, as he slammed into the rocky wall. He grunted from the collision, yet without the vines surrounding him, he would've been smashed to a pulp.

Gripping a thick vine, he hauled himself up. Hand over hand, he pulled himself higher. The lip of the crevasse loomed, and sweat dripped into his eyes.

Finally, he reached the rim. He grabbed it and heaved himself over the top. A moment later, the bridge collapsed. It fell into the crevasse, landing with a crash that sent birds wheeling into the sky with alarmed cries.

Ben splayed on the ground, panting, clutching the solid earth beneath him as the cage of vines that surrounded him fell away.

Fuck. He'd come close to dying before, but that was during wild storms, when his mind had been too hazed with the need to keep the ship afloat and on course. This, though, hollowed him out.

Alys, Susannah, and the quartermaster gathered around, peering down at him.

"I've never thanked anyone for using magic before," he rasped.

"Her." The second-in-command jerked her head toward Alys. "She did it all."

Ben stared at Alys. Her face was taut, her hazel eyes bright in her ashen face.

"You—"

She held up her hand. "Would've done the same for any of my crew. And we're losing daylight the longer we stay here, kissing our own arses."

Beneath her sharp words there was relief, curling like feathers on the wind.

He'd leapt in front of her without thought, protecting her from an unknown threat. And now she'd saved his life. The vines that had woven across the ravine were less tangled than whatever bound Alys and Ben together. No matter what lay ahead.

CHAPTER THIRTEEN

"Y OU ARE WHITE as paper," Stasia said in a low whisper. She trotted to keep up with Alys, who had again taken the lead. Ben was just behind them, with Susannah keeping a close eye in the back, in case anything decided to attack from the rear. Though the creatures that inhabited this island had been peaceful so far, at any moment they might see Alys and the others as a threat.

"I like to think of my complexion as *pearly*." Alys slashed through the dense underbrush, using more force than her body had to give. It had been taxing enough to create the vine bridge with the help of Stasia and Susannah, but to create the cage and hold the end of the bridge on her own had completely drained her.

"You need rest," Stasia insisted.

"On the ship. For now, we keep going."

Stasia grumbled in Greek as she fell back. She took up her position behind Ben, shooting him a wary glance.

Alys marched ahead, following the sound of the water's voice. It was a welcome distraction from her own thoughts. She'd acted without thought to save Ben. The moment she'd seen the bridge give way, she'd rushed to help him. Now she paid the price. Her legs were weak beneath her, and her arm ached as she cut through foliage and vines, and she needed to sit a minute to catch her breath.

164 EVA LEIGH

But she couldn't let him see how little she'd mastered her magic. She had to keep going, presenting the face of an intrepid and tireless captain.

If he felt it, he didn't say. At least he had some sense of caution. Or self-preservation.

"Cap'n." Susannah appeared beside her and pressed something into her hand.

They paused long enough for Alys to examine what Susannah had given her. It was salt beef, as well as one of the small sugary cakes that Josephine occasionally gave the crew as a treat.

"I didn't ask for this."

"For a year, I've been sailing with you," Susannah whispered as they resumed marching, "and back home, we learned the measure of our magic together. Including what we need when we've pushed ourselves too much. Since I can't give you a cuddle right now," she added with a smile, "a bit of food and sugar will serve."

Alys nodded her thanks as she took a bite of the salt beef. It was tough and briny, but exactly what her depleted body required. "You and Stasia need it, too. And give some to him as well."

"He didn't use any magic," Susannah noted.

"He's human, and humans need sustenance."

"Aye, Cap'n."

Everyone kept walking as Susannah handed out rations. All conversation ceased as the simple meal was consumed. It was a far cry from the fresh, hot food Josephine provided for the company when aboard the ship. Damn if Alys didn't crave a bowl of her peppered mutton stew.

Ben meditatively chewed on the strip of meat Susannah had given him, yet his gaze was alert and attentive to his surroundings, ready in case a new threat emerged. His beard was nearly grown in now, making the blue of his eyes all the more crystalline, and his dark hair was loose about his shoulders. The crispness of his clothing was nearly gone. He reached up

THE SEA WITCH   165

to slacken his neckcloth, revealing his throat, and there was a sheen of sweat in the hollow just at the base.

"Something's amiss?" he demanded, catching her looking at him.

"Haven't I seen you at the Wig and Merkin, drinking ale with Rodrigo Flores?"

He scowled and straightened his waistcoat. Why stroke his ego by telling him that it pleased her to see him like this, rough and disheveled? He'd been attractive as a neat, spruce naval navigator, but now he was rugged, verging on wild.

Alys took a large bite of sugared cake, sating one hunger for another.

He sucked in a breath, and stared at her. Her cheeks warmed even more. *Hellfire.*

She tipped up her chin in defiance. So, she had begun to find him attractive—it didn't matter. All animals had the urge to mate. But there was a difference between her and a feral beast. *She* had control over herself.

His throat worked as he swallowed tightly.

She held up a hand, and everyone stood still.

"I hear it, too," Ben said.

"Water over stone," Susannah added.

Following the sound, everyone pressed forward, until they came to a shallow creek. It tumbled across wide smooth rocks, its banks narrow and pebbled.

"Small for a waterfall," Stasia noted.

"Its source might be what we're seeking," Alys mused.

"We can go upstream." Ben nodded toward the volcanic peak, still rising above them. "Likely, there's a waterfall coming off that mountain."

There were nods all around, and they trekked along the creek's rocky bank. They hadn't gone far before everyone came to a halt to behold a fresh spring bubbling up from the rocks. The voices Alys had conjured quieted.

"We have our source." Alys planted her hands on her hips. "Nothing more."

"Back the way we came," Ben said decisively.

Stasia growled, "I think you are *enjoying* yourself, navy man."

"We're *all* eager to find Little George's fail-safe," he answered. "And tramping around a rugged island jungle has far more merits than sitting idly on my ar—er, behind."

"Call an arse an arse," Alys said. "I'd hate to think of yours doing nothing all day but looking pretty."

He blinked. "That might be the first time anyone's called my buttocks *pretty*."

"You haven't been keeping the right company," she replied.

"Shall we *go*?" snapped Stasia.

Turning, they went back the way they'd come, following the creek as it wended its way down the mountain. It widened and roughened, until it turned from a gentle stream into a broad, surging river. The sound beat against their ears after the quiet of the jungle.

Then, suddenly, the river dropped off into nothingness, the open sky spreading beyond it. There was a loud booming noise.

Alys edged her way forward until she reached the lip of a precipice. The river spilled over the edge, becoming a huge roaring waterfall. Sheets of white foam rushed downward with monstrous force. Just as she'd seen it in Ben's dream.

The toe of her boot dislodged a stone and it went tumbling downward. She followed its trajectory as it spun through the air, until she could no longer see it. Likely, it was lost somewhere in the churning spray far, far below.

"Behold, the Weeping Princess," she said over her shoulder.

Ben, Stasia, and Susannah all cautiously approached and peered over the edge, and Stasia swore in Greek. It was easily two hundred feet down to the base of the waterfall, which plunged along a sheer rocky cliff. Large boulders were strewn at the base. At one point in the past, part of the mountain slope

THE SEA WITCH   167

had broken free, exposing countless rocks to crash to the ground below, where water now churned and foamed.

"We've a climb ahead of us," Ben said gravely. "I'll take the lead down."

"The hell you will," Alys countered.

He rolled his eyes. "Only a madman would use a massive, sheer drop as a means of escaping. Besides," he added before she could object, "this island isn't known to anyone, and marooning myself here without a knife or firearm is a certain way to die slowly."

She regarded him suspiciously.

"And," he went on, "if I'm in the lead and you fall, I can catch you."

It was her turn to roll her eyes. "Strong you may be, but if I'm falling, you aren't going to pluck me out of the air and cradle me to your manly bosom. *I'm* going first. However," she added, stroking her chin as a thought leapt into her mind, "we don't have to climb."

"There's no other way down," Ben said.

"For *some* people," Alys countered. "We aren't *some* people."

Susannah held up a hand and it was wreathed with warm gold light.

Ben said, dryly, "Not all of us. Climbing's my only option."

And have him possibly slip and fall an even greater distance than back at the ravine?

"I've enough magic for the both of us," Alys said. When he only sent her a doubting look, she added, "We'll go down together. If you fall, so do I. My neck's too pretty to snap."

Hopefully, her words held more faith than she felt. Though over the past year she had been working more on understanding her magic, never before had she tried to use it in this way. She'd conjured the wind to help her fly from St. Gertrude, but she had only needed to make *herself* soar. Ben was not only another person, he was a tall man with muscle.

He also wouldn't simply wait for them at the top of the waterfall, and he'd stubbornly insisted on climbing, leaving her with only one option.

Turning to Stasia and Susannah, she said, "I've done this before. We summon winds to hold us as we go down. Can you do that?"

Susannah nodded readily. "On moonless midnights, I'd practice off the roof of the granary. It was a wonder, tasting that kind of freedom. I never wanted to come back down to land. My home was with the gulls and cormorants."

Stasia, however, grimaced. "Such a skill is new to me, and I dare not attempt it here."

"Susannah," Alys directed, "you'll take Stasia with you, and I'll manage the sailing master."

Ben and Stasia exchanged a look—the first time they had ever been in solidarity together.

"Trust me," Alys said, "and trust Susannah."

She held out her hand to Ben. He stared at it for a long moment.

"There's no poison in my flesh," she said wryly.

Slowly, he threaded his fingers with hers, and his palm slid against hers. His hand was large, nearly engulfing her own, and the heat and callused texture of his skin rubbed against her flesh, equally rough from labor.

Yet there were parts of her hand more delicate than she expected, to be able to feel him against her skin with such sensitivity.

She sucked in a breath. So did he.

They both stared down at where they were joined. Golden magical light sprang to life around her hand, and it coursed up her arm . . . and his.

His jaw tightened, yet he didn't pull away. If anything, he gripped her hand tighter. A faint hint of his interest and curiosity danced.

THE SEA WITCH

By silent agreement, together they stepped to the edge of the precipice. Her heart beat in her throat. Mixing fear and excitement strengthened her magic.

She looked out over the green valley that spread before her. Farther beyond was the azure sea stretching toward the equally blue sky. Drawing in a deep breath, she reached out to the winds that were ever present in the Caribbean. She drew them toward her, calling upon them the way one would call to old friends. And they were her friends . . . They filled the sails of her ship so she and her crew could traverse the waters, doing the work and living the lives they were meant to.

Come to me, she silently beckoned.

She waited several heartbeats, and then with words that were not words, the winds answered.

We are here.

Wind blew across her face and gusted against her body, filling her coat up so that it flapped behind her like wings, her hair wild. It grew in strength, rising up, surrounding her and Ben.

Hold us, she urged the winds.

The gusts increased even more, buffeting them. Spray from the waterfall flecked across their faces.

"Now," she said to Ben.

Breathing in, they stepped off the edge of the cliff.

They fell, spinning. They hurtled down too fast. And then the wind grew stronger, pushing against them. It barely held them aloft as they tumbled. The ground rushed closer.

And then—it was over. They both stumbled when their boots touched the rocky soil. The winds gave one swirl around her before shooting upward. At the very edge of the precipice stood Susannah, calling the wind to her, as a frightened Stasia clung to her hand.

Energy danced through Alys's body. Where was the exhaustion that often followed working a challenging spell?

"When can we do that again?" Alys asked eagerly.

"I never thought . . ." Ben said softly. "I didn't believe I would ever fly. It was . . ." His eyes were warm and brightly blue as he gazed at her. "Terrifying . . . and . . . incredible."

Awareness shimmered between them. Awareness of him as a man, and her as a woman. He was bigger than her—yet she could meet his strength with her own. They both knew it.

Her gaze went to the lapel of his coat. The dark blue garment was fraying, but most of the brass buttons remained. Slightly ragged as his coat was, it still marked him as a sailing master for the Royal Navy.

She was a pirate. A witch.

Abruptly, she let go of his hand, realizing only then that she'd still been holding it. She turned away, ignoring a throb in her chest.

Alys gave her attention to Susannah and Stasia, descending from the cliff. They drifted down, rather than half fell, as Alys and Ben had. Susannah's braids slipped from the binding that held them back, and floated around her in elegant cursives. Stasia seemed too terrified to concern herself with the fact that her loose trousers fluttered like sails.

Susannah clearly had more practice and skill when it came to flying.

"Steady as she goes, my girls," Alys called up. "Nearly there."

"Say *nothing* . . . until I am . . . on the ground," Stasia growled.

Susannah was silent as she controlled the wind, but as she drew closer to the earth, she appeared joyous, like someone coming home.

Finally, they all stood on the rocks, having reached the bottom of the precipice.

"When the sun turns into a block of ice," Stasia muttered. "*That* is when I will fly once more."

Seeing Stasia frightened by anything was a rarity, but in addition to being Alys's second-in-command, Stasia was also her friend, and so Alys kept any remarks to herself.

THE SEA WITCH 171

They faced the waterfall, which appeared even more towering and thunderous than it had from the top of the precipice. Water sheeted down in a heavy pour, slamming against the rocks that lay at the bottom. It held a cool scent with the fragrance of stone beneath. Since coming to the Caribbean, she'd seen many waterfalls. The first one had dazzled her. But *this* left her stunned. It was beautiful and terrible and somehow it was the key to Little George's fail-safe.

Alys recited,

"A golden, holy key you seek to open the stone heart,
But first, you must be penitent.
Bow at the feet of the Weeping Princess
And behind her vale of tears, you will find your way."

Everyone looked around, taking in the thick jungle that encircled the pool at the base of the waterfall. It was just as densely wooded here as elsewhere on the island. The breeze churned up by the thundering water made the trees dance as if they were revelers honoring the forest gods that made them.

The pool itself appeared about forty feet across, pale green around the edges and then a deep emerald in the middle, revealing that it was quite deep.

"Little George was a wily bastard," Alys said. "He wouldn't leave the fail-safe out for just anyone to find."

"How is it determined who's *just anyone?*" Ben peered into the green shadows surrounding them.

"We'll split into two groups and search the area. Stasia and Susannah, you take the north quadrant."

Her crew nodded and, with their hands on the butts of their pistols, marched into their assigned portion of the jungle.

"We'll search around the waterfall," she said to Ben.

They walked the perimeter of the pool at the base of the waterfall, searching for some hint or sign of the buried trove.

She examined rocks both large and small, toeing some aside or else rolling them away in the hopes of uncovering even the smallest item that might be the fail-safe. Ben did the same, looking beneath the bracken that grew in the dampness.

They went in wider and wider arcs as they investigated. And yet, no matter how intently they searched . . .

"I'm finding fuck-all," she said after some time. Crossing her arms over her chest, she added grimly, "Beginning to think Little George was having us on, a final laugh from the depths of hellfire."

"An infamous pirate like George Partridge isn't the sort who fails to deliver on his threats, or in this case, clues."

"And yet there's nothing *here*."

She sensed his frustration match her own. Together, they glared at the thundering water that fell in a surging misty curtain.

"'Behind her vale of tears, you will find your way,'" she quoted.

They turned to face each other.

"*V-e-i-l* not *v-a-l-e*," they said in unison.

"The water forms a veil," he exclaimed, "and behind that . . ."

"We might find the fail-safe."

She looked at the waterfall. A shadow loomed behind the cascade of water, a large dark hollow midway between the rocks at the base and the top of the cliff. It appeared to be about twenty feet wide and ten feet high.

"A cave." She tugged on Ben's sleeve and pointed. "There, in the stone behind the waterfall."

"Damn—I missed it before."

"The water keeps it hidden. We'll climb to it."

They approached the rocky cliff next to the waterfall. Alys gripped a boulder and pulled herself up. She wedged her boots into the stone to give her more force moving upward. Beside her, Ben did the same. They were silent as they climbed, slowly ascending. Sun-warmed rocks dug into her hands, but her palms were callused, her fingers strong, and she held tightly as she went up.

THE SEA WITCH 173

They climbed for what seemed like forever, nearly a distance of a hundred feet. At last, they were perpendicular to the floor of the cave. There was a slim gap between the cliff and the water plummeting downward, just enough to sidle through toward the cave—if they were careful. Yet the rocks were damp and would prove hard to hold onto, and if they got caught in the waterfall, they'd be pulled off the cliff and dashed against the boulders below.

Her magic guttered like a candle. If either she or Ben fell, she had no power left to stop them from falling.

After taking a steadying breath, she edged sidewise. Her fingers clutched at the rocks made slick from the spray. She pushed down hard with her boots on the footholds to keep from slipping. The waterfall's roar drowned out all other sound, filling her head with thunder. She kept her focus on the stones and handholds directly beside her as she sidled toward the cave.

Alys chanced a quick glance to make sure Ben was still beside her. His face was set in concentration, his hands splayed upon the rocks. His gaze caught hers and he gave a brief nod.

She continued on. The waterfall now bellowed behind her, cool and ravenous. She pulled herself tightly against the cliffside.

Finally, her fingers felt the edge of the cave's opening. She held her breath as she climbed the last remaining feet before clambering in. At last, she was inside the cave.

She sat heavily, then scrambled back to give Ben room. Once his hand appeared around the lip of the rock, she exhaled, but only when he was fully inside did she allow herself to breathe easier.

He splayed on the ground, spread-eagle, his chest rising and falling with great heaving gulps of air. Alys crawled until she was right beside him. Her hair hung in long wet strands around her face.

He turned to look at her, and they stared at one another, both panting. Their breath mingled in the small space between them.

174   EVA LEIGH

"Not as . . . adept with cliffs . . . as I am with rigging," he gasped.

"A fair showing, all the same."

"From both of us."

A tiny smile played about his lips, and she couldn't help herself from smiling back. But then their smiles fell away. All she had to do was move her body slightly and she could stretch herself atop him. His clothing, like hers, was soaked. They would be able to feel every muscle and curve.

Her regard flicked down the length of him. His breeches clung to the taut lines of his thighs.

She dragged her gaze back to his eyes, burning sharp blue even in the shadows of the cave. He levered himself up on his elbows and reached for her.

Alys never considered herself a coward. Not until that moment.

She lurched to her feet. Then turned her attention to the cave, created by years of water wearing away at the rock. In the dim interior, the craggy surfaces were slick from mist that was flung from the water. It was a space perhaps fifteen feet deep. At first quick glance, it seemed bare of anything resembling what might serve as a fail-safe. No enchanted objects, no chests holding scrolls with spells. The cavern echoed with the constant roar from the crashing water at the opening.

A fascinating space. Not nearly as fascinating as the man behind her. Yet she couldn't turn back to him. Couldn't finish what every part of her wanted.

"No fail-safe anywhere," he yelled above the noise.

She glanced in his direction. He'd gotten to his feet and also studied the cave. Thank the stars he hadn't tried to hold her again. Because she just might have let him.

"It could be hidden," she suggested. "Buried."

He slapped his hand against the walls. "Solid stone. It's as you said. There's nothing to be found here except Little George's idea of a joke."

THE SEA WITCH

175

"Let's start looking."

She ran her hands over the sheer rock that made up the walls of the cavern, searching for anything loose that could possibly hide the cache. After a moment, he did the same, passing his palms along the craggy surface.

Her hand glided over something smooth. It was so unlike the other jagged rocks that she passed her fingers back over the expanse. Yes, it was flat and polished, the area roughly the size of a platter one might use for serving a roast. Her fingertips brushed against delicate lines in the stone.

"Ben," she called.

He was immediately at her side.

"Words," she explained. "Etched into the rock."

His hand passed over the faint carving. "It's too dark in here to read it."

"I lost my flint somewhere in the climb." She reached for her magic, calling forth the light of a firefly. Yet it sputtered and died. She tried again, and again the light failed. "I can't get my magic to hold. Seems Little George put a block of some kind in here, something that keeps my magic from working. But," she added, "we can pry it loose. It's brighter at the mouth of the cave. We can try to read it there."

She wedged the tip of her dagger between the polished stone and the jagged rock. With the heel of her palm, she pounded on the hilt to create a lever that would pry it free.

"A little more," he urged.

Tension mounted as she continued to work at the buried stone, and grew even more as it began to work its way out of the rock. Her boots slipped on the ground as she pushed. The blade of her dagger nicked her thumb, but she ignored the drop of blood that ran down her hand. Swelling apprehension grew, as she kept digging out the polished rock. His eagerness danced with hers in rising waves.

"Yes, yes," Ben said eagerly. "That's it."

The smooth stone leapt from the wall. She grabbed it before it tumbled to the ground.

They both gave an elated shout, turning toward each other and beaming in triumph.

And then his mouth was on hers.

She immediately pressed her lips to his. He cupped the back of her head to angle her better to taste more of her, going deeper. She still held the stone, but pressed into him as she kissed him with equal hunger.

A sudden burst of energy blasted between them. They were thrown through the water and out from the cave. Pushed out of the cavern, they flew through the air.

She had a fleeting glimpse of his astonished face as they soared briefly before plummeting down into the deep pool at the base of the waterfall.

Dark green water surrounded her. For a moment, she was suspended in the pool, stunned. The polished stone in her hands pulled her to the bottom.

Her lungs burned. With quick, forceful kicks, she swam upward, fighting the downward drag of the rock in her hands. She broke the surface and took a deep breath.

"Ben," she shouted, swiveling her head to find a sign of him. Nothing.

A beat of her heart later, he emerged from the water, gasping, just as stunned as she had been.

He pushed his hair out of his eyes and looked around. When he caught sight of her, they swam to the edge of the pool. Clothes soaking, water squelching in their boots, they trudged up the bank. They had a moment to stare at each other, drenched and dazed, before Stasia ran up, with Susannah right behind her.

"Captain," Stasia exclaimed. "What the hell happened? Has the fail-safe been found?"

The magpie on her shoulder twittered.

"What are those?" Susannah added.

THE SEA WITCH

She pointed to the dark markings on Ben's skin, winding across the back of his hands and up his neck. They stood out in bold relief as they formed arcane patterns that twisted and curled over his flesh. He stared at them, shocked.

"These only appear when my skin touches seawater." He turned accusing eyes to Alys. "What did you do? What magic are you using on me?"

She looked up toward the cave behind the waterfall, where they had been moments earlier until some power had blown them out with explosive force.

Bewildered, she said with a shake of her head, "That magic belonged to you alone, Sailing Master."

CHAPTER FOURTEEN

BEN GAPED AT Alys. She stared back.

He shook out the cuffs of his coat, but it was a lost cause. His garments had been drenched too many times to look at all presentable. Between that and his loose hair and grown-in beard, if any of his superior officers saw him, they would be horrified. Lieutenant Oliver would be particularly annoyed seeing him so bedraggled.

He gritted his teeth at the train of his thoughts. What the hell did it matter what Oliver felt? There was no value in a clean-shaven jaw when Alys had just accused him of something he could never, would never, believe about himself.

"What just happened requires magic," he snarled at her. "I have none."

"Then what the fuck are those?" She pointed at his hands.

He didn't want to look again, and yet he did. There they were, the markings that had haunted him since he was nine years of age. His fingers strayed to his throat, and though he couldn't feel anything, the markings had to be there, too.

"There's no sense in any of it," he threw back. "*Your* magic caused . . . whatever the hell that was."

"Magic and I are old friends," she answered. "I know its ways. Including when it begins in me. And this time, it didn't. The source was you."

THE SEA WITCH 179

"When we . . ."

He glanced toward Susannah and Stasia, watching them both with alarmed confusion. Only if the fires of hell licked his heels would he admit in front of them that he and Alys had kissed.

"*Did you locate the fail-safe?*" the quartermaster demanded.

Alys held up the stone as everyone gathered close to peer at the writing on its surface.

She read aloud, "'Find what you seek in the shelter of Sir Fenfield's nephew's cousin's daughter's son's table.'"

"And?" Stasia pressed.

"And nothing."

"That's not the fail-safe," Susannah said flatly.

"Another fucking riddle." Alys glared at the stone in her hands. As she did, the edges of the polished rock began crumbling into fine powder. It spread across the stone, until it was nothing but dust in her hands. She cast what remained of the dust into the pool, and it sank through the water to settle at the bottom.

"More of Partridge's magic?" Ben asked.

"I destroyed it," she answered. "Can't have anyone read it and follow us."

"What does it mean?" Susannah wondered.

The trees ringing the waterfall's pool shuddered. Shapes moved in the green shadows, and a low rumbling echoed out from the forest. The quartermaster's familiar flapped its wings in alarm.

Whatever creatures inhabited this island now stirred, and they didn't sound pleased.

Alys drew her cutlass, and Stasia and Susannah cocked their pistols. Ben searched for something to use as a weapon, and had to settle for a sharp piece of rock. He clutched it tightly and it dug into his skin. Damn if he didn't wish for his own blade or flintlock.

"There's a creek that runs from the waterfall," Alys whispered, nodding toward the running water. "We can't go back the way we came, so we follow it. Hopefully it'll lead us out of here."

Silent nods were exchanged. Single file, with Alys in the lead, they hurried along the bank of the creek. Thick jungle gathered on either side of them with lengthening shadows that deepened as dusk approached.

Rustling sounded in the vegetation. Deep growls rolled out from the cover of the trees.

"Don't run," Alys cautioned everyone.

Ben walked quickly to catch up with Alys. "I count half a dozen creatures following us. Large ones."

"There are eight of them," she answered lowly. She pulled on a tree branch, and used her cutlass to lop it off. Pinning his gaze with hers, she handed him the limb. "Stay alert."

"One of your daggers would be a better weapon," he noted.

"I've little doubt you can defend yourself with that."

Clearly, she still didn't trust him enough to arm him. He hefted the branch, his fingers wrapped around the rough bark. Ben gave it an experimental swing, wielding it like a club. It would have to do.

The quartermaster and Susannah glanced at his weapon before looking toward Alys with questions in their eyes. Alys's set expression didn't move.

Silently, the women resumed their speedy march. Ben fell back, striding quickly behind Alys, his gaze constantly in motion as he attempted to track whatever followed them and lurked in the darkness. Long shadows loomed like dusk-hued ghouls.

Stasia and Susannah also peered into the gloom. A tense silence fell, broken only by the continued growling from the unseen creatures and the sound of the creek running over rocks as they followed it down the slope of the hill.

At last, the forest parted to reveal a narrow strip of shore. Thirty feet of sand stretched between the forest and the sea.

THE SEA WITCH 181

Ben didn't exhale. They still needed to get off the beach and away from this island.

"Go," the second-in-command said to her familiar. "Tell Thérèse and Cora where we are, and urge them to hurry."

The magpie gave a quiet chirp, as if it, too, was aware of the things slinking in the darkness. With a flap of its wings, the bird took to the sky and wheeled off to the other beach, where the jolly boat was grounded.

"They need the speed of Hermes," Stasia muttered, glancing behind her at the jungle.

The sky deepened to violet with approaching night. A scattering of stars appeared above, while behind the forest loomed darkly. The heat of the day hadn't abated, pressing down with a crushing hand.

More rustling and snarling sounded.

Ben joined the quartermaster as she took a defensive position facing the fringe of the jungle. Alys and Susannah watched the beach. Everyone crouched low with their weapons at the ready.

His stomach was taut in anticipation, and Alys's tension vibrated through his consciousness. No one spoke.

The sound of oars in the water drew his attention. The jolly boat had arrived, and perched on the prow was the magpie.

Before the small vessel could reach the sand, everyone on land charged through the surf to reach it. Ben slogged through the water, his movements slowed by the waves pushing against him. The women moved quickly, and panic skittered along his shoulders as they clambered into the jolly boat.

They began to row.

Still in the water, he grasped the edge of the jolly boat as it pulled away from the beach. His arms strained with the force of trying to hold on. He would be left behind.

And then hands were grabbing his coat, pulling him up and over the edge of the boat. Alys and Susannah gritted their teeth as they hauled him in. He tumbled to the bottom of the small vessel. For a moment, he lay still, his breath coming in ragged gulps.

He sat up and sent a glance toward the jungle.

Several large dark shapes emerged from the forest.

"Row, damn it," Alys snarled at the two women on the oars.

As the pirates put their backs into it, Alys, Stasia, and Susannah lifted their hands and held them above the water. They murmured words he couldn't understand, but the surf around the jolly boat glowed. It shimmered as if lit by underwater candles. The vessel moved, propelled through the water as if by a dozen oars.

Ben stared at the beach as it shrank behind them. The shapes were at the edge of the water now, watching their departure. After several moments, they retreated back into the jungle.

He didn't permit himself an exhale.

EVEN THE MAGPIE remained quiet on the voyage back, perched on the quartermaster's shoulder and rubbing its beak back and forth across the Greek woman's cheek. Stasia stroked the bird's chest feathers, her gaze steely as she stared back at the island they had just fled from.

Ben's attention remained fixed on Alys. Her eyes were shut, and though it was full dark now and he couldn't see her clearly, her weariness was tangible and pulled at him, dragging down his own heavy and aching limbs.

Finally, they reached the *Sea Witch*. Shaken and exhausted, they clambered out of the jolly boat and up the ladder hanging portside. In the lamplight, Alys appeared even more drawn, but the moment her feet touched the top deck, her shoulders straightened, she raised up her chin, and confidence radiated from her.

Only he knew differently. Beneath her poise, she ached with fatigue, but there was a determination that her crew would never grasp that their captain was just as fallible as any of them.

THE SEA WITCH   183

The curious crew gathered around, full of questions.

"What did you see?"

"Did you find the fail-safe?"

"By and by," Alys answered, holding up her hand, "all will be known to you." Another crew member stepped forward, and Alys said to her, "Inés, we're in need of Josephine's skills. Hearty food and plenty of ale and rum. Whatever works best for balancing. Have them brought to my quarters."

"Aye, Cap'n," was the brisk answer, and she trotted off to obey Alys's orders—whatever *balancing* might entail from the ship's cook.

Alys turned to Stasia. "You and Susannah to my quarters for balancing. I'll want Polly and Luna there as well. We've much to discuss."

"Yes, Captain," the quartermaster replied briskly. She and Susannah climbed down the companionway, leaving Ben and Alys behind.

Alys motioned another member of the crew forward. She spoke lowly into the other woman's ear before the crew member hurried away. A moment later, the woman returned. Holding a pair of manacles.

Ben's heart sank. Even so, he held out his wrists.

Alys took the manacles. Her gaze was on his as she fastened them on him, and he stared back. The iron was heavy and abraded his skin, even as his gaze drifted to her mouth.

He'd tasted her. And she'd been hungry for him. Yet the manacles now binding him were proof that nothing had truly changed. She still didn't trust him, and he couldn't fault her.

He had lost sight of his objective, misled by unwanted desire. A mistake he couldn't, wouldn't make again.

Ben glanced down at his ankles, awaiting the shackles, too. But when he looked toward Alys, a question in his eyes, she gave a minute shake of her head.

He exhaled. Something *had* altered.

Yet now that his usefulness on the island of the Weeping Princess was over, she might send him back down to the brig. And then he'd have no chance to destroy the fail-safe.

"The clue that Partridge left behind," he said. "You'll need my assistance in deciphering it."

She raised a brow. "Very kind of you, Sailing Master, offering your services."

Back to *Sailing Master*. As though the manacles around his wrists weren't proof enough that they stood at opposite ends of the law, and their kiss was a momentary madness never to be repeated.

"It's a foolish man who doesn't search for any opportunity to prolong his life."

Her eyes narrowed. He held motionless beneath her regard, her skepticism scouring him. He smoothed out the convolutions of his mind, his emotions, becoming a pond on a windless day. Glassy and reflective, giving away nothing beneath the surface.

At last, she jerked her chin toward the companionway. "To my quarters."

"Aye," he said, then added, "Captain."

She nodded, as if calling her by her official rank was her due.

He followed her down from the upper deck. The markings had faded from his skin. Thank God. Talking about them was the very last thing he desired. Not with her crew present, at least.

They didn't speak on the way to her cabin. His gaze stayed on her back and the glossy fall of her russet hair. He rubbed the pads of his fingers together, evoking the memory of the heavy strands he'd felt only hours ago.

Pain pulsed in his chest. He shoved it aside. Selfish and reckless desires had no place. Not here, not now. Not ever.

Reaching her cabin, she pushed open the door.

The quartermaster and Susannah stood in the middle of her cabin, embracing.

THE SEA WITCH

185

"They'll want some privacy," Ben muttered.

Instead, Alys walked up to the two women and wrapped her arms around them both. She laid her head down on Susannah's back, closing her eyes as she inhaled deeply. The three women seemed to melt into each other, gently caressing one another, breathing together.

"I'll step out . . ." Ben started to pull the door shut.

"Belay that, Sailing Master." Alys didn't open her eyes as she spoke. "Drop anchor."

"You're—"

"Balancing."

"Ah. Yes. I see." Ben didn't see at all, but she'd commanded him to stay, and he wouldn't disobey her.

He stood awkwardly in a corner, trying not to watch them, and yet unable to stop his gaze from wandering to the trio of women. A golden glow began emanating from the three witches. Dimly at first, surrounding their bodies in a soft haze, before strengthening. In gradual increments, the light gained potency, engulfing them in a brightness that forced Ben to shield his eyes from its intensity.

A single musical note rose up, the combination of their three voices in a low sweet tone. The music shivered through the air and along Ben's skin, the hairs on his nape and forearms standing up as an unseen energy charged him.

And then they stepped apart. The light faded, yet that energy continued to reverberate throughout the cabin. The three witches stood taller, no longer strained and faded with weariness. Alys's eyes were bright as she nodded at Stasia and Susannah, just as their gazes seemed sharper, clearer than he'd ever seen before.

Ben could only stare at them, mystified. Tingling danced along his skin. The quarters brimmed with energy, and invisible waves spilled from the open window to whirl across the sea. Where it would stop . . . there was no knowing. Out to the farthest corners of the known world, perhaps even into the unknown world.

A tap sounded on the door and Luna the navigator as well as Polly poked their heads in when Alys bid them enter. They were followed by the crew member Faith and another woman with olive skin, braided brown hair, and capable hands, whose apron proclaimed her to be the ship's cook.

"Gather round, little birds," the cook urged as she and Faith set bowls brimming with stew on the table. They also laid out loaves of fresh crusty bread—a true luxury at sea—a plate laden with cheerful oranges, and bottles of rum and jugs of ale. The cook and her mate filed out, leaving them with a true feast.

Everyone collected around the table. His mouth watered at the sight and smell of so much hot food that carried the scent of browned meat combined with herbs, but Ben hesitated. Yet Alys tipped her head in his direction, indicating that he, too, should join them for the meal.

Wordlessly, ravenously, they began to eat. Cups were filled, drained, and filled again.

Though Ben was hungry, and the food proved once again that the ship's cook was excellent, he ate slowly. To this point, all his meals had either been taken on his own or with only Alys for company. Yet here he was, breaking bread with members of a pirate crew.

Damn, more buttons were missing from the front of his coat. The remaining buttons had dulled, too. The cuffs were frayed and much of the braided trim was gone. Could he ask for a sewing needle to make a few repairs? The chain between his manacles swung every time he reached for his cup.

His coat wasn't a sail that was necessary to make the ship function. No needle, then. Not unless he was supervised. And she wouldn't spare a member of her crew to watch him mend his unravelling clothes.

THE SEA WITCH

His metal cup held his reflection, and he fought a grimace at the sight of his beard growing thickly on his jaw.

Not shipshape. Not by a league.

He maintained his rigid posture as he ate, while Alys, Stasia, and the other women hunched or leaned over their food. A few wiped their mouths on their sleeves. Crumbs were scattered and droplets of ale and rum landed on the table, soaking into the wood. Someone belched audibly. They would all have been disciplined by Admiral Strickland for lack of decorum.

As they ate and drank, Alys, Stasia, and Susannah grew even more alert and animated. It was as though the long exhausting and terrifying day on the island of the Weeping Princess had never happened. Impossible not to grow bolstered from Alys and her crew's energy. Moments earlier, Ben had been certain he'd fall asleep the moment he climbed back into his hammock. Now, he felt he could climb the rigging and barely tire.

"No complaints about the quality of our food aboard a pirate ship, Sailing Master?" Alys asked.

He looked down at his hand, swiping a piece of bread through the last of the gravy at the bottom of his bowl.

The other women chuckled.

"Women aren't much tolerated on naval ships," he said, "but your cook would be welcome, and heartily."

"Josephine would be flattered by such praise," Alys answered, "to be so graciously *tolerated*."

She stood from the table and walked to the window running along the back of her quarters, where the dark sea rose and fell. Everyone's attention was on her, and not the reflection of the moon upon the waves.

"A crafty scoundrel, that Little George," she said thoughtfully. "Made us work to find what we sought."

"A clue to the fail-safe," Susannah said.

"'Find what you seek in the shelter of Sir Fenfield's nephew's cousin's daughter's son's table,'" Alys recited.

Looks were shared around the cabin.

"I have no knowledge of this Sir Fenfield," the quartermaster said darkly.

"A landowner," Ben said quickly.

"What else do you know of him?" Alys demanded.

"He lives well from investments, in Bermuda, and has no truck with pirates."

"That you are *aware of.*" Stasia crossed her arms over her chest.

"It's not Sir Fenfield that interests me," Alys interjected. "But his nephew's cousin's daughter's son."

"Whoever that is." Luna the navigator threw up her hands.

"He had a nephew by marriage, a man called John Abernathy," Ben mused. "Abernathy had another uncle . . . Samuel Wyle. And two sons. One died . . . Cholera, I think, but the other lives, Ralph Dunwood. He dwells on an estate located on an island off the coast of Tortola."

"Did he have children?"

"I believe so," Ben said slowly.

"Their names," Alys demanded.

Ben could only shrug.

"Tell me more about Dunwood and this island he lives on. Have he and his kind dwelt on there long?"

"His grandfather came to the Caribbean around 1660. Him and his offspring, they've kept close to the area."

"There'll be a parish record, then," Alys said.

Ben slowly rose. "To learn exactly *who* his nephew's daughter's son would be." He turned to Luna. "We'll review the charts together and I can show you which island he lives on, and the location of the town and church that would have the parish records."

"Go, both of you," Alys said with a jerk of her head. "To the chart room and set a course."

THE SEA WITCH   189

"Aye, Captain," Ben answered.

Only when she smirked at him did he realize that this was the second time tonight he'd ceded to her authority.

He quickly left her quarters, following Luna to the chart room.

Stay useful. Help her find the fail-safe. And then demolish it.

With each step, he recited his objectives like a refrain in a hymn. Reminding himself. Shutting away the memory of the kiss as if stowing it in a heavy iron lockbox. Yet the safe couldn't contain the recollection of her mouth against his, no matter how hard he tried to imprison it.

CHAPTER FIFTEEN

Balancing always left Alys humming with more energy than she knew what to do with. Had she been on land, she would have found someone to share her bed for several enthusiastic hours, which either quieted the tumult in her blood to a low roar or, depending on who she fucked, filled her with even more vitality.

She wasn't on land, and she always adhered to her dictum of not sleeping with her crew. Briefly, she considered touching herself for some quick help. It had been too long since her last climax and her body demanded release. Kiss or no kiss, she wasn't about to have Ben return to her quarters while she was in mid-frig. Even if that kiss had hinted at an unpredictable—and shared—attraction.

She took lovers only for the night. Anything beyond that . . . She'd been married before. Alys had been obedient to men's whims and desires and demands. She'd been forced to grind by the yoke of affection.

Already, she felt Ben's interest in her sharpening. And while she might want his body, she couldn't risk anything more with him. His naval coat was frayed, but he still served the King. And he was hiding something from her.

She called for a pitcher of warm water, and it was brought with a basin, cloth, and cake of honey-scented soap that had been

THE SEA WITCH

taken from an English merchantman. They were all luxuries, but after tramping around the island of the Weeping Princess in dense heat, being flung from a waterfall, and fleeing unknown creatures, she could use a bit of bathing.

Alys placed the basin on the little table near the foot of her berth. She poured half the ewer's contents into the bowl. The water giggled as it filled the porcelain. Turning her back to the door, she removed the dagger from her belt, pulled off her coat, jerkin, and shirt before undoing the band of linen wrapped around her breasts.

The bindings fell away. She scratched at her red itchy flesh. Then she dipped the cloth in the water, before rubbing the cake of soap on its fabric, pulling up a lather that smelled of honey on a summer day.

Grime from the day rinsed off her body. As a pirate, there wasn't much time or means for luxuries like a soaking tub, so she had to take what delight she could from this smaller indulgence. What a series of calamities the day had been.

Including the kiss.

She touched her lips.

A knock sounded on the door, and she dropped her hand from her mouth. No sense in dwelling on something that couldn't go further.

"Enter," she called.

"Luna said I was to come back and— Jesus God." Ben's strangled voice carried across the cabin.

He'd turned his back to her, facing the now closed door. His back and shoulders were ramrod straight.

"You're a veteran of these seas for many years," she said wryly. "Surely you aren't shocked by the sight of someone bathing."

"It's the *who* that's naked from the waist up that has ensnared my attention."

If he couldn't control himself at the sight of her partially nude, well, that was *his* concern. Besides, he was manacled, and

192 EVA LEIGH

her dagger was close at hand. Should he get too free with his hands, stabbing him was always an option.

With a shrug, she resumed bathing.

"The course has been set?" she asked.

"We'll arrive at the island in three days, barring inclement weather." His voice was gruff. "Luna's an excellent navigator. She'll get us there."

"A prize, that Luna. Earns her share and a half. I'll never let anyone take her from my crew."

A strained quiet descended, interrupted only by the sound of her dipping the cloth in water and abrading it across her skin. Even Samuel had walked out of the room whenever she bathed. "*Shameful*," he used to say, his hand over his eyes. "*Where's your modesty? Your self-respect?*"

"*But you're my* husband," she'd answer.

"*Eve*," he'd mutter as he fled, and she'd stare down at her nude body, the Massachusetts cold pebbling across her pale vulnerable skin.

Ben still faced the door.

Briefly, she considered sending him out of her quarters. Yet she'd had enough of enforced modesty.

She tugged off her boots and then, after a moment's hesitation, shucked her breeches. The air in her cabin pressed dense and warm on her now completely naked flesh.

She washed her sex, her movements quick and impersonal. It *had* been a long time since she'd given herself a release, and the rubbing of the cloth on her cunt made hot sensations rocket through her—but he didn't deserve the honor of watching her pleasure herself.

Still, even with his back to her, his arousal was hot and sharp, a whetted edge.

Once she was satisfied that she'd gotten herself clean, she grabbed a fresh cloth and washed her face.

"Those markings on you," she said in the silence.

THE SEA WITCH

He said nothing for a long while. Then, "I wasn't born with them. They appeared when I was nine."

"Appeared."

"After . . . an attack."

"The octopus," she recalled. "In the dream."

Again, he did not speak. Uncertainty thrummed. He didn't know if he could trust her.

Finally, he said, "Father was at sea and my mother was always distracted when he wasn't home. As though part of her was on the waves, with him. There were tide pools near our home in Port Royal. I loved to go to them and be amongst the sea creatures that lived there. I would roll my breeches up and wade around, looking at the corals and fish and all manner of things living there."

Her hands stilled in their movements. There was a rare openness in his voice, a vulnerability she sensed in throbbing pulses.

His head was bent, his hands curled into fists at his sides as he continued to speak, the words coming from him as if he cleaned an old infected wound.

"I liked . . ." he cleared his throat " . . . to pretend I was a pirate."

She said nothing, but he glanced quickly at her, feeling her shock.

"I would take leaves from the black-bead plant and float them on the water, pretending they were my fleet of buccaneer ships. That's what I was doing when—"

He drew in a ragged breath.

"The octopus had disguised itself as one of the rocks," he said lowly. "I hardly knew what was happening until it was too late, and by then I hadn't any voice to shout for help, not that any would have come for me. Here I was, playing at being a pirate, when my father risked his life to hunt them. The attack was retribution. Or so I thought. Maybe . . . maybe it was."

194 EVA LEIGH

She threw on her shirt and her breeches, but stayed where she was.

"I didn't know octopi could attack a human," he went on. "I'd never seen it or heard about it. But this one did. I still feel the lash from its tentacles, its ink covering my skin."

The vivid dream surrounded her, and she was there with him, his pain and fear and isolation, left alone to fend for himself against something that wasn't supposed to be his enemy. Twisting tentacles wrapped around his arms, his legs. For whatever reason, this animal had unleashed itself upon him, and he'd had no means of protecting itself.

"It went on forever," he continued. "Seemed that way. And then, as quickly as the attack began . . . it ended. The octopus shuddered and shriveled. It died, its body swaying with the movement of the tide pool. I was so afraid it would come back to life I just stared at it for what seemed like an eternity. But then I knew it was dead and couldn't hurt me anymore. The salt water stung my skin as I tried to wash the ink off. It left behind the markings you've seen. They faded, but from that day to this, they appear when salt water touches my skin."

"Today, at the waterfall, it was freshwater, not salt."

His expression was unreadable, yet his bewilderment formed a fog in their connection. "Much of today mystifies me."

Their gazes held.

He'd revealed something of himself to her, yet there was more he kept hidden, secrets and motivations. Especially after their kiss, remaining wary around him was vital.

But she wasn't in the navy, or one of those pirate captains that reveled in their captives' misery. She could be cautious *and* considerate.

"Some clean water remains in the pitcher," she noted. "There are more fresh cloths, too. I'm certain you're as eager to bathe as I was."

THE SEA WITCH   195

He glanced with longing toward the ewer and basin. "Privacy might be as rare on a pirate ship as it is a naval one."

"These are *my* quarters."

A debate raged behind his eyes. Finally, he muttered, "The hell with it," before striding toward the table that held the bathing supplies. He held out his manacled wrists. "I'll need these off."

From between her breasts, Alys pulled out the key, dangling on a cord. She also grabbed a loaded flintlock and pointed it at him. With the muzzle trained on the center of his chest, she walked to him and unlocked the manacles before taking several steps back.

He rubbed his wrists, and then shrugged off his tattered coat. Neatly, he laid it over the back of a chair, smoothing it carefully with his hands. She bit the inside of her cheek. In the name of the constellations.

The linen of his shirt pulled tightly over his shoulders. His hands hovered over the buttons of his waistcoat.

"Missish behavior from a member of His Majesty's Navy?" She snorted. "With my own eyes, I've witnessed people cut wide open, their guts spilling over their boots. The sight of a bare male torso is hardly cause for me to require sal volatile."

She crossed her arms over her chest. His gaze shot to her breasts, pushed up and against the thin fabric of her shirt. Well, if she was going to insist on seeing *his* chest, she might as well afford him the same privilege.

Still, he hesitated.

She exhaled. "Pick one: cleanliness or modesty. I can't keep myself and my crew safe and look away."

After a moment, his fingers moved over the buttons of his waistcoat. Though his hands were rather large, his fingers were deft as they undid the buttons, and she held her breath as his waistcoat opened. Finally, he shrugged the long garment off, and placed it atop his discarded coat.

That left only his shirt. His gaze holding hers, he reached behind his head and tugged until he pulled the whole garment off.

"Well," she said, her brows lifting. "A pleasant surprise."

"I . . . uh . . . climb the rigging frequently to take readings. And practice my swordsmanship."

"I see the proof."

Living in a fishing village as she had, she'd seen many men without their shirts. Since becoming a pirate and taking lovers, she'd also seen her share of naked men. Even so, she could appreciate that life at sea had left Ben lean and athletic.

A flush spread across his cheeks. "As bad as watching someone be eviscerated?"

"Slightly less bad." She tipped her chin toward his chest. "No sign of the markings."

"And there won't be, unless we're washing with seawater."

"We can't use our fresh stores."

Ben poured water into the basin, before dampening the cloth. He ran it down the length of his arms, across his chest, and along his stomach. Light from the lamp gleamed on his now wet flesh.

He'd been bold enough to chase after her in St. Gertrude, and hale enough to climb halfway up the waterfall of the Weeping Princess. Yet his body told a story of a man who pushed himself. A thin creased line across his left bicep and a round puckered mark on the back of his right shoulder revealed there was more to the tale of Benjamin Priestley.

The more she learned of his story, the more she wanted to discover. And, as she watched, markings appeared on his skin, lines in unknown configurations tracing over his flesh.

His gaze shot to her.

Ah, damn. She couldn't hide her feelings from him.

"The markings . . ." She cleared her throat. "On your skin. They appear to be some variety of pattern. Writing, almost."

THE SEA WITCH

197

"If they are, I've never learned what they meant." His voice had gone deeper. He worked the soap into a lather and spread it across his torso before rinsing. "Perhaps you recognize them."

"I don't."

That wasn't true. She'd seen such figures before . . . yet she couldn't remember where.

He paused again, hands hovering over the fastenings of his breeches. When he glanced warily at her, she sighed loudly.

She spun her hand in the air, calling forth the webs woven by the garden spiders that gathered in the vegetable patch behind her old cottage. Filaments made of tawny light zigzagged across her quarters, spanning the distance between her and Ben, caging him in a narrow space.

Plucking one strand, a loud chime sounded. "You move toward me," she said to him, "or reach for something to arm yourself, I'll know."

Then she turned and faced the wall.

The sounds of his boots being removed filled the room, followed by the unmistakable noises that came from removing his breeches. A cloth was dipped in water, and then silence.

She quickly glanced over her shoulder. He faced away from her, treating her to the sight of his naked arse, taut and flexing. The markings covered his entire body and highlighted his long, hale form.

Alys made herself look away.

"What happened at the waterfall," she said. "When we were thrown from the cave, that energy came from you. And then the markings appeared."

She heard splashing. He was likely rinsing himself. The goddess of the moon help her.

"Never before has that happened."

"A link is likely, between the appearance of the markings, even without salt water, and that magic—"

"Not magic," he said at once. "It's impossible."

"I can see the feathers on a gull perched on the topmast, and I *know* what I saw at the waterfall."

"That can easily be explained."

"Explain it to me."

He threw the cloth into the basin, and water sloshed. "Six and twenty years I've lived, on land and on sea. Not once in all that time have I shown any supernatural ability. And for good reason. I do not, and never will, wield any magic."

"You—"

"This topic is no longer open for discussion."

It sounded as though he dressed himself quickly.

She turned around to find him in his shirt and breeches—a disappointment. With a wave of her hand, the web disappeared.

He stalked to his hammock. "Talk all you desire, but there will be no response from me."

Glowering, he climbed into his hammock, folded his hands across his stomach, and squeezed his eyes shut.

"By all the constellations," she said on an exhale, "men can be the veriest children."

He remained obstinately mute.

After using magic to douse one of the lamps, she went to her berth, then pulled off her breeches. She caught him staring at her before he slammed his eyes shut once more.

Shaking her head, she climbed into her bed and slipped beneath the covers. Sleeping was the last thing she wanted to do at that moment, but even with balancing, she needed rest.

A moment later, she rose from her berth and grabbed the manacles.

He didn't speak, only held his wrists out again. She fastened the bonds around him before returning to her bed.

His breathing didn't slow, and neither did hers. They both lay awake, late into the night.

THE SEA WITCH

BARE TREE LIMBS shook overhead, rattling like bones from the chill January wind. The sky stretched in an uninterrupted span of iron. Columns of smoke rose from the chimneys of low stone cottages in a desperate attempt to beat back the marrow-deep cold. Distantly came the sounds of the ocean pounding against the shore, angry and relentless. Above that rose men's voices, even more angry and relentless.

Terror plunged through her.

She was in Norham. Today, they would drag Ellen from the prison and hang her from a branch of the oak that stood outside.

I can still stop it.

She hiked up her skirts and ran. Her breath was frozen and harsh in her lungs as she sped as fast as she could toward the heavy stone structure where they held Ellen.

The town whipped by her in a blur of gray and brick. She splashed through icy puddles, uncaring whether her buckled shoes were soaked and ruined. If she pushed herself hard enough, ran fast enough, she could beat the mob and reach Ellen first.

Yet as she neared the prison, hands erupted from the ground. Men's hands, clutching and demanding. They gripped her skirts and her cloak, holding her back. They were legion, bursting from the ground like grasping vines. She fought against them, yet no matter how she struggled, kicking them away, prying them off of her, there were always more and more. She would never reach Ellen in time.

Her magic could get her there. She summoned the sleek elusiveness of a cat. Twisting, muscular and fluid, she writhed and spun herself away from their clutches. Finally, she was free.

The ground churned beneath her as she sprinted, and then, with a final burst of speed, she reached the prison yard.

The mob gathered in a crowd around the base of the oak tree. And Ellen . . . Ellen was already gone. Her body swayed in the cold wind.

Alys screamed, sinking to her knees in the mud. She was too late.

Someone gripped her shoulder, pulling her to her feet, leading her away.

"Again," Ben said, his voice in her ear. "You failed her again."

Alys shot up, blankets twisting around her as sweat clung to her skin. Her breath was jagged in the quiet of the cabin. Her gaze ricocheted around her quarters, seeking comfort in familiar things. Her desk. The bottle of rum atop a table. A roll of charts propped in the corner.

Ben's eyes gleamed in the moonlight as he watched her. He was here, too, just as he'd been in Norham in her dream.

"Who—" he began.

"Go back to sleep."

"But, I saw her before—"

"Quiet, or I'll cut your tongue from your head and have it stewed." She grabbed her dagger and held it up so that its blade shone in the moonlight.

He pressed his lips together and lay back. Yet he didn't close his eyes.

Neither did she. She lay in her berth until the first pink rays of dawn crept through the widows. She attempted to distract herself, recalling past raids, and ports of call. Yet for all the exhaustive details she tried to bring to mind—counting the number of jewels taken from a French merchantman, the haunting music played on a bamboo flute in a tavern in Maracaibo—nothing turned her heart from the unavoidable truth.

She and Ben . . . they were woven together in a mystifying tapestry. Any hope that they might somehow become untangled from each other faded with each passing day, and night.

CHAPTER SIXTEEN

BEN WOKE THAT morning to find Alys already up and dressed. Her gaze was shielded as she watched him rise.

He knew better than to press about what he'd seen in her dream last night. It didn't stop him from wondering.

"Any chance of getting a razor to rid myself of this?" He rubbed his chin, though the rattling his manacles gave him his answer before she shook her head.

"You won't pass muster on a naval ship with that beard," she answered coolly, "but you'll make a fine addition to a pirate company."

"My happiness knows no bounds."

A tap sounded on the door. At Alys's permission, Cora stuck her head in. Cora tossed her head back to flick brown curls off her face as she pushed the door open with her broad hip.

"Breakfast for you and the sailin' master, Cap'n." Cora held up two bowls, and the scent of honey, milk, and oats drifted across the cabin.

Alys grabbed her bowl on her way out the door. "I'll take mine topside. Watch him while he eats, and then bring him to the upper deck when he's ready."

Ben's stomach clenched to hear him spoken of with such remove. Treated like a pet spaniel no one wanted, a responsibility to be fed and exercised, and naught beyond that.

"Aye, Cap'n." Cora set the second bowl on the table and stepped back before motioning for Ben to begin eating.

He took his seat and went through the mechanical motions of breaking his fast. Spoon to bowl, then to mouth, swallow porridge, and repeat the process.

It didn't matter how she behaved toward him. They weren't friends. He had his goal, and he'd hold fast to it. She couldn't feel betrayed if they meant nothing to each other.

But *who* was the woman in her dream? And the dream they had shared before? She had a face very similar to Alys's. And it surely had something to do with why she left Massachusetts.

It was a private agony, one he wouldn't normally be privy to, were it not for the way they had infiltrated each other's dreams. She needed to speak of it to someone, unburden herself, or else the sickness of sorrow would consume her from the inside out.

"Susannah's not a gossip but I managed to drag an account out of her," Cora said, leaning against the bulkhead. "Nearly got yourself killed on that island."

"We were *all* in danger."

"Don't come over all stiff naval officer," Cora chided affably. "Susannah said you made a fine showin' of it. Tryin' to protect the captain. Grabbin' yourself a club and lookin' like a right fighter. And you didn't show a lick of fear, not even when monsters were chasin' you down."

"Merely performing my duty." He couldn't stop himself from puffing his chest, then rolled his eyes at himself.

"Hurry up and eat, Sailing Master. Thérèse promised she'd show me how to summon that prickly spell of hers. I've got this—" she held up her hands and a cascade of red sparks fell from her fingertips "—but it never hurts to add somethin' to the arsenal. You know," she added with a pointed look, "in case a prisoner gets out of hand."

Ben finished his porridge quickly. He washed up before Cora ushered him out of the captain's quarters. As he made his way

THE SEA WITCH   203

topside, Alys glimmered inside him, drawing him up through the ship, until he surfaced on the top deck.

She was on the quarterdeck, yet she didn't so much as glance in his direction.

Something heavy settled in his gut. Perhaps he'd eaten his breakfast too quickly.

Luna approached, bearing a backstaff and compass. "Shall we, Mr. Priestley?"

He exhaled. *This* he knew. Navigation. Charting and mapping. At least when it came to his official duties, he could find his way.

SHORTLY AFTER SEVEN bells, the wind gusting across the deck kept the worst of the day's heat at bay, and Ben turned into the breeze, letting the sweat on his brow dry.

A shout went up from the crow's nest.

The crew member quickly climbed down the mainmast and hurried to Alys, standing on the quarterdeck with her second-in-command and Polly, the first mate. Ben followed the lookout, curious to know what she'd seen.

"I spotted something flying toward us," the woman said. "It's no gull or some other seabird."

"A familiar?" Alys asked her second-in-command. Stasia only shrugged in bafflement.

"Off the starboard bow," the lookout added.

Following the lookout's pointing finger, Ben peered at the spot in the sky. Sure enough, the bird seemed to be on a direct course for the *Sea Witch*.

Alys pulled out a spyglass. "A bird of prey. Black-and-white feathers, hooked beak, a scissor tail."

She handed the spyglass to Polly. "A kite of some kind," the first mate said. "Exhausted, too, by the way it's flying."

A minute later, the kite circled the ship, crying out as if in distress. Many members of the crew gathered closely as it landed on the quarterdeck railing before collapsing to the planks.

Alys rushed forward, gathering the kite carefully in her hands. She spoke in soft coos as the bird made feeble, weak sounds. Ben had never seen such an extraordinary sight, both a wild raptor permitting anyone to touch it and Alys's tender care of the animal.

"Water, and a cloth," she called over her shoulder. "Meat, cut into small pieces. And a blanket. On the double."

After a few moments, someone appeared with everything Alys had demanded. Gently, Alys wrapped the kite in the blanket, and dribbled water into its beak. With even more care, she fed the animal pieces of meat, one at a time, seemingly uncaring about the kite's sharp beak plucking the food from her fingers.

"Easy now, girl," she crooned softly. "You made it. You're safe."

Patiently, solicitously, Alys tended to the bird. More crew members gathered around, murmuring comments and suggestions, until Stasia barked that they needed to see to their duties, or else she'd make them pick oakum. They scattered, leaving Alys, the quartermaster, Ben, Polly, and Luna.

The kite seemed to gradually recover its strength, reviving enough to shake off the blanket and perch on Alys's arm. It ruffled its feathers before settling down.

"What's your name, lovely?" Alys said.

To Ben's shock, the bird responded with a cry.

"Hello, Anwuli," Alys said, her voice still low and careful. "You've come a very long way to find us. I'm Captain Tanner."

The kite cried out several times, and the women all nodded, as if they understood it. Ben glanced at them in bafflement.

"Yes, yes, I see," Alys said pensively, her brow furrowed. "When?"

Anwuli made another noise.

Alys turned to Luna. "How long will it take us to get there?"

The navigator pursed her lips in thought. "A day, day and a half, if we push with a few spells."

"What do you think?" Alys asked the quartermaster.

THE SEA WITCH   205

"A different mission from what we typically do," came the reply.

"We'll put it to the crew," Alys said.

"They will seek to know what their captain wants."

"I think . . ." Alys rubbed her chin. "Who are we, if we refuse? No better than the men keeping them prisoner and treating them like commodities."

"What—" Ben began, but Alys held up her hand, cutting him off.

"Take a vote," she said to the quartermaster.

Stasia strode away. Alys continued to tend to the kite, stroking it and murmuring soothingly. A few moments later, the quartermaster returned.

"They all vote *aye*," she said.

"Set in a course and speak with Hua," Alys said to Luna.

"Aye, Cap'n." The navigator hurried away.

"We'll do our part," Alys said to the bird. "All you need to do now is rest." She turned to her second-in-command. "Tell the company to ready themselves for something new."

"Tell them *what*?" Ben demanded when Stasia climbed down the companionway and began speaking to the crew.

She glanced at him as if she'd forgotten he was there. "We're making an alteration to our course."

Alarm shot up his back. "The fail-safe—"

"Has to wait. This takes precedence."

"Explain to me what *this* is."

She stroked the chest feathers of the kite as she set it on the railing. The bird closed its eyes and nestled down. A moment later, it appeared to fall asleep.

"Anwuli is a witch's familiar," she explained. "The witch, Olachi, is being held captive by Richard Kinnear."

"The *Jupiter* patrols past his compound. Even from the ship I could see that the walls surrounding the fortress were exceptionally thick. At least four feet, if I were to hazard a guess. Keeping intruders out."

206 EVA LEIGH

"Keeping his *merchandise* in." Her lip curled in disgust.

"I . . . ah."

He wasn't innocent. Naivete couldn't last when this place was your home. Obviously, he knew how much of the Caribbean's economy worked. Human beings treated as commodities to be bought and sold and worked until they died. And it sickened him. Yet he was only one man. He'd walk quickly past the auctions with his gaze firmly on his boots.

Say Strickland *had* negotiated with Kinnear to patrol, would the admiral even listen to Ben's protestations?

There's nothing I can do to stop it. So Ben used to tell himself.

"Kinnear and his men plan to sell Olachi and almost fifty other women they've kidnapped off of ships around the Caribbean."

Ben gazed at the hot blue arch of sky. But it held no answers. Nothing to give countenance to the fact that the Royal Navy assisted in cruelty. And he . . . he was tacitly part of that.

"Olachi's going to liberate herself," Alys continued. "The other captives, too. She needs a big enough vessel to ferry everyone away. Anwuli was sent to find me and the *Sea Witch*. For a week, that poor bird's been flying, looking for us."

She nodded in approval as Hua turned the wheel to a new direction. The crew were also adjusting the sails for their new course, following Polly's shouted instructions.

"Little George's fail-safe." Ben's entire purpose on the *Sea Witch* was to find and destroy the fail-safe, but this new direction unbalanced his plans. "What of that?"

"Helping Olachi and her fellow captives comes first now."

"Your treatment of slave ships, the navy has reports. I've read them. But I've never heard about anything else, not the kind of mission you're talking about."

After a moment, she said, "For us, this is new. But, saying no . . . refusing to help . . . it makes us no better than the men who buy and sell people. Standing by when we can do *something* . . . we can't do that."

THE SEA WITCH

He studied her through the spyglass of this new information, seeing things he never had before. What else had he missed? What hadn't he understood? "This isn't . . . what I expected."

"That's between yourself and your own beliefs." She was already striding away, heading toward her second-in-command and calling for a council in her quarters. Her purpose and determination glinted like knives.

The kite opened one eye and regarded him warily.

He held up his hands. "In this, I'm merely an observer. A very mystified observer."

"Come on, navy man." Cora approached with a spiky glowing ball of magic dancing on her fingers. "Back to the captain's quarters. She doesn't want you topside."

Ben followed her down the companionway, his head whirling with everything he'd learned. Alys and her crew . . . today they had become more than pirates in his eyes. There was far more to them than he'd ever believed.

Yet he was still a prisoner. That, at least, hadn't changed.

THAT EVENING, AFTER he'd been fed, Ben was taken above for a turn around the deck and some air. Dorothea was the crew member assigned to watch him. Gray shot through her sandy hair, and she had an elaborately embroidered eye patch. As she escorted Ben, she kept up a slow melodious tune in German. Yet her hand rested on the butt of her pistol and she insisted Ben walk ahead of her.

"All right, Jüngling," she said with a jerk of her head. "Back into your cage."

They headed toward Alys's quarters, yet when he and Dorothea got to the door, the second-in-command opened it before he could. Stasia stood with her hand braced on the doorframe, her arm barring him entrance. Just beyond her, he could see Alys and several members of her crew standing around the table, a sheet of parchment spread before them. Someone had drawn a diagram of a walled coastal fortress. The kite perched on the back of a chair, occasionally crying out, with the women all listening attentively to it. The air was thick with tension, and the women all wore serious, focused expressions. No one glanced in his direction, not even Alys.

"Find somewhere else for him to be, Dorothea," the quartermaster said curtly.

"I'm a sailing master," he offered, then raised his voice so Alys could hear, "but I know something of strategy."

"We will keep that under advisement," Stasia said in a voice that indicated she would do nothing of the sort. "Take him to the brig until the morning."

"Can I not at least sleep on the top deck?" Ben hated the imploring note in his words, but the idea of being confined again made his body taut as a lute string.

"And waste a member of our crew to guard you?"

"Someone guards me, anyway," he protested.

"He can sleep on the top deck," came Alys's flat command. "Guarded."

Stasia's look of displeasure couldn't stifle Ben's happiness at the prospect of a few hours beneath the stars. The second-in-command shut the door in his face.

Dorothea took him back topside.

"You will sleep here." She kicked a coil of rope toward him. "And that is your pillow."

His only companionship that night came from Dorothea guarding him, the other women on watch, and the span of stars arching overhead. Through the night, he sensed Alys's resolve.

Busy footfalls awoke him before dawn. As he rubbed grit from his eyes, he watched one of the crew paint a symbol onto a cannonball. The symbol itself looked like a lightning bolt with a few additional lines surrounding it. The crew member gave no explanation when she caught Ben observing her. Instead, she marched away with the heavy shot in her hands.

THE SEA WITCH 209

His guard had been replaced, Inés for Dorothea. The Latin woman's expression was stoic as she pushed a bowl of porridge into his hands. As he ate, the company raced back and forth across the top deck. Judging by the winds, they were soon approaching land.

Alys appeared, deep in consultation with Stasia. She looked every inch the captain, her gaze clear and resolute as she issued orders that her crew quickly obeyed. If anyone ever doubted that a woman could command a ship with authority, they had only to see Alys Tanner directing her crew in the moments before battle.

The kite and the magpie took flight. Shielding her eyes against the sun, the quartermaster watched them go, until they disappeared.

Later, at dusk, two members of the company approached Stasia with drawn cutlasses. Ben recognized the narrow-framed woman as Jane, who moved now with none of the wariness she'd shown when he had spoken to her before. It was easy to recollect Thérèse's tattoos and extraordinary hair. Stasia closed her eyes and gripped Jane's blade between her palms. A green glow shimmered to life, enveloping the metal. There was a scent like the air after a lightning strike. The same process was repeated for Thérèse.

Jane presented the second-in-command with a handful of bullets. She laid her hand over them, eyes still closed, until the projectiles also emanated green light. After Jane and Thérèse took the bullets back, they charged their weapons with gunpowder. They each loaded their pistols with glowing bullets and packed them down with ramrods.

Jane left, and then Alys wrapped her arms around Stasia, with Thérèse embracing both of them. They all leaned against one another, eyes closed. The same radiance from the other night surrounded the three women. It grew brighter and brighter, forcing Ben to train his gaze elsewhere. By the time the glow diminished and Ben could look again, Alys, Stasia, and Thérèse had stepped back and were again brusque and efficient.

210   EVA LEIGH

Just after nightfall, the magpie returned. It perched on the quartermaster's shoulder and twittered excitedly into her ear.

"All has been made ready," the second-in-command said to Alys. "When the moon reaches its zenith, they will begin."

Alys looked up at the sky, as did Ben and Stasia. The moon hung low over the horizon. It would reach its high point in an hour. Whatever it was that Alys and her crew had planned, timing would be critical.

Ben pressed a hand against his stomach, yet it leapt and quivered as the moon rose in the night sky.

A strip of land appeared on the horizon. They drew closer and closer, until Ben could make out a beach and the walled fortress beyond it. The citadel was low and brutal, thickly walled, an ugly hulk squatting two hundred feet from the water's edge. A few high cliffs jutted out and partially covered the walls, scuttling any attempts to fire on the fortress from the water.

Nausea rose in Ben's throat. There had been a time, not long ago, that he hadn't allowed himself to consider the implications of Kinnear's trade. Yet looking at the enslaver's compound, evasion was impossible. Cruelty was baked into the heavy walls, designed to keep human beings penned in like cattle.

And the navy had *negotiated* with him, to protect his *business*.

"Time to help our sisters," Alys said when Stasia, Jane, and Thérèse approached.

As Alys climbed down into a waiting cutter, she sent Ben one searing look. And then she was gone, off on her mission.

CHAPTER SEVENTEEN

Nearing its zenith, the moon gleamed in the night sky. It wouldn't be much longer now.

Alys was on one oar, Stasia, Jane, and Thérèse on the others. With Eris on her shoulder, Stasia whispered under her breath, calling forth waves to push the mostly empty cutter quickly toward the shore. Thérèse added her own spell, spoken lowly, to muffle the sounds of their oars and dull the sound of the cutter's prow through the water. Even so, Alys's breath came quiet and shallow.

Silently, they made their way to the beach. Tiny lights ahead drew Alys's attention. Torches lined the heavy walls surrounding Kinnear's compound. Against the flickering flames, she counted silhouettes of five guards on top of the walls. They stood ready, yet no one seemed in a state of alarm. Not yet.

A forty-foot-wide strip of beach met them as they landed. Alys readied to jump from the cutter. Magic still clung to the cutter, muting their splashes as they eased out of the boat. Soundlessly, they dragged the cutter onto the sand.

Alys nudged Stasia, then pointed to a dock jutting out into the way. An unmanned cutter was tied to the pier, rising and falling as it sat upon the water.

From their own boat, Alys grabbed a small ceramic pot and boar-bristle paintbrush. She tucked the brush into her belt,

212   EVA LEIGH

double-checked that her pistol was primed and ready and then pulled tatters of shadows to cloak her and her crew so that even as the moon glowed, darkness engulfed them.

Sand muffled their steps as they crept up the beach. Kinnear's fortress emerged from the gloom, its bulky black shape growing more menacing the closer they got to it. The walls loomed, easily twenty feet high. A massive oaken door kept the compound secure. A guard tower stood atop the wall. Flickering torchlight revealed two sentries beside the tower, leaning on their long guns, and their voices drifted down to where Alys and her crew slunk closer.

". . . ready to find me some company . . ."

". . . in Bridgetown . . . heard they've . . . can't walk straight for a week . . ."

Alys and Stasia pressed against the wall beside the door, and Jane and Thérèse took the other side. The heavy stone was cold and jutting against Alys's back.

The moon slid higher in the sky. Only a matter of minutes before it reached its peak.

With shadows still clinging to her, Alys hurried to the giant door. She opened the small ceramic pot and the sharp scent of oil and ground tamarind rose up. After dipping the brush into the pot, she began painting a lightning bolt and angled stripes on the door's thick wooden planks.

She couldn't render the symbol and keep the shadows around her and the crew. The darkness around them sifted away.

At the same time, the moon reached its highest point.

The ground beneath her feet shuddered. An explosion ripped through the night. Shouts rose up on the other side of the door, and gunfire popped.

It had begun.

Alys hurried to finish painting while sentries on the wall above fired into the compound. Someone cried out.

As Alys worked, Stasia, Jane, and Thérèse moved away from

THE SEA WITCH 213

the wall. They aimed pistols at three guards gathered atop the barricade, then fired. The men pitched forward as magic-charged bullets pierced them.

Three more guards ran along the parapet and fired down at Alys and her crew. Stasia threw up a shield, and the bullets ricocheted off the spell, slamming into the wall and sending down chips of stone.

At last, the symbol was finished.

"Take your positions," she called to her crew.

She and the others sprinted away from the door. They hurled themselves down into the sand. Alys raised up and threw a magical flare of light into the sky.

From far off came the sound of the *Sea Witch*'s cannon booming. A streak of green arced through the sky. The cannon ball went wide, a blaze of light trailing after it.

Harsh laughter sounded from atop the wall.

"Can't even fire your guns proper," one of the guards jeered.

A rushing sound filled the air. The cannon ball, painted with its own lightning bolt, veered in its path and flew over Alys and her crew's heads. It now charged directly toward the symbol painted on the door.

The ground shook again and another explosion shook the night as the magically-charged cannon ball slammed into the door, flinging rocks and splintered wood high in the air and across the sand. Alys and her crew threw their arms over themselves, burrowing into the sand

When the debris stopped falling, Alys lifted her head.

A massive hole now stood where the door used to be. Part of the wall was gone, too, the guard tower collapsed, and two sentries' motionless bodies splayed in the sand.

Nearly a score of women poured out of the compound. Some wore panicked, fearful expressions. Others looked fiercely determined.

214 EVA LEIGH

Alys and her crew leapt to their feet. Thérèse and Jane ran toward the fleeing women, ushering them down the beach and toward the waiting cutters.

As her crew tended to the escapees, Alys and Stasia plunged through the smoldering remains of the door, into the compound.

People were everywhere, running in confusion. Flames engulfed numerous buildings that squatted inside the fortress walls. The sky was lit with a reddish glow from livid fires. Smoke poured dark and thick into the sky. Coughing, Alys pulled the kerchief from her hair and wrapped it around her nose and mouth.

A bulky man charged at her, his blunt sword raised. She whirled and fired her pistol. The man fell to the dirt.

Women in ragged clothing dropped torches as they fled toward the huge hole in the wall.

"Boats wait for you at the beach," Alys shouted at the women.

The escapees moved in a group out of the stronghold and down the sand.

Frightened neighing echoed around the compound when over a dozen horses ran from the burning stables. Alys and Stasia dodged the panicked animals, and slapped their haunches to urge them toward the beach. The horses galloped through the hole and disappeared into the night.

Huge flames danced atop the disintegrating roof of a large two-story building, built in a more elaborate style than the rest of the structures in the compound. A smaller squat building also blazed. A section of its wooden wall collapsed, revealing rows of cots crammed side by side.

An African woman stood outlined against the flames. Richly woven, brightly patterned cloth hung in tatters around her. Her posture tall and regal, she threw a torch into the open doorway of another dormitory. She wore her mass of loosening braids like a crown as she watched the destruction. Above her, Anwuli dove and swooped, as if guarding her mistress.

Alys and Stasia ran to her.

THE SEA WITCH   215

"Olachi?" Alys asked.

"I am she. And you must be Captain Tanner." Olachi spoke with the accent of the Igbo people.

"I am. And my quartermaster, Stasia Angelidis."

Stasia and Olachi exchanged quick nods.

Alys handed Olachi the long dagger that had been tucked in her belt, and a primed pistol. "I bring you a present. Two presents, actually, if you count the *Sea Witch*."

"I will count her amongst my gifts," Olachi answered. "I sprang the locks with magic, but we could not flee without a ship to carry us away. You see what I did with our captor."

Richard Kinnear lay in the dirt, staring without sight at the sky.

"We have a boat," Stasia explained, "and there is an empty one tied to a pier just up the beach. Everyone is out?"

"My friends are accounted for," Olachi said, looking around the compound.

"What about him?" Alys nodded toward a cage that stood within the yard. A man was locked within it, his clothing filthy and ragged, his hair a dark lank curtain around his face. He gripped the bars and watched the fighting intently. "He with you?"

"That man was here when we were brought in. I heard one of the guards call him . . ." Olachi searched her memory " . . . Pasquale."

In disbelief, Stasia demanded, "Luca Pasquale?"

Alys shared a look with her second-in-command. In a sea teeming with infamous figures, Luca Pasquale was notorious.

"I have never seen this mage with my own eyes," Stasia admitted.

Alys turned to Olachi. "Have you done what you need to?"

Olachi gazed around the burning compound. "I have."

"Go, now," Alys urged. "Get to safety."

When Olachi raced through the hole in the wall, Alys hurried to the cage holding Pasquale, with Stasia close at her heels.

216   EVA LEIGH

The mage stood in the cage. He stared at them from behind his grimy curtain of hair. Gaunt and filthy, it looked as though he hadn't been properly cared for in a very long time. Yet he smiled, as if meeting them in a raucous tavern, surrounded by wenches and fragrant wine, instead of dead mercenaries and the smell of gunpowder.

"Hell of a party, Captain Tanner," he said, his Italian-accented words polished.

"You know of me," she replied, surprised.

"Rare birds, pirate witches," he answered.

"You are wanted by no fewer than five governments," Stasia exclaimed. "Seven pirate captains have sworn to cut off your head, if they ever cross your path."

"I'm a lucky bastardo." He eyed the bars surrounding him. "Safe and secure in these luxurious accommodations." With a wink, he said something to Stasia in Greek, and she turned pink.

She snapped at him in the same language, but his response was to give her a lopsided smile. Stasia reddened even more.

Even Alys's heart gave a small leap in response to his dangerous smile.

"The hell *are* you doing here?" Alys demanded.

He rolled his eyes. "I've got a price but this time I couldn't be bought."

"Athena only knows why you refused," Stasia said.

"I don't use my power to secure human cargo."

"An unfortunate attack of ethics?" Stasia barked out a laugh.

"Every now and again." He shrugged. "My coat was white when they locked me in."

Alys grimaced at the dull gray hue of his coat. Unlike other mages, however, he wore no black sash.

"We have to *go*," Stasia urged her when the roof of a nearby building collapsed in a shower of flaming beams.

"If we leave him here," Alys noted, "he'll die."

THE SEA WITCH

"Most probably," Pasquale agreed jauntily. He held up a wrist encircled by a dull metal band. "I can't take this off, and it makes magic as useless as a drunken man's cock."

Stasia made a face. "Your charm is just as flaccid."

"With the right motivation, I'll rise to the occasion." He smirked.

"No supper for you, children," Alys snapped at both of them.

The mage turned back to Alys. "What's it to be, Captain? Let me roast, or set me free?"

Alys placed her hand on the bars.

"Is this wise?" Stasia asked.

He pressed a hand to his chest and looked wounded. "Oh, no, pirates think I'm untrustworthy. I'll soak my pillow with my tears."

"Can you open it?" Stasia demanded, ignoring Pasquale entirely.

Alys kept her hands on the bars. Summoning the deft maneuverings of a bee, she channeled that energy into the lock. She worked and manipulated the tumblers, navigating the metal until, at last, the lock sprang open.

She pulled open the cage door. Pasquale immediately stepped out.

"Here," Stasia said testily. She placed her hand on the bracelet and it glowed an angry red. Pasquale hissed, but made no complaint.

The bracelet fell to the ground, split in two.

Pasquale drew in a breath. One moment, he was a man, the next, he was a sleek and handsome falcon. He flapped his wings once, twice, before taking to the air with a shriek. Then he flew into the night without even a backward glance.

Alys and Stasia sped through the hole in the fortress wall, and then down to the beach. Women were scrambling into the waiting boats, assisted by Jane and Thérèse. Olachi had commandeered the boat moored at the dock, and helped the freed captives to climb in.

"Have we got everyone?" Alys shouted to her.

"They are all here," Olachi called back.

With the cutters full, and each captive safely aboard, the boats put out to sea. As depleted as the witches' magic was, they summoned a last burst of power to help them reach the *Sea Witch* faster.

Cheers rose up from the cutters, fifty women celebrating their freedom. Alys looked back at the burning fortress, the flames writhing high against the night sky.

Many hands helped them onto the ship. The crew was already waiting with water and bandages and food. There was barely any room on the top deck as the freed women took up all available space. Space was made so wounded escapees could lie down upon the deck as the crew draped them with blankets. Fatima, the ship's doctor, moved steadily through the injured, caring for them with calm skill.

One hand pulled Alys up, helping her onto the top deck. Alys looked up into Ben's set and stern face. His gaze flicked over her, a pleat of concern between his brows.

Turning away from him, she cupped her hands around her mouth. "Raise anchor and make for open water!"

As the crew scrambled to carry out her orders, Alys strode to Olachi, who bent over two women sitting on the deck. One of the women had her eyes closed and her head resting in the other's lap. Olachi pressed a cloth to the escaped prisoner's side, stanching the flow of blood, though the woman's dark brown skin looked wan. There were bits of ash in her natural curling hair. It appeared that a bullet had grazed her ribs. Yet she bore her wound without complaint.

She opened her eyes and spoke to Alys in a lyrical language.

"Effia wants to know if this ship is better than the last two she sailed on," Olachi translated.

THE SEA WITCH

219

"This ship will take you to wherever you want to go," Alys answered. "And our doctor's going to heal you."

After Olachi provided a translation, Effia gave a small smile before closing her eyes again.

"Did everyone make it?" Alys asked Olachi.

"We lost no one. But a dozen are wounded. The spells I know are for diplomacy and the settling of disputes. I know little of healing magic."

"Fatima," Alys called.

Composed as always, the ship's doctor appeared beside her, carrying a painted wooden box that gently rattled with tools and bottles. Fatima's hair was covered by a black scarf and her amber eyes flashed with incisive knowledge. She had rolled back the sleeves of her loose black shirt, revealing sepia forearms that were well-toned from her careful, precise work.

"Captain," Fatima said with a nod.

"Your report, Doctor."

"Twelve of our guests have serious lacerations. There are a few minor scratches on some others."

"And the landing party?"

"Thérèse and Jane are unharmed. But I have to see to the gravely hurt."

Effia seemed to understand the conversation, because she spoke to Olachi.

"She says she can wait for the doctor," Olachi translated. "She says there are others who are in greater need."

Fatima hesitated, but at Effia's nod, the doctor strode away.

With a fresh cloth, Olachi continued to staunch Effia's injury. Fortunately, this cloth was less red-stained. A moment later, Susannah knelt beside Effia.

"May I?" Susannah asked, gesturing to show she wanted to place her hand on Effia. "I'm not the doctor, but I have trained as a healer, and can help as we wait for Fatima."

Olachi translated, and Effia gave a small nod. Susannah

pressed her palm over the laceration. Susannah closed her eyes. Golden light enveloped her hand, and the light flowed into the other woman. When she lifted her palm, the seeping wound was sealed into a dark crease across Effia's skin.

"Imeela," Olachi said to Susannah as she inclined her head. Drawn but looking satisfied, Susannah took Olachi's hand between her own.

Alys turned and stared when Ben offered her a tankard. She eyed its contents.

"Ale," he explained. When she hesitated, he took a sip before handing it to her. "I left the poison out this time."

She drank deeply, watching him over the rim of the mug. Of all the things she expected from him, concern about her ranked at the very bottom. Especially after Kinnear's fortress—which Ben and the navy had once protected—was now in flames. Yet the sailing master seemed determined to defy her expectations.

With sails billowing, the *Sea Witch* sped away from the smoking remains of Kinnear's citadel. A thick smear of black billowed darker against the inky night. The wind carried the smoke away from the ship.

CHAPTER EIGHTEEN

"LOOK LIVELY!" DOROTHEA snapped.

Ben stepped to the side, out of her path, as she quickly carried blankets toward the freed women.

On the *Jupiter*, he understood the routine. He wasn't in the way, familiar with how the ship operated and what was expected of him.

Now, activity bustled around him, and he'd no idea where to be or what he was required to do. The ship's surgeon moved from patient to patient, women either sitting or lying. Fatima was methodical, precise, yet she murmured calming words to her patient as she labored.

He'd witnessed the aftermath of battle before. Dr. Glynne would work his imprecise art, stemming the flow of blood as it spattered across the deck, hastily sewing up wounds or digging out bullets as men screamed and clutched at the cups of rum they were given to try to dull the pain. The deck always reeked of iron and gunpowder, with shit and sweat stinking beneath. Warne, the *Jupiter*'s mage, would assist, sprinkling caustic potions on those that were most severely injured, muttering incantations over others. Yet Warne always looked irritated by his labors, as if he had other more important matters to attend to besides injured marines and seamen.

On the *Sea Witch*, Fatima saw the injured first, cleaning lacerations and providing sutures or bandages. Then, half a dozen witches stepped in. They placed their hands upon the patients' wounds, and golden light flowed from the witch into the injury. As they did this, the wounded women's expressions eased. They sighed in relief and nodded thanks to their healers.

Cora rose from healing one of the captive women, and went to the railing near Ben. She stretched her sturdy arms and groaned in relief.

"The mage on our ship," Ben said. "He only treats officers' wounds. The rest is left to our surgeon."

"Ah, well, mage magic is important magic," Cora said with a shrug. "Only the finest of injuries for them. I suppose I'm not high up enough to warrant being picky about whose blood I'm staunchin'."

"There's a spell, then, for healing?"

"Don't know about specific spells. No one ever showed me how to mend anyone. We witches, we don't get much in the way of proper learnin'. I suppose you'd call it trial and error."

She went to a bucket and lifted the dipper to her lips. Water dribbled into her mouth, yet there was a tightness to her expression and her skin was pallid. Until Faith, the cook's mate, appeared with a sugared cake and handed it to Cora, who devoured it in two bites.

Some color filled Cora's cheeks and she exhaled. "Not a full balancing, but it'll do for now."

"Then how do you do it? Fashion a healing spell, I mean."

"If it's a cut, I think about how the oriole weaves its nest. Bringin' all these little bits together until it's all safe and secure. I do that with the cut flesh, weavin' it together. Might not always be pretty. It can leave a beauty of a scar."

"A scar is better than blood everywhere and disease seeping into the flesh," Thérèse threw in wearily. Golden light

THE SEA WITCH

drifted around her fingers, fading as she took one of the cakes offered by Faith. "Step aside, monsieur le navigateur. We are still working."

Ben hung back, keeping to the railing. He had no place here, yet no one took him down to the captain's quarters. In truth, almost no one paid him any attention at all.

Alys glanced in his direction every now and again, her expression opaque, just as it had been when he'd given her ale.

Well, it made sense that he'd see to her. As captain of this ship, his fate was in her hands, and she was the key to hunting down the fail-safe. Once he had that, he'd carry out his duty. Yes, that was exactly why his worried attention kept drifting back to her.

Like Dorothea, several members of the ship's crew circulated with blankets. They draped them over the newly freed women. Bony shoulders poked up from their ragged clothing, and cheekbones stood in stark relief on their faces. Josephine handed round mugs of steaming soup, which were consumed in eager gulps before being quickly replenished.

The liberated captives shot him cautious glances, their attention ricocheting between his threadbare naval coat and the manacles at his wrists. He offered them nods, which were not returned.

Some of the women looked weary. A trio of them gathered at the gunwale to stare at the waves and excitedly point toward the horizon. Red angry flesh encircled their ankles from where shackles had chafed, but those were now gone. Two of the escaped women laughed, while the other leaned against one of her comrades, a contemplative expression in her eyes.

They had been captives, goods to be sold.

That was what the navy worked with Kinnear to preserve. What Alys and her crew now fought against. What Ben had supported by not doing anything to stop it, as the *Sea Witch* had.

A quartet of the freed captives took their blankets and made pallets upon the deck. They rested their heads on each other's bellies as they looked up at the sky. One by one, they fell asleep.

The sky lightened with the coming of dawn. The stars winked out.

The woman who appeared to be their leader moved from cluster to cluster of freed women, speaking lowly to them. Ben heard one of her comrades call her Olachi. Alys approached, with Stasia and the first mate beside her, before the trio broke away to stand near the capstan.

Ben slowly drifted nearer. When no one stopped him, he moved closer.

"We have been held for nearly a month," Olachi was explaining. Circles of exhaustion surrounded her deep sable brown eyes, yet she seemed resolute to remain awake. Anwuli perched on her shoulder, nuzzling her with her beak. "Some were taken from their homes, others, like me, from ships bound for the Caribbean and the Americas."

"Anything you want," Alys said at once, "you and the others can have it. We've stockpiles of gold at the ready. We can take you to any port in the Caribbean, and from there, you can sail wherever you want."

"There are some of us who will gladly accept your offer," Olachi answered.

"What is it *you* desire?" Stasia asked.

"A ship for myself," Olachi replied immediately. "Not so long ago, I was stolen from my home. I had been council to the Omu, advising her as she governed women's concerns. I knew nothing of combat, or how to make my magic a weapon. Mediation and peacekeeping, that was what I knew. But that was taken from me. Everything was taken from me."

Ben's gut clenched. Yet he wouldn't back away, making himself listen.

THE SEA WITCH

"With my own ship," Olachi continued, "I will find other vessels laden with those bound for enslavement and free them. And destroy anyone who profits from the sale of human beings. If they think there is anywhere safe for them, they will find themselves quite mistaken."

"We can get you a ship," Alys answered firmly. "It'll take some doing, and it might not be possible right away, but we can do it. I have to ask . . . why did you send Anwuli to us? We're only pirates."

"You are more than that," Olachi said. "And it was a risk, but I thought, if anyone might listen to us, it would be a ship of women."

Alys tipped her head. "We're honored. *I'm* honored to have such faith put in me."

Olachi nodded, then struggled to suppress a yawn. Her kite also yawned.

"I have been planning our escape for weeks," she explained. "Have hardly slept for . . . I cannot remember when I last let myself dream."

"You've been shouldering a great weight for a long time," Alys noted.

"The other women who were captive with me," Olachi said, "they relied upon me. They rely upon me still."

"Who do *you* rely upon?" Polly asked.

Olachi gave a faint smile. "Myself, but I must admit, it is rather nice to have someone at my back, fighting with me."

"You don't have to fight on your own," Alys vowed. "Now it's time to rest."

At Alys's look, Polly held out a hand. "Come, I'll find you both somewhere to sleep. I can give you my berth."

"I will sleep here, with the others."

"We'll discuss more later in the day," Alys said.

Olachi placed her hand on Alys's shoulder, her gaze abundant with solemn significance, then let Polly lead her toward an empty part of the top deck, where more blankets were piled. Together, Polly and Olachi made a pallet and then Olachi lay down. Her kite settled on her chest as Polly slipped a rolled-up blanket beneath Olachi's head. She waited until it was clear that Olachi was asleep before drifting toward the quarterdeck to confer with the helmswoman.

Alys jerked her chin toward the companionway. "My quarters." She grabbed the chain between Ben's manacles and tugged. "You, too, Sailing Master."

He walked between Alys and Stasia, careful not to step too loudly upon the upper deck lest he wake the sleeping women.

Once they were back in her cabin, Alys slumped in a chair, seemingly weary beyond imagining.

"This was a good night," the quartermaster said, pouring herself and Alys a mug of ale.

Ben went to decant himself a mug. The second-in-command didn't stop him, her gaze impassive, so he filled his cup, and then drank.

"It doesn't seem like enough," Alys exhaled.

"It is not," Stasia agreed.

"But perhaps, it's a beginning," Alys said.

"Where will you find a ship for them?" Ben asked.

"Concern yourself with yourself." Alys said this without heat. Unlike Olachi, she couldn't smother a large yawn. After draining her mug, she got to her feet. "Stasia, find your own berth and rest. That's an order."

"Aye, Captain." Stasia slipped from the cabin, but not before giving Ben a meaningful glance. Then she was gone.

Alys pulled off her boots and threw them to the floor. Then she reached for the fastenings that ran up the front of her breeches.

Ben turned away. He strode to his hammock and clambered in. Last night, sleep was impossible. He ought to try it now.

THE SEA WITCH 227

"My magic's too exhausted for me to shutter the windows," she grumbled.

He rose and pulled the shutters closed. The sounds of the ship came as a low murmur, along with the lapping of the waves against the hull. Dawn settled around the ship.

LATER IN THE day, two bowls of hasty pudding were brought to the captain's quarters. They were redolent with the smoky scent of maple syrup, and sunset-hued slices of mango fanned over the tops. Ben eagerly took a seat at the table to break his fast.

He was careful not to look up from his bowl when Alys sat at the table, too. They silently ate together, spoons scraping against wood as they consumed their breakfasts. It was almost peaceful.

"Did you sleep well?" Inwardly, Ben grimaced at the inane question.

She shrugged. "Well as anyone can hope."

At the least, they hadn't been in each other's dreams. God knew what other secrets about him she might learn. But then, he could discover more about her.

Dreams or no, he could still delve deeper when it came to the enigma that was Captain Alys Tanner.

"It's a heavy burden you carry," he said. "Seeing to the welfare of the women you rescued."

"I didn't rescue them. We only gave them a ride after they freed themselves."

He took a drink of small beer. "The women you gave a ride to. Finding a ship for their leader." Cautiously, he added, "Locating the fail-safe."

She said nothing.

"If you're still looking for it," he amended.

"Never left my mind." She took a final bite of hasty pudding. "We'll reach Domingo later today."

He straightened. "Where the parish record is. It will tell us more about Sir Fenfield's family."

She raised her eyebrow. "*I'll* be tracking that down, yes."

"Not alone," he said at once. "You'll have me as escort."

Alys stood. From the floor, she picked up the shirt she had worn during the assault on the fortress. She pointed to the blood that had left dark rusty stains across the fabric. "This didn't belong to me. I've no need for anyone's protection."

"But you'll need a bridegroom." He collected their bowls and stacked them.

"The hell I will," she shot back. "Been married once before. That's a meal I don't need to swallow again."

"The best means of learning the identity of Sir Fenfield's nephew's cousin's daughter's son is to search the parish records at the church. Posing as an engaged couple will get us the information we need. We'd review the record to ensure no consanguinity prior to our marriage."

She eyed him. "Been giving this some thought."

"I give everything some thought."

She straddled a chair and studied him. He held himself still under her examination. The more he pressed, the more she would resist. When the matter at hand was something he wanted very much, the best strategy was cautious neutrality.

It wouldn't be possible to fully disguise the fact that he did, in truth, fear for her safety.

"Be pretty," she said at last. "That's your only role. Talking's my task."

"Understood," he answered, pleased with how indifferent he sounded.

"Now we go topside, Sailing Master."

On the upper deck, the freed women were sitting and talking, or standing at the gunwale to watch dolphins leap through the waves alongside the ship. They laughed at the sleek creatures'

THE SEA WITCH

antics. Many of them seemed much more spirited than last night, and some even no longer needed bandages on their wounds.

More wary looks were thrown his way as he followed Alys to the quarterdeck. There, the plan on Domingo was outlined to the second-in-command, who looked with suspicion at Ben. Yet she didn't object.

Instead, Stasia went below, and then returned a quarter of an hour later with two tiny cups of something as thick and potent as night. As she did this, Alys strode away.

To his astonishment, the quartermaster handed him one of the cups. He took a sip. It was as though someone had taken five cups of coffee and boiled it for an hour, to reduce it to a thick liquid that could fell a titan.

She stared at him pointedly.

"It's a wonder anything else has the temerity to call itself coffee," he answered.

She gave a solemn nod. "I can tell your fortune in the grounds when you finish."

"My thanks. I'd rather meet my future as it comes. Any attempt to circumvent fate inevitably meets with disaster."

She didn't smile at Ben, but she didn't scowl at him, either. He'd take what victories he could. This test, at least, he'd passed.

As he struggled to swallow his next sip, Alys reappeared on the quarterdeck.

Ben choked on his coffee. "Gown."

What a prime specimen of eloquence he'd become.

Alys stared down at herself with an expression that bordered on revulsion. It was a relatively simple dress of printed calico, with ruffles on the sleeves and down the stomacher pinned to the bodice. He'd seen far more revealing and ornate gowns on many other women. Seeing *this* woman in such a garment made him stare. Particularly, he was fascinated by the freckle-dusted skin rising above the low square neckline, and the curves of her collarbones, and the hollow of her throat, and the swell of her breasts, and the—

She cleared her throat, and he dragged his gaze back up to her face.

"Needs must," she answered, disgusted.

"You look . . ."

She raised a brow.

"Careful, Sailing Master," Stasia said under her breath. "The next few moments will determine the duration of your life."

"Like a captain on an extremely important mission," he finished.

Alys lifted her chin and sailed away.

He plucked at the grimy cuff of his coat. "Most bridegrooms don't look like a half-drowned dog."

"You look like a *fully* drowned dog," the quartermaster said. "I shall see what our stores can provide. Now, I have duties that require my attendance. Inés," she called down to the woman in question, "you are to watch him."

As Inés escorted him off the quarterdeck, he exhaled. At least he wasn't being shut back up in the captain's quarters. Perhaps some progress was being made in his efforts to get the crew to trust him.

Even if he would betray them all.

The freed women gathered in small groups. A few played a dicing game with members of the crew, using a collection of objects for betting, including coins of every origin and denomination, sparkling many-hued jewels, and strands of pearls. After the newly freed women won seven rounds in a row, it became clear that the crew purposefully lost so their guests might take all of the winnings.

One woman braided another's hair. Another read a book aloud to a quartet of women, who listened with rapt attention, though one had her head on her raised knee and her eyes closed, as if to imagine the scenes of adventure being described to her.

THE SEA WITCH   231

In the midst of this, Olachi sat calmly near the windlass. Her comrades approached her frequently. Judging by the way Olachi listened, her head slightly tilted, her expression thoughtful, the women were posing questions, which were carefully answered. As Olachi offered her counsel, the ship's cook approached at regular intervals. Josephine handed out cakes and fruit to the liberated women. Yet she shyly presented Olachi with steaming fresh biscuits, wedges of golden cheese, and quartered guavas artfully arranged on wooden platters.

Only yesterday, they had been in chains. In no small part because of the Royal Navy. Because of men like him.

Ben rubbed his forehead. God above, the world was a complicated place.

A group of the crew practiced fencing. Some of the liberated captives had joined in. They moved back and forth across the busy deck as they honed their swordsmanship. The familiars darted between their legs, mistaking the practice for play, until they were corralled by Dorothea, who entertained the animals with a display of butterflies made of light.

Thérèse appeared, holding a coat. "Put this on."

He held out his wrists, still encircled by manacles. When both Thérèse and Inés looked at him with wariness, he said levelly, "I'm accompanying the captain ashore and playacting the role of her bridegroom. It might look a trifle irregular if I am chained."

"Couples do all sorts of things to keep the bedroom interesting," Thérèse replied.

Well. "I can't change my coat with my hands bound like this."

After a moment, Thérèse gestured in the air as green light danced along her fingers. The manacles' lock sprang open.

Ben removed the manacles and rubbed his wrists. His arms were suddenly lighter than feathers, and he almost believed he could take flight—although, after his last experience with flying at the waterfall, that option wasn't particularly appealing.

Still, he exhaled to be free of the iron bands abrading his skin.

Inés took the manacles, but held them at the ready.

He shed his old coat, which Inés also took. What had once been his pride was now shabby and stained from being submerged in seawater. Half the buttons were missing, the golden trim unraveling into filaments.

Exhaling, he pulled on the new coat. It was rather tight across the shoulders and arms, and too short, but it was clean and had all its buttons and trim, and for that, he was grateful.

Striding by, Alys caught sight of him in his borrowed coat. "Been eating more beef? Someone had a growth spurt."

"It was either this, or resemble the underside of a ship that hadn't been careened in a decade."

"Barnacles are so becoming on a man."

"I've dueled men for lesser insults, and beaten them." In truth, he'd only practiced his fencing with voluntary sparring partners, though he *did* often win.

"You haven't fought *me* yet." She turned away in a rustle of skirts, her hair a satiny red curtain around her shoulders.

Shortly after two bells, the island appeared as a fringe of green on the horizon. The *Sea Witch* put in at an uninhabited stretch of sand a mile from the town's harbor, and Ben and Alys rowed themselves ashore. They beached the jolly boat before making their way through a forest, dense with gumbo-limbo and ironwood trees. The forest was welcome and cool after the scorching heat of the day, noisy with the raucous laughter of woodpeckers.

Soon Ben and Alys stepped into full sunlight again. They crossed open meadows and skirted around a yam field before emerging at the edge of Domingo's only town, imaginatively named Domingo Town.

It was a typical settlement, with clay and redbrick buildings with both thatched and tiled roofs, demonstrating the prosper-

THE SEA WITCH 233

ity of the island's inhabitants. People of many colors walked along well-packed dirt roads, and donkey-drawn carts trundled up and down these lanes, laden with local and imported goods. A few carriages brought over from the Continent also added to the traffic. There were shops and offices, and taverns that seemed to cater to a more subdued clientele than the pirate-infested saloons in St. Gertrude or New Providence.

"All Saints," he said, pointing to the church's elaborate spire rising at the center of Domingo Town.

She whistled. "Bit nicer than what I'm used to. Norham's church was made of plain clapboard, held together with guilt."

"I've never been to Massachusetts."

"I'm sure you'd be welcome there far more than I ever was. You've been to Domingo Town before?"

"Long enough to be impressed by All Saints' baroque style and stained glass. The wealthiest local citizens are its benefactors. But I'm less impressed by the shop selling charts and outdated maps that leave off half the known world."

Alys took a step into the town before Ben pulled her into a remarkably clean alleyway.

"I don't have the time or desire for a back-alley tryst," she said flatly.

Something poked him in the chest. A small dagger had appeared in her hand and dug between the second and third button of his waistcoat.

He pointed to a nearby wall, where sheets of paper had been pasted, bearing the likeness of several disreputable men. But he gestured to one in particular, with the word WANTED blazed across it. Beneath that was an illustration of a woman, the hair helpfully colored in with red ink. Beneath that, there was a banner proclaiming REWARD FOR INFORMATION LEADING TO THE CAPTURE OF CAPTAIN ALYS TANNER, £200.

"My hair isn't that shade," Alys insisted. "Still, two hundred pounds is a flattering amount."

"You fail to see the significance of that handbill."

She rolled her eyes. "We'll use disguises."

"I can obtain a veil from one of the clothing shops, and we should powder your hair. Also—"

"Ben," she said, and he quieted immediately. "There's another way to hide who we are."

"*We?* No one is offering two hundred pounds for me."

"It's likely that the navy's also put out word that you're missing. And you've been to Domingo Town before. They'll know you here."

He scratched his chin. Even though he was fully bearded now, there was always the chance someone might recognize him. "How are you going to disguise us?"

"Firstly," she said, crisp, "I'm going to need you to stop talking."

He shut his mouth. Once she seemed satisfied by his silence, she pressed her hand against his chest and closed her eyes.

Surely, she could feel how, beneath her palm, his heart pounded from her touch.

Yet she made no remark. Instead, her lips moved in a silent stream of words. A soft glow encircled her, shimmering along her skin. He forced himself to remain still as the glow expanded, enveloping him. It tingled along his flesh, as though hundreds of moths alit upon him with delicate legs and fluttering wings.

Her features shifted beneath the glow. Her nose became thinner, her cheekbones lowering, her mouth changing, full lips compressing into a little bow. Her bosom grew rounder and her hair shifted from glossy deep russet to flaxen curls.

More tingling glided over his face. He lifted his hand to touch his features, yet they felt the same to him.

The glow dissipated, the tingling stopped, and she stepped back with a long exhale.

"No more Captain Alys Tanner," she announced. "Go ahead and greet Miss Abigail Williams."

"A remarkable disguise," he said. "What of mine?"

THE SEA WITCH   235

She smirked and nodded toward a nearby puddle. "Tell me you recognize yourself."

He went to the puddle and exclaimed when he gazed into its reflective surface. A man with waves of tawny hair, wide-set brown eyes, and a pointy nose looked back at him.

"I feel the same." He touched his face once again.

"Glamours exist only on the surface. Beneath the illusion, we haven't changed. Here." She took his hand and brought it to her face, gliding his fingertips along her cheeks and lips. "Feels no different."

"No different," was all he could manage, his voice hoarse.

Her movements stilled, and she stared up at him with eyes that weren't hers, yet beneath the change of shape and color, there was the spark that belonged to her alone, charging the air between them.

A bray came from a donkey pulling a cart full of kegs. The noise pierced the bubble of intimacy surrounding them. She stepped back, and he did the same, nearly tripping over an empty crate in his haste to put distance between them.

"The church," he said gruffly.

"The parish records," she said at the same time.

He moved toward the street, then stopped to hold his arm out to her.

She stared at it with a puzzled frown. "My feet work just fine."

"Any man in love would offer his woman his arm when walking with her," he explained.

She continued to study his proffered arm, as if it contained a hidden danger. "I, uh, don't have experience with it."

Now it was his turn to stare at her. "You've been married."

"Samuel liked it better when I walked behind him."

A low curse escaped Ben.

"But you're an expert in wooing," she said quickly.

"There was a girl I courted. *Tried* to court, in Havana. Beatriz,

236   EVA LEIGH

a chandler's daughter. I had such plans, you know. Romantic notions of us on the water, and she'd be dazzled by my seamanship. In truth, Beatriz wasn't much impressed with a warrant officer, and refused to go out on a cutter I'd hired for the day."

"So, we're both new to it."

"Today, we'll both have the full sweetheart experience."

With an encouraging look as much for himself as her, he offered his arm once more.

Slowly, cautiously, she took it. Her fingers rested lightly on his sleeve, and his body tightened from even this slight pressure.

"The hell with this timidity," she muttered.

Her grip tightened around his arm, and they both sucked in a breath at the feel of her holding him firmly.

"Damn, Sailing Master," she exclaimed, squeezing his forearm. "Another surprise. You're hard as marble."

Did his disguised cheeks turn as red as they felt? "Time to get this mission underway."

"I'M GOING TO be struck by lightning," Alys said under her breath as they crossed the threshold of All Saints into the narthex. A sudden quiet descended as the heavy carved door shut behind them, the clatter of traffic and human voices fading. The vestibule smelled of cool stone and herb-scented linen.

"God is very busy," Ben answered. "He surely has other concerns besides smiting a few sinners in a corner of the Caribbean."

"Except one sinner's a witch, and I've been told with great authority that such a person isn't welcome."

"Opinions founded on ignorance. I didn't know much of witches, not so long ago. You might be the first witch I ever talked to." Certainly, she was the first witch he'd ever touched. Ever kissed.

"And now you'd set a place for me at your table?" She shot him a dry look.

Inside, the church was bright, lit by windows lining the nave.

THE SEA WITCH   237

Rows of oak pews faced the pulpit and altar, and the chancel was decorated by carved wooden arches. Light shone through a stained glass window depicting the Annunciation, more evidence of the wealth of the church's benefactors.

Ben moved to the font to dip his fingers in the holy water before crossing himself.

"This place isn't safe for me," Alys muttered, pulling away from him.

"Good afternoon, sir and miss." An elderly man in a clerical collar approached them. "I am Reverend Gardiner. How may I be of assistance?"

Alys went to Ben and wove her fingers with his.

"Miss Abigail Williams," she sang, "a pleasure to meet you. I wish to be married to my darling Thaddeus." She fluttered her lashes at Ben. "Been courting me forever, but Thaddeus finally asked my father. And he gave us his blessing," she added with a very atypical squeal.

Ben made himself look down as if abashed.

"Felicitations," Reverend Gardiner said, beaming. "We'll need to read the banns, of course."

"Of course," Ben agreed.

Breathlessly, Alys said, "Before we do that, we need to ensure that there's no chance . . . that is . . . our families are very *close* . . . and we'd hate to think that there could be any *problems* . . . being so *close* . . ."

"Yes, I see, my daughter," the reverend intoned. "We cannot have any besmirching from consanguinity."

Ben nodded eagerly. "You understand, Reverend."

"Can't be kissing cousins, can we?" Alys giggled.

It was all Ben could do to keep from gaping at her. Never had he heard her actually *giggle*.

"The parish register will have the answers you seek." Reverend Gardiner waved them toward the back of the church. "I keep it in the sacristy. This way."

238   EVA LEIGH

The reverend ambled up the aisle, leading them to a plain door beside the altar.

"Thaddeus?" Ben whispered when he was certain the old man couldn't hear him.

"It was either that or Zebediah," she whispered back.

Reverend Gardiner unlocked a door and then gestured for them to enter. It was a small chamber containing sacristy credens, with wide shallow drawers that held vestments. There was also a piscina for washing, and a taller heavier cabinet. The reverend used another key to unlock it. From a drawer, he pulled out a thick leather-bound book, tooled with gold adornments, which he set upon a table.

"The answers you seek are in there," he said, smiling.

"I'll look, Thad," Alys twittered.

She stepped to the register and flipped through the pages. She read for a long while, with Ben and the reverend occasionally exchanging polite smiles.

"Oh, here's my cousin Hecuba," she said, "and here's your great uncle Boaz."

Ben watched her expectantly. The answer to Little George's clue had to be in this book. What would they do if it wasn't? The Caribbean was vast, abundant with tiny islands, hidden coves, secret locations. All the things that made it so appealing to the lawless. But the fail-safe *had* to be out there, somewhere.

Alys continued to read, making her way through three years of records. And then she glanced up at Reverend Gardiner. "I'm not seeing any shared kin, but just to be sure, might I look at the older register?"

"This is all we have," the old man answered quickly. "There was a fire, you see, three years ago. A candle tipped over, and alas, the register was lost. We were all quite despondent."

"That *is* a shame," Ben said. "Is it enough, dearest Abby?"

"I'm certain it will be fine," Reverend Gardiner interjected. "I see no reason why you two should not be married."

THE SEA WITCH 239

Alys ran to Ben and threw her arms around his neck. "We can be wed, dearest, dearest Thaddy."

As his hands came around her waist, she lifted up on her toes. Their lips met.

Her mouth was soft and nimble against his. One brief peck turned into a longer deeper kiss. He pulled her closer, his palms warming as he held her. She pressed snug against him.

He hadn't expected she'd be so sweet. Or how right it felt to have her in his arms.

"Well," Reverend Gardiner boomed with strained joviality, "we know this will be a most *fruitful* union."

Ben and Alys broke apart. Her eyes were dazed, her disguised lips slightly swollen from their kiss, as surely his were.

"We'll come back to discuss the banns," Ben managed when she appeared unable to talk. "Thank you, Reverend."

He grabbed Alys's hand once again and tugged her out of the sacristy, down the aisle, and then out of the church. Together, they stood blinking in the bright sunlight as traffic moved around them.

For a moment, neither of them spoke. His breath came quickly. Hers, too. She brought her hand up, fingers lingering on her lips. Currents of lightning shot along his limbs.

Words attempted to form but broke apart before he could speak them.

Finally, she said thickly, "When I looked through the register, I used magic to search out the answers we needed. But they're not in that register. They're in the older one."

"The reverend said it was destroyed in a fire."

"The register exists," she said, "but it's kept hidden elsewhere in the church."

"We should come back."

"When there's no chance of anyone being there."

"The church should be empty tonight."

"Until then, we'll need to find somewhere to hide. Somewhere private." She let out a shaky breath.

"You're trembling." Her tremors reverberated through her hand, all the way up his arm.

Even with her disguise, she looked drawn and tired. "It's the glamour. I can't . . . I can't hold it much longer."

Her hair had already begun to shift from blond to red, and her lips were filling out, taking on the shape of her own mouth. God knew what he looked like.

"Come." He led her hurriedly down the street. "I know where to go."

He prayed he could get them to safety in time.

CHAPTER NINETEEN

I F ALYS APPEARED ill, she'd only attract unwanted attention from the people they passed, so she forced a placid smile on her face and hoped no one could see the clammy sweat beading on her forehead. Standing upright taxed her to the limits of her strength. Yet she made herself do it, holding Ben's arm.

"Don't know why . . ." She struggled to speak. "Done bigger spells than this . . . never got me this bad."

"Have you ever held the glamour for this long?" His voice sounded far away, even with him right beside her.

She shook her head, but that made the world tilt, so she kept her head still. "Not alone. Not shared with another person. It's far, where we're going?"

"Not far at all. We've arrived." He guided her up a step, past a painted wooden sign that read THE TWO CATS INN. They moved inside, and she had a vague impression of a neatly appointed taproom with a few patrons, as well as a sitting area where a man perched on the edge of a chair as he read a newspaper.

"What might I do for you?" a middle-aged woman in an apron said, coming forward. She had light sepia skin and a few tendrils of tight black curls escaped the kerchief wrapped around her head. "Our kitchen is closed but I could find some bread and cheese and ale, if you so desire, and you can dine in our taproom."

"My wife and I require a room for the night," Ben answered.

"Of course, sir. It'll be a shilling for one night's stay."

Ben patted his pockets. "I, uh . . ."

"Here. And here. For food." Alys fished out two shillings from her own pocket and handed it to the innkeeper. "Room."

The landlady blinked at Alys's terse words. She squinted at Alys's face, which was no doubt looking a bit wobbly as the glamour slipped away.

"Right away, please," Ben said firmly.

"This way." The innkeeper led them up a narrow steep staircase, which made Alys's normally strong legs burn. At the top of the stairs, they found a T-shaped hallway lined with closed doors. The landlady passed several of them before turning down a corridor and unlocking one.

Ben pushed the door open, revealing a snug chamber with a dormer window. It was full of plain but well-made furnishings, including a dresser, washstand, and bed. The walls had been painted a cheerful yellow, but through Alys's blurry vision, the color appeared more sickly than sunny. She gripped the doorframe to stay upright.

"Everything satisfactory, sir?" the innkeeper asked, standing in the hallway.

"We'll need that food brought up as soon as possible," he answered. Before he shut the door, he added, "My thanks."

The moment the door was closed, Alys sank to the floor. She blinked groggily as the room spun—but no, it was Ben, gathering her up in his arms and carrying her to the bed.

He laid her down upon the mattress, and quickly got to work removing her buckled shoes. His hands upon her feet, even through her stockings, shot tiny filaments of energy up her legs. But it wasn't enough.

"You need balancing," he said, studying her gravely.

THE SEA WITCH   243

"Know what . . . balancing is?" she mumbled.

"Not precisely. It helps you replenish your magic, and involves touch. Food, too."

"Quick study, Sailing Master."

He rolled her onto her back and braced his hands on either side of her head. The glamour was thinning now, and the humble-featured man she'd transformed him into was quickly disappearing. His own face emerged like a proud oak from a stand of scrub trees.

She reached up to run her fingers along his angled jaw. "You, but not you." She touched her own face. "Me, but not me."

There was a knock at the door. "Brought you bread, cheese, fruit, and ale, sir."

"Leave it in the hallway," he called.

"As you like." There was a sound of a tray being set down, and then retreating footsteps.

He leaned over her, concern written across his face. "I'll be right back."

"Watch me fly from the room the moment your back's turned," she slurred.

The bed creaked as he rose. She stared at the beams on the ceiling. Despite the cleanliness of the inn, someone had missed a cobweb, but Alys didn't mind a spider here and there. They were her sisters, after all, some of them devouring males when they no longer served them.

Ben reappeared, holding a tray laden with food. As soon as he returned, Alys released her final tenuous hold on the glamour, exhaling with relief when she no longer had to keep it up.

His face was fully restored to its original likeness, handsome as a hawk. He set the tray on the bedside table before using a few pillows to prop Alys up.

"Open." He held a piece of apple to her mouth.

"Can feed myself," she protested, but then her protests died when he popped the morsel of fruit between her lips.

244 EVA LEIGH

She closed her eyes and groaned at the sweet taste. Flavors were always amplified whenever she ate anything during balancing. She'd been known to polish off an entire plate of iced cakes as she revived her magic.

When he fed her a piece of sharp cheddar, she moaned.

"What?" she demanded as Ben stared at her, his gaze heating.

"It doesn't signify." He shook his head. "Here's more."

When he moved to place more food in her mouth, she turned away. "Can feed myself."

He handed her pieces of apple, cheese, and bread, which she steadily ate. They were quiet like this for a while, the sounds of traffic coming faintly through the window, and voices below in the taproom and footfalls upon the wooden floor.

"The woman in your dream," he said after some time. "The one who was . . ."

"Hanged." Could she trust him with this? "My sister. The gentlest person you'd ever meet. She'd bring animals home if they were sick or wounded. Always gathered wild herbs and collected mushrooms. She could speak with birds."

"And she taught you?"

"Before she could, she was executed by a mob three years ago for being a witch. Speaking with birds, that's something I made myself learn, and I taught others. After she was gone."

He pressed the mug into her hands, and she swallowed some ale. "I'm sorry."

"Either you hide the fact that you're a witch, or they kill you. We all know this."

"Time doesn't make any of it easier," he said gently.

"I go over it. Again, and again." She nudged his hand away when he tried to give her more apple. "I could've learned their plans sooner and urged her to flee. I could've escaped faster to reach her before the mob pulled her from the prison."

"Escaped?"

THE SEA WITCH   245

"Samuel locked me in the cellar that morning. Said he loved me too much to let me risk my life for someone guilty."

"Christ."

"I finally kicked the door open and ran but . . . I didn't make it in time. They were gathered around her body when I reached the prison. Well, you saw it. It's why I left Norham, otherwise it would have been my body swinging from a noose."

"Jesus. Alys." His voice was tight.

"I failed her. It won't happen again."

Ben was quiet for a moment. "I keep thinking . . . if I find his murderer . . ."

Her eyes were hot, and she blinked to clear them. "Then he'll forgive you."

"I'll forgive myself. Maybe it's a futile hope. Maybe . . . it's all I have. Alys." His hand rested on her shoulder. "Look at me."

"I don't want to forgive myself." She pressed her hand over her eyes. "Leave me be, Sailing Master."

"Ben." His voice was gentle. "There's no one here but us. You can call me by my name."

"Ben." She sat up a little. "A good name. Solid. Dependable."

"Alys," he murmured. "A good name. Sounds like music."

She made a face. "A dirge."

"A hymn," he insisted. "Something soaring."

She opened her eyes as a rueful laugh escaped her. "I'm not very good at flying."

"You fly high enough. You made *me* fly. Roughly, granted, but it happened."

"Susannah knows her way through the skies better than me."

"Susannah didn't help me to soar. *You* did."

"Kept us alive, at least." She shifted uncomfortably.

He was instantly alert. "In pain? I've asked too much of you with my questions."

"I'm used to your prying."

"Ah," he said with a nod, "you must be on the mend if you can make fun of me."

"Inch by inch, I'm getting better. Not enough to take up the glamour again."

"Is there something else we can try? To balance you?"

She hesitated. Then took his hand in hers and brought it to her cheek.

"Touch." she said. "The best way to balance."

He was briefly still. Then he stroked his palm along her skin. Energy faintly sparkled within her.

"We could do more," she murmured. Her gaze flicked to his mouth. "If you're willing."

After a moment, he leaned close. His breath was warm over her. The moment held, stretched out.

Slowly, slowly, he brushed his lips across hers. The lightest of touches, and yet it made her purr. He was warm and soft and firm.

"Tell me yes, Ben." Her words were husky as they rasped across his mouth. "Tell me this is what you want."

"I want this. I want *you*." He cupped her head with his hands, angling her so that their mouths met. They kissed deeply, taking long drugging tastes of each other. She held tightly to him as he pulled her closer.

"Touch me," she urged.

"Tell me where. Show me what you like."

She again took his hand in hers and stroked it down her throat. She glided his palm over her collarbone before moving lower and then—

She moaned when she brought his hand to cup her breast through her bodice. His hand was large, surrounding her completely.

"Ah, God." He gave a low rumble.

He dipped his hand beneath the neckline of her bodice to find her nipple. His fingers were callused and the rasp against

THE SEA WITCH

her flesh made her writhe. When he gave her nipple a slight pinch, she arched up with a cry.

"Too much?" he asked, pulling back.

"Keep going."

He seemed to grow more confident, caressing her with rough care.

"The feel of you." He growled against her neck, then licked the flesh there. "Your *taste*."

"Ben," she panted.

A glow began to emanate from her, golden and radiant. It enveloped them both as it grew in strength. As it expanded, so, too, did her power, coursing through her like liquid lightning.

Arousal and desire rose sharply. Her own pleasure climbed higher, stoked by the flame of his hunger.

"I need more," she said breathlessly. "Will you give it to me?"

"I'll give you whatever you want."

"Your hand on me."

"Between your legs?" His cheeks were flushed, his eyes fever bright.

"My cunt. Yes."

He kissed her again, his tongue stroking against hers. She moaned her encouragement when he began to gather up her skirts.

"Take off my stockings," she murmured.

He quickly undid her garter and slid her stocking off to cast it aside, all reserve gone.

"May I touch your legs?" he asked.

"Goddess, yes."

His hand skimmed up her calf, then higher, past her knee, along her thigh, drawing patterns of pleasure on her skin. She'd never thought her legs were particularly sensitive. They served a purpose, taking her from one end of her ship to the other, allowing her to climb into the rigging, kicking away enemies in the middle of a fight. Yet now they were responsive. She writhed like a cat as his caresses grew more confident.

"Don't need to linger," she gasped as she twisted against him.

"No rushing. I may be balancing you, but this is for me as well."

"Damn you." She moaned.

"If this is my path to damnation," he growled, stroking her thigh, "then I forsake the Kingdom of Heaven."

"I—" She lost the ability to speak as his fingers grazed over her sex.

His hand stilled. "Is this right?"

"It's very, very right. You can . . . go between my lips. Touch me deeper."

He did as she instructed, and they both groaned when he found her slick and soaking. "Fuck."

Yet for all his eager caresses, he didn't touch her exactly as she needed.

"Here," she said, guiding his hand toward her clitoris. "This is where I need you most. Circle it, rub it."

"Like this?"

She bowed up. "By the stars, yes. And at my entrance. Press against it."

He joined his mouth to hers, stroking her as commanded. His navigator's hand learned her geography, all the places that made her cry out, all the topography that made her arch and writhe. His confidence in pleasuring her seemed to grow from moment to moment, and the more he touched her, the brighter the glow emanating from her became, filling the room.

"More." She gasped. "Fill me."

He sank one finger into her passage. "Is this enough?"

"Another finger."

When he did as she instructed, widening and filling her, she bowed up at the feel of him. "There's a place deep inside me. Swollen. Stroke it."

He rubbed over the aching, enflamed place within her. She clutched at him and cried out.

"Yes, there," she gasped. "There."

THE SEA WITCH

Yet it still wasn't enough. She thrashed, desperate for something to bring her over.

"What do you need? How can I give you what you want?"

"This is good . . . this is . . ."

"It isn't." His voice had firmed with determination. "Tell me. Anything. I'll do anything."

"Your mouth on my cunt," she said on a tortured groan.

"Never done it before," he confessed, his eyes blazing, his features sharpening.

"Treat it like the most delicious meal. Something you'd want to eat every day for the rest of your life."

She lay back, and he swallowed hard as he looked down at her uncovered sex. The blue of his eyes disappeared as his pupils widened. A muscle jumped in his jaw.

With deliberate intent, he rose and then placed himself between her legs. He didn't seem to care that half his body hung off the bed. All that appeared to matter to him at that moment was her bared cunt.

He wrapped his arms around her thighs, widening them, then he fused his mouth to her. He lapped at her sex, consuming her, teasing her clitoris with his tongue as his fingers continued to pump in and out of her. She bowed upward, but he held her hips with his other hand, pinning her to the bed. Keeping her in place so that she had nowhere to go, no choice to make, accepting and basking in the pleasure he gave her.

She guided his head, placing him where she ached. "Lick. Suck. Yes. Like that."

He was a very good student.

Sounds poured out of her, moans, pleas, cries. He rumbled against her, half encouragement, half bliss. She sensed him everywhere. His hunger, his freedom from the restrictions that held him back.

Release came in a firestorm. Wave after wave harrowed her. Yet he didn't stop, carrying her over the edge again. Once more.

And again. With each climax, more power built within her, the light surrounding her almost blinding. But he kept going, as if greedy for her pleasure.

At last, she could take no more, and she panted, "Enough."

He stopped at once. When he looked up, his face was glossy with her arousal, and his eyes blazed.

She pulled him up and they kissed deeply. The taste of her own pleasure was on his lips.

"I want it all," she breathed, reaching for the fall of his breeches.

"You'll have it."

His hand tangled with hers as they struggled to undo the buttons.

"Ben," she said, glancing down.

He pressed more kisses to her throat. "Alys."

"Ben. Stop."

He went still.

"Look," she urged. "Your hands."

He held them up, and they both cursed.

His markings covered the back of his hands, and climbed up his throat. Sitting back, he dragged off his coat and waistcoat, then pulled open the neck of his shirt. More of the dark lines twisted and curved over his chest and shoulders, tracing patterns on his flesh. The contrast between the figures and his skin was even more stark in the glow of her balancing.

"We're over a mile from salt water." He tugged off his shirt to reveal the dark lines all over his torso and arms. "Why now?"

"I've seen them in the past." She pulled her skirts down to sit up as she finally remembered why they seemed familiar. "Months before I met you."

"What do you mean?"

"These lines and patterns. I've seen them once before." She traced her finger over one arrangement of figures on his deltoid. He flinched away from her.

"Where?" he demanded.

Her gaze held his. "In a mage's spell book."

CHAPTER TWENTY

BEN REARED BACK. "You didn't tell me."

"I hadn't remembered," Alys protested. "Not until now. The way you moved a moment ago—it jogged my memory. We took the book from a merchant ship months back."

Light from Alys's balancing had begun to fade, and deep shadows filled the room. Even in this darkness, he couldn't stand the sight of his markings any longer. He pulled on his shirt and paced to the window. Night loomed over Domingo Town, the buildings forming black shapes against a violet sky, and the first stars appearing like indifferent gods.

His body and mind were still in a riot from pleasuring Alys.

Never had he been so uninhibited with a lover, more himself in those moments than he had ever been, and hell if he didn't love that feeling. *She* showed him how to make that happen. Because he'd wanted nothing more than to give her pleasure.

His joy had evaporated the moment he saw his markings.

He braced his hands on the window frame. "I want to see this book."

"I don't have it anymore." Her voice came close behind him, but he kept staring out the window and its view of dusk descending over town. "Nobody aboard the *Sea Witch* knew the language it was written in, so I bartered it with a mage for texts

252 EVA LEIGH

we could read. That's why I couldn't quite recall—it wasn't in my possession long."

He wheeled around. "I—"

Bells rang out, shattering the night's calm. Loud, clamorous bells that signaled danger.

Ben immediately pulled on his waistcoat and coat, and Alys stuffed her feet into her shoes, not bothering with stockings. Panicked footsteps sounded in the hallway outside, mingling with people's confused, nervous voices.

Alys's balancing light had faded entirely, so Ben wrenched open the door to their room and stepped into the corridor. He grabbed the arm of a man attempting to hurry past.

"What's going on?" Ben demanded.

"A chickcharney has been spotted on the edge of town," the man yelped. "Been over a decade since such a beast bothered us, but it's here now. Hurry, sir. To the shelters."

Ben released the man's arm and he scurried away. More people pushed past, rushing to get to safety.

Alys shouldered her way out of the room and together they joined the throng pouring out of the inn. But instead of following the crowds heading to the shelters, Alys tugged Ben in the opposite direction. Toward the church.

"No one's around," she explained. "Now's our chance to find that register."

"And risk an attack by a chickcharney, whatever that is."

"Resembles an owl, long legs, red eyes, tail that can grip things, and stands about yea high." She held her hand three feet off the ground. "It can be kind to travelers, but something's riled it."

"If the creature's riled, the last thing we want is to cross its path."

She sprinted to a nearby clothesline and snatched a coral-colored petticoat from it. "Use this to beguile it, and whatever

THE SEA WITCH

you do, don't laugh at the chickcharney. Or it'll twist your head right off."

"With that image in my mind, it's not likely I'll do much laughing."

Alys grabbed his hand and together, they ran against the human tide. She was much nimbler, darting between gaps in the crowd, while he had to muscle his way through as he clutched the petticoat in one hand.

As they ran in the opposite direction, the throng began to thin. The bells stopped as well, signaling that everyone had taken shelter. No lights shone in storefronts, no torches or lamps burned on the street. Darkness and silence smothered the town.

Finally, Ben and Alys reached the steps of All Saints church. No one was around, only them and the shadows. And the looming threat of a creature that could remove Ben's head from his neck like pulling an apple from a tree branch.

Ben tugged on the church's door, but it held fast. Alys knelt down to place her hand on the doorknob.

"There's a spell for everything, it seems," he said dryly.

"Magic's got many uses. I can't speak for mages, but a witch will do what she must to keep herself safe. But," she added, "these'll do the job without taxing my power." She pulled two thin pins from her hair and held them up with a smile.

He shook his head as she set about picking the lock. As she worked, he kept his attention on the dark streets, alert should anyone—or any*thing*—pass by.

"A pistol or cutlass makes for better protection than a petticoat." He gripped the yards of fabric, crushing the cotton in his fist. "The creature that's out there—"

"The chickcharney," she said, focused on her task. "It's found on Andros in the Bahamas, but a few have been spotted here. We once rescued a witch from Domingo. She told us about

254   EVA LEIGH

it. Had us all shivering in our berths for a week. Now, silence yourself and let me concentrate."

He said nothing further as she continued to manipulate the pins within the door's lock.

"Easy, my sweet one. A little more, and then—" She grinned up at him when there was a clicking sound. "The Norham schoolmaster impressed upon us to be always humble. But, the hell with that."

She stood and shook out her skirts before opening the door and slipping inside. Ben followed, shutting the door behind him. They were plunged into the darkness of the narthex, and beyond that, the stillness and shadows of the nave. Though they had been there only a few hours earlier, the church was now vast and echoing, made more eerie with the knowledge that a creature lurked outside.

He stepped into the aisle between the empty pews. "Small as this church is, we'll still have a devil of a time searching for the parish register."

"*Here*'s where my magic comes into play." She cupped her hands and whispered into them with words he could not understand.

As she spoke, a small glow appeared between her fingers. She opened her palms and the glow hovered above them. Soft pinkish gold light illuminated her face and a small area surrounding them.

In this glow, she was a being of brightness and shadow, lovelier than any moonrise.

"I summoned the light of a firefly and combined it with a bee's sense of direction." To the ball of light, she added, "Go, my friend. Lead us to what we're looking for."

The glowing sphere darted away and they chased after it. It shot up the aisle, then into the chancel at the front of the church. They hurried in pursuit. It alighted upon the freestanding wooden altar, faintly humming.

THE SEA WITCH 255

"In here." She laid her hand atop the fair cloth draped over the altar.

It had been years since he'd last attended a mass. Even so, he asked forgiveness from whatever deity might be observing as he removed the altar covering. He carefully folded it and set it on the front pew before returning to the altar.

"There's a kind of puzzle mechanism carved into the wood." He placed the petticoat on a pew, then glided his hands over the altar panels. Several of the pieces seemed to be grooved, fitting into each other. He slid them back and forth, rearranging them. At first, nothing happened when he did this.

But then he slid the pieces into a different configuration, forming the shape of the church's layout. And then, there was a satisfying *snick*. One side of the altar popped open. Gently, he removed the wooden slat and also placed it on the pew.

Alys reached into the open space within the altar. She pulled a leather tome out, nearly identical in appearance to the register they had seen earlier. At once, she sat cross-legged on the floor and opened it, placing her hand on its pages.

"There's no reason for Reverend Gardiner to lie about this register's existence." Ben crouched down beside her.

"I can't read this language, but these entries look suspect." She flipped to the back of the register and pointed to a page covered in columns of numbers, with words written beside them.

"Latin." He muttered, "These are records of trades. Spices for brandy. Flour for bolts of cotton. Christ."

"Something else?"

"The good reverend is a thorough recordkeeper. He's documented how the town fathers have been embezzling hundreds of pounds over the course of decades. I suspect Reverend Gardiner plans on using this evidence to blackmail the leaders of Domingo Town, should it ever be necessary."

"Small wonder he insists this was destroyed in a fire. Still . . ."

"We're after a different prize."

Alys flipped back and forth between pages in the register. "Here's Ralph Dunwood . . . his daughter, Miss Olivia Dunwood . . . who married William Lambert . . . and they had a son . . ." Her voice trailed off.

"What?" Ben demanded. "Who was her son?"

She looked up, her expression wide and disbelieving. "Lethal Lambert."

"Olivia Dunwood named her son *Lethal*?"

Alys gripped his sleeve. "That's not his name. Well, it *is* his name. He was christened Charles Lambert, but he's been known as Lethal Lambert ever since he skewered French Henry with Henry's own cutlass. Born into wealth but turned pirate when he learned his father had bankrupted the estate."

Ben rubbed his forehead, attempting to keep track of all the twists of Lethal Lambert's life. "And *he* has the fail-safe."

"The clue at the waterfall said it was at Lambert's table." She rose, leaving the register on the floor.

"A tabletop mountain? Perhaps an arithmetic table."

Also standing, Ben left the register where it was. Let the parishioners of All Saints discover Reverend Gardiner's record of blackmail.

"Lethal Lambert's family owned an estate near the Bahamas, but it was sold to pay their debts." Alys started down the aisle, back toward the door. The ball of light followed her, a faithful servant. "After New Providence became law-abiding, Lambert used his prize money to buy the estate back and turn his family estate into a haven for pirates. Every now and again, he'll throw a massive party. Feasts that would rival any king's."

"Sir Fenfield's nephew's cousin's daughter's son's table," Ben said wonderingly. "And that's where we'll find the fail-safe. God willing."

"*Goddess* willing."

They reached the narthex, and she held up her hand. The ball of light perched on her palm.

THE SEA WITCH 257

"Thank you, friend," she murmured to it.

The glowing ball hummed before winking out.

"The *Sea Witch* should be waiting for us where we left it," she said. "Town's deserted. It'll be easy enough to reach our landing spot." She pushed the door open, took two steps, then lurched to a stop, throwing her arm in front of Ben.

The chickcharney stood in front of the church.

CHAPTER TWENTY-ONE

Alys had warned Ben to keep from laughing at the chickcharney. But now the awful, impossible urge to guffaw climbed up her throat.

The chickcharney did indeed look like an owl with unusually long legs, and in that, it was almost ridiculous. Round face, short hooked beak, tawny feathers. As ordinary as any bird seen flying through the night. Yet from under its wings emerged spindly human-shaped arms topped with three-fingered talon-like hands. They flexed as if searching for something to grasp and twist.

The creature had a long thin tail, almost like a monkey's tail, and it snapped back and forth, cutting through the air. Its red eyes blazed in the darkness as it glared at Alys and Ben.

It took three steps closer. The talons on the ends of its hands glinted as he reached for them, ready to snap off their heads.

"We need weapons," he growled.

"Couldn't fight it if we wanted to," she hissed back. "Use the petticoat. Wave it around."

He did as she commanded, swishing the coral-colored skirt back and forth in slow hypnotic movements. "I feel like an ass."

"Healing your injured pride is easier than replacing our severed heads."

He seemed to have no argument against that, so he continued

THE SEA WITCH

to flutter the petticoat. Gradually, the chickcharney's eyelids and hands lowered, and it sank to the ground as it made soft contented noises.

"Slowly, now." Alys took Ben's hand.

They eased past the creature, its head swiveling around to track their progress. Ben kept moving the petticoat back and forth as he and Alys backed away. A step. Another step. Until they were in the shelter of an alley.

The chickcharney's head turned away, no longer interested in them.

Alys and Ben ran. They ducked through the lanes and back streets of Domingo Town, all uncannily empty, echoing with their footsteps. At last, they reached the edge of the settlement. Plunging across the fields, they sped, hand in hand, until they came to the forest. They didn't stop running through the dense vegetation, following game trails. Trees loomed, menacing all around them. Ahead was the pounding of surf against the sand. Neither Ben nor Alys stopped to look behind them to see if the chickcharney followed, praying to the stars that the creature had found something else to draw its attention.

She cursed in relief when they came out of the forest to emerge on the beach. Waiting for them was the jolly boat, and Eris, perched on one of the benches. The magpie flew over to land on her shoulder.

"Please tell me that your mistress and the ship are nearby," she pleaded.

Eris chirped an assent.

"They're waiting for us," she informed Ben. "But keep that," she added when he tossed the skirt aside. "I'm sure someone aboard will be happy to get a new petticoat."

He scooped it up and deposited the underskirt in the jolly boat. Together, they pushed the boat into the water, then climbed in. They both took the oars to row them past the surf, and farther out into the dark cove.

260 EVA LEIGH

A hundred feet into the bay, a lamp appeared. Too low to be a star.

A handful of more lamps glowed to life. The outline of the *Sea Witch* gradually took shape with each new lamp being lighted.

They brought the jolly boat alongside the ship, then climbed up the ladder when it was rolled down in welcome.

Stasia stood ready when Alys stepped onto the top deck. Olachi was with her, along with Polly, Luna, and Effia.

"We have news," Stasia said.

"So do we," Alys answered.

"A ship for me has been found," Olachi said, her eyes bright with purpose.

"A naval ship," Stasia added. "A forty-gun, fourth rate frigate in the Royal Navy."

Beside her, Ben went still. Alys didn't look in his direction.

"It'd have all the necessary weapons to attack enslavers' ships," Alys said.

"And the size to accommodate all those we'll free," Olachi noted.

"The ship was spotted on its way to investigate what happened back at Kinnear's," Stasia went on. "We can intercept it."

"Which ship?" Ben asked, his voice low.

Before Stasia could answer him, Alys said quickly, "Is it far from us?"

"Half a day's sailing," Luna explained.

"Set a heading," Alys said. "We'll come up with a plan, and then the crew needs to be made ready."

"Which. Ship," Ben pressed.

Alys didn't answer him. Instead, she grabbed the pistol tucked into Stasia's belt—and pointed it at him.

"The hell?" he demanded.

"To the brig."

"Alys—"

THE SEA WITCH

"Now."

When he didn't move, Stasia unsheathed her cutlass, then Polly brandished a dagger, and Luna aimed her own firearm at him. Olachi and Effia watched, their expressions guarded.

Slowly, Ben raised his hands. With Alys behind him, the muzzle of her pistol trained on his back, he climbed down the companionway.

"You know the way," Alys said flatly.

"You think this is necessary." His back was to her as he descended lower into the ship. "What we did . . . at the inn . . ."

"Not the first time I've made an error in judgment."

He spun around, and she pressed the muzzle of her gun against his chest.

His expression was disbelieving, then hardened. "An error."

Heat rushed to her face and through her body. "I needed balancing. You provided a service. Willingly. I thank you for it."

Pushing the words from her mouth, wounding him like this . . . her chest ached.

"Giving you the touch and pleasure you needed isn't an offense that requires throwing me in the brig," he said tightly.

"The risk's too high. Having you roaming free when we attack the naval ship."

"Then manacle me."

"You could still sabotage us. Or join them. A hundred possibilities. Keep walking."

He turned and continued to make his way toward the brig. "As if you couldn't know what I think, what I feel."

"We can lie to ourselves as much as anyone else. You could be halfway to the magazine, not even knowing you intended to blow up my ship, before either of us realized what was happening."

"It's *my* treachery that worries you. *You're* the one with a pistol aimed at my back."

"The safety of my crew and ship come first."

They had reached the brig. Alys grabbed the key from the hook and unlocked the bars. With a jerk of her head, she motioned for him to step inside. He backed in, his gaze never leaving hers, his eyes cutting. She ignored the frost between them as she closed the door to the cage and locked it.

Lowly, he asked, "Is that all you're keeping safe?"

She stepped away. "You're in this cage, but in truth, I'm setting you free."

"This doesn't look like freedom." He gripped the bars.

"Locked in here, you're free from having to make a choice. Them, or me."

Without another word, she walked from the brig, all the time fighting the need to look back.

CHAPTER TWENTY-TWO

A LYS CLIMBED DOWN the side of the *Sea Witch* and slipped into the water. With its glamour, the *Sea Witch* now appeared to be a damaged merchant ship, limping as it approached the *Ajax* of His Majesty's Royal Navy. The naval ship seemed to believe that a listing merchantman couldn't harm them, so the *Ajax* allowed the *Sea Witch* to come closer.

No one aboard the naval vessel would anticipate or notice a lone figure swimming toward them. All the attention was fixed on the ship in distress, so Alys made her way without anyone raising an alarm or, worse, trying to pull her onto the ship.

She hadn't the ability to swim *and* maintain a glamour. None of her crew could cast a spell over her appearance, busy as they were maintaining the *Sea Witch*'s disguise. So, it was without concealment that she made her way toward the *Ajax*. Meanwhile, the *Sea Witch* maintained its own glamour, resembling an impaired ship requiring help, and sailing slowly toward the *Ajax*. No hostile actions could be used by the witches aboard. All their focus had to be on keeping the glamour going. Only when the illusion was dropped could they begin to fight. It was a precarious balance to get close enough to the *Ajax* for the right position, while being unable to use their best method of attack and defense.

264   EVA LEIGH

Alys finally reached the naval ship. The frigate towered above her, creaking and groaning as it rode the waves.

With the British crew distracted by the approach of the disguised *Sea Witch*, she began to clamber up the side. Knives were tucked into her belt, and her sword hung from a baldric as she pulled herself up, hand over hand. A year ago, she'd done almost the same thing in the frigid waters of Cape Ann. But now she climbed the *Ajax* with far more strength and confidence than she'd had back then.

She edged past cannons bristling from their gunports and heard the voices of the men on the gun deck.

At last, she reached a porthole wide enough to wriggle through. She tumbled into a storage hold, stacked with barrels and crates. Climbing to her feet, she peered out the door. A few seamen made their way along the passageway, and she ducked back into the hold, waiting for them to pass.

"Don't know why we're bothering with that merchantman," one of the sailors grumbled as he passed. "They can sail. No need for us."

"Captain Isley never turns down a chance to make himself look like a hero," another answered.

"Why drag *us* into it?"

The voices faded as they walked away. When they were gone, Alys checked to ensure no one else was in the passageway. It was clear, so she darted out.

From a pouch hanging on her belt, she pulled a sealed vial containing a sprig of herbs. Olachi had given them to her that morning, a collection of ordinary things taken directly from cook Josephine's pantry as well as from the Fatima's supply of herbs used for healing. Thyme, lemon balm, feverfew, barberry. Typical as these plants were, Olachi had insisted that it was this specific combination that created a desired effect. Yet they needed a catalyst.

Alys uncorked the vial. She snapped her fingers. A tiny flame

THE SEA WITCH

265

appeared on the tip of her index finger, and she touched the fire to the herbs within the vial. They immediately started smoldering. A thin wisp of sharp vegetal smoke curled up from the glass.

Concentrating on the smoke, Alys whispered, "Take me to where magic is strongest."

The smoke drifted up in a narrow column. For a moment, it seemed the spell hadn't worked. But then the smoke snaked down the passageway. She followed where it led her, along the corridor, up a companionway, then along another passageway, before it stopped in front of one closed door.

Alys corked the vial, extinguishing the miniscule blaze. After drawing her cutlass, she pulled open the door and rushed in. She quickly shut the door behind her.

It was dim within, a heavy curtain over the porthole, and it took a moment for her eyes to adjust to shadows. There was a narrow berth, a small desk holding numerous scrolls and books, and a cabinet whose drawers were overflowing with countless objects. Feathers, animal bones, polished stones, seashells, metal amulets, even an assortment of human teeth. The room smelled of ash and loamy soil.

This cabin belonged to the ship's mage. But the mage himself wasn't within it. She'd have to wait.

She took a step deeper into the cabin, toward a long narrow wooden box. Thorny vines had been carved into the lid and sides. Inside were two rows of small bottles sealed with a plug of pale wax. She held one up. A reddish glow emanated from it, the glimmering contents swirling hypnotically.

Cautiously, she returned the bottle back to its case. The constellations only knew what it contained. Fumbling about with strange magic never ended well.

The cabin door swung in abruptly. Brandishing her cutlass, she spun to face a man with close-cropped blond hair, gray eyes, a black sash, and a malevolent smirk.

"I believe you're looking for me," the mage said.

Alys summoned a shield on her arm just as the mage flung a cutting spell at her. Most of the sharp energy bounced off her shield, but what got past sent a rain of hot stings across her face. Ignoring the pain, she shot a bolt of power into her cutlass and attacked.

Her blade clashed against a lance of cold fire, thrown by the mage. Alys leapt onto the berth, gaining a height advantage, but he flung more spikes of icy flame at her. She ducked and shielded herself. The spikes slammed into the bulkhead, leaving burnt scars.

She feinted as if she intended to strike high, and when the mage tried to block the blow, she dove low, slashing at his legs.

He snarled in pain as she cut across his thigh and he shot another slicing spell at her. While she ducked away, he darted across the cabin to the narrow wooden box. He flung open the lid and pulled out a bottle. With his dagger, he cut off the wax seal, then put the bottle to his lips. He downed its glowing contents in one swallow.

Alys threw herself at him. Too late. Whatever the liquid inside the bottle was, it filled the mage with a surge of energy. His eyes glowed red. Fiery power seethed around him, and the force of the energy enveloping his body flung her backward.

The deep cut across his leg instantly healed. The sight of his own flesh mending made him grin.

"Fuck," she muttered.

"Exactly," the mage replied.

He stabbed his fiery fingers at her, but she had already leapt away. She yanked the box of potions off the table and threw it to the floor. Bottles smashed on the wood, spilling their glittering contents. The air filled with the smell of iron and fire.

The mage's face contorted in anger. Trying to fight him now in his cramped quarters was a surefire way to get herself killed.

THE SEA WITCH

Shoving to her feet, she wrenched open the door to his cabin and darted into the passageway. He followed her, throwing spells that made the walls instantly crumble. She moved backward, blocking with her shield and slashing with her cutlass. Frightened seamen scurried out of their path and huddled in doorways as the fight continued.

The mage's attacks forced her up the companionway until they emerged on the top deck. More stunned sailors darted out of their way. A man with a long dark blue coat and powdered wig—clearly the captain—gaped at her.

Alys glanced to see the still-glamoured *Sea Witch* coming closer to the portside of the *Ajax*. Close enough to board.

It was impossible to wait any longer.

She stomped her boot onto the deck. It boomed like a thunderclap, causing the seamen to cover their ears.

At that same moment, the *Sea Witch* dropped its glamour. No longer a damaged merchant ship, it sailed in all its piratical brilliance. Its decks were laden of women of every color, armed with firearms and cutlasses, magic encircling hands as witches prepared themselves for battle. Stasia and Olachi both held pistols and cutlasses as they stood at the head of the crew.

Their flag, a black banner depicting a woman wielding a sword beneath a crescent moon as she danced upon the waves, flapped defiantly in the wind.

"To the guns," the captain of the *Ajax* shouted. "Fire at will!"

Gunners manned the cannons, loading and aiming them.

The witches flung up a shielding spell. It encircled the ship just as the *Ajax*'s cannons fired.

All the cannonballs slammed against the shield, then tumbled harmlessly down into the water.

Grappling hooks were immediately flung from the pirate ship to the naval vessel. Led by Olachi and Stasia, the crew swung onto the *Ajax*'s deck, their weapons forming bright arcs of magic between the ships.

268   EVA LEIGH

A series of thumps followed as, one by one, the crew landed on the Ajax's deck.

Marines gaped at the women as if they were gorgons who had turned them to stone. Women in trousers, laden with weapons and magic, glared back at them.

"Attack," the captain shouted.

Seamen grabbed whatever weapons they could. Some had short daggers, others seized cudgels. Marines hefted rifles.

The mage threw glimmering spells toward their weapons, charging them.

Pops sounded as the marines' guns fired. Stasia and Olachi threw up another shield, protecting the pirates from gunfire.

The marines and armed seamen charged through the smoke of the discharged firearms at the pirates, dodging and evading. Each witch darted toward their attackers. Once they were close enough, the witches placed their hands on the backs of the sailors' necks.

Marking each witch's hand was a crescent moon. The symbol had been painted on their palms with a mixture of honey and burnt valerian.

The marked men collapsed to the deck, dazed and motionless from the skin-to-skin contact. Women without magical power dashed forward, binding the men's hands.

The mage spun around, anger bright in his cold eyes. He reached for a pouch hanging from his belt.

Blade out, Alys sprung toward him. Her cutlass slashed through his belt, and, using the tip of her sword, she flung the belt to the other side of the deck.

The mage kicked her in the stomach. She gasped as she flew backward.

He clapped his hands together, sending out waves of invisible force. The ship rocked.

"A signal," she shouted to her crew. "For reinforcements."

THE SEA WITCH 269

The mage chuckled. "Enjoy your last moments alive, witch."

Alys ran at him. He pulled his cutlass, charged with glowing green energy. He leapt at her and she spun to evade his sword. She parried another strike, jolting from the force of his magic-infused weapon. Regaining her balance, she countered with her own blow. The mage snarled as they fought past the forms of dozens of marines and seamen littered the deck. Groggy and stupefied, they could only mutter and flop bonelessly as pirates bound their hands.

One of the seamen still on his feet turned a swivel gun toward the *Sea Witch* and prepared to fire.

Gritting her teeth, Alys hurled lightning toward the swivel gun. The gunpowder in the weapon ignited and it exploded.

Pain blazed in her thigh. She screamed as the mage's power-charged cutlass struck her in the leg. The wound was exactly where she'd cut him.

She buckled from the pain as his weapon remained stuck in her leg.

"Retribution tastes sweet." He loomed over her, his hands upraised with the red light of a killing spell.

"Like honey." She pulled the sword from her thigh and stabbed it through his foot. The blade sank through the leather of his boot, into flesh, muscle and bone, and into the deck.

The mage screamed. Yet when he tried to leap back, his pinned foot kept him trapped.

With her own cutlass, she stabbed into the center of his chest. The mage looked down at her sword, stuck between his ribs. He tried to pry the blade from his body, then fell backward. His lifeless eyes no longer glowed. His body went slack as his foot remained pinned to the deck. Blood, tainted with the glittering gleam from the potion, pooled on the wood.

Alys panted and stared at the mage's body. Her leg buckled beneath her as blood poured from her wound.

The captain took a step toward her, his rapier raised.

"I would not." Olachi pressed the tip of her cutlass against the captain's throat. Slowly, he lowered his sword.

"She has a far better use for your ship," Alys said to the captain, and Olachi nodded.

One by one, the remaining conscious seamen and marines laid down their weapons. They raised their hands in surrender.

Stasia was at Alys's side, supporting her when she could barely hold her own weight. "Let us finish this."

"Get the navy men in the jolly boats and cutters," Alys commanded her crew as more blood flowed down her leg. "Lively, now. The hourglass quickly empties."

The women did as they were instructed. They loaded the *Ajax*'s crew into two jolly boats and two cutters. The boats lay low in the water, overfilled with the crew.

The captain was the last one set into a cutter. Just as he climbed into the small vessel, both the *Ajax* and the *Sea Witch* jolted.

"Good. Fucking. God," Alys growled.

Everyone, even the sailors and naval officers, cried out in alarm.

The sleek, sharp scales of a leviathan broke the waves. Circling the *Ajax* and the *Sea Witch*, it twisted and spun in the water, long and serpentine, and impossibly huge. Its head, the size of a jolly boat, breached the surface. Glowing eyes with slitted pupils stared up at her. Opening its enormous mouth, rows of teeth like cutlasses flashed.

This was the nearest she'd ever been to a leviathan. Alys had seen one from a distance, back in St. Gertrude, when one had destroyed the *Diabolique*. This close, the size of the beast stole her breath. Fighting a creature such as this was hopeless.

Only one leviathan was known for attacking ships. Where that beast was, the naval flagship wouldn't be far behind.

"Those that sail with the *Sea Witch*," Alys shouted, "to the ship. *Now!*"

THE SEA WITCH

271

Women began swinging back to the *Sea Witch* in a mad rush. The others, who wished to stay with Olachi and join her mission, remained behind.

Alys winced as Stasia helped her limp to the ropes connecting the *Ajax* and the *Sea Witch*. She grabbed one of the ropes, but a hand on hers stopped her.

"Ije oma," Olachi said, her dark eyes warm. "Safe journey."

"And to you," Alys answered. "We'll see each other again."

"Of that, I do not doubt."

Olachi stepped back, and Alys hoisted herself up before swinging across the gap between the two ships. As she flew through the air, she looked down at the leviathan. Agitated, its tail lashed the churning water. Its open maw gaped, dark and terrifying. Its sharp teeth glinted in the sunlight. The creature could easily swallow her whole.

A moment later, she landed awkwardly on the deck of the *Sea Witch*. Searing pain shot up her leg but she kept standing long enough to make sure that everyone who wanted back on the *Sea Witch* was aboard, and those who intended to sail with Olachi were on the *Ajax*.

The leviathan bumped its head against the two ships with greater force, sending both vessels rocking violently. Crew clung to the railings as they fought to stay on their feet and not tumble into the water, where death awaited.

The ropes lashing the ships together were frantically cut just as the leviathan made another pass between the ships. Both vessels shuddered and rolled from the impact. The *Ajax* and the *Sea Witch* needed distance between the two ships.

"Enemy vessel approaching, Cap'n," Susannah cried. "Off the starboard bow!"

Stasia shoved a spyglass into Alys's hand, and Alys used it to look starboard. She cursed.

"The *Jupiter*," she growled.

The first-rate one-hundred-gun man-o'-war sailed right for

them. The full-rigged sails billowed, the wind charged with a mage's power. Within moments, the massive ship would be upon them.

Another beast swam beside it.

"A kraken!" Stasia shouted. Fear laced her voice.

"Not possible." Alys aimed the spyglass and cursed.

The gargantuan beast's tentacles stretched far, far behind it as it cut through the water. The kraken's huge reddish bulbous head broke the surface. Even from this distance, there was no mistaking the predatory intent in its yellow eyes.

Alys's mind whirled. There had to be *something* they could do. Or else there'd be no surviving the attack of a leviathan, a kraken, *and* the naval flagship.

Rage poured into her, hot and acidic. She couldn't fail her crew, or Olachi and the other freed women.

"All witches," Alys shouted to the women aboard her ship as well as the *Ajax*. "Send your voices to the bottom of the sea! We've been hunted and hounded, made to feel ashamed, killed for who we are. Bought and sold. Now's the time. Scream. All of your fury, put it into your screams! Send them silently to the bottom of the sea."

Witches on both vessels opened their mouths. Alys screamed, too, for herself, for Ellen, for Stasia and Olachi and the women of Norham and women everywhere. She screamed her outrage and grief and defiance.

Dozens of women released their fury at a world that refused to understand or accept them.

The witches of both ships shrieked noiselessly, their faces darkening with the venting of centuries of suppressed anger. Even the familiars opened their mouths on silent cries.

Alys clenched her fists as she used her magic to gather the screams and guide them as they sank deep beneath the water. Sweat poured from her as she struggled to shape them into a

THE SEA WITCH 273

massive sphere, large as a house. All of their voices collected within the bubble.

The *Jupiter* grew closer, its guns trained on the *Sea Witch* and the *Ajax*. The kraken's tentacles rose from the sea, ready to wrap around the hull and masts. The leviathan opened its maw.

Alys and crew braced for the attacks.

The bubble of screams broke the water's surface and burst, releasing the voices with deafening force. The crew aboard the *Jupiter*, and the sailors in the jolly boats and cutters, covered their ears and grimaced in pain. The creatures halted, frozen in place.

The force of their fury pushed into the *Jupiter*. The naval vessel was swept backward on surges of water, while the leviathan and the kraken were pushed away on the churning sea. A hundred feet separated the flagship and creatures from the *Ajax* and the *Sea Witch*.

"My witch sisters," Alys cried, "summon the winds to make our escape."

Her magic had been taxed to its limits, yet Alys joined her crew as she called upon the strongest winds to fill the sails of the *Sea Witch* and the *Ajax*. They roused them from every corner of the Caribbean, all the breezes and gales and gusts. Anything that could help them flee promised destruction.

Winds gathered, filling the *Sea Witch*'s and *Ajax*'s sails with a surge. Propelled by the blasts of air, the two ships cut through the sea and away from each other. It was as though they had been shot from a cannon. Distance grew between themselves and the naval flagship. A quarter mile, a half mile. A mile.

The *Ajax* sailed off on its own course.

Only when the *Jupiter* and the creatures disappeared over the horizon did Alys permit herself to exhale. Pain from her wound returned in a rush, coupled with her exhaustion in the wake of using so much magic. She gripped the rail to keep

274 EVA LEIGH

herself upright. Around her, witches sank down to the deck, while other members of the crew nursed wounds sustained in the battle.

Fatima led a group of crew members to mend injuries for some, and balance others with food and gentle, careful touch.

Alys pulled off her coat, then tore the sleeve of her shirt into a long strip. She bound the fabric around her wounded thigh. Blood immediately soaked through the linen.

When Fatima approached Alys, she waved the doctor off. "Others need more attention."

"I suppose this blood on your thigh and dripping onto the deck belongs to someone else," Fatima said.

"The crew first," Alys growled. When the doctor looked as though she might argue, Alys added, "Don't make today the first time you disobey a direct order."

Fatima shook her head, but moved on to attend to the rest of the company.

A moment later, Stasia was at Alys's side. "I have unfortunate news."

Alys braced herself. "Tell me."

"Josephine left to join Olachi," Stasia said somberly. "We are going to need another cook."

A ragged laugh escaped Alys. "You're always saying that no one here can brew decent coffee. Now's your chance to take the tiller."

"Coffee is the extent of my talent in the kitchen. It is one of the reasons why I left my village. I would rather sail a ship than roll grape leaves to make dolmades. Do not put too much weight on your leg."

"I have to." Alys groaned as she limped toward the companionway. "There's something I must do."

CHAPTER TWENTY-THREE

Her second-in-command knew when it was a fool's errand to argue. Stasia let her go as Alys slowly, awkwardly, climbed down the companionway, and then went lower into the ship. She hobbled to the brig, where Ben stood, gripping the bars of the cage.

His gaze shot from her face, which was surely ashen, to the dark crimson stain on the bandage around her thigh.

"Where's your damned doctor?" he demanded. "Get her here immediately."

"Fatima's busy."

"The captain's health should be her priority."

"I decide what's important on my ship." She pointed a finger at him. "How many more sea creatures is the navy adding to their arsenal?"

"I . . ." His brow furrowed.

"A leviathan *and* a kraken," she said through gritted teeth. "With the *Jupiter*. A hell of a surprise."

"Damn," Ben muttered. "Warne spoke the truth."

"No surprise for you, it seems." She kept her weight off her leg as much as she was able, but she refused to hold the bars of the brig to support herself. "You said nothing."

"The *Jupiter*'s mage and I are not friendly. When he speaks,

I never know what to believe. Distorting the truth is one of his favorite games."

She clenched her jaw to keep from crying out in pain. "Letting us know we might be facing two creatures instead of one would've been somewhat helpful. Annihilation was very likely."

"When was I supposed to tell you? En route to you throwing me into the brig? I only knew which ship you planned on commandeering when I spotted the *Ajax* through the porthole. The same for the *Jupiter*. I'd no knowledge of them sailing to the *Ajax*'s aid. How could I?"

"The kraken and leviathan don't care who's aboard the *Sea Witch*," she fired back. "If this ship goes down because of them, you go down with it."

"I didn't know the *Jupiter* would come to the *Ajax*'s aid. The way you escaped from them, and their creatures . . . that scream . . . the *rage* within it."

"The crew aboard the *Sea Witch* have reason to be angry. *I'm* angry."

Doubt vibrated between them. "I couldn't be certain if . . . if I could trust you with the information about the beasts. Especially with these bars between us."

"And now?"

"Now . . ." He drew in a ragged breath. "To think of the Royal Navy exploiting those creatures . . . giving their might to help bastards like Kinnear . . . stealing the freedom of those women, and others like them . . ."

They regarded each other in silence.

"The poles have reversed," he went on, "and I've no idea what side of the globe I'm on."

She studied him for a long moment, even as her blood seeped through the bandage. His expression mirrored the pain she felt.

"I believe you." She unlocked the brig. When he continued to stand within its confines, she pulled the door open.

THE SEA WITCH   277

He took a tentative step forward. She grabbed a set of manacles from where they hung on the bulkhead; he didn't look surprised.

"Because I didn't tell you about the other creatures?" he asked heavily.

"I don't know if you're keeping anything else back from me," she said.

He said nothing, and in that pause, she had her answer. Yet he held still as she fastened the manacles around his wrists.

"To my quarters." She jerked her chin toward the door.

"I could carry you," he offered.

She shot him a look that would castrate a minotaur. "My crew only sees me on my feet, and it stays that way."

"Aye, Captain."

He stepped into the passageway, and she followed.

"It's critical we find the fail-safe," she said, limping behind him. "If we don't, disaster follows for anyone seeking to live free upon the water."

"Subjugating not one but two creatures to the Crown's will."

"How many more will they control?" she pressed.

"I don't know." He shook his head. "I didn't join the navy for this."

Hobbling to her cabin made Alys's head spin. They passed many crew members, some of them bearing evidence that Fatima and her helpers had worked on them, while others still bore a residual glow from having been recently balanced. They all saluted as they passed. Alys did her best to stand as straight as possible, and not let her face contort with the agony she felt.

Only when she was safely inside her quarters, easing herself down onto a chair, did she allow herself the luxury of groaning. Manacled, Ben awkwardly poured a mug of rum, then handed it to her. She drank it down in one swallow.

"From the porthole in the brig," he said, refilling the cup

and handing it back to her, "I saw the seamen and captain of the *Ajax* in the cutters and jolly boats. You spared them."

"All we had need of was the ship." She gripped the mug tightly. "Killing the captain and crew served no purpose."

"No purpose to spare them, other than mercy."

She shrugged. "Death's messy and often not necessary."

"Few in your position would see it that way."

"And for my efforts, the navy's put a two-hundred-pound bounty on my head."

His mouth flattened.

She drained her cup once more, letting the rum burn round the hard edges of her pain.

"Now I'm questioning my decision to destroy all of the mage's potions." She dragged her sleeve across her mouth. "In a trice, my leg would've healed and I could climb the rigging as much as I pleased."

"You saw the box?"

"The one with vines carved in the lid. It reeked of sulfur but when he drank one of the vials, it was as though he'd been turned into a demigod."

"Dragon's blood." At her raised eyebrows, he explained, "A poetic name but there's no actual blood of a dragon in it."

"I've heard nothing of such a brew."

"The naval mages keep much of their . . . skills . . . a secret from the rest of the crew."

"Yet *you* know."

"A mage from the *Destiny* came aboard the ship, and I overheard a conversation between him and Warne." At her sardonic look, he said, "I've never trusted Warne. I was . . . monitoring the situation."

"*Monitoring.* A spruce naval word for *eavesdropping.*"

"Learning takes many forms, including listening in to conversations I wasn't privy to."

"And you learned . . . ?"

THE SEA WITCH 279

"Mages drink dragon's blood to heal and increase their magic, and to ingest it brings power at a great cost. They become the tinder that burns hot and bright, but devours the fuel too fast. Trims down their lifespan. Few mages who take dragon's blood live past five and fifty. None of them seem to care, though. They'd rather be triumphant at that moment than accept their limitations."

"They brew the potion themselves?"

"It's supplied to them, but what it contains, where it comes from and who makes it . . ." He spread his hands. "My *monitoring* didn't help me glean more information."

"These are the things witches are forbidden to learn," she said moodily. "When I told you about the kraken and the leviathan, you said you didn't join the navy for that. What *did* you join for?"

He was quiet for a long time. He took the silver cup from her and refilled it with rum. When he offered it to her and she shook her head, he drank the liquor himself, his manacles rattling as he did so.

Perhaps he might refuse to answer.

But then—

"I *wanted* to be a ship's navigator on privately funded voyages of exploration and discovery." He stared out the window, his gaze turning faraway. "Learning new coastlines, pristine geographies. Seeing things I never thought I would ever see. It made the world less mysterious, but also . . . more enchanted."

"And your naval captain father thought otherwise."

Bringing his gaze back to hers, the wistfulness drained from his eyes. "There was no choice. Not really. Except . . . as I said, I wasn't officer material." His mouth twisted. "My father smashed our plates and china curios when I failed to make officer. Mother never said anything, just swept up the debris. But I angled to become the master's mate aboard his ship, and that, he allowed. Allowed, but never . . . never accepted. Never approved."

"And now you're a sailing master. One of the best in the navy."

He inclined his head. "Traveled all the way to London to take the oral examination before a senior captain and three sailing masters."

"A far journey," she noted.

"A worthwhile one. I received my warrant, yet promotion is never guaranteed. I did get it. Though I don't know if he'd be proud of me." He grimaced. "*I'm* not. Not anymore. My skill as a navigator . . . it abets things . . . things I can't countenance any longer. It's all falling away like so much rotten flesh from a corpse."

"We cut off diseased limbs," she said softly. "It keeps the infection from spreading."

"It *has* spread." His words were hoarse. "They have the leviathan bound against its will, and now they've added the kraken. No one can stand in their way. God knows where it will stop. If it will stop. It's not going to end with protecting the Crown's interests. There won't be any resistance left. Whoever isn't enslaved . . . they'll be dead."

"There's only one way to bring an end to it."

"Using the fail-safe."

They were silent together, worry and doubt and apprehension shuddering between them.

There was a kind of comfort in their shared anxiety.

A knock sounded on the door, and when Alys bid them entrance, Stasia came in briskly.

"Fatima tells me no one will cross the River Styx," she said, crisp. "Nothing to be amputated, no one lost eyes. A few days, and everyone will be healed. We will recover." She glanced at the crimson stained bandage around Alys's thigh. "Everything is shipshape topside."

"I want you above," Alys commanded, "where you're needed."

THE SEA WITCH

Moments after Stasia left, there was another knock on the door.

"Captain?" came a voice on the other side. "It's Fatima."

Ben strode across the cabin and pulled the door open. "Doctor."

Shouldering past him, Fatima carried her bag under her arm. She went to stand beside Alys's chair. "I'll need you on your berth."

Alys cursed. "Don't think I can stand. Not now."

Cautiously, Ben approached, offering his arm. "Might I?"

"Tell no one of this." Alys aimed this at both Ben and Fatima.

"The silence between the patient and the doctor will be preserved," Fatima answered.

"Gossiping with the crew is not one of my diversions," Ben added.

He helped Alys to her feet and remained solid as she leaned heavily against him, and they slowly made their way to her berth. She swore the entire journey.

Slowly, she lowered herself onto the mattress. Fatima bent over her leg and unwrapped the drenched bandage. Alys clenched her teeth as Fatima examined her wound.

"I must clean it," the doctor announced, "and then sew it shut."

"As you please," Alys said.

"We can summon someone to cast a numbing spell," Fatima suggested.

"After all the magic we've used today?" Alys shook her head. "Everyone's exhausted. More rum will do."

The filled cup was in her hand instantly, courtesy of Ben. Once she drained it, he filled it again, and she downed all the rum within it. As she attempted to drink herself insensible, Fatima put on a pair of spectacles and prepared her instruments.

To distract herself from the agony coursing through her, Alys studied the medical tools. They were beautifully engraved metal instruments of many shapes, delicate and precise works of art, forged by experts to perform complicated and important work. They were adorned with red enamel flowers and vines, the color of the lacquer likely chosen to hide any blood. Fatima had brought them with her when she had joined the crew, saying they had once belonged to her great grandfather but had passed to her when none of her male relatives expressed an interest in pursuing medicine. She had added to her collection over the course of the year, and had taken tools from some of the vessels they'd captured—always careful to let the ships' doctors keep the most essential equipment so they could continue to perform their duties.

Fatima helped Alys strip off her boots and ruined breeches. Then, with her leg completely bared, the doctor bent over the wound, her curved needle and catgut ready.

Alys reached out her hand. At once, Ben took it. He held her firmly through the whole painful procedure.

DESPITE FATIMA'S URGING that what Alys needed was rest, she called a gathering together in her quarters. Luna had brought a chart of the area, and spread it on the table.

Alys sat, while Stasia, Polly, Luna, and Ben stood around the table, as everyone contemplated the map, showing them all the possible routes to Lethal Lambert's enclave.

"The *Jupiter* and its creatures stand between us and our destination," Stasia mused. "Now that they are riled, there is no way past them. They will patrol in widening circles and be ready to attack with their beasts."

"You look like you've got an opinion," Alys said to Ben.

After a pause, he said carefully, "Another route is possible."

"Show us."

"We take this route, and stay clear of the *Jupiter*." He pointed to a narrow channel that ran between a series of islands.

All the women exchanged speaking glances.

THE SEA WITCH

"What don't I know?" he asked.

"This." Alys tapped her finger on the largest island, which formed a jagged, rocky coastline. "The cliffside location of the Redthorns' monastery."

Just saying their name caused a ripple of unease to travel around the table.

"Redthorns." Ben shook his head.

"Mages of the deepest and most fanatical devotion," Alys explained. "They hide themselves away from the world. Study the darkest magic. To them, the natural world's theirs to exploit and defile."

"Why call themselves Redthorns?" Stasia asked.

"I can only speculate," Alys answered.

"For all their piety, they can be bought," Polly added. "They act as mercenaries for whomever can afford them. In battle, they never leave survivors."

"Not very holy." Ben frowned. "They're monks?"

"So it's said," Alys replied.

He muttered a curse. "I may have seen them."

When he hesitated to speak, Alys waved toward him. "If there's something you know, we need to hear it."

"This must have been . . . three months ago? We were at sea, about a day from San Domingo. It was late, but I don't know what hour. No one rang the ship's bells. I remember thinking that was odd. I struggled to wake up, and when I left my quarters, everyone was asleep. *Everyone.* I managed to get myself on the top deck. Even the watches slept at their posts."

He continued, "A schooner came alongside us. The ship seemed made of darkness. Instinct had me hide myself as a trio of men in monastic robes boarded. Huge men. Their hoods were up, so I couldn't see their faces."

"None of this is pleasant to know," Stasia muttered.

"Warne and Lieutenant Oliver, they were awake. They met the monks and took them to the admiral's quarters,"

Ben continued. "They were sequestered for an hour, perhaps two, and when they came back on deck, they carried a small strongbox. They sailed away. The watches woke up, and I hurried back to my quarters. Neither Admiral Strickland, Oliver, nor Warne ever spoke of it."

"Did you ask them about those men?" Polly asked.

"I suspected I wasn't supposed to see or know about them, so I kept my silence."

"They're allies, then, to the navy," Alys said bleakly.

"We face them," Polly said, "or run right into the *Jupiter*'s arms."

"With its kraken *and* leviathan," Luna added.

"And a hundred guns," Ben noted.

"Magical monks, or sea creatures and a first-rate man-o'-war." Alys exhaled in the grim silence. "Seems that the Redthorns are the slightly less horrible option."

"The monastery has the high ground." Stasia's words were foreboding. "They will see our ship pass by their abbey and attack. Even with the number of witches aboard our vessel, we will be unable to defend ourselves against whatever magic and spells they aim at us."

"Couldn't you sail around them?" Ben asked. He pointed to the other islands near the Redthorns' monastery.

"For a navigator," Stasia said tartly, "you know precious little of this area."

"The navy seldom sails in this territory," he fired back. "I didn't get the opportunity to chart it."

"That archipelago is called the Broken Serpent," Luna said darkly. "It's made up of miles of rocky islands surrounded by shallows. You can't get through them on a full-displacement ship such as ours."

"The only way out is through," Polly said. "We'll need a diversion."

THE SEA WITCH

285

Alys nodded. "A party will make its way off the *Sea Witch* here." She pointed to a location on the peninsula that was a short distance south of the monastery. "We'll approach the abbey, provide the needed distraction to let the *Sea Witch* sail past, undisturbed, and then rejoin the ship here."

She rapped her knuckles on a spot north of the monastery.

"I'll lead the landing party," Alys said.

"Is that wise?" Stasia glanced at her injured thigh.

"I'm the fucking captain," Alys snapped, "and I'll manage."

Stasia held up her hands in acceptance. Alys resisted the urge to glance at Ben.

Continuing in a clipped voice, she said, "Stasia, Susannah, and Thérèse will make up the rest of the group. Polly, you have the bridge while I'm ashore. We'll run the *Sea Witch* through the strait at midnight."

Ben frowned, but wisely said nothing to contradict her.

"There's something you should know about that area," Luna added. "The tide's too low after dark for the *Sea Witch* to clear the channel."

"Then we go just before dawn," Stasia said.

"The last tide before sunrise is too violent," Luna said. "Our ship would be smashed against the cliffside. We'll have to catch the tide before dusk. There'll be enough water to pass through the strait, but not so violent that we'll wreck."

"A daylight operation."

"That climb will take an hour at least," Luna pointed out.

Alys planted her hands on her hips. "What choice have we?"

"If the winds hold, we'll reach the Redthorns' monastery tomorrow, just after three bells," Luna explained. "Exactly in the window we need to navigate the strait successfully."

Another thoughtful silence fell.

"Rest well tonight," Alys said. "Dismissed. Oh, and, Stasia," she added as everyone filed out, "find someone to serve as our cook. We'll need to dine abundantly this evening to shore up our power."

"We may dine abundantly," Stasia said, pausing on the threshold, "but we will not dine well. Josephine's culinary ability was unmatched. She could roast a lamb even better than my yiayia."

"At least Olachi and her crew get the benefit of Josephine's ability." Alys sighed.

When the last of her crew had left her quarters, Alys permitted herself to slump in her seat.

"Find someone else," Ben said in the silence.

She glanced up at him as he stood close. "Step back, Sailing Master. You're casting a shadow."

He moved back, but looked defiant.

"What I hated the most about being married," she continued, "was being told what I could and couldn't do."

"You're injured," he pointed out. "Leading a party against these fanatical Redthorns could cost you your life."

"I'm the captain. When it comes to missions this important, I'm the one in command." When he opened his mouth to argue further, she held up her hand. "I'm not asking your permission. This is what's going to happen. Any more comments or complaints will see you sleeping in the brig."

His jaw flexed, but after a long silence, he said, "Understood."

She pushed herself up to standing and limped to her berth. "Until our supper of questionable quality arrives, I'm going to rest."

She lay down on her side, her back to him.

A minute passed, and then his heavy footfalls sounded, approaching her. "You didn't want to tax the rest of the crew, the ones that fought or used magic. But I've been idle. No duties are demanding my attention. If you're in need of balancing . . . I find myself conveniently available."

She hesitated. "Fine."

THE SEA WITCH 287

The berth dipped with his weight as he lay down behind her, snugging his body close to hers. His warm breath brushed along the sensitive fine hairs along the back of her neck.

She stiffened. Cuddling with her lovers wasn't something she indulged in, and balancing with witches wasn't the same as this . . . this intimacy. Yet when he continued to lie with her, simply cupping his body to hers, she exhaled. In gradual degrees, her own body relaxed.

Soft golden light enfolded them. Energy flooded her, warm and healing, filled with a sense of purpose, a purpose that had been shifting and evolving. It shored up her own flagging resolve. At that moment, she was capable of doing anything.

She would need that strength to face what was next.

CHAPTER TWENTY-FOUR

Close to dusk, Alys, Stasia, Susannah, and Thérèse were rowed in to a thin beach at the base of a cliff. As soon as their boots touched the sand, the jolly boat returned to the *Sea Witch* in preparation for its treacherous passage through the strait. Whether or not the ship survived its journey depended on Alys and the rest of the landing party.

To reach the Redthorns' monastery first required a long climb up the steep rocky bluff. A flash of soreness ran up Aly's leg, yet it still held her weight. That morning, before pulling on her breeches, she had examined her wound. The flesh was now marked with a pink puckered line, bisected by Fatima's unneeded stitches, which the surgeon soon removed.

Never had Alys healed so quickly before. Even after balancing.

Except last night, Ben had been the one to balance her, his body close and solid against hers until sunrise.

"We climb to the top," Alys said now to her waiting crew. "Looks to be about sixty feet high."

"Poutana," Stasia muttered.

Alys sent her friend a sympathetic look. "Then we make our way along the ridge, until we reach the Redthorns."

They all looked toward the monastery. At this distance, a quarter of a mile away, it appeared deceptively small. Alys pulled

THE SEA WITCH   289

out her spyglass for more detail. The monastery was made up of several stories built atop a stony cliff, topped with a deeply pointed slate roof. Yet more of the hermitage had been built into the side of the bluff, boasting arches that opened onto a long balcony running the length of the building. One cannon sat on the balcony. There was no railing to impede the gun's firing. The cannon faced the strait, ready to blast anyone foolish enough to try to pass.

Alys passed the spyglass to Stasia. After Stasia looked through it, she handed it to Susannah, who then gave it to Thérèse. Once Thérèse assessed the monastery, she returned the spyglass to Alys.

Waves lapped against Alys's boots. The tide was rising, giving the *Sea Witch* the needed water level to navigate the strait. Alys and the rest of the landing party had to move quickly.

"Fly up?" Susannah suggested.

"We need to save our magic," Alys answered. "Are we all good to climb?"

"Are *you?*" Stasia sent a pointed glance toward Alys's thigh.

Alys gave her leg one last test to make sure it could bear her weight. "It'll hold."

Gripping to the projecting stones, she aimed her gaze to the top of the cliff and began to climb. The rest of the crew followed. No one spoke as they ascended—except Stasia, who cursed steadily in Greek the entire way up.

Finally, they reached the top. Alys's newly healed leg throbbed, yet it continued to bear her weight. Stasia briefly knelt in the soil and brought a handful of dirt to her lips before she rose to standing.

Keeping low, Alys, Stasia, Susannah, and Thérèse crept along the top of the rocky bluff. Alys's thigh ached as they skulked up the gradual incline, sloping upward toward the monastery. Half a mile away, the *Sea Witch* began to sail through the narrow

290   EVA LEIGH

passage. Soon, the ship would be visible to the monastery. Alys
and her crew had to be well inside the structure by the time that
happened, or else . . . disaster.

She and the others skirted around windswept scrub and jagged
rocks, an air of worry hanging low, almost smothering. Sweat
clung to Alys's back as they scrambled toward the monastery.

They drew closer, and then came to an abrupt stop.

A menacing wall of thick thorny vines rose up, tall as a single-
story building, deep enough that they couldn't see through, and
stretching out on either side as far as the eye could see. Tightly
entangled, the vines were bluish black, shining as if dipped in
viscous oil. The thorns were the size of fingernails, pointed
and curved to hook into something and hang on. Stasia tried to
clear a path by pulling the vines away, then snatched her hand
back with a curse.

Blood dripped down her punctured fingers and palm.

Alys drew her cutlass and slashed at the foliage. Yet her blade
glanced off the vines, leaving not a single mark on the vegetation.

Susannah darted off to one side of the thicket. When she
returned a moment later, her face was grim. "There's no end to
them. And no other way inside."

"We might use magic to pry these things open," Stasia said.

"They seem too tough to be forced to do anything." Alys
studied the thorny vines.

"We make them change directions," Thérèse suggested. "Al-
ter how they grow."

Alys and her crew shared a nod before they faced the thicket.
"Concentrate," she urged them. "Flow into the vines, curve
and curl with them."

Silence fell as the four women focused on weaving their magic
into the vegetation. The more Alys eased into each turn and twist
of the vines, the more the plants accepted her guidance.

A rustling sounded. The vines began to twist apart.

Alys stepped into the small space now open within the thicket

THE SEA WITCH

wall. She slowly moved forward as she and the other witches encouraged the vines to untangle. As she pushed onward, Stasia and the others stayed close behind her. Thérèse brought up the rear, holding the foliage open just enough so that they could all walk through. With each step forward, the vines behind them closed. The thicket curved overhead, nearly blocking out the remaining daylight.

Thorns surrounded them. The way was tight as they wove through the corridor. Their faces and clothes were soon covered with scrapes, and all the while, they fought the vines' demand to grow back together again.

Hisses and curses rose up from her crew.

"Fuck these plants from hell," Stasia snarled lowly.

Finally, daylight appeared ahead. Inhaling, Alys stepped from the vegetation into open space. She moved to the side as the rest of her crew emerged.

As soon as they were free, the foliage twisted back into place with a loud snap. A scrap of Thérèse's coat was hanging from one of the thorns.

"I liked that coat," she muttered, examining the tear in her clothing.

They now stood in a strip of cultivated land that stretched between the thorns and the monastery itself. Flourishing plants lined up in several raised beds. Some of them bore fruit, evidence that they were well cared for.

"Kitchen garden," Susannah said.

"The dishes these crops season are poisoned." Alys examined the leaves of the plants, careful to keep from touching them. "Hemlock, nightshade, foxglove. Enough to fell an army."

"Or nourish Redthorns," Thérèse noted.

"Hecate save us," Stasia muttered. "We are to *engage* these monsters?"

Alys strode to an arched door set in the monastery wall. She drew her cutlass before opening the door as quietly as possible.

292   EVA LEIGH

At one end of the vaulted room, a tall hearth stood with smoke-stained bricks and a large heavy pot bubbled above a smoldering fire. Shelves stacked with jugs, cups, bowls, and cannisters lined the walls. Down the center of the room stood a heavy table. Here and there were more bowls, and cooking knives set aside from their tasks. The air carried the scent of roast meat and bitter almonds.

She and her crew quickly moved from the empty kitchen and turned into an adjoining room. Another trestle table ran the length of the chamber, with three large rough wooden chairs on either side. An empty bowl sat at each place.

"We'll expect six of them," Alys whispered to her crew.

Deep-set windows lined one of the walls, facing out toward the strait. Alys exhaled—the *Sea Witch* wasn't yet in the passage. Shadows darkened the strait as the day drew toward its close. The tide was rising, but it would ebb soon. It wouldn't be much longer before their ship was vulnerable in the strait. They had to hurry.

A staircase led down from the refectory. Narrow and dank, it loomed close as they descended. They emerged in a corridor with open doorways on one side, and more windows set in the opposite wall.

Alys led her group from room to room, peering inside to ensure no one was within. Narrow cells were bare of furnishings, save for a single cot in each one, covered in a rough blanket, and a shelf set into the wall holding a few books. The only sunlight in each cell came from the window out in the corridor, turning each monk's sleeping quarters into a grim hollow of shadows.

A bundle of thorny vines huddled at the foot of every bed. The floor beneath was stained with dried blood.

"This must be why they're called Redthorns," Susannah whispered. "They flagellate themselves with these thorny canes."

The final cell was much larger, with multiple cots lined up, and a thick door bearing a substantial iron lock.

THE SEA WITCH

"There were only six places at the table," Alys murmured. "So who are these beds for?"

"Guests?" Thérèse supposed.

"Who don't eat with the monks?" Alys shook her head. "There were prisoners here. But they're gone now."

Alys stepped to a window facing the sea. It revealed the *Sea Witch*, sailing as quickly as it could through the channel. "If I can see our ship, so can the Redthorns."

They crept down spiral stone stairs and emerged on the bottom floor of the monastery. It was one cavernous hall carved directly into the cliff, with ceilings beamed with broad timbers. The chamber stretched into darkness. A few tall open doors led to a balcony. Hanging from the wall nearest the staircase were six maces, almost as long as Alys was tall. Topping each one was a cylindrical head, ringed by giant iron thorns.

Alys gulped at the brutal weapons. At least they were hanging here in their armory—the Redthorns were currently unarmed . . . hopefully.

Six enormous men stood on the balcony, surrounding the cannon. Black robes draped from their broad shoulders. Red cowls topped their black robes. Slanting rays from the sun glinted on the shaved sides of their heads. The rest of their hair hung in long matted locks. A tattoo of a thorny vine encircled each monk's neck.

"Do they recruit only from the ranks of giants?" Stasia whispered. "The *size* of them."

The monks were indeed massive, over a foot taller than any of her crew, with wide shoulders. All of them were gathered around the largest cannon Alys had ever seen. Runes covered its barrel—which pointed at the *Sea Witch*. Cannonballs were arranged beside the gun, along with stacks of powder kegs.

A monk loaded a glowing magic-charged cannonball into the artillery. He hefted the heavy projectile as easily as she might hold a pebble.

With dark sorcery imbuing the weapon, her ship would never survive being hit.

Alys and her crew dipped their hands into pouches hanging from their belts. They threw forged iron nails at the Redthorns.

At the same time, Thérèse flung a spell as they flew through the air, transforming them into angry gleaming hornets made of magical energy. Buzzing, they surrounded the monks, attacking the men.

The Redthorns didn't swat at the insects, didn't curse, even as the hornets drew blood. Instead, the men turned, facing Alys and her crew.

The monks rushed inside as they attacked. They snapped their fingers and maces flew from the wall into their hands.

Susannah used gusts of wind to swoop overhead, her cutlass slashing as she darted through the air. Yet the ceiling and its beams hampered her movements and kept her too close to the bald monk's swinging mace. Tables were scattered throughout the chamber, and Thérèse cast a spell to pull metal bolts from them. She flung the bolts at an advancing monk, this one with gray mixed in with the black of his hair. Yet when the bolts pierced him, he simply pried the metal from his body and tossed them aside. Stasia used her magic to flip two of the tables onto their ends. The tables screeched toward the Redthorns, forming a protective barrier between them and the crew.

Relentless, the monks pressed forward. But two Redthorns lumbered out onto the balcony to aim the cannon at the *Sea Witch*.

Alys spotted tables with laboratory equipment, and on them, glass flasks with multicolored liquids and tubes of potions and powders. She lunged toward the vials. A monk, younger than the others but still massive and menacing, blocked her path.

Susannah swooped down from above. She picked up three vials and threw them at the foot of the cannon.

THE SEA WITCH 295

Dashing out from behind an upright table, Stasia summoned a lightning strike. It hit the compound at the base of the gun and ignited a powder keg.

A deafening explosion shook the room and rocked Alys back on her heels.

The section of balcony shattered into chunks of stone. One of the Redthorns was sprawled on the balcony, missing half his head.

The other monk still stood. But his right arm was gone. He turned and lumbered toward the remaining powder kegs, tracking streaks of his blood across the stone.

Head buzzing from the deafening explosion, Alys swayed on her feet. She backed into metal bars. Spinning around, she faced a cage, a fox inside staring at her with haunted eyes. More cages filled this section of the chamber, each containing different animals. Hawks and sparrows, monkeys, wolves, rabbits, even deer. They were missing patches of feathers and fur. The animals all regarded Alys warily, as if anticipating terrible harm. Farther behind the cages were tables the width and length of a human, with leather straps where a person's wrists and ankles would rest.

Four Redthorns charged into the chamber, maces at the ready.

Alys needed to distract them. She raced along the rows of cages and Stasia joined her. Together, they quickly undid the locks, one after the other, and the cages' doors all swung open. For a moment, the animals within them remained where they were, too stunned to move.

"Flee," Alys cried to the creatures. "You're free now."

The creatures burst from their confinement. Hawks shrieked and wolves howled as the air was filled with fur and feathers.

But the chaos of the animals' flight stymied the monks' efforts to attack. Soon, the cages were empty, the animals all gone, leaving everyone to face the Redthorns with nothing to curtail the monks' assault.

Alys sprinted from the laboratory into the last section of the long chamber. Tall shelves filled with books lined the walls, and more books were piled upon tables used for studying.

The four Redthorns charged, brandishing their maces. Stasia used her magic to flip two more tables onto their sides. She maneuvered them with the wood groaning across the floor, protecting them from the Redthorns' maces.

A small book lay open on the floor. On the pages were illustrations of something that looked very familiar.

Ben's markings. This tome contained diagrams of the markings on Ben's skin. And this time, the language of the text was one she recognized. She couldn't read it, but someone on her ship would be able to.

She snatched the book up.

Alys peered past the monks blocking the tall doors. The *Sea Witch* continued to sail through the strait. The monk with salt-and-pepper hair joined the mangled Redthorn at the cannon, and they began to prepare it for firing. The ship was still within range.

"We have to get to the gun," she shouted to her crew.

The blond monk leapt, but instead of jumping toward Alys and her crew, he sprang up. Susannah dove out of his way as the Redthorn attached himself to the ceiling. Like an insect, the monk scuttled across the beams. The tables Stasia had used as a defensive wall were useless.

In a moment, the blond monk would be right over their heads. They had no means of holding him back, and no way of reaching the cannon.

A bird of prey's screech sounded, and a falcon soared through the open doors. Still in midair, a glow surrounded it, then it transformed.

Into Luca Pasquale.

The mage smashed his body into the Redthorn on the ceiling. They dropped to the ground, landing on their feet in the

THE SEA WITCH   297

midst of the library as the monk's mace spun away from his hand.

Pasquale had changed his grimy clothing for an elaborately ornamented black coat, black braid and jet buttons decorating nearly every available surface. His shirt was spotless, with lace at the cuffs and throat. His dark hair, now clean, brushed his shoulders, and he'd trimmed his wild facial hair into a neat beard that framed a smiling mouth.

"My thanks for coming to our aid," Alys said.

"My thanks to *you*." The mage stepped toward her. "Been waiting for you to attack these bastardos and distract them."

"How'd you know we'd be here?"

"Following you is an easy thing from the air. And there was but one way for you to come, after that lovely skirmish with the navy." He plucked the book from her hand.

"I need that!" Alys growled.

"I need it more," Pasquale answered.

The broad monk moved forward to attack.

Pasquale gripped the wide Redthorn by his neck. As he clutched the monk, his hand transformed into massive talons. The mage snarled as he dug his claws into the monk's flesh.

The monk scrabbled at the lace encircling Pasquale's throat, uncovering the mage's skin. Encircling Pasquale's neck was a tattoo of a thorny vine.

Yet the monk's attempts to grab him did nothing to stop Pasquale from tightening his talons.

Alys had seen her share of bloody, gruesome combat, from beheadings to limbs being hacked off, but even she winced at the scream and then gurgle as Pasquale's talons ripped out the Redthorn's throat.

Pasquale's eyes blazed, his jaw locked tight. He watched the Redthorn fall to the ground, then kicked the body away with one gleaming boot. His talons transformed back into a human hand, now covered in blood.

Beyond, the *Sea Witch* continued its navigation of the strait. The monks manning the gun loaded it with a glowing cannon ball. There was no time left.

"Bring it down," she said lowly to her crew, glancing toward the stone that made up the back wall of the chamber.

She and the other witches rushed past the mage.

"Take wing, Pasquale," Stasia snapped at him.

As they ran, Alys and her crew shot hurling spells at the stone wall. The entire monastery shook violently. Rumbling filled the air as massive cracks spread through the rocks. Stones and boulders, freed from the interior of the mountain, rolled in a slide through the chamber. The two Redthorns in the library tried to lunge for Alys and her crew, but were quickly pinned to the ground by falling rocks. Dust from the walls formed thick clouds to obscure their writhing forms.

The chaos seemed to wake Pasquale. He transformed once again into a falcon and flew out the closest door, the book in his talons.

"Fuck," Alys growled. The likelihood of ever seeing that book again, and the answers it contained, was nil.

Alys and her crew dove out the doors to the balcony just as the roof buckled and the rock wall caved in. More stones poured through the doors onto the balcony, sweeping into the cannon and the two Redthorns beside it. The balcony itself shuddered as it collapsed.

There was only one way to get out alive.

Alys and the witches jumped into open air. Immediately, they fell. The cliffside whizzed past and the strait raced toward them as they plummeted.

Susannah flung out her hands. Wind gathered, swirling around the crew. It gained strength from moment to moment, until they all spun and rolled upon wild eddies of air, buoying them up just enough to keep from complete freefall.

THE SEA WITCH   299

The *Sea Witch* grew closer and closer. And then, Alys and her crew landed on the deck, rolling in a dizzy jumble. They had made it through the strait. Her crew greeted their arrival with cheers.

A pair of sharp resounding bangs reverberated across the wooden planks, splintering the cheering into stunned silence. From her sprawl on the deck, Alys lifted up to find herself staring up at the two remaining Redthorns. They were covered in dust and blood.

The sons of bitches had survived the collapse of the monastery's roof, and had flown down to the ship.

Over a dozen witches massed around one of the monks. Snarling, he swung his mace. The crew remained just out of striking distance, and began attacking him in waves. Nets of magic held him in place. Some witches thrust with spells of lightning or ice. Others, led by Inés, slashed with their cutlasses. Each hit struck deeper into the monk.

The remaining Redthorn stood in front of Alys. His black and gold eyes were maddened with fury, his mouth twisted.

Raising his mace, the monk readied himself to smash the weapon down on her. Alys lifted her cutlass and gathered her last scraps of magic to shield herself.

The metallic sheen of a cutlass's blade emerged from the center of his chest. Stunned, the Redthorn stared down. Blood welled, darkening his robes. The blade retreated.

The monk turned to face whoever had possessed the audacity to stab him.

Ben stood with a crimson-streaked cutlass in his hand. His face was tight with determined rage. His shirt was open, revealing the intricate markings coursing down his chest, up his arms, and covering the backs of his hands.

"You . . ." the Redthorn gasped in a gravelly voice. Recognition glinted in his eyes. "The first."

"What?" Ben frowned. "First *what?*"

The monk shook his head, and moved back toward Alys, raising his mace once again.

Ben darted in front of Alys, sword outstretched. But the Redthorn ignored him and made a staggering attack at Alys. Before the blow could come down, Ben thrust his cutlass into the hollow of the Redthorn's throat. The monk dropped his mace and clawed at his neck. When Ben withdrew his blade, a river of blood poured forth. The Redthorn gurgled and gasped, looking at Ben with confusion. Then he fell with a hard thud.

The other monk also lay dead upon the deck.

Ben's chest heaved with the force of his breath, his legs bracing wide upon the deck. The fury left his face, replaced by shock.

She took a step toward him.

The ship rocked, jolted from a sudden impact.

"A creature," Cora cried. She stood at the gunwale and pointed into the waves.

Alys, Ben, and the rest of the company raced to the railings. A massive beast with red scales and two long curving tusks swam beside the ship. It had the head of a boar, with long pointed spines sticking up along its back. Whatever it was, she'd never seen its kind before.

It kept ramming against the *Sea Witch*.

"Is it with the navy?" Polly demanded.

"Don't see any naval ships nearby," Susannah answered. "The beast's acting of its own will."

"I cannot hold it back," Stasia said as her hands moved through the air, purple light cascading from her fingers.

Alys turned to her crew. "Feed it the Redthorns."

The company swarmed around the dead monks. As one, they hefted the bodies up, carried them to the railing, and heaved the monks' remains overboard.

THE SEA WITCH   301

The bodies splashed next to where the creature butted its head against the hull. It wheeled in the water and dove for the corpses, leaving the *Sea Witch* in peace.

Moving away from the railing, Alys strode to Ben. He stood still as she unlocked his manacles. He didn't react when his bindings clattered to the deck.

"I've never . . ." His eyes were wide.

"First time you've killed anyone."

He nodded.

"I wish it didn't get easier," she said.

CHAPTER TWENTY-FIVE

The seawater in the basin changed from clear to pink and then to a rusty red as Ben bathed in Alys's quarters. He emptied the basin out the window twice and refilled it with water. He'd stained three cloths, but he couldn't consign them to the ocean. They were heaped beside the bulkhead, to be taken away later. Whoever did the laundry aboard the *Sea Witch* was surely familiar with getting blood out of fabric.

Ben stared down at his now clean skin. Though his markings now stood out in bold relief, the last traces of the Redthorn's blood were gone.

Not so. His clothing bore permanent traces of what he'd done. An oxidized pattern heralding a decision he could not, would not, undo.

Alys had disappeared after their brief encounter on the top deck. His gaze kept straying to the door.

Without the manacles weighing down his movements, he pulled on his breeches. God, fresh clothing would be incredibly welcome. But what would those garments be? The ensemble he wore as a naval navigator? Or something else?

He turned his wrists this way and that. Red chafed skin glowered at him. He might always bear the reminder on his flesh of the time he'd been held prisoner aboard the *Sea Witch*. He wasn't held captive any longer. His sword through the monk's

THE SEA WITCH

303

chest and throat was the closing of a door. On one side of the doorway was his life in the Royal Navy. On the other side . . . he didn't know.

Alys strode into her quarters.

"Shipshape." Like him, she appeared to have bathed, her wet hair spread on her shoulders. She wore a linen shirt and laced bodice of deep wine-colored twill, along with her favored leather breeches and tall boots. The bodice had the added benefit of lifting her breasts, freckled half-moons rising above the neckline.

He held himself still as she approached him.

When she stood less than a foot away, she asked, "May I touch you?"

"You may."

His chest heaved as she ran her hand over his pectorals, tracing the patterns.

Their gazes locked as she continued to touch his flesh, skin against skin. She drizzled more water down his arms. Her fingers skimmed along the corrugations of his abdomen. His muscles twitched.

"I wanted to see these again." She eyed his markings, and traced the patterns that twisted and wove across his body. "Remind myself of what they looked like."

"I hate them."

She laid her hand against his chest. Her eyes widened, no doubt because his heart pounded against her palm. "I saw them, back there at the monastery."

"My markings?"

"In a book in the Redthorn's library. I'd recognized the language this time. It was the same as the parish register at the church in Domingo."

"Latin." He straightened. "You brought books back with you."

"Not that one." Regret flashed across her face. "Someone took it."

"Who?"

"A powerful mage. Got no fealty to anyone. Only himself." She added, frowning, "I'd heard, once, he had an allegiance, but that's long past."

"Who's this mage?"

"Luca Pasquale. Good fortune to you in finding him. This sea's too vast, and he's as manageable as a hurricane."

Ben swore. "The Redthorn . . . seemed to recognize me. Said something about me being the first. And that's two books now that had illustrations of these things on my skin. There's a riddle written on my flesh."

"We'll find the answer." She said this like a vow, her hand on his chest pressing against him firmly.

We, she had said. Not *you*. *We*.

He covered her hand with his.

"I was going to destroy it. The fail-safe." When her expression didn't change, he said, "My plan was to help you find it."

"And make sure no one could use it." She didn't slide her hand out from beneath his.

"No anger? No recrimination?"

"I didn't keep those manacles on you because I thought they looked pretty." She glanced down at his chafed wrists and clicked her tongue. "Fatima will have a salve for that. Should heal up within a few days, even if the salve stinks like rotten haddock."

He stared at her. "At the least, throw me back in the brig. *I was going to betray you.*"

"Betrayal doesn't look like your cutlass through a Redthorn's chest and throat. And it doesn't sound like you confessing your plan, either. A plan that sounds abandoned."

"It is," he said firmly.

"I can't be angry on account of you trying to carry out your duty. But," she added, pressing her fingers against him as if she

THE SEA WITCH 305

could learn the truth of his heart through touch, "I don't know what your duty is now."

He hauled in a long rough breath. "At the Weeping Princess waterfall, we took that step over the edge, hoping we'd fly to the bottom and not smash against the rocks below. This feels like that."

"You flew, didn't you?"

"It was more of a controlled plummet, but yes. And I did it because . . ." He swallowed. "Because you were with me, and I trusted you."

There were so many colors in her eyes. Moss and amber and the tiniest flecks of summer sky. The whole of the world contained in her irises, and that world was warm, brimming with life.

"Trust your own judgment," she answered. "Trust yourself."

A knock sounded on the door.

"Got the things you wanted, Cap'n," someone in the passageway said.

Alys stepped back, her hand sliding out from beneath his. To the door, she called, "Bring them in."

Ben moved to slip on his grimy shirt.

"No need for that," Alys said to him as Jane and a crew member named Cecily marched into her quarters, their arms laden with garments. To the crew, Alys instructed, "Put them on my berth."

Only Cecily glanced in his direction, her gaze skimming quickly over his bare but marked torso, before she turned her attention back to laying out each article of clothing. They appeared to be very ornate clothes, with gold braid, shiny buttons, and brocade fabric.

"Here's everything we could find, Cap'n," Cecily said with a deferential nod. "Something's got to work amongst all this."

"We'll find what we need," Alys answered. When she looked toward the door, the crew took this as a clear sign of dismissal, and they filed out, carefully shutting the door behind them.

306   EVA LEIGH

Ben moved toward her berth to examine the clothes. "These are men's garments."

"What we're searching for is at Lethal Lambert's table. His estate is . . . wild."

"How wild?"

"When he's throwing one of his parties, orgies have been known to break out. Yet Lambert likes everyone to be clean. The blueblood in him."

"We've both bathed," Ben noted.

"Tomorrow afternoon, we reach Lambert's island," she explained. "I suppose you'd call it an enclave for pirates. He's a man who values prosperity, or at least *looking* prosperous. To take a seat at his table, you've got to look like you're thriving."

"Wait . . ." Ben held up a hand. "Orgies?"

"It *can* turn into one."

"So, you've . . ."

A corner of her mouth turned up wryly. "It's a careful line I walk, as a witch and a female pirate. Having others watch me fuck wouldn't do my reputation any favors."

Ben exhaled and the knot in his gut unraveled. They weren't virgins, either of them. Yet at the mental image of her eagerly participating in a public bacchanal, his jaw turned to iron.

"Lambert might be having a party, he might not, but he always likes a festive mood," she continued. "With you beside me at the pirate refuge, the right rigging is needed."

Forcing his jaw to unclench, Ben picked through the assortment of coats, waistcoats, shirts, neckcloths, and breeches. They all were of excellent quality, and came in every hue and fabric. Amongst the coats, there was a vivid emerald green with golden braid, a deep aquatic blue trimmed in peach ribbon, and a rich claret adorned with black soutache, like calligraphy written upon the silk.

Something she had said snared his attention. "A pirate refuge. Then I'm to pose as . . ."

THE SEA WITCH   307

She slanted a look at him. "Lambert's quite particular about who he lets feast with him. Only the Brethren of the Coast."

"This choice is dizzying." He examined the array of coats on her berth. They were far more elaborate and ornate than anything he'd ever worn.

"One of them must call to you," she answered carefully. "When you played pirate, how'd you see yourself?"

His heart kicked within his ribs, and he rubbed at his chest.

"This one." He stroked his fingers along the cuff of the claret coat, with its dark braid scrolling in mysterious patterns.

"Bold, sensuous," she said with approval. "Daring, with substance."

She searched through the waistcoats and grabbed one that was black with silver embroidery, which she handed to him.

"A good pairing," he said. "Unexpected."

"But they work well together, despite the odds." She stroked a finger down the lapel of the coat. "Give them a try."

He took one of the clean shirts and pulled it on. Then he donned the waistcoat, followed by the coat.

"I take it they fit well," he said dryly, seeing the smile bloom across her lips.

She opened a trunk and pulled out a large flat object wrapped in a silk blanket. Unwrapping the blanket, she revealed a mirror of decent size, framed in carved and gilded wood. She held it up for him.

He started at his reflection, the first time he'd seen himself in a long, long while. His beard was thick and dark, his hair loose, and in these small details, he was no longer a warrant officer in the Royal Navy. No longer neat, trim, tidy, but wilder, closer to the living pulse of the sea than ever before. His eyes held knowledge of things that the other Benjamin Priestley did not possess.

"They suit you."

Her admiring words broke his stunned reverie.

He stepped back to see more of the ensemble. It was all he could do to keep from turning and preening at the reflection of a dangerous, daring man looking back at him. But then . . . fuck it.

He turned. He preened.

"You look a fearsome, dashing pirate," she added, eyes bright.

"I do." He loved the way the fuller skirt of the coat flared when he moved. It was dramatic and dashing, as she'd said. And the coat itself clung to his shoulders, just as the waistcoat hugged his torso. The embroidery glinted and gleamed like a blade. Everything fit exquisitely. It was as if all the garments had been made specifically for him.

He stopped in the middle of his posing. "I cannot fathom why a ship entirely crewed by women has an assortment of men's clothing at the ready, clothing that's too big for any of them to wear. You must have taken them from captured ships."

"Not quite." Twin stains of pink rode high on her cheeks, yet she didn't glance away. "They were left behind. By guests."

"Guests."

"*My* guests. I send them packing soon after their usefulness is over. Items are forgotten in my haste to get them down the gangplank."

He stared down at the garments. "Which *useful* person did this coat belong to?"

"Don't remember." Still, she returned his regard boldly, without apology.

He looked into the mirror again. "Whoever owned these clothes before, they likely didn't wear them half as well as I do."

"There's something else you need." She set down the mirror, and then unlocked a cabinet. From it, she pulled out a finely tooled leather baldric, which she handed to him.

She grabbed a cutlass from the cabinet, with an ornate bell guard.

"A gift from a Spaniard?" he asked.

THE SEA WITCH 309

"Taken from a galleon with too many guns but not enough brains." After taking a deep breath, Alys held the baldric and cutlass out to Ben.

His hands remained at his sides.

"You'll need this," she said. "At the enclave."

"You're arming me."

"If you set foot inside Lambert's without a weapon," she said flatly, "you may as well bid a fond farewell to your life."

Slowly, he reached out and took the items. They made satisfying weights in his hands. He unsheathed the sword, revealing intricate etching along its curved blade, and gave it an experimental cut through the air.

"You wield that blade well," she said.

"During combat, sailing masters are stationed on the quarterdeck. We don't fight. Too valuable to risk. But I practiced every day."

"Thirsting for action?" she asked.

"Perhaps it's better in theory than practice." Heaviness settled in his chest. Only a few hours had passed since he'd first ended someone's life.

"The only blade I'd picked up was the one I used to gut mackerel and bass. Turning pirate, you've got to be skilled with a sword. I thought I'd hate it but . . ."

"You do it so well."

She didn't say anything, but pride radiated from her like sunlight.

He sheathed the cutlass and buckled on the baldric. The missing part of himself slid into place.

He gave her a simple nod of thanks. She returned the nod.

"Let's hope you won't have cause to use it," she said.

"I—" He straightened. "Dupont or Sanchez or Best might be at Lambert's refuge."

"Ben." She stood in front of him. "Tread carefully at Lambert's. Ask too many questions of the wrong people—"

310   EVA LEIGH

He dragged in a breath. "And risk our mission."

"And risk *yourself*," she corrected. "A misplaced word or hint to a hotheaded buccaneer means you'll quickly join your father in the afterlife."

"If you're looking for my promise that I won't seek answers," he said, "I can't give you one. I owe justice more than that."

"You owe yourself more than a quick death from a buccaneer's blade. I should leave you on the ship."

"I'll swim to shore." He stared levelly at her. "There's no choice in the matter."

She held his gaze until, at last, she gave a short nod. "Do what you've got to, but for the love of the sea, take care. Be cautious."

"I'm always cautious." Except when it came to anything related to her.

He strode to the door, but when he reached it, she said, "More swaggering."

"More what?" He turned back to her.

She waved toward his lower body. "You walk like a naval officer. Like the admiralty's rammed up your arse. Trying to get from one end of your chart to the other with the most economy. Pirates, well, we're not so direct. It's the journey, not the destination. Wreaking havoc along the way."

"All of that in simply the way I walk."

"All of that. Where's the cocksure arrogance? *You*'re in command of the seas. No one can kill you, and everyone wants to fuck you, even if they hate you."

"It's only walking."

She moved to stand in front of him. Her expression was unexpectedly focused, thoughtful.

"When I first came to the Caribbean," she said intently, "I was terrified."

"I can't imagine you terrified of anything."

"A year ago, everything here was new to me. Never captained a ship before. To be responsible for a crew of this size . . .

THE SEA WITCH

Josephine thought I didn't like her cooking, I hardly ate a bite of it. Piracy was something we had to learn for ourselves. No one would show us the way."

She continued, "I hadn't raided a ship, or knew what it was to be a pirate. I only knew that going back to Norham wasn't possible. I would've been hanged, true, but also, I couldn't be the person they wanted me to be. Walking behind my husband. Silent until spoken to. Dutiful and useful and obedient to *their* wishes."

Her gaze turned introspective. "Here, in these waters, I could remake myself in the image of who *I* wanted to be. But," she added, "that didn't mean I knew exactly *how* to do that."

"That's why you were afraid."

"For myself, and the safety and success of the women relying upon me. By the stars, I was so damned frightened when I led my first raid. For all that, nothing scared me more than the first time I walked into a pirate tavern, buccaneers on every side of me. These men, they didn't honor any law. But even with them, I was an outsider."

"A female pirate is a rarity." He held himself still, as if any motion or stray gesture might tear open the cocoon of trust that surrounded them.

"What do you think the odds are of meeting a pirate who's also a witch?" she asked.

"I wouldn't take that wager."

"Every step into that tavern was a risk. If they found out how green I was, how unsure, they would've killed me."

"You're alive today, speaking with me now," he observed. "You survived that gauntlet."

"By telling myself I deserved to be there. That all the things, all the people, I wanted to be was in me. I had let them surface. I told myself that I was Captain Alys Fucking Tanner, and no one could stop me, not my dead husband, not the men of Norham, not the Royal Navy, and not the pirates who sailed these seas. I told myself all that, and *this* is how I walked into that tavern."

She strode from one end of her quarters to the other. There was a loose, rolling motion in her hips, enthralling in its rhythm and movement. It was both dangerous and alluring, utterly confident. She cleaved the world apart.

"There's a gate in yourself," she said. "Open it. You once played pirate, but now you can *be* a pirate. Be *yourself*. As wild and unruly as you want."

When he hesitated, she said, more softly, "You're safe with me."

He breathed in deeply. With his family, he'd been a dutiful son, following his father to a life in the navy. He'd inhabited his identity as sailing master, putting on armor and a mask every moment that he was on board.

Alys . . . she saw beneath all of this to the man beneath. And she hadn't turned away, wasn't disgusted or horrified.

Brashness and courage and all the things he never let himself feel coursed into his limbs and filled his heart.

He strode from one side of the cabin to the other. Each step gave him more and more power.

"A beautiful thing to see," she said, pride in her eyes.

Ben stalked to her. Wrapping his arm around her waist, he pulled her to him.

He kissed her. Deep and hard and thorough, devouring her, claiming her. Whoever owned the coat he currently wore, they didn't matter. Because *Ben* was here with her now.

He nipped at her bottom lip. Her hands came up, sliding along his chest, to weave her fingers behind his neck.

Ben released her. Her eyes opened, and her gaze was drugged and unfocused.

With one final look, he swaggered out the door. Danger lay ahead. He might survive it. He might not. Yet with her beside him, he could face anything.

CHAPTER TWENTY-SIX

"Y OU AND I met in Tortuga," Alys explained to Ben as he rowed them toward the dock at Lambert's island estate. "Well, off the coast of Tortuga, when we both attacked the same Spanish merchantman, bearing gold and jewels bound for Barcelona. We argued over who'd take the prize, but in the end, you yielded to my superior skills as a pirate, and the *Sea Witch* took the majority of loot. And I took you to my berth."

She spoke quickly, her gaze fixed on the approaching dock. The *Sea Witch* had anchored some distance from the shore, and it was left to Ben and Alys to row themselves in. Numerous other ships were anchored just out of firing range, including sloops and schooners favored by pirates who relied upon their sleek lines and shallow hulls to sail quickly and take refuge in precarious coastal shoals.

Ben gripped the jolly boat's oars. Pirate vessels loomed on every side. He spotted Diego Sanchez's ship, as well as Louis Dupont's. They were here. One of them might have murdered his father.

But Ben was a killer now, too.

Like him, Alys was all edgy energy, one hand on the grip of her cutlass, the other clenching and unclenching in her lap. Unease almost visibly emanated from her. For all her restlessness, she looked every inch the pirate queen. Her coat was black brocade adorned with bright brass buttons and scarlet braid. Beneath this, she wore a crimson waistcoat topped with jet trim, and a wide leather belt encircled her waist, capped with a large buckle. Her polished black boots rose up over her buckskin covered thighs, and she wore her auburn hair loose. A red plume fluttered atop her tricorn, announcing to everyone that she would not be content to hide in the background.

If someone had asked him a month ago that he might ever find a pirate attractive, he would have sent them immediately to a surgeon to be bled and have their humors balanced. Now . . . looking at Alys in all her piratical regalia . . . there was no one like her.

For all the power she exuded, he couldn't disregard her uneasiness.

"My memory is excellent." He oared them closer to the dock. "We've reviewed the tale of how we *met* three times already."

"Can't leave important details to chance."

"You fear Lambert won't welcome you to his refuge."

"Women like me, we aren't accepted at his enclave. Not really." She scowled. "Like most men, Lambert's afraid. Wary of witches, suspicious when it comes to women aboard a ship in anything other than a recreational capacity. It's the same when it comes to his refuge."

"How many times have you been here?"

"This'll be my third."

"You survived then, and you will again. But there's a difference this time. *I'm* with you." He started. "It's *me* that's got you in a state. You're worried about me."

"I'm not in a state," she fired back. Then, surly, "I'm *slightly* concerned."

"Should I be pleased or insulted?"

"Don't bother with it," she said through clenched teeth.

"I can handle myself. Already, I can walk like a pirate."

THE SEA WITCH

315

Her tight mask gave way, and her eyes gleamed with trepidation. "There's a difference between walking like a buccaneer and being amongst them. Ben," she said, her gaze holding his, "other than the servants, and hired company, the only people at the enclave are pirates. Not that long ago, every buccaneer was your enemy."

His jaw hardened. "I meant what I said aboard the *Sea Witch*. I'm not so thirsty for pirates' blood that I'll put us in danger."

"These men love brawling and fighting," she pointed out. "Doesn't take much to get them going."

"I won't challenge anyone to a damned duel, if that's what's unsettling you."

"Ben." Her gaze held his. "If you're hurt . . . if something happens to you . . ." She cleared her throat, and glanced away. "I don't want to have to drag your corpse back to the jolly boat."

At her gruff words, he gave her a reassuring nod. "When you row back to the *Sea Witch*, I'll be right there beside you, alive. That's my vow."

She exhaled and offered him a wry smile. "I should know better. The man who chased me onto my ship, climbed the mainmast of my ship while in irons, scaled a waterfall, and killed an unkillable Redthorn—a man like that, well, he won't go down easily."

He glanced over his shoulder and tipped his head toward the approaching dock.

"We've a contingent waiting to greet us," he noted. "Three people, armed with pistols and blades."

"Lambert's majordomo, Janssens. The other two are part of the group who keep order on the estate. *Order*'s a relative term."

Turning back to his task of manning the oars, Ben rowed the jolly boat to the dock. Dozens of other jolly boats and cutters were tied to the dock, final proof of how many other people were at the enclave. He tossed a line to one of the guards, who tied them to a cleat with quick practiced movements.

"Captain Tanner," said a man with ruddy cheeks and a long full wig. His accent marked him as from the Lowlands of Europe. "An unexpected surprise."

"Surprises are always unexpected, Mr. Janssens." Alys stood and planted her hands on her hips. "That's what makes them surprising."

"Arriving with a guest." Janssens eyed Ben. "We have not had the pleasure of meeting you, er . . ."

"Prowse." Ben climbed onto the pier and helped Alys up. "Bloody Ben Prowse."

He tried to imbue perfect ease and confidence in his voice, making certain to look at Janssens as if he expected to be given his due.

"The Terror of Madagascar," Alys added. She looked at Ben with pride, and patted her hand on his chest. "Bloody Ben and I have been sharing a berth for months now."

"Well . . ." The majordomo looked uncertain. "If you are willing to vouch for him, Captain Tanner . . ."

"I wouldn't have him in my berth if I didn't trust him," she snapped. "And I wouldn't bring him here if I feared betrayal."

"As you please, Captain Tanner," Janssens replied with the smooth cadence of one well used to pirates and their quick tempers. He waved toward a path that wended through a grove of copperwood trees. "I believe you know the way."

Alys tossed him a doubloon before sauntering down the pier, toward the house. As Ben strode past the majordomo and the two scowling guards, he gave them all a jaunty salute, before hurrying to catch up with Alys's long easy strides. Even here, simply walking away from the pier, she imbued her gait with self-assurance. Regardless of any uncertainty she struggled with in her heart, the confident pirate captain was a role she inhabited well.

"That went well," Ben said as they continued on the path.

"The first obstacle." Her gaze was fixed ahead. "More await."

THE SEA WITCH

317

They emerged from the copperwood trees onto a broad . . .
Lawn was too lofty a term for it. Once it might have been a
neatly tended and trimmed terrace. Now, it was overgrown
with all manner of plants, both native and imported, including fever grass, sea marigold, and paradise plum shrubs. They
formed a sprawling expanse leading to an enormous manor
house. The structure itself was built in the colonial style, with
tall columns supporting a portico at the front, two stories
boasting lofty windows protected by shutters, and a sharply
pitched roof. Like the lawn, the house itself had likely seen
more well-tended days, as vines grew wildly up the sides, and
large patches of paint had stripped away from the exterior
walls like peeling skin. Several shutters hung askew, and a few
of the windows were broken.

People lolled on the front veranda, and draped themselves
on the steps leading to the front door. Most of them appeared
unconscious—or dead. Bottles were strewn around them. One
of the loungers stirred and sat up. He shouted something unin-
telligible as he pointed at Alys and Ben.

"We caught Lambert throwing one of his bashes. This one's
a real ripper, too. Look lively, Bloody Ben," she said under her
breath and winked at him.

Taking in a deep breath, he took Alys's hand in his.

He kept his pace deliberately loose and long-limbed as he
swaggered toward the manor. As they approached, music lurched
out of the open front door, a cacophony of fiddles, drums, and
woodwinds.

Bleary-eyed revelers watched as he and Alys climbed the
steps. The pirate who had pointed at them had used up his remaining sobriety and now observed Ben through half-slitted
eyes as he lay, spread-eagle, on the stairs.

A middle-aged man in a gold brocade coat came out of
the manor. A woman hung on each of his arms. One of them
petted the fringe of light brown hair that ringed his head.

He possessed the mealy features that came from aristocratic breeding. His nose was red with broken capillaries, but his eyes were sharp as he took in Alys and Ben coming toward him. He walked as though, at one point in his life, he'd had a dancing master.

"Tanner," he said neutrally.

"Lambert," she answered. "We're in need of your famed hospitality. We came at the right time, too. Even your legendary parties can't compare to this one."

"Word about what happened to Fontaine has been spreading across the Caribbean." Lambert's words were smooth and cultured, clearly the product of a public school education back in England. "A fate that might await every pirate. If our time on this Earth is short, then by God, we'll end our days in a blaze of revelry."

"And what a revelry it is," Alys agreed.

"Kept yourself busy." Lambert eyed Ben and their linked hands.

"New friend."

"Bloody Ben Prowse," Ben replied. Did pirates shake hands? Unlikely, so instead he gave Lambert a sly smirk.

"The Terror of Madagascar," Alys added helpfully.

"I've never heard of you," Lambert fired back.

"Only been in the Caribbean for a month," Ben answered, "but a hell of a month it's been." He grinned at Alys, and she grinned back, making clear for Lambert's benefit what they'd been doing for four weeks.

"Fucking and fighting, eh?" Lambert snorted. "The Caribbean's been ablaze with word of you and what you've been up to. Stealing Kinnear's women for sale, wiping out his whole operation. There was nothing but smoke and bones remaining after you quitted the place."

Alys shrugged. "Kinnear had what I wanted, and I don't ask for what I want when taking's much swifter."

THE SEA WITCH

319

"Like that naval ship? The *Ajax*? Just snatched it away from His Majesty without a by-your-leave. What I can't make sense of, though, was why the crew was spared."

"Who'd tell the tale if I killed everyone?"

Lambert abruptly turned to Ben. "Who did you sail with in Madagascar, Prowse?"

Ben rifled through his mental catalogue of the pirates sailing off the eastern shore of Africa. "Captain Mission. And Baldridge. Then I captained my own ship before growing weary of that sea. Plenty of opportunity in the Caribbean. And fair wenches." He smirked at Alys.

She gave him a rude hand gesture.

"One man aboard the *Sea Witch*." Lambert looked dubious. "A change from the usual policy."

"There's plenty of cock in these waters," Alys answered. "But finding cock of quality, why, that's another matter."

Ben made himself grin, even though it wasn't often that he had his cock discussed so freely. Come to think of it, no one *ever* talked about his cock in public.

"Charming talker that you are, Lambert," Alys said breezily, "you're an even finer host. The best part's inside. It's roasting today and I've got a powerful thirst. Besides," she added with a cajoling smile, "I've boasted to Bloody Ben here all about your hospitality. He should sample it, don't you agree?"

Ben held his breath as Lambert scratched his chin in contemplation, clearly in debate.

"None of your infernal witchy magicking while you're under my roof," Lambert said pointedly.

Alys peered past him, through the open door, and into the house. "Braga and Moreau are inside. You give them the same dictate?"

"Mages' magic is different from witches' magic," came the retort. "Purer. Educated."

Alys rolled her eyes, before saying, "As you like, Lambert."

320 EVA LEIGH

"I'll keep her in line," Ben said, and received a discreet elbow jabbed into his side.

"I'm smelling the fine work of your kitchen." Alys sniffed at the air. "We lost our cook on the last raid, and I'm panting for decent grub."

"Go on, then," Lambert grumbled, waving them inside. "Most of the bed chambers are taken but any unoccupied one is yours."

"There, you see." Alys grinned up at Ben. "The finest host in these or any waters."

Ben clapped Lambert on his shoulder. "She told the truth about you, Lambert. My vow to you is that I'll not drain your cellars. Well," he amended, moving past their host, "I won't drink *all* of your wine."

"Wily bastard." Alys laughed. "You said nothing about his rum."

Lambert scowled, but there was no heat in it. "Inside, you two."

Still holding Alys's hand, Ben stepped over the threshold and into madness.

There might have been a time when Lambert's manor house served as a model of dignity and colonial grandeur. That time was long past.

In this last-ditch attempt at carousing, people were everywhere, hanging off the landing, brawling in the foyer, dancing in the salon. Paintings on the walls had been defaced with every known substance and several unknown substances. Some wag had drawn horns on distinguished patriarchs and eyepatches on blushing ladies. Tables listed and chairs lacked backs and seats. Tapestries hung in tatters like the ghosts of horrified ancestors.

Music and voices mixed into a discordant combination that, after the relative quiet of life at sea, rattled inside Ben's head in shards of broken pottery.

THE SEA WITCH

Pirates surrounded him. They were literally everywhere, men who obeyed no laws but the ones they made—and bent—for themselves. In this place, with their world on the verge of ending, too, they indulged in every lawless, self-indulgent impulse. They drank, fought, danced, ate, and, in a few corners, fucked. It was unimpeded profligacy.

A dark and edged heat burned in his throat and behind his eyes.

God, it would be so much simpler if he could merely hate them, as he used to.

And yet . . . a filament of envy knotted in his chest. They were so free. Yet their freedom had a cost that others had to bear.

But to taste that liberty for himself . . .

He'd denied himself for so long. And for who? For what? A navy that was complicit in countless crimes? Or the need for vengeance?

His head spun.

Alys pressed a tankard into his hand. "Drink this."

He eyed the contents, then took a sniff. It held the malty tang of ale. He drank.

Fortunately, it *was* ale, its flavor and mildly alcoholic sharpness grounding him in the midst of complete anarchy.

"It's a hell of a talent you have," he said. "To know what I need. Even when I don't."

"You looked on the verge of setting this house on fire."

They'd moved through chambers and corridors, emerging in a massive hall that was two stories tall. A huge staircase stood in the middle of the chamber, reaching up to the second floor. A catwalk ran the perimeter of the second floor, and people hung off the railing, shouting down to the revelers below. One gargantuan long table ran the length of the room, laden with plates and goblets and countless platters of food. Roast meats, pies in hot water crust pastry, fruit from every corner of the Caribbean.

322   EVA LEIGH

Anything a gluttonous pirate could desire was provided by a
steady stream of weary-looking servants who marched out from
a doorway that likely led to the kitchens.

"This is . . . a considerable amount to absorb," Ben admitted
to Alys.

Revelers danced at one end of the chamber, but nearly two
dozen people were splayed in tall-backed wooden chairs set up
along both sides of the table. Women perched on pirates' laps,
and half of the buccaneers had their boots propped up on the
table as they ate with their hands.

Mixed amongst the crowd were mages, distinguished from
the pirates by the embroidered black sashes wrapped around
their waists, just as naval mages wore the same sashes. Some
drank and ate with the same abandon as the buccaneers. Others practiced fashioning illusions of light and shadow for the
crowd's amusement, creating scenes of seafaring battle or fairies
cavorting lewdly as the throng cheered and clapped.

"*I'm* overwhelmed," Alys confessed. "Not a woman amongst
this crowd who isn't part of the hospitality. I belong here as
much as a pearl earring belongs on a boar."

As she and Ben walked, stares followed them. Some were
curious, but a goodly amount blazed with hostility. Yet Alys
wasn't the only one of their pair that attracted attention. Suspicious glares were aimed at Ben.

"I seen you before." A pirate with a long braided beard staggered forward, blocking Ben's path. He narrowed his eyes.
"The Wig 'n' Merkin."

"What pirate *doesn't* go to the Wig and Merkin, Smythe?"
Alys rolled her eyes.

A quick chill of panic danced down Ben's back. He'd been
with the navy at the tavern on St. Gertrude, raiding the gathering
as they'd assembled to pay tribute to Little George Partridge. If
any of these buccaneers recognized Ben as a member of the navy,
he'd be flayed and roasted and served as the next course.

THE SEA WITCH 323

"A favorite haunt of mine," he answered with bravado. "Good rum, better wenches."

Smythe didn't smile. He continued to study Ben through red-rimmed eyes. "Wasn't that long ago."

"At Little George's wake," Ben replied.

"His letters," Smythe said, shifting his attention to Alys. "Everyone's talking about 'em. He was an underhanded bastard. Workin' with the navy. And there was that thing, that fail-safe. God, the screams from Fontaine's crew . . . That could happen to any of us now." He took a steadying drink.

"Nobody's safe," Alys said.

"Not without that fail-safe," Smythe shot back. "Van der Meer was sure you knew where to find it."

"Van der Meer sells horseshit by the ton, Smythe" Alys answered.

Smythe seemed to accept this, but his wary watery gaze turned back to Ben.

"You were there? When the letters were read?"

"We were having ourselves a fine celebration," Ben said, "until the navy showed up and spilled my drink in my lap."

"Damn navy," Smythe muttered. "Always spoiling a good time."

"We left together," Alys added, giving Ben's chest a playful nudge with her shoulder. "Through a window. I imagined we'd both wake up with broken necks."

"Our necks are still sound, love," Ben said with a wink, "even if the navy wants to stretch them."

"Or have their leviathan swallow you," Smythe added sourly. He looked at Ben with suspicion.

"You're blocking the grub, Smythe." Alys moved to shove the pirate aside.

Before she could, a man with rings in his ears and a knee-length embroidered tunic pushed Smythe away.

"Be off with you, maggot." The man spoke with an Arabic accent. "No one has the stomach to be downwind of your breath."

Smythe started to argue, then glanced at the jeweled and curved scimitar at the newcomer's waist, before staggering off.

Alys tipped her chin in thanks. "Always a timely appearance, Karim."

"In a mansion full of tedious people," the corsair said with a sigh. "Smythe reigns supreme as the most tiresome."

"And yet, you keep returning to Lambert's."

Karim's smile flashed. "I remain optimistic that someone worthwhile will appear, and lo," he added, gesturing at Alys and Ben, "my hopes have been fulfilled." He bowed to Ben. "Karim Samali, your servant."

"Ben Prowse." He bowed in return.

"Most of the people here have a weeklong advantage over you, as far as debauchery is concerned."

"Including you?" Ben asked.

Karim pressed a hand to his chest. "In this, I am deficient. I only arrived three days ago, and so my debauchery is somewhat lacking." He waved away a servant offering cups of wine.

"Have faith, Karim," Alys said with a smirk. "You'll catch up."

The corsair bowed before sauntering away toward a beckoning dancer.

Once Karim had gone, Ben permitted himself a small exhalation. Lambert's refuge was a pit lined with knives. One misstep and Ben and Alys would be sliced to bloody chunks.

"Now," Ben murmured to Alys as they watched the depravity unfolding, "we've merely to find the answer to Little George's clue. And survive the night. Not certain which is more difficult."

"When it comes to piracy and magic, everything's a voyage through a hurricane. But," she added with a grin, "that's what makes it fun."

CHAPTER TWENTY-SEVEN

A LYS WAS TORN.

Torn between hunting down whatever it was that Little George had hidden here in Lambert's refuge . . . and pulling Ben into a corner to kiss him.

He'd been coming slowly undone over the course of the last few weeks. A lost button here. A scruff of beard there. Little by little, he'd changed from a naval officer into someone wilder. He was freer, too, a scoundrel, all bravado and boldness.

Now, to see him clad in the clothes of a pirate, ornate coat and tall boots and loose hair, watching him strut and swagger around Lambert's estate as if he owned the place, well . . . She almost fanned herself.

Suspicious looks were aimed in Ben's direction, but they gave way to admiration and, in several cases, pure lust.

Who could blame someone for desiring Ben? He was in every way delicious. Like a knife coated in honey. You wanted a lick, and it didn't matter if you cut yourself in the process.

Yet she was the captain, damn it. The responsible one.

"Magic's going to surround whatever Little George has hidden here," she said for Ben's ears alone. "I'll call to it, using my own power."

"Lambert seemed disinclined to any displays of your magic,"

EVA LEIGH

Ben answered lowly. "And mages surround us. Surely, they'll know if supernatural power is afoot."

"Hard as it may be to believe," she answered with a smirk, "I *can* be subtle when I have to."

"No one else here is subtle," he added when a tankard flew past his head. Ben snatched it from the air, and then held it out for a passing servant to fill with ale.

Alys slipped behind one of the large potted palms that dotted the edge of the chamber. Ben stood in front of her, sipping from his tankard as he watched the room.

Alys closed her eyes to block out any distraction from the wild feast. She searched out the blazing spark of magic within herself. It always burned, and now she encouraged its flame to rise higher. Once it gleamed more brightly inside her, she urged it to locate all other sources of magic that dwelled on Lambert's estate.

At once, her magic quivered with awareness, finding each of the mages carousing both within the manor house and elsewhere on the grounds. It was a sprawling estate, abounding with frolicking mages such as Braga and Moreau. She had to play a careful game, locating the mages without alerting their supernatural senses to her own magic, but she let her power dance as lightly and loosely as a spark on the breeze.

She exhaled when none of the magic users became aware of her. That, at least, she could manage.

But what of the fail-safe? Or was something else here that would lead her and Ben on to another step of their quest?

She searched for more of the magic that had encircled both the clue at the Weeping Princess waterfall as well as the magic that lingered in the parish register at Domingo. It shivered and shone, just at the edge of her awareness.

Yet when she reached for it, her senses glanced away, like light reflecting off a mirror, unable to find purchase. Again and again, it happened. She grasped it, but then it slipped away. She

THE SEA WITCH

pushed against whatever shielded it from her, only to fall back, repelled.

"Damn and hell." She opened her eyes.

"Not here?" Ben asked.

"It's here. But Little George placed a barrier around it. A strong one." Frustration tightened her voice. "I don't have enough power on my own to break it."

His brow furrowed. "We can bring someone from the *Sea Witch* here, add their magic to yours."

"One witch is the limit for Lambert. Can't ask a mage, either. They'd find out what we're after. But . . . there's another way." She placed her hand on his chest. "You."

A startled laugh escaped him. "Surely you've better sources of magic than my carcass."

"Your markings. There's more to them than either of us truly fathom. I've seen illustrations of them in two magic books. That Redthorn, he recognized the markings when they appeared on your skin."

"Before I killed him." Ben exhaled. "If my markings were in mages' books . . ."

"They've got to be magical, somehow." She peered at him when a crease appeared between his brows. "Disgusted?"

"Confused . . ." He shook his head. "It's as though I've heard other people sing but never carried a single note. And then suddenly, I'm on stage at the opera. But I don't know the song."

"Magic can be a gift," she said softly. "If you let it. I'd be half the person I am without my magic."

"Even if you were stripped of your magical ability, you would still be extraordinary."

She'd been in the midst of a pirate feast before, and had seen every kind of outrageous behavior, shamelessness and immorality in abundance. There wasn't a single human act she hadn't witnessed and grown jaded to.

For all that, her cheeks heated.

"We've got to bring forward whatever magic you possess," she pressed on. "And that happens . . ."

"When you and I are . . . close."

"Our kiss at the waterfall," she said. "And in that room at the inn in Domingo."

"And when the Redthorn threatened you." He scowled. "I don't want anyone here endangering you."

"There's a much better way to get your magic going." She looped her arms around his neck and pressed her body to his. At once, he tossed the tankard aside and his hands clasped her waist as his eyes darkened. "Objections, Bloody Ben?"

"None at all." His voice had gone rough. He backed her against the wall, and one of his hands cradled her jaw. Her pulse was urgent beneath his touch.

She lifted onto her toes, straining into him with her hands on his shoulders. His lips found hers.

They didn't waste time with beginnings. Their mouths opened at once to each other. She met his tongue with her own, twining against him.

She forgot everything but the feel of Ben and riding the waves of desire that rose and crested and crashed.

A bottle smashed near them.

They broke apart with a gasp. He still held her, and she continued to cling to him. Their panting breaths intermingled in the narrow space between them.

Her fingers traced the dark markings now climbing up his throat and twisting across his chest, revealed by the open neck of his shirt.

"Glad my theory's correct," she breathed.

"That voice in me, the notes yet to be sung," he said, low and urgent. "They're searching for a way out."

She wove her fingers into his hair. "The spark of your magic. I sense it, too."

THE SEA WITCH

"It's . . . strange," he said slowly. "Different." At her nod, he went on, "Is it enough? Can you use it?"

With her own magic, she reached for his. The power inside him rose up, tentative. Unsteady. She didn't back down, instead stretching toward him with careful patience. Slowly, his magic glowed brighter. Awakening like a creature that had long slumbered at the bottom of the sea and now swam to the surface. Meeting hers, growing more vivid, stronger.

She inhaled sharply. Joining her magic with other witches had always filled her with power and joy, to be part of something greater. Yet this was surging and vital, encircling her and Ben, taking each of their strength and becoming fiercer. She'd been complete in herself, but this lifted her higher. She could touch stars.

"Ben," she gasped. "It's . . ."

"Strange. Wonderful."

She wanted to explore every corner of the sky with him, from Polaris to Pegasus, and swim through the hidden depths of the ocean, to the coral reefs off Cozumel to deep water caves of Bermuda.

Again, Alys felt for magic Little George had left behind, hidden behind a blockade. She summoned the light-gathering of a prism, collecting her and Ben's power, concentrating it and aiming it toward the barrier.

The blockade shuddered and shook. Yet it held.

She focused her and Ben's magic even more, strain pulsing through her body.

Suddenly, she felt the barrier shatter into fragments like tiles liberated from their mosaic.

She moved away from the wall of the large hall, nudging him to follow her. Walking along the edge of the massive noisy chamber, she would stop and start as she searched for the magic's origin.

Ben kept pace beside her as she stepped toward one of the dancers. Gold shimmered on the woman's ankle as she twirled, and Alys went closer. Yet as the dancer spun, Alys moved away, still seeking.

Swirling music pulled on her, and she strode toward a gathering of performers. They banged on drums and sawed at fiddles. A man shook a tambourine.

Yet magic wasn't here, either.

She turned away and faced the long table running the length of the hall. At the very end, a roast was being carved by none other than Lambert himself in a display of flamboyant hospitality. In one hand, he held a fork with long tines. His other hand gripped an ornate gold-plated carving knife. Patterns and words were engraved into its blade, and small holes dotted its surface.

"A golden holy key you seek to open the gates," she whispered to Ben.

"Not *holy*," he answered, understanding dawning in his face. "*Holey*."

"The golden key to the fail-safe—it's a damned carving knife."

BEN WATCHED WITH Alys as Lambert cut into another hunk of roasted meat. Servants carried the slices to waiting guests, and additional staff brought out more platters bearing meat waiting to be carved.

"There's no end to the parade of food requiring Lambert's attention," Alys observed grimly.

"People have to sleep at some point," Ben said.

"Or pass out." She eyed the casks of drink being rolled out to serve thirsty pirates.

"We'll have to outlast them." Ben turned away to feign interest in the music. He grabbed two tankards, handing one to Alys, and they both took distracted sips as they scanned the large chamber.

THE SEA WITCH 331

A cluster of pirates gathered around a dancer. They clapped and called out encouragement as she whirled. The men ranged in age, but judging by their weathered skin, all of them had been on the sea for a long while, and they tipped their chins in silent greeting as Ben and Alys joined them in watching the dancer.

"Tanner." A pirate with thick sideburns gave a wary nod to Alys.

"Blue John," she answered.

When the other pirates looked to Ben, he said, "Bloody Ben Prowse."

A few of the pirates eyed the markings on his neck and chest, still vivid after kissing Alys, but no one commented on them.

"That there be Stagfoot Reeder," Blue John said, gesturing to another buccaneer, who also nodded at Ben. Continuing around the circle, Blue John went on, "He be Fred Fowler. Esteban Jimenez. Louis Dupont."

Careful to keep his expression smooth, Ben took a sip of ale. "The same Dupont that sailed with Captain Tarrier?"

"Don't know Tarrier," the Frenchman replied.

"Shame, that," Ben said with regret. "I would've congratulated you for raiding the HMS *Valiant* with Tarrier."

Speaking the name of his father's ship in the presence of these pirates tasted acrid, so Ben took another drink of ale.

"Not me, confrère." Dupont's gaze remained on the dancer. "Nor Tarrier."

"They talk nothing but respect in Maricaibo and Cartagena of Tarrier," Alys said.

"He engaged the *Valiant*," Ben said, doing his best to sound offhand. "Killed her captain."

Dupont continued to watch the dancer as she kicked and twirled. "Whoever Tarrier is, he didn't battle the *Valiant*. No pirate did."

Coldness crept down Ben's spine.

332   EVA LEIGH

"No way to know that for certain," Alys said.

Dupont snorted. "The captain of the *Valiant*, Priestley, I think was his name? A name that struck fear into every member of the Brethren of the Coast. If any pirate killed him, they would've spread that tale from one end of the sea to the other. No one's said a word of it."

"Perhaps they're afraid," Ben suggested. "That the navy will come after them if Priestley's death was pinned on them."

"Ami," Dupont said, his lips curled, "I don't know about the waters you've sailed, but here in the Caribbean, hiding our kills isn't how things are done. This was, what, five years ago?"

Ben pretended to consider the matter. "April," he said after a moment, and then, "1714, or so I'd heard."

"I was sailing my ship toward the north coast of Jamaica." Dupont scratched his chin in thought. "The *Valiant* was heading there, too. But when my crow's nest spotted the *Jupiter* sailing to the same heading, we turned tail."

"No one sails against the *Jupiter*, and their leviathan," Blue John said darkly. "Not if they want to live. Poor bloody Fontaine."

The other pirates muttered in agreement.

"A ship of hell, the *Jupiter*," Fowler chimed in. "Should've called it the *Pluto*."

"We faced them, after St. Gertrude," Alys said. "They came to aid the *Ajax*, and damn if we didn't barely make it out with bleeding scratches on our souls."

Fowler's lip curled. His fair skin had been roasted by years in the sun, and his blond hair was almost colorless. "I'm talkin' about hell for them that served on it. Once, I was one of 'em."

Ben had never seen Fowler aboard the *Jupiter*, not while he'd been aboard. But then, Fowler possessed the stoop shoulders and sagging flesh of one who'd served the navy for many years.

Alys knocked her tankard against the mug in Fowler's hands. "A twenty-one-gun salute for surviving."

"Ain't no joke, lass." Fowler grunted. "I was an able sea-

THE SEA WITCH   333

man on the *Jupiter*. Was aboard that day, off the north coast of Jamaica."

Ben forced himself to breathe slowly and he let his gaze roam around the chamber, moving from the chandelier to a plate of roast goat to a man throwing knives at a vase.

"Tarrier's going to have to eat his words," Ben said casually.

"Whoever this Tarrier is," Fowler said, "he wasn't nowhere around. It was just the *Valiant* when the *Jupiter* came up alongside. This was afore Strickland became admiral. The Royal Navy was looking for someone to head the Caribbean fleet. Priestley and Strickland, they were both vying for the spot. I was damned surprised that Strickland himself was rowed over."

"Why surprised?" Alys asked.

"Strickland and Priestley were as friendly as two eels in a bag. Hated each other. But when the *Jupiter* and the *Valiant* met, Strickland and Warne went aboard. And when they came back, Strickland, he . . ." Fowler took a drink, but it didn't wash away the disgust twisting his features. "Had blood on 'im."

"Then he sounded an alarm," Alys prompted.

"Did no such thing," Fowler retorted. "He went down to his quarters and the *Jupiter* sailed away."

Ben pushed out a laugh. "An admiral killing a captain."

"Strickland was a commodore then," Fowler threw back.

"But you didn't *see* it," Alys insisted.

"Didn't need to see it to know what happened." Fowler glanced warily around before saying lowly, "'Specially after I heard it was reported the captain of the *Valiant* was killed by pirates."

Blue John, who'd been silent through this, let out a low whistle. "Hell. Navy killing navy."

"Where's the sense in it?" Dupont exclaimed.

"There's sense in it," Fowler insisted. "Strickland, every six months, he used to sail us into a strait between these cliffs. There was a building, big and gloomy, on one of the cliffs. He'd

334   EVA LEIGH

send a cutter out with a dozen seamen on it. Two weeks later, the *Jupiter*'d come back, and collect them."

"Those seamen . . . they must have said what happened," Ben said.

"Silent as the bottom of the sea." Fowler shuddered. "Whatever Strickland was doing, sending those seamen off, the admiralty wouldn't like it. And I'm guessing Priestley, he got wind of it, somehow."

"Priestley was going to tell the admiralty," Alys deduced.

"I knew one day," Fowler continued, "it'd be me on a cutter, sailing to that pile of bricks on the cliff. And when I heard that Strickland said pirates killed Priestley . . ." He scowled. "My next shore leave, I hared off. Signed articles with Flores, and stayed well away from His Majesty's Navy."

Ben barely remembered how to breathe as he dazedly moved away from the group of pirates. The world blurred around him. There was a roaring in his head that had nothing to do with music or human voices. His whole body was stiff and awkward, lumbering around like an automaton that had lost its key, and his shattered thoughts littered the tile floor. Everything was in chaos and nothing made sense.

"Ben. Ben!"

Alys materialized before him. She took one look into his face before grabbing hold of his hand and leading him into a corner. The feel of her skin against his was his only anchor.

When they were in the relative privacy and calm of the corner, she cupped his face with her hands and stared into his eyes. "I'm here."

"Strickland took me aboard his ship," Ben choked out. "Encouraged me to go to London to test for becoming his sailing master. He knew I wanted to find my father's killer. He *knew.* The whole time. And he . . . The fucking bastard *commiserated* with me. Told me he wanted to bring the murderer to justice. But it was him. And Warne."

THE SEA WITCH   335

"We don't know if we can believe Fowler."

"There's no reason for him to lie." Ben dragged his hands through his hair. "What a goddamn *jest* that must have been for Strickland and Warne. How they surely laughed as I tracked buccaneers across the Caribbean, certain one of the pirates was the murderer. But it was Strickland . . . with some kind of pact with the Redthorns. Sending them men for . . . God knows."

"There were tables," Alys said. "At the Redthorns' monastery. With straps to hold men down."

"Jesus Fucking Christ."

The world would collapse. The floor would open and swallow him whole. Any of these things were possible. And yet none of them happened. The feasting and dancing continued around them, oblivious to the fact that Ben's entire existence had crumbled.

He shook his head. As if that tiny gesture could somehow restore everything to rights.

Alys guided Ben to the massive staircase leading to the floor with the bedchambers. Shouts and catcalls followed them as they climbed the stairs, and he threw everyone a grin to keep up the pretense of two pirate revelers about to unleash their carnal impulses in one of the bedchambers. More hoots and yells of encouragement came from the buccaneers still carousing in the main room. He barely heard them.

He placed one foot in front of the other, step after step, holding tightly to Alys's hand. He could not let go. He would not. Once he did . . . there was no telling what would become of him.

They reached the top of the stairs, and were met by a door-lined catwalk running the length of the floor. Where the catwalk reached the farthest wall, it was met by another walkway. Windows above this section revealed the darkness outside.

She turned and guided him past room after room. From behind the closed doors came grunts and cries and the banging of headboards against walls. They peered into an open door. Two people inside the room were energetically fucking. They didn't even notice Ben and Alys.

Alys moved on, and headed to an open door at the farthest end of the walkway. The room was mercifully empty and surprisingly clean and tidy. It held a large bed with four posters and a canopy, a chaise upholstered in wine-colored moiré, as well as a few other pieces of furniture. A square of deep indigo night shone through the window. Golden braid trimmed the canopy. A statue of a faun had lost one arm, and it cast a stubby dancing shadow against the wall. There was a painting showing an English country scene, and someone had drawn a shepherd fucking a dairymaid from behind, clearly not the original artist.

She pulled him into the bedchamber and closed the door, shutting out the sounds of revelry and sex.

Ben threw open the window to let in fresh air, but all that met him was a heavy hot breeze. Alys flicked her fingers, and a weighty chest slid in front of the door to ensure no one came inside. The relative quiet of the room left too much space inside his head for clamorous, agonizing thoughts.

"I'm going to find Strickland. And Warne." He clenched and unclenched his fists. "And kill them both."

She nodded. "My blade will join yours."

"It's not your fight."

"Of course, it's my fight." She stood in front of him. "Someone needs to guard your back."

With rough hands, he scrubbed at his face. "Everything I've known about myself, they're all lies. Fabrications that shored up illusions."

She reached beneath his shirt to press her palm against his bare skin. The feel of her flesh on his dimmed the chaos closing in on him.

"It's a curse, and a gift," she murmured. "The chance to remake ourselves well away from anyone's beliefs of who they want us to be, and what the world demands."

THE SEA WITCH

He stared at her, his only anchor in the midst of a maelstrom.

"When we set sail, it's *our* course to set," she went on softly, intently. "Where we go, it's up to us."

"Not so simple," he said hoarsely.

"I never said it was simple," she answered. "It's risky as hell. That's why few try. But the reward," she added, her mouth curving, "it's bigger than any treasure, any prize we claim."

Pressing his forehead to hers, he breathed in deeply. She carried the scent of night-blooming flowers and the summery, salty fragrance of a life lived upon the sea.

"I want to believe you," he rasped.

"*I* believe me." She pressed her lips lightly to his. "It can hold us both, but there's going to come a time when you won't have need of my belief. You'll know it enough on your own."

"I'll always have need of you," he said urgently.

Something panicked and restless flashed within the hazel of her eyes. He almost took the words back—but they were true, and he couldn't lie. Not to her. She deserved complete honesty and he would give it to her.

"Before now," he said, "no one ever gave me permission to be myself."

"You don't need permission. Not from me or from anyone."

"Yet *you're* the only person who told me I didn't require it. *You* let me exist as who I'm meant to be."

The fear in her eyes faded.

He curved one of his hands around the back of her head. Their gazes held. She didn't look away or back down. She never did. Even when she was afraid, she met her fear.

"Impossible, extraordinary woman," he growled. "I've wanted to throttle you and bed you in equal measure. For so long, I've wanted you. At night, when you're on the other side of your quarters, I lay awake in my hammock, just . . . just aching. For you. You've laid claim to each part of me, and have ever since I tried to rescue you at the tavern in St. Gertrude."

"No one owns anyone," she breathed, "and I don't need rescuing."

"And if *I* need *you*?"

"For tonight," she said, bringing her mouth to his, "you have me."

CHAPTER TWENTY-EIGHT

At first, the kiss was gentle, the soft meeting of her lips to his. Alys wrapped her arms around Ben's shoulders, holding him tightly as they kissed. She gave him tenderness and he took it.

But then they kissed deeply in rough, drugging tastes. One of his hands splayed just above her arse and the other gripped her hip.

"The chaise," she said.

He staggered backward to the chaise, still holding her. He sat down heavily and she went with him. She straddled him as the kiss continued.

"Alys." His voice was a growl. "I want . . . I need . . ." Yet he seemed to hold himself back.

"More," she gasped

"Yes."

After tugging off her boots, she hooked her hands into the lapels of his coat and pulled it down his shoulders. At the same time, he fumbled for the buttons of her waistcoat and cursed in frustration from the countless fastenings. Why the hell had she worn such an elaborate garment?

"These . . . damn . . . buttons," he snarled.

"Tear them off," she panted. "Just do it."

340   EVA LEIGH

He hesitated for a moment. She took his hands and placed them on her waistcoat.

Ben pulled on the two sides of her vest, and buttons flew in every direction.

"I've never done . . . *that* before," he confessed. "Wanted to."

"You want more," she urged. When his gaze dropped to her chest, she took his hands and brought them to her breasts.

She moaned as his hands cupped her breasts through the fine lawn fabric of her shirt.

His thumbs stroked back and forth to tease her nipples into aching points.

"Pinch them," she encouraged.

He did so, lightly, and she arched back with a cry.

She pulled back long enough to strip away her coat and waistcoat. Warm, humid air touched her skin as she whisked off her shirt.

He bent close to her breasts, his mouth hovering over one of her nipples. "Can I?"

"Goddesses, yes."

She cried out when he took the nipple in his mouth, tonguing it. He gave her other breast the same attention, and she pressed his head against her. His mouth was hot and wonderfully greedy as he lapped at her like a forbidden treat.

"Unfair," she gasped. "I'm exposed, and you're as secure as a fortress."

"You're a pirate," he said with a rakish grin. "So plunder me."

Sitting back, she managed to peel off his coat, and his waistcoat, before removing his shirt and throwing it to one side. His upper body bare, she indulged herself, running her hands over his shoulders, down the lengths of his arms, along his chest. His markings stood out boldly against his skin. She ran her tongue along them, tasting the brine of his flesh and basking in the steady stream of curses that flowed from him.

THE SEA WITCH

"The upstanding, dependable naval sailing master," she murmured with approval, "undone at last."

His eyes flashed. "You think you cannot lose control, Captain Tanner?"

"I'd like to see you try to make me, Mr. Priestley."

The world spun and she was on her back, splayed on the chaise, as he loomed over her. His face was taut and his eyes dark.

"Never offer me a challenge, Captain Tanner," he said, his voice rough. "Unless you want to provoke me."

"What'll you do?" she taunted. "*Navigate* me to death?"

His lip curled. "I'll discover your geography, Captain. Without and *within*."

Before she could hurl a retort, his lips were on hers. He braceleted her wrists with one hand. With the other, he tugged off her breeches, stripping her as effectively as a hurricane stripped a tree of its leaves. She was completely bare now, her naked flesh pressed between the silk of the chaise's cushions and his body.

His gaze fell to her lower abdomen. Gently, he touched the coin-sized marking on her belly, a small figure of a bow and arrow. "What's this?"

"A symbol of Artemis," she explained breathlessly. "The Virgin Hunter. A spell painted on with henna. It prevents me from conceiving."

"You cannot—"

"Not so long as Artemis's mark is upon my skin. There's no danger of pregnancy."

His pupils widened. "I can come inside of you."

"I damn well insist upon it."

She pulled her wrists free from his grasp and dug her nails into his shoulders. Their mouths met once more.

He trailed his hand down between her breasts. He paused long enough to toy with her nipples, rousing them into taut points, before gliding down her stomach and going lower. As their kiss lingered and heightened, he sifted through the hair between her legs, then continued on. He stroked the seam of her sex.

She pushed her hips up, desperate for a deeper touch.

"A cartographer must discover every part of the geography, Captain."

"Enough of this survey, Sailing Master," she snarled. "*Touch me.*"

He licked into her mouth. "Is that a command?"

"Ben, *now.*"

She cursed with pleasure when his long finger delved between her lips, and his oath joined hers. "Fuck."

In response, she arched up again. His rough fingertip grazed her clitoris, and when she moaned, he stroked her there again, and again.

"Mark me," she urged, "like an animal marking its mate."

He dragged his mouth from hers. He skimmed his lips along her jaw, and down her throat. She gasped when he bit her neck, just as she wanted.

As he did this, he sank two fingers inside her. His thumb caressed her clitoris in time with the pumps of his hand. She lifted her hips in encouragement and he worked his hand faster, fucking her steadily as he stroked her clitoris. The sharp sting of his teeth on her neck only heightened her pleasure.

The climax struck her. She bowed up with a cry.

Yet he didn't stop. If anything, her release only urged him on, his efforts strengthening as he relentlessly chased her pleasure. He growled when she cried out with another orgasm and another.

Vision hazy, she watched him pull back just enough to slip his fingers from her. He gave his fingers a thorough lick, his eyes heavy-lidded, before painting her nipples with the slick combination of his saliva and her arousal. Then he swept his tongue over her nipples, drawing one and then the other into his mouth, until she whimpered.

THE SEA WITCH 343

"Fuck me, Ben."

"Is that what you want? My cock deep inside of you, filling you up?"

"Yes, by the tides, yes."

His gaze fierce, his hand shaking, he tore open the placket of his breeches. He exhaled when he freed his cock, and Alys licked her lips.

"What a gorgeous cock you have, Mr. Priestley," she breathed.

"It wants you. *I* want you." He fisted his cock. The sight of him with his shaft in his hand brought a rush of renewed wetness in her sex.

"Let me touch it."

"Another time," he panted. "Now, I need inside your . . . your . . ."

"My cunt." Her words were breathless. "You can say it."

"Inside your sweet cunt."

By the stars, his profanity urged her legs to spread wider.

His gaze fastened on her sex as he lined up his cock with her opening. He gripped himself as he stroked his shaft up and down, coating himself in her arousal. Then, with one thrust, he plunged into her. All the way to the hilt.

She couldn't stop the cry that escaped her. He hadn't lied. He truly did fill her up, completely, absolutely. Her body stretched around his thickness.

"I'm hurting you." He started to draw away, but she hooked her ankles behind his back, holding him in place.

"I swear by all the seas," she panted, "that I'll commit murder if you pull out now. A moment. That's all I need. One moment for me to learn what it means to have you truly inside me."

He nodded, the cords on his neck standing out from the strain of holding himself still.

Gradually, her body relaxed. The initial pain faded. Pleasure took its place.

"Kiss me," she commanded eagerly. "Then fuck me."

"Aye, Captain." He took her lips, his mouth ravishing hers. His hips began to move. Patiently, steadily. Each thrust jolted through her body. He saturated her senses as he plunged in and out.

"Harder now," she urged.

His eyes blazed and his hips surged in fast thick thrusts. The chaise shook beneath her.

"Give me your hand," she panted. When he did, she brought it between their bodies, to her clitoris. She commanded, "Stroke it, with each drive of your cock."

A climax overtook her. Exploding through her, hot and gleaming. Yet he hadn't achieved his own release.

"Want to try something," he huffed. At her questioning look, he said, "From behind."

"I order you to do it." Her command was breathless.

He pulled her up off the chaise. She was boneless in the aftermath as he stood and positioned her so that she was draped over the chaise's curved arm. He stood behind her, his hands clasping her hips with enough force to bruise.

She loved it. Loved what she could make this restrained, disciplined man do.

"Hold tight," he rumbled.

She did, gripping the upholstery. He notched his cock to her entrance, and then plunged into her.

"Oh, goddesses," she gasped.

"The gods can't help us now," he said, his voice hoarse.

The chaise buckled beneath her and she clutched it for support, even as she pushed back to meet his thrusts.

She glanced over her shoulder to watch him. His eyes were half closed, his mouth open as he panted with each stroke.

"Come with me, Flame," he urged.

"I can't," she moaned. She'd lost count of how many orgasms she'd already had.

"Let me try."

THE SEA WITCH 345

He released one of the hands gripping her hips, bringing it around between her legs. He caressed her clitoris as he continued to fuck her.

She came again with a long moan.

"Alys," he snarled. "I'm—"

"Inside me, Ben," she commanded. "I want all of it."

His breath gusted over her back as he pressed himself tightly against her, each tremor moving from his body into hers. A smaller softer climax glided through her at the feel of his release.

He pressed his damp face against the nape of her neck, lavishing kisses on her skin. "Beautiful, beautiful Alys. My Flame. I didn't know it could be like this."

She closed her eyes. It was too much. *He* was too much. And the awful thing was that she couldn't wait to do everything again. With him.

Finally, he pulled out, and her body missed him already. Her legs had lost all stability but before they could buckle, he swept her into his arms and carried her to the bed. After tucking her beneath the covers, he stripped off his boots and breeches, then strode to a stand that held a pitcher and basin. Through drowsy eyes, she admired his nude body, covered with his intriguing markings, as he poured water into the basin, dampened a cloth, and then brought it back to the bed.

She purred as he gently, thoroughly cleaned his seed from her, before cleansing himself. He cast the cloth aside as he climbed into bed and gathered her against him. Her hand pressed over his heart, feeling it pound beneath her palm.

Tenderly, he kissed her forehead.

Fear uncoiled in her, a serpent awakening from its slumber.

"Ben," she gulped. "We can't—"

The building around them shook and dust filtered from the ceiling. An inhuman roar pierced the night.

CHAPTER TWENTY-NINE

A LYS LEAPT OUT of bed, and Ben did the same. The furious, outraged animal roaring reverberated in Alys's gut as terror climbed up her back.

She dressed quickly, and strapped on her cutlass. Ben pulled on his clothing, concealing his markings, which still covered his skin. He grabbed his blade. The walls of the manor shuddered so violently that cracks spread through the plasterwork.

After using magic to push the chest out of the way, Alys pulled open the door to reveal pirates in all states of dress crowding in alarm along the catwalk. Chunks of ceiling and wall slammed down onto the tile floor, shattering it and barely missing fleeing buccaneers. Panicked yells joined together in a cacophony as people screamed.

Alys joined Ben on the catwalk. He reached for her hand, and she took it. Together, they wove through the throng. When she stumbled over a pile of rubble, Ben steadied her and helped her to keep moving. They, along with the crowd, headed toward the stairs leading to the ground floor.

A crashing noise made her turn. The manor's outer wall cracked open and split apart, and a pair of huge claws ripped the wall away. The head of a massive creature pushed its muzzle into the manor, right by the room Alys and Ben had just been in.

THE SEA WITCH

"Holy fucking stars," Alys gasped.

The beast was a cross between a feathered bird and a scaled lizard, with a gleaming sharp beak at the end of a long reptilian face. Golden eyes glinted with rage.

A man tried to spring past the creature, but a stone falling from the ceiling knocked him down. The beast snatched the pirate in its beak, then tossed him aside.

Alys froze as the beast turned its yellow eyes to her and Ben.

"It's searching for something," she breathed. "Some*one*."

A man bellowed, "*You*."

She turned to face Lambert. Her hand went to the grip of her cutlass. "Me?"

Their host advanced, his face twisted in fury as he blocked their path to the stairs. "Magic seeks magic."

"There are dozens of mages here," she countered.

"The monster wants *you*, witch." Lambert pointed at her. "*You* brought it here."

Drawing their swords, six pirates collected behind Lambert. The other guests surged down the stairs, buccaneers and women running.

"We should give it what it wants," one of the pirates with Lambert shouted.

"Push her back! To the monster!"

Alys and Ben glanced at the creature behind them, ripping out more chunks of the building, and the armed angry pirates ahead of them. She and Ben shared a look, coming to a silent agreement, and pressed toward the pirates.

A pair of buccaneers moved in front of them, a square-set man facing off against Alys and a tall man against Ben.

Her opponent struck first, and she blocked his strikes. Knocking his guard low, she then punched him in the face with the bell of her cutlass.

With quick decisive strikes, Ben drove his opponent into

the railing at the edge of the catwalk, where the pirate then teetered. He glanced behind him nervously as he nearly fell over the balustrade, the floor fifteen feet below.

Before the off-balance pirate could fall, Ben grabbed him by the front of his coat. The man tried to jab with his cutlass, but Ben spun, throwing the buccaneer toward the creature behind him. The pirate scurried to a corner, cowering as the beast's claws narrowly missed him.

All the while, the creature continued to roar and tear down the walls in its search. The floor juddered and everyone battled to keep standing.

Lambert and four more pirates remained, blocking Alys and Ben from reaching the stairs.

"Straight down the middle," she commanded Ben.

"Aye, aye, Captain," he answered.

She and Ben attacked with a flurry of slashes.

Gritting her teeth, Alys traded strikes with a pirate, and their cutlasses rang out above the creature's roars. As she fought, Lambert attacked.

Ben stepped between her and Lambert, wielding his blade.

With all the force of her body, Alys kicked her opponent in the chest. Cursing, he crumpled.

Ben pushed Lambert back. There was just enough room to give Ben and Alys access to the stairs.

She raced down one section of the stairs, until she reached a landing. Reaching deep into herself, she summoned the destructive force of an earthquake. She turned to launch the spell at the stairs.

Yet Ben was still on the steps, fighting with Lambert and several of his men.

"Get to the landing!" Alys shouted at Ben.

He was a whirl of steel and fury as he attacked Lambert, fierceness in his eyes and his movements. It wasn't pretty, his combat, but it was beautiful.

THE SEA WITCH

Lambert and his cohorts edged backward in an effort to dodge Ben's strikes. With enough space to move, Ben leapt down to the landing.

With Ben now beside her, Alys cast her spell, pushing the force from her body as she groaned from the effort. The marble stairs between the landing and the catwalk shuddered and then shattered, breaking into pieces that rained onto the floor below.

She and Ben sprinted down the remaining steps. They reached the ground floor of the main hall. The long feasting table was abandoned. Plates and goblets and cutlery were scattered across its surface and over the floor.

"The key," Alys called to Ben.

The glint of gold was everywhere, but a pointed item near the head of the table caught her eye.

"That's it," she cried.

The house shook again. More stone fell as the creature broke through the wall on the opposite side of the hall. Its scaled arm reached through the hole and its claws dug trenches in the floor as it struggled to reach them. Hot green breath gusted around the chamber.

The table lay between them and the beast. With one of its talons, the creature punctured a hole in the wooden surface and began to drag the table toward it.

Alys leapt aboard. She fell to one knee as the creature pulled the table toward its snapping beak, but with her experience on rocking ships she regained her balance and stood.

She dove for the key, and her fingers wrapped around the handle. The beast's claws swiped just above her arm. She pulled back with the knife in her hand, and she rolled off the table to land on her side. Ben helped her to her feet. She tucked the carving knife into her belt.

"Run for the beach." She kept her voice low so only he could hear.

At his nod, they sprinted out of the main chamber and into the corridor that led to the front door. The manor shook as the creature continued to tear at the walls.

The front door loomed ahead. As she and Ben sped toward it, Janssen blocked their way, along with a duo of guards.

"Damn it," Alys groaned at the prospect of facing off against the majordomo and his ruffians.

"You and your filthy witch magic," Janssen snarled, raising a cutlass. "Ruining my master's home. We should never have let you cross his threshold."

"There's no knowing what the creature wants," Ben answered as he and Alys both stood with their blades at the ready. "It could be your master, Janssen."

"His family's been here for generations, and they've never faced an attack from a monster. Not until tonight. Until *she* came here." He glared at Alys as he advanced on her.

"You want filthy witch magic, Janssen?" Alys shot back. "Choke on it."

She flung out her hand. A torrent of thick dark sludge sprayed as she conjured up the foul-scented muck that collected in bogs and ponds at the end of summer. She sent it spewing all over Janssen and his brutes.

The men fell back, clawing at themselves and retching. The smell nearly made Alys gag, too. Her eyes watered. Ben made an agonized sound.

As the men heaved, Ben shoved them out of their path. He and Alys leapt out the front door and hurried down the steps, darting into the forest.

Roaring sounded, far too close. Birds took flight as the trees suddenly splintered apart behind them. The monster had turned its attention away from the manor.

It chased them.

Alys and Ben sprinted through the woods. She chanced a glance behind her, to see the creature relentless in its pursuit,

THE SEA WITCH 351

scuttling after them. Trees crashed and there was a terrible thundering of the beast's beating wings. Yet the wings seemed incapable of giving the creature flight as it continued to scramble toward them in a serpentine motion.

They burst from the tree line to tumble out near the pier. The jolly boat was still tied up, and together, they ran full out for the vessel. The pier rattled beneath their boots.

"I'll row," Ben shouted as they reached the jolly boat.

They both leapt into the small vessel. He hacked at the rope with his cutlass. The creature emerged from the forest, its feet slamming down on trees and breaking them apart like they were slender reeds. The beast was fully visible now. It was the length of three horses, with a powerful body, a beak that could easily swallow an entire human, and a long tail topped with spikes.

Its eyes blazed with wrath. And it headed straight for them.

"*Now*, Ben," she yelled.

With a snarl, he dropped his cutlass and grabbed the oars.

Summoning the swiftness of dolphins, she imbued the jolly boat with their speed.

The stars protect them if the beast could swim.

They shot away from the dock just as the creature reached the end of the pier. The beast snapped at them. It nipped the stern, rocking the boat.

As they sped toward the waiting *Sea Witch*, the creature crouched on the pier, roaring and shrieking at the nighttime sky. Frustrated, the beast slashed its claws through several of the tied-up boats. Shattered timber flew into the sky and splashed in the water.

When they were a hundred yards away, the beast gave one last bellow of anger before slinking away. It disappeared into the darkness, its tail lashing out and felling trees.

"By all the tides," Alys breathed as they neared the *Sea Witch*. "I've aged a hundred years this past quarter of an hour."

"What did the creature want with you?" Ben continued to row them toward the ship, their speed all the faster from the assistance of her magic.

"Maybe the navy sent it," she surmised. "They may see me as an even bigger danger to them now, and they can't let that threat stand."

"They must know you're in pursuit of Little George's fail-safe. They're afraid."

"I weep for them," she said, scornful. Then, with more warmth, "You fought well."

He gave her a nod, though he looked abashed. "We fought well together." He exhaled. "Practice and actual combat are assuredly not the same."

"I'd never know you hadn't spent years brawling with pirates."

The jolly boat finally reached the *Sea Witch*. They climbed the rope ladder as the crew gathered on the top deck to help them up. Once they were aboard, Stasia came forward, her face expressionless except for the tight set of her mouth.

"Lambert certainly knows how to throw a feast," her second-in-command said.

"We didn't care for the entertainment he provided," Alys answered.

Stasia glanced toward Ben and her brows lifted. Shooting her own look at him, Alys understood why her second-in-command had reacted.

The way Ben gazed at her . . . his relief at seeing her safe, and the care in his eyes . . . There'd be no mistaking what had happened between them.

Her hand went to the carving knife tucked into her belt. "In my quarters."

THE FAIL-SAFE KNIFE lay in the middle of the table. Alys gently ran her fingers over it, the residue of tingling on her skin. The

THE SEA WITCH

handle had been fashioned into the shape of a siren with abundant hair and a tempting but sinister smile. Intricate engravings of seaweed worked their way across the blade's surface. Holes of different sizes had been punched into the blade as well. She squinted to see that tiny numbers were also etched into the gold-plated silver, as fine as spiders dancing across the surface.

Alys, Stasia, Ben, Polly, and Luna all gathered around the table. Everyone looked haggard, their faces drawn with weariness. Sunrise was only a few hours away, but no one would sleep until the riddle of the carving knife had been untangled.

"If we need to cut lamb into delicious morsels," Stasia said, standing opposite Alys, "we are now well-equipped for the task. Beautiful as this knife is, I cannot see how it is worth risking your life for it."

Eris, perched on Stasia's shoulder, made a chirp of agreement.

"There's far more to this knife than one would guess." Alys tapped each of the holes in the blade. "Not random, these. They form a pattern."

There was silence, and then Ben spoke.

"A constellation."

"Hydra," Luna said.

"Curious location to place a constellation." Stasia bent closer to study the knife.

Alys started. "It's a chart."

"A celestial chart," Ben said. "We line it up with Hydra . . ."

"Then we know where we're headed," Alys continued.

"Except that constellation isn't visible this time of year," Luna noted.

"But here," Polly said, tapping the numbers *31–10*. "A date, perhaps. None of the other numbers match the calendar. This could be the Thirty First of October. Five months from now"

Alys grabbed the knife and held it up, moving it this way and that.

"We position the blade to where Hydra would be on All Hallows' Eve," Alys said.

"And then?" Stasia pressed.

Still holding the knife, Alys gave her a wry glance. "Then, the *and then* will hopefully reveal itself."

The ship slept around them as the group moved to the top deck, which was largely unoccupied except for the morning watch.

In the wake of the harrowing time on land, Alys drew fresh salty sea air into her lungs. Her body still continued to throb warmly in the aftermath of the pleasure she and Ben had shared, even following the terror of their flight.

Ben all but glowed with care and tenderness.

She handed Luna the blade, and the navigator held the carving knife up to the black star-dusted sky.

"There," Luna said after adjusting its position and angle. "That's where Hydra would be on All Hallows' Eve."

"And there." Ben indicated the tip of the blade, angled toward the dark horizon. "The knife points the way to where we're headed."

"It's a chart, guiding us to our next step." Alys shook her head. "I keep thinking I know the limits to Little George's cunning. And I keep being proved wrong."

"What *is* the next step?" Stasia demanded as Eris chittered with agitation. "The end of our journey, or another kataramé-nos clue?"

Alys leaned against the railing and folded her arms across her chest. "There's no way of knowing."

Everyone was silent as they contemplated this.

"Luna," Alys went on, "set our heading and then inform the helm."

"Aye, Captain." Luna sped down the companionway, as if eager for her charts.

THE SEA WITCH

"Polly, find your berth and get some sleep," Alys said. "Stasia, you do the same. We'll need rest before facing . . . whatever it is that we're going to face."

Stasia gave a clipped nod and followed Polly as she went below.

Alone with Ben, Alys allowed herself to droop with weariness. He was beside her at once, offering his strength and the sturdiness of his body. For a moment, she allowed herself to lean against him.

She tried to push back to stand on her own, and fought a yawn. "Didn't get much service out of that bed at Lambert's."

"We made fine use of the chaise."

"Look at you. Preening like you've got the biggest cock to ever sail the Caribbean."

"You did call it *gorgeous*."

When he moved to wrap his arms around her, she eased away.

"Everyone's asleep," he said.

She glanced toward the upper deck. "There's the watch, too."

"You've had men aboard this ship before. Brought other lovers to the *Sea Witch*. But," he said, wry, "none of them were in the Royal Navy."

"*Were*, not *are*?"

"Going back's impossible. And I don't want to. That's not what I know, anymore. What I do know . . ." Closing the distance between them, he cupped her jaw with his hand. "I know *you*, Alys Tanner."

He looked into her eyes, his own gaze warm and affectionate.

"That's where the danger lies," she said flatly.

"No danger with me." He stroked his finger down her cheek.

"Come." She took his hand from her face and led him to the companionway. "I've no desire to collapse in a heap on the top deck, dead to the world. More than anything, we need sleep."

He walked beside her, and she kept her fingers woven with his. Save for a few creaks and the water lapping against the hull, the ship was quiet as they made their way to her quarters.

Desire—she knew what it was.

She'd sailed its dark and wild seas many times over the course of the past year, knew its swells and rough waters, the danger and excitement from its shoals and shores. The first time she'd ever gone to bed with a man who wasn't Samuel, she'd been dizzy with eagerness and fear, trembling with a combination of nerves and enthusiasm. She could get what she wanted for herself, demand exactly what it was she needed, accepting only what it was *she* craved.

Nothing had to be suffered in silence. Nothing had to be endured. She wasn't a cup to hold someone else's release. She wasn't subject to someone's affections. She commanded the ship of her own pleasure. Whoever didn't like her terms found themselves back on shore.

She'd taken lovers from one coast of the Caribbean to the other, only picking the men who caught *her* fancy.

She was glad to welcome her lovers to her berth, and even more grateful when they left and she was the self-contained captain once more. As their sweat cooled on her skin, none of them left any lingering trace of themselves on her heart. They didn't cage her with claims that they felt deeply for her. She certainly felt little for them.

They couldn't touch her.

But Ben . . . Oh, constellations above, Ben.

Now she knew what it was to have Ben as her lover. He'd been eager and open to learning. He took her lessons and gave her pleasure. Yet beneath the passion, there'd been something terrifying.

She wouldn't name it. Naming it gave it power and truth.

AFTERNOON SUNLIGHT SLANTED through the long window in Alys's quarters as she and Ben reviewed the chart Luna had pulled, showing their course.

THE SEA WITCH

357

She had awakened in his arms only a few hours ago, and a vague sense of shame had crept over her. The fact that she'd slept so late weighed in her gut like so much ballast. She was always on deck by the crack of dawn, and now, here she was, lying abed like a paying passenger, not the captain of a whole damn ship.

It wasn't Ben's fault that having him hold her as she slept lulled her into the deepest, most profound sleep of her life.

Thank the stars he hadn't offered her more sweet, soft kisses, or tender, caring smiles. She didn't have any defenses against them. Instead, they were both purposeful and focused, over their meal of charred stew—a new cook was *definitely* in order in the wake of Josephine leaving—and now, as they studied the chart.

"Here's where we're headed." She ran her finger across the map, skimming over the painted waves, until a cluster of tiny dots on the chart stopped her progress. "You know it?"

"The Caribbean is rife with miniscule uninhabited islands," he said, examining the map. "Half of them don't appear on any chart. This archipelago could contain a score of more islands, some no bigger than a dozen yards across."

"Hell." She braced her hands on the table as she leaned over the map. "Little George has already proved himself a cunning bastard. It's no small task to find the one island we need."

"Doubt, from the captain who raided a Redthorn monastery, and fought a dozen pirates in Lambert's house?" Warm and large, his hand covered hers.

She dragged in a breath. Before she could speak, there was a knock at the door.

"Enter," she called, relieved.

Stasia opened the door and stood on the threshold. Her face was set and serious, even more so than usual. "I need you on the quarterdeck."

358   EVA LEIGH

At once, Alys followed her second-in-command up the companionway and higher, until they stood on the quarterdeck. Ben was right behind her, and the three of them gathered at the railing, where Eris perched. A seagull was beside the magpie, both birds twittering to each other.

"A problem has sailed into our path," Stasia said without preamble. She nodded toward the seagull. "This is Bembe, and he has news."

"What's he seen?" Alys asked.

"That ship of yours," Stasia said to Ben. "The naval flagship."

"The *Jupiter*," Ben supplied.

"It sails between us and where we are heading," Stasia explained. "We circled back toward the Hydra formation, and when we did that, they must have tracked us from our last encounter with them."

Grimly, Alys said, "With its leviathan and that other creature they have bound to their will. Fuck."

A heavy silence fell as they contemplated what this meant.

"The previous time we faced that ship," Stasia said, somber, "we survived, but barely."

"We outrun them," Ben suggested. "Same as before."

"They'd follow," Alys said. "And we'd take them to the next step in our search for the fail-safe."

"Find another route?" Stasia mused.

Alys shook her head. "We don't know the precise location we're going. If we try a different course, we could be completely thrown off and never find what it is we're looking for."

Another taut quiet descended.

"We've got no options," Alys said darkly. "Got to move forward, but if we do, we're sailing right into destruction."

"Not if the *Jupiter* is set on a different course," Ben said.

"We cannot be sure *where* they will go," Alys countered. "Not unless . . ." She stared at Ben. "No."

His expression was resolute. "I'll return to the *Jupiter*, tell

THE SEA WITCH

them I've escaped, and feed them false information so they sail in a completely different direction."

"There's another way," Alys said.

"There is not," Stasia said. "What the sailing master says makes sense. If he goes back to his ship and leads them astray, we have the best chance of finding what it is we seek."

"We could summon as much wind as possible, outrun them."

"A huge gamble," Ben said. "They've two creatures to do their bidding. They could swim faster than the *Jupiter* and catch us as we try to flee."

"We could try to wreck the *Jupiter*, use our magic—"

"Even all the witches aboard our ship could not destroy a naval man-o'-war," Stasia pointed out.

Alys forced out a breath and set her hands on her hips. "Fine. We'll send him back."

She didn't remember going below, but suddenly she was in her quarters. Behind her, the door shut quietly but firmly.

Wheeling around, she faced Ben, who stared at her with a stoic expression that made her stomach clench.

"I'll find a way to return to you." He took a step toward her, cautiously, as if afraid she might bolt.

"You can't be sure of that."

"I know it as sure as I know the beat of my own heart." He reached for her hand and placed it on his chest, where his heart did pound steadily. "Nothing in this world or the next will keep me from you, Flame."

"Please, don't." She hesitated before carefully resting her body against his. "Say nothing of that. I can't . . . I can't bear it."

"But it's true," he answered gently. "Shutting your ears to it doesn't make it less true."

"I won't allow it. It's . . ." Her palm hovered above his chest. "Love's a prison."

He cupped his hands around her face. "What your husband gave you . . . that wasn't love. It was ownership."

"The same thing."

He bent close and pressed his lips to hers. "Not with me."

"You can't say that," she choked. "You can't tell me such things and then leave."

"Reaching that fail-safe is imperative. This is how I can make certain you do it."

"The hell with the fail-safe."

"We both know its significance," he said gently. "When you get the fail-safe, then *you* are safe. And that's all I want. Your safety and happiness."

"Damn you, Benjamin Priestley," she growled. "I wish you'd never chased me through St. Gertrude."

"I'll chase you off the map, to where the dragons live."

She closed her eyes. "I've lost so much, so many. What I want most, I fear the most."

"A peculiar thing about fear," he said softly. "Running away from it doesn't take the danger away. We're always at risk. Everyone at every moment."

She couldn't think of it. She wanted nothing but the certainty of his body and hers.

"Kiss me." She threaded her fingers into his hair. "Kiss me and let's pretend, for just a little while, that nothing and no one else exists. There's only us. Us and the sea. And it's enough."

CHAPTER THIRTY

Their lips met, and the kiss was deep and lush, tasting of honey and loss. Ben cupped her head. He consumed her as a man might savor his last drink of summer wine before a long barren winter.

As they kissed, they tugged at each other's clothing.

"I want all of you," he growled into her mouth. "There isn't a part of you that I don't want to feel."

He would come back to her.

It was awkward and clumsy, yet in a few moments they were stripped bare. His markings were visible now. His hands stroked along her body to touch her curves and hollows and sinews and scars. No one felt like her. He gripped her arse and pulled her tightly against him.

When she gave him a shove, he willingly went, tumbling so that he half lay on her berth, his legs splayed wide as he leaned back on his elbows. She stood between his thighs. Her hair was loose around her shoulders, a flaming curtain that spilled over her rising and falling breasts. Her eyes blazed and she was everything powerful, all the stars and tides.

"Witch of flame," he rumbled. "Pirate queen. *My* queen."

That seemed to please her, a small-edged smile curving her lips.

"Let me serve you, my queen," he said, his voice a rasp. "My heart is yours. My body belongs to you."

He reached for her, but she knocked his hand away.

"If your body's mine," she said huskily, "then I'll take my pleasure with it."

"Anything," he vowed.

He stared as she lowered to her knees. Yet there was no submission in her, only a claiming of what she wanted. Her hands stroked up his thighs, digging into the straining muscle.

Her eyes avid and commanding, she wrapped her fingers around his cock.

"Fuck." His hips bucked up.

She held him tightly, her fist going up and down with almost punishing strength. The pleasure . . . He'd never known anything like it. And when she lowered her head to take him in her mouth, he swore and sweated. The sight of her swallowing him down was too much . . . he would lose all control . . . and yet he couldn't look away. Couldn't close his eyes. She was too beautiful, too powerful, licking and sucking him.

"So good," he panted.

She sucked harder, her hand clasping him with the strength of a woman who lived on the sea. Low in his spine, the hot tightness of a climax gathered.

"Not yet, not yet." With a groan, he pulled from her mouth.

She rose from her knees and climbed over him. He lay back, clasping her hips. With her hands spread on his chest, she positioned herself over his cock, lining the head up with her opening. Their gazes locked.

Slowly, she lowered herself down to impale herself on him. For a moment, she was still, her breath coming in quick gasps, but then she began to move.

She rode him, slowly at first, her hips moving up and down as she angled herself exactly how she wanted. Pink washed through her cheeks and flushed her body.

THE SEA WITCH 363

"You're so beautiful," he said, hoarse. Whatever happened to him after this didn't matter—not when he'd seen something so perfect as Alys in ecstasy.

Her breasts swayed with her movements, and he lifted up enough to take one of her nipples in his mouth. He lightly bit the point, making her gasp. Her hips ground down as she rubbed her clitoris against him. Undulating cries slipped from her mouth.

With short fierce movements, she rode him, her thighs taut. Sweat slicked both of their bodies. His own hips jerked up to meet her and the cabin was filled with the sound of flesh against flesh, and their intermingled moans.

He gritted his teeth, determined to last as long as he could. Yet he didn't relent, not when her body went still as she came. He reached down and stroked her clitoris with his thumb, summoning another climax from her, and then another.

This might be their last time together for a long while. Perhaps evermore.

Only when she bowed forward, her hair hanging in her face as she panted, did he allow himself to let go.

His orgasm tore through him, jagged and unrelenting. He arched up as he held her tightly and her fingernails dug into his chest.

"All of you," she gasped. "I want it all."

On and on his climax went. He was annihilated and reborn. And she held him within herself through everything, until he was wrung dry.

He was still inside her as she draped herself over him. His arms looped around her waist and he closed his eyes.

"I care for you, Alys," he murmured into her hair. When she was silent, he held her even tighter. "You can say the words, or not, but it changes nothing. I care for you."

Something damp dropped onto his pectorals. A droplet, and then another. Her tears.

His chest seemed to cleave apart. There was no taking his words back, and he didn't want to. But causing her pain, any pain, was a knife that carved him from the inside out.

He opened his mouth to say . . . he didn't know what . . . only he had to comfort her from the agony that was caring for another person.

The ship jolted violently. Shouts sounded above.

They were being attacked.

"FOR THE LOVE of the tides," Alys snarled as she stood, throwing on her clothing "can't we have an uninterrupted moment?"

She braced herself as the ship gave another powerful lurch.

"The stars align against us." Ben kept his balance as he, too, struggled to get to his feet. He dressed quickly, his shirt covering the marking that still curved over his skin. "If I had faith in such things."

She staggered toward the door, pulling it open as she did her best to stay upright while the ship listed from side to side. Ben was close behind her. They both scrambled up the companionway to stand on the top deck. Crew members fought to keep on their feet, clinging to whatever was fixed and solid so they didn't pitch into the sea.

No other ship was nearby, and the skies were clear of any storm.

"They just set upon us," Stasia said, lurching toward Alys and Ben.

"*They*," Alys echoed.

Stasia glanced toward the rail. "The creatures."

Alys tottered up to the quarterdeck and peered over the rail. She cursed.

A pair of large sea creatures, the size of jolly boats, rammed into the *Sea Witch*'s hull. The top half of the beasts looked something like a beetle, with mandibles, antennae, and legs, while the bottom half had the long length, tail, and scales of alligators.

THE SEA WITCH   365

Their black iridescent bodies were glossy and forceful seawater churned around them.

"I've never seen creatures like them," Ben said, gripping the railing as he, too, watched the beasts slam their heads into the hull, over and over again. The sea creatures moved to assault the hull beneath the quarterdeck.

"Eris has not spotted the *Jupiter* nearby," Stasia said, lurching toward them. "Nor any other naval ship. These beasts act of their own accord."

Alys's teeth rattled from the force of the impact. They'd break the ship apart soon. "We've done nothing to make them angry."

Ben darted down from the quarterdeck and ran toward one of the guns.

"Don't fire on them," Alys shouted after him. She wouldn't harm any animal or beast unless absolutely necessary. As long as her ship remained intact, she refused to hurt the creatures.

Ben didn't seem pleased by her order, but he obeyed.

And then . . .

The creatures swam away from the quarterdeck. They moved to the part of the ship where Ben stood before resuming their attack, battering themselves into the hull.

"Ben," she shouted.

"I see it." Experimentally, he ran to the prow. The creatures followed him. And when he sped back toward the middle of the ship, the beasts did the same.

Alys hurried toward him.

"It's me," he said grimly. "They want me."

"They're not getting you," she said at once.

"I should—"

"No. There's another way." She glanced over the railing. "We can lure them off with something. Food, perhaps."

Ben rubbed at his jaw, and his markings were still visible along his neck. As she watched, the dark patterns began to fade.

366   EVA LEIGH

A moment later, they were gone, and his skin returned to its original unmarked state.

The ship leveled. Alys looked over the gunwale.

The creatures turned and swam away. They seemed entirely disinterested in the *Sea Witch* as they vanished beneath the water.

Everyone aboard the ship collected themselves, murmuring.

"What the hell was that?" Thérèse demanded.

"I've never witnessed anything like it," Dorothea said, furrowing her brow.

"There's no explanation," Susannah mused, as Inés wrapped a protective arm around her shoulders.

But there was an explanation.

Ben turned to Alys and spoke quietly. "My markings, my . . . magic." He looked down at the backs of his hands, now free of the patterns. "They appear when you and I are . . . close. We knew that at Lambert's, when we kissed to summon my power to help you find the carving knife. And every time we've kissed or been intimate, my markings show up."

His gaze moved to hers.

"At the island of the Weeping Princess," Alys said grimly, "creatures followed us to the beach."

"When we were in the room at the inn at Domingo," he added. "The chickcharney appeared. And when the Redthorn attacked you—"

"You killed him, we kissed, and two creatures appeared. Then, at Lambert's enclave, a beast attacked the manor. It was searching for someone."

"For me," Ben said darkly. "There's something about my markings appearing when you are near me . . . It summons creatures, makes them angry."

She slammed her fist on the railing. "Fucking Luca Pasquale. Taking that book. We could've learned something."

Frustration rose acidly within her.

THE SEA WITCH

"I have to return to the *Jupiter*." His words were both resolute and somber. "Sooner rather than later. I'll take the cutter and should intercept them soon."

"There's time," she said at once. "We need to review our plans, and provision you, and—"

"Alys." He stepped closer to her. "I must go. Now."

She fought to swallow down the burning lump in her throat. Her body was too small to contain the battle brewing inside her. It was as though a frantic, furious being was caged within her own skin.

"Go, then." Her voice came out clipped and sharp as a cutlass. She moved away from him. "We'll gather enough supplies, water, and food to keep you provisioned. And we'll summon winds to move you along faster. They won't last very long, the farther away you get from the *Sea Witch*, but it should be enough to speed you to the *Jupiter* quickly."

He reached for her and she stepped back.

When it became clear she wouldn't go to him, he exhaled. Expression hooded, he slowly nodded. "As you like."

"It isn't what I like," she answered. "Not at all."

CHAPTER THIRTY-ONE

It took far too short a time to outfit Ben for his voyage back to the *Jupiter*. Alys cursed her crew's efficiency as the cutter was loaded with adequate food and water to get him to the flagship—it was a delicate balance, since it had to appear as if he'd escaped.

Flasks of water and a crate of hardtack and salted meat were loaded into the hold, small enough to be jettisoned when he got close to the naval ship.

As she and Ben watched the last of the provisions loaded into the cutter, he shrugged out of his coat and waistcoat.

"It will look suspect if I present myself to Strickland resembling a pirate." He folded the garments and set them aside. For good measure, he tore several places on his shirt and rubbed a bit of grime on the fabric.

"They suited you well." Alys resisted the urge to sigh as his transformation was stripped away.

Cora brought forward his old coat and waistcoat, much shabbier than when he'd first set foot on the deck of the *Sea Witch*, and he put them on.

"Like wearing someone else's skin." He grimaced.

By the hard set of his shoulders, his wide stance upon the deck, and the new toughness in his eyes, he wasn't the same

THE SEA WITCH 369

man he'd been all those weeks ago when he'd first burst into her life like a fusillade.

Alys clenched her jaw. Every moment, he slipped further and further away from her, and he was still aboard her ship.

"Give me two days from today," he said. "I'll try to send word that the passage forward is safe."

"You'll be surrounded on all sides by the navy." He wouldn't be safe. Something could happen to him, and she'd be too far away to do anything about it, unable to help him.

"Have no doubt that I'll find a way," he answered, stepping close so that no one around them could hear.

"My doubt isn't for *you*," she said in a low voice, "or what you're capable of. It's the rest of the world that I don't trust."

"We only have ourselves."

"But is it *enough*?" she demanded.

"We're connected, intertwined. Nothing's concealed, everything is exposed."

"I don't know if it's going to last, when we're no longer together. It might fray apart like so much rope."

"If I could promise that it will hold, I would."

"Captain." Susannah came forward. "We're ready for him."

"Yes, all right," Alys clipped.

Glancing back and forth between Alys and Ben, Susannah eased away.

"Please, one goodbye." Ben embraced Alys, his hold strong and steadfast.

She held herself stiffly, her arms at her sides. She couldn't let herself press against him, rest her cheek on his chest, grab on and grip him tightly.

He cupped her jaw and looked into her eyes. "I care for you, Alys. And you feel something for me, too, whether or not you say the words. We're joined now, in our dreams, and in our hearts. That will always guide me back to you."

"Please," she choked. "Please go now."

He pressed a kiss to her forehead, and then another one, softly, on her lips. "We will see each other again."

Then he was gone, climbing over the railing and down to the waiting cutter. She stood at the gunwale to watch him.

He seated himself at the tiller, and untied the boat from its rope anchoring it to the *Sea Witch*. When this was done, he gazed up at her, far above him. The blue of his eyes was the same blue as the water, and now even that would be ruined for her, because she would never again sail upon the sea and not think of him.

Stasia shouted, "Witches, we summon the winds."

"Aye, aye," came the answering cry.

Alys couldn't join the magical members of her company as they called upon the winds to fill the cutter's sail. Instead, her hands knotted into fists and her throat burned when the sail billowed and the boat pushed away from the *Sea Witch*. The cutter grew smaller and smaller. Even as Ben steered the boat, he looked back at her.

She still felt him within her, the strands of him braided with her own heart. His worry. His determination. Yet they stretched and grew muted, distance dampening the peaks and depths of his emotions inside her.

The cutter turned into a dot, and the glow of Ben's presence inside her became a tiny flicker of light in the midst of darkness. It disappeared over the horizon, and finally Alys turned away.

BEFORE THEY COULD sail to the next step in the search for the fail-safe, it was essential that the ship reprovision. Stores of water and food were getting dangerously low, and the stars only knew when there would be any allowance of time to replenish them.

It also gave Alys something to think about besides the fact that Ben was no longer aboard the *Sea Witch*. She'd avoided her

THE SEA WITCH   371

quarters all day, his presence everywhere in her cabin. He was either standing at the table where they would review charts and discuss their course, or else he lay in the hammock, asleep but wary, or he stretched across her berth.

She was in her quarters, briefly, when Jane came in and began taking down the hammock.

"Leave that." Alys didn't like the snapping tone of her voice, but it had come out before she could stop herself.

Jane blinked at her. "If that's what you wish, Cap'n."

"It is," came Alys's clipped response. She stalked from her quarters, fleeing from Jane's confused look.

Ben was gone, though no one knew for how long. There was no need to keep the hammock if he wasn't around to use it.

But he *might* need it. He could be back within a few days. And then where would he sleep? There was always the possibility that they'd share her berth, yet it was narrow and hardly held two people, especially someone of his size. They'd keep the hammock for a while, and maybe she might have her berth widened so that both of them could fit into it comfortably . . .

Alys marched up to the quarterdeck and took the helm from Hua. Better to give herself something to think about besides these fucking circles that had her spinning and spinning.

Had he reached the *Jupiter* yet? Was he safe? Did he think of her at all or, now that he was back aboard his naval ship, did he consider his time aboard the *Sea Witch* a temporary madness, best soon put behind him? Though she was aware of him, she could no longer sense him as acutely as she once had.

"Fuck," she snarled to herself.

She let the wind in her face and the motion of the ship upon the waves do their best to chase away her endlessly cycling thoughts. And yet there was nothing in the whole of the Caribbean that could possibly wash away the heartache gripping her.

With relief, she put in at the island of Saint Bernadine. There was a decent-sized town there, sympathetic to buccaneers and a safe place for a pirate ship to reprovision without worrying about any naval ships or governments to make life difficult. She docked the *Sea Witch*, and immediately members of the crew hustled down the gangplank to assist Cecily in securing food and drink for the ship. Everyone else was given two hours of much-needed shore leave. A skeleton crew remained behind, with the promise that the next time they docked, they'd be given several days of sanctioned leave.

Alys stood at the gunwale. Stay on board, or go ashore? On one hand, she didn't have the stomach for the revelry Saint Bernadine offered. On the other, the *Sea Witch* was haunted everywhere by Ben's presence.

She stalked down the gangplank, Stasia at her side.

Saint Bernadine boasted a low mountain in the center of the island, with the town crouched at the base of the peak, like an imp at the foot of a demon. The town bustled as goods were loaded on and off ships, and taverns did brisk business, filled with pirates eager for a little pleasure after hard weeks at sea, and tapsters eager to take their ample coin. The air was heavy with salt and sweat, music and laughter and shouts clanging together.

Alys's head throbbed, and her chest ached even more.

"Go on," she said to Stasia, waving her hand toward an open-air tavern. "Find a warm and willing soul to share a bed with for a few hours. Nobody with any sense will refuse such an offer."

Stasia eyed the people in the tavern, many of whom eyed her back with interest. She cut a sleek and dangerous figure, dressed in a long dark coat, her eyes lined with kohl, and Eris perched on her shoulder. Yet she gave everyone a dismissive shrug.

"When I take a person to bed," she drawled, "I prefer a more expansive window of time."

"In Kingston, you grabbed Pretty Daniel Delacroix and hauled him into an alcove with a convenient couch. You were there for no more than a quarter of an hour."

THE SEA WITCH   373

"He was not worth more than fifteen minutes," Stasia answered. "All show, with minimal performance."

Alys glanced at her friend. "I don't have need of accompaniment."

"All the same," Stasia replied, "I am precisely where I want to be."

"I'm only walking to the top of the mountain." Alys stopped and faced her. "There's surely more entertaining use of your time than hauling your carcass beside mine."

"We have had an abundance of entertainment these past few weeks. Parleys, searches for waterfalls, helping captives free themselves, battles with naval ships, *more* battles with Redthorns, sea creatures attacking the ship." Stasia looked at her steadily. "A sedate walk is exactly what I require."

Alys exhaled, even as her friend's loyalty warmed her. "Follow whatever wind carries you."

She marched ahead, keeping her strides long. Yet Stasia could walk at a brisk pace, too, and soon they had left the town behind as they neared the foot of the mountain. Trees and low scrub dotted the base, thinning out as the mountain rose higher.

Once, this tropical landscape had been new and strange to Alys, so different from the thick forests of pitch pine and black oak of Massachusetts. Yet now, she knew it as well as she knew her own freckles, and she strove to find comfort in the gumbo-limbo and palm trees that swayed in the hot breeze.

Neither she nor Stasia spoke as they ascended the mountain, which was a relief. Stasia seemed to understand that Alys had no desire to talk, and so the noise of the town faded, replaced by bird calls and animal sounds and wind in the trees, with nothing else to interrupt the silence, save an occasional twitter from Eris, wheeling overhead.

She glanced back at her friend. Something seemed to preoccupy Stasia, her gaze turned inward even as her feet remained steady on the rocky terrain. Perhaps Stasia thought of her own past, and whomever she left behind in the Mediterranean, and choices which led to heartbreak.

Swallowing the urge to ask her friend, Alys concentrated on placing one foot in front of the other. That was all anyone could do, keep moving forward in the face of pain, no matter the cost.

They finally reached the top of the mountain. Together, they stared down at the town, now a collection of poppet-sized toys, and the azure bay full of anchored ships of all sizes. The sight of so many masted vessels, all dedicated to a life outside the law, briefly lifted the heaviness within Alys. And yet . . . what did any of it mean, all the plunder and freedom, when at the end of each day, there was nothing but unwanted solitude? When the person you cared for faced terrible danger, and you couldn't do anything to help them?

She turned to face the other side of the island. It was more rugged, lacking a town on its craggy shore, and almost completely uninhabited. Beyond the rock-strewn beach stretched more cerulean water.

Alys pointed to a lone ship sailing toward the island. "She's flying a skull and sickle. It's John Lynne's ship, the *Bold Fortune*."

"A right bastard, that Lynne," Stasia said dourly. "Always trying to cheat the tavern wenches out of their share of coin."

"See there," Alys noted, pointing to a vessel approaching the *Bold Fortune* with exceptional speed. Guns bristled on its decks, and it flew the Union Jack. "Damn—that's a naval ship."

"Saint Bernadine has been safe from the interference of the Royal Navy."

"Today marks the end of that, and, hell, the ship isn't unaccompanied." Alys pulled a spyglass from her belt and pointed it toward the water beside the naval vessel. A reddish bulbous body broke the surface of the waves, and long tentacles trailed behind. Judging by the shadow in the water, whatever it was possessed massive size. "A sea creature."

THE SEA WITCH

"Is it the *Jupiter*? That is the only naval ship that subjugates beasts."

For a brief moment, Alys's heart lifted into her throat, that Ben might be so close. Yet she peered closer. "It's too small to be the flagship. This is some other vessel."

Stasia let out a low curse. "The threat your naval man spoke of, that the navy was adding more creatures to its arsenal, it is true."

"God*damn* it," Alys bit out. "They're setting upon the *Bold Fortune*."

Within moments, the naval ship was beside Lynne's vessel. Distant booms thundered as the two ships fired upon each other. Several gigantic thick tentacles rose up from the water and wrapped around the *Bold Fortune*'s masts and hull. The sea creature crushed the timbers of the masts, and the hull collapsed in on itself as if it was a rotten melon. Through her spyglass, Alys watched members of the pirate crew leap overboard in a desperate attempt to save themselves, only to be dragged beneath the water by more tentacles.

"By the tides," Alys breathed. "There's no stopping the navy now. Not without the fail-safe."

"We must get aboard the *Sea Witch* and flee," Stasia growled. "Fast as we can."

"And warn everyone else."

There wasn't time to summon winds to hasten them down the mountain, so they sped back as fast as the uneven terrain would allow. At last, they reached the base of the mountain, and raced into town. As they entered the marketplace, Alys grabbed a pot being sold by a tinner, along with a wooden spoon. She banged on the pot furiously.

"Everyone," she shouted when people stared at her in confusion, "get to your ships. Have your mages summon every wind to speed your escape. The navy approaches."

"We can fight 'em off," someone yelled. "More of us than those bloody prigs."

"They have a kraken," Stasia bellowed.

The entire town went silent. Then, chaos.

People ran in every direction. Pirates poured out of taverns and brothels, some of them barely dressed, and tumbled in terrified confusion toward the wharf. Alys, Stasia, and the *Sea Witch*'s crew joined in the exodus, jostling their way through the crowd to reach their ship.

Alys waited at the foot of the gangplank, making certain that none of her company was left behind, shouting as she waved each member of the crew onto the ship. Once she was certain that everyone was aboard, she finally slammed up the gangplank. The rope securing the *Sea Witch* was untied and the gangplank was drawn back.

"Get us the fuck out of here, Hua," Alys yelled up to the woman at the helm. "Witches, we need that wind, and no dallying. Everyone with magic, topside, *now*."

Stasia repeated the order at an even greater volume. The members of the crew that possessed magic gathered on the deck and formed a circle as they concentrated on gathering every wind and breeze available to push their ship out to sea. Different ships were attempting to do the same, but they had the power of only one mage per vessel.

The *Sea Witch* shot away from the wharf, slipping through the clogged traffic, while the remaining vessels struggled to sail to safety. As her ship raced into open water, Alys stood on the quarterdeck, using her spyglass to look back toward the harbor of Saint Bernadine. The naval ship wheeled around the island toward the vessels still attempting to flee. Beside the Royal Navy vessel swam the kraken, its eyes dulled by the spell that bound it to a naval mage.

She pitied the creature, but the fact that it acted against its will did nothing to dampen the destruction it was forced to cause.

THE SEA WITCH

Finally, Saint Bernadine disappeared over the horizon.

"Rest now, witches," Alys ordered. "You've done your part."

The women collapsed to the deck, exhausted from using their magic for such an extended period of time.

"See that they're balanced immediately," Alys said to Stasia.

The second-in-command strode about the deck, gathering up crew members to provide the touch necessary to restore the witches' strength. Spiced rum cakes which had been purchased ashore were handed out, and mugs of lime-spiked ale. The ship soon glowed with the energy of two dozen witches being balanced.

Anxiety clung to the *Sea Witch*, heavy as a fever.

"They'll come for us, too, won't they, Cap'n?" Dayanna asked uneasily.

"We'll stop them before that happens." Alys hoped her voice sounded confident, because inside, she was a mass of kelp, knotted and stranded upon a beach, left to rot in the sun.

She cast her gaze ahead, toward the beckoning horizon. Somewhere out there, Ben was doing his part to ensure they were successful, and they could find the means to sever the Royal Navy's command over sea creatures. If he didn't achieve his goal, she prayed the stars were merciful.

Ben was now a candle flame glimpsed through thick and cloudy glass. There was no way of knowing his thoughts, his heart. Whether he was safe or not. If she could help him.

She stood to lose everything that mattered to her: her crew, her ship, and Ben.

CHAPTER THIRTY-TWO

THE SEA WAS metallic and blinding. The last time Ben had been alone on a vessel, he had yet to join the navy, and had been a boy sailing his family's sloop in and around the waters surrounding Port Royal. He'd loved the freedom of it then, the notion that he could go anywhere and learn new truths about the sea. He wasn't a naval captain's dutiful son, forced to become someone he didn't want to be.

Instead, he'd become Bloody Ben—the very same name he'd used when playing pirate as a child. But as a grown man, Bloody Ben's life was filled with adventure, and a woman unlike anyone he'd ever known.

A sense of duty had always made him return home. To the codes and conventions that tried to shape him into the man he was supposed to become.

Now, he was alone again at sea.

Yet instead of the soaring joy of liberty, his heart remained aboard the *Sea Witch*. With Alys. She hadn't given him the words he longed to hear, yet the anguish in her eyes as she watched him go, her hair streaming like crimson silk in the wind . . . those memories he clung to. In the middle of the Caribbean Sea, they were all he had.

He'd gripped the filaments of her emotions inside him, once a curse, now his sole means of holding tight to the person who'd

THE SEA WITCH

come to mean everything to him. They were still intertwined, yet distance made the connection grow faint. Even so, that it even continued was his sole source of salvation over these past days.

He'd been sailing in the cutter since yesterday, and spent the night on his own. The day was still bright, but night was only a few hours away.

He followed the course he'd set, his gut churning with apprehension. That apprehension turned icy when the dark shape of the *Jupiter* appeared ahead of him. He recognized every line and mast, could name each of the crewmen gathering at the gunwale as his cutter approached. He discreetly threw all his provisions overboard, in case anyone questioned how an escapee managed to grab food and water before fleeing for his life.

The kraken and leviathan swam beside the ship, both of them eyeing him pass as unease tightened his limbs. His cutter was a toy compared to the creatures, fragile and easily broken. His muscles tensed as he sailed closer. The ship's mage controlled the beasts, yet it was always possible that Warne nursed a vendetta against him. The bastard had been with Strickland when Ben's father was killed. He could turn the creatures into weapons with a wave of his hand.

To be certain, Ben fluttered a white cloth over his head, ensuring that even if they didn't recognize him from a distance and with his appearance so altered, someone aboard the ship would realize that he meant them no harm.

Soon, he drew up beside the *Jupiter.* He stood to squint up at the crew gaping down at him.

"That's the sailing master," someone exclaimed.

"Can't be him," came the reply. "That bloke looks half feral, and Priestley ain't wild."

A bewigged head poked over the railing. "The devil? Is that you, Mr. Priestley?"

"Aye, Mr. Oliver," Ben called up to the second-in-command.

"Thought you were dead." Oliver sounded slightly disappointed.

"I'm indeed alive. And ready to rejoin my ship. Sir," he added belatedly. The word *sir* sat like a square of metal upon his tongue.

"Get him aboard," Oliver commanded the nearby seamen.

A ladder was lowered, and in short order Ben climbed up and once again stood upon the deck of the *Jupiter*, the ship that had been his home for the past five years. Everything was the same, and its very sameness pressed between his shoulder blades. Order and consistency were the enduring characteristics of the Royal Navy, ensuring their nation's supremacy on the sea. What Ben had once loved most about the navy now was a bitter poison. There was no room for dissention, or freedom of thought: you were inserted into an existing machine and did what you were ordered to do. Otherwise, you were flogged.

Seamen gathered around him in a wary, awed circle, whispering amongst themselves. Ben stared back. Even when Captain Gray arrived, Ben remained silent. He would reveal nothing. Not until—

"Mr. Priestley."

Ben stiffened at the sound of Strickland's voice. When the admiral strode forward, looking every bit as commanding and domineering as when Ben had last seen him, Ben forced himself to salute rather than slam his fist into Strickland's red craggy face.

"Sir." The word came out of him sharp and edged as a dagger. He struggled to breathe, making his inhalations and exhalations as long and slow as possible.

Standing in front of Ben was the man who had murdered his father. And just behind Strickland loomed Warne, the mage who was complicit in the killing.

Never had Ben drawn upon more self-control than he did at that moment, his heart pounding, his muscles aching with the force he exerted to keep from wrapping his hands around

THE SEA WITCH   381

Strickland's neck and squeezing until all life left the admiral's body and his soul shot straight to hell.

"Last we saw of you, Mr. Priestley," Strickland said, "you'd dived overboard to chase after that witch whore Tanner."

Ben's jaw throbbed from the pressure he exerted on it. "I was in pursuit of Captain Tanner, sir. That is true. I found myself aboard her ship—"

"The one full of witches," a seaman exclaimed.

Mutters and curses rose up from the assembled men, some spitting upon the deck and others crossing themselves.

"Sir," Ben ground out, "if I may request that we continue this debriefing somewhere that affords us more privacy."

"My quarters," Strickland answered.

"Dismissed," Oliver shouted at the crew. "Make yourselves useful. Anyone lollygagging or found lingering at keyholes will receive ten lashes. Twenty if you don't disperse immediately."

Sailors hurried in every direction, attempting to show the quartermaster that they were occupied with their duties. Once they had gone, Ben followed Strickland, Gray, Oliver, and Warne down the companionway to the admiral's quarters.

The ship that had been his home swallowed him like a prison. He longed to run back topside, jump overboard, and sail the cutter back to the *Sea Witch*. Yet he had a mission to carry out, and he'd be utterly useless to Alys if he failed in that objective.

Merely bringing her to mind made his back straighten and his steps decisive. This was for her. Everything was for her. Hazy as their connection was, it still burned within him.

Strickland strode into his quarters and leaned against his desk, arms folded across his chest, as Ben stood before him. Gray, Warne, and Oliver positioned themselves nearby. Long ago, Ben had stood in the exact same place, arguing that he should join Oliver on St. Gertrude. What deity could have possibly foreseen where that decision would take him?

"Give us your account, Mr. Priestley," Strickland commanded.

382   EVA LEIGH

"I did follow Captain Tanner to her ship, the *Sea Witch*," Ben said. "Hubris, perhaps, to think that I could capture her aboard her own vessel, but duty impelled me, especially after she destroyed my charts and maps."

His words tasted acrid, speaking of Alys this way, yet in order to protect her, he had to continue.

"I was taken prisoner immediately," he went on. "They threw me in the brig, and there I remained for God knows how long."

"You look hale enough," Oliver said dismissively. "Captivity didn't disagree with you."

"I was fed," Ben answered. "And every day I was permitted a half an hour on the top deck for closely supervised exercise and air."

"A ship full of women," Warne sneered. "Witches. They must've been panting for cock."

Ben fought to keep his feet anchored to the floor, lest he launch himself at Warne and slam the mage's head into the bulkhead. "No one abused my person."

Warne snorted. "They all love cunt, anyway. You wouldn't offer much temptation."

"I can't speak to what company the crew of the *Sea Witch* preferred," Ben went on, his jaw clenched.

"You were aboard when they took the *Ajax*," Strickland said. "Yet you didn't prevent them from seizing the ship."

"I was one man," Ben answered. "And confined to the brig. There was nothing I could do to stop them."

The admiral seemed to accept this explanation, which was, in fact, true.

"They treated me with as much dignity as anyone can hope for when held as a prisoner aboard an enemy ship," Ben continued.

"If your captivity was so pleasant," Oliver jeered, "why escape? That is," he added, peering at Ben closely, "if you *did* escape."

Ice prickled along the nape of Ben's neck. "There was nothing

THE SEA WITCH

383

about my circumstances that gratified me. I needed to return to my ship, my duties."

"How *did* you manage to slip free, Mr. Priestley?" Captain Gray asked.

"As I said, I was permitted a brief period of exercise and air each day." Since Ben had left the *Sea Witch*, he'd gone over his story many times, and recited his tale with as much authenticity as he could muster. "I was closely watched, but I deliberately cultivated the behavior and attitude as a model prisoner. It had the effect I sought, and in time, the guards were more permissive. They would leave me unattended for a few minutes as they socialized with the other members of the crew."

Strickland, Gray, Oliver, and Warne continued to listen, and nothing on their faces seemed to express disbelief, so Ben continued.

"The ship had anchored off the beach of an uninhabited island for reprovisioning. Members of the crew were going to venture ashore to hunt and search for fresh water. They would take a cutter to navigate the shoals. Through persuasive talk, I managed to convince the crew that I was adept at finding potable water, and would make a good addition to the party going ashore. When we did reach the island, it became apparent that a squall would soon be upon us. The group ventured inland to search for shelter. I slipped away through the foliage and made my way back to where the cutter was beached. I saw the *Sea Witch* raise anchor and sail out of the bay to ensure that they weren't damaged on the shoals or rocks during the storm. Moments later, the squall hit, and I used it as cover as well as harnessing its power to sail off as quickly as I could manage."

"Surely the witches went after you," Warne insisted. "They have an abundance of magic at their disposal to aid in their pursuit."

"By the time the squall had passed," Ben said, "and they gathered their resources to retrieve their crew from the island,

I imagine that it was only then that my absence was discovered. They were assuredly faced with a choice whether or not to pursue me. At that stage, I was likely closer to the *Jupiter*, which meant that if they did give chase, they would find themselves within dangerous distance of this ship. Even when the *Jupiter* had only the leviathan as escort, that would certainly deter them from getting close. And so," he concluded, "it appears they let me go."

Silence fell, broken only by the sounds of the crew going about their duties and waves slapping the hull. Ben held himself still as he endured Strickland's penetrating stare. It was the admiral that Ben had to convince. Gray, Warne, and Oliver mattered less, yet even they needed to be assured that Ben's story was genuine.

Finally, Strickland straightened, unfolding his arms as he approached Ben. He stood directly in front of Ben. He was within striking distance.

Do it, a voice in Ben's head whispered. *Draw his cutlass and run him through*.

Warne or Oliver would slay Ben within moments of striking the admiral down, and he couldn't kill one without also eliminating the other. Both were equally responsible for his father's murder.

Ben had another objective: protecting Alys and eliminating the Royal Navy's escalating threat to the Caribbean.

And so, he held himself still and returned the admiral's gaze, strangling his own need for vengeance.

A minute passed. And then another.

"Welcome back aboard, Mr. Priestley," Strickland said gruffly. He clapped a hand on Ben's shoulder, and Ben barely managed to keep from lashing out at the admiral's touch.

"It's good to be back, sir."

"You showed exceptional resourcefulness and courage," Strickland added. "And now you must use the knowledge you

THE SEA WITCH

gained during your captivity to tell us where to find Tanner and her harpy crew. We'll show that upstart woman and her company of shrews that they cannot trifle with the Royal Navy. Not now, when we have so much power at our fingertips, and can erase any trace that they ever existed."

Needles of fear wove beneath Ben's skin. Between the manpower and firepower of the *Jupiter* and the strength and might of the leviathan and the kraken, the *Sea Witch* could never survive an engagement.

"I need a map of this region, sir. That is, if we have any left, after the witch's destruction of my charts."

Strickland shot Oliver a pointed look, and the lieutenant scowled but stalked from the cabin. A few moments later, he returned with a chart.

"We managed to replace some of the maps and books of charts," Oliver grumbled as he laid it out atop a table. "At considerable expense, I might add."

"I won't accept blame for something I had no hand in," Ben replied.

"If you hadn't chased that Tanner cunt aboard the *Jupiter*," Oliver fired back, "she wouldn't have deemed it necessary to set half the ship on fire."

"You—"

"Enough," Strickland clipped. "Arguing like fishwives when we could be learning important intelligence."

"Yes, sir," both Ben and Oliver muttered.

Ben bent over the map. He resisted the impulse to look in the location where Alys and the *Sea Witch* were located. Instead, he pointed in the opposite direction.

"Here," he said decisively. "They were sailing toward Hispaniola. I believe they intended to wait for a merchantman en route to Spain, and relieve that vessel of its cargo of gold and jewels."

"They may be witches." Warne chuckled. "Yet to the last, they're nothing but thieving piratical scum."

386   EVA LEIGH

Ben would never tell the mage, or anyone in the navy, about why Alys and her crew raided ships. The Royal Navy didn't care.

"Excellent work, Mr. Priestley," Strickland said.

"The state of your clothing is disgraceful," Oliver barked. "You need a shave, and must change immediately."

"I will gladly do so, Mr. Oliver," Ben said calmly. "I assume everything in my quarters is still where I left it."

"It is," the lieutenant said through clenched teeth.

"Will you excuse me, sir?" Ben asked the admiral.

"Dismissed, Mr. Priestley."

Ben saluted again and backed out of Strickland's quarters, closing the door behind him. He briefly lingered at the door.

"Not sure we can trust him." Oliver's voice was muffled by the closed door.

"He has no reason to lie to us." That was Strickland.

"Maybe the Tanner bitch ensorcelled him," Warne's jeering voice threw in.

"Were he anyone other than Priestley," Strickland mused, "I might believe that. But the sailing master cares only for navigation. Nothing else is worth his interest."

"He *is* fond of his charts and maps," Captain Gray noted.

"Keeps to regulation and order," Strickland went on. "Whatever wiles that pirate witch might possess, they would find no purchase in the soil that is Benjamin Priestley's heart."

"The vulnerable organ I'm thinking of isn't his heart," Warne said, a smirk in his words.

"Fine," snapped Strickland. "Go and speak with him, Mr. Warne. See if there's anything more you can learn, any flaws in his tale."

"Aye, sir."

Ben hurried away from the door, keeping his footsteps as light as possible to avoid detection. He made his way to his quarters, which he shared with two lieutenants. The other members of

THE SEA WITCH

the crew were currently not in their cabin, so Ben was alone as he pulled out his sea chest for a fresh coat and waistcoat.

As he laid the garments on his berth, Warne entered his quarters. The mage leaned against the bulkhead and watched Ben without speaking, all the while his long pale fingers plucked at the black sash around his waist.

Ben discarded his tattered coat and waistcoat. As he did so, he shot Warne a wary glance. There had always been a strain between Ben and the mage, so he didn't have to feign warm camaraderie with Warne now.

He pulled out his shaving equipment. The straight razor was an odd weight in his hand. Lighter than a cutlass. And yet, there was a time not that long ago, when all he'd wanted was to be given some means to shave himself.

He went to the small mirror hanging on the bulkhead. The man looking back at him wasn't the sailing master, wasn't Bloody Ben. He was someone else. A man without a place in the world.

He whisked soap into foam and lathered his cheeks.

"An anomaly," the mage said, his voice almost disinterested. "A ship crewed and captained entirely by women. And not merely women, but witches."

"Indeed," Ben answered with just as much disinterest. It took some time to shave, his cheeks and jaw slowly revealed with each stroke of the razor. After wiping his face with a towel, he stowed his shaving gear.

He slipped on his fresh waistcoat and did up the buttons. It was looser in the abdomen now, and snugger across the chest.

"Not many have had the opportunity to observe that many witches so closely," Warne continued.

Ben made a noncommittal noise as he shrugged on his coat. He kept his expression neutral, though he preferred the ornate and dramatic pirate's coat he'd worn at Lambert's refuge. This plain naval coat was now tight in the shoulders and arms.

He turned away and discreetly pressed a hand to the center of his chest. He felt Alys there most.

Removing his hand from his chest, he faced Warne. "You seem to think I've information on the habits and practices of witches, but the majority of my time was spent confined to the brig."

"And what of the time you spent on deck? That precious half hour where you had a degree of liberty."

"Witches haven't the luxury of formal schooling," Ben answered. "Compared to what mages are capable of, they're hardly a threat. Although . . ."

He leaned closer to Warne and lowered his voice. "I overheard two of the witches talking when I feigned sleep. There *was* talk of cursing me."

"Unsurprising," Warne said. "An underhanded and unscrupulous lot, women who use magic. They'll exploit anything to gain the advantage and keep men in their power."

As opposed to decent and upright mages, who subjugate creatures against their will?

"They mentioned something about placing markings upon my skin," Ben continued. "Some kind of patterns and shapes."

Warne lifted an eyebrow.

"Naturally, I was terrified of such a thing," Ben said, attempting to imbue his words with as much unease as possible. "I wouldn't even know what such markings could do to me. They must be a common practice amongst those who wield magical power."

He waited, hoping Warne might take the bait.

"Likely something only done by witches." Warne's expression shuttered, but not before a flicker of some recognition glinted behind his eyes. "Such a practice isn't done by mages. Not that I've ever heard. You had a narrow escape, Priestley, if the witches didn't execute their plan and put such cursed markings on you."

"Narrow, indeed," Ben answered blandly. He had always been careful to make certain no one observed him whenever he came in contact with seawater. Warne had never seen his markings, nor had anyone aboard the *Jupiter.*

He feigned a yawn.

"Apologies," he said. "I cannot recall a moment where I had a decent night's sleep, and after the tumult of the last few days, I find myself unable to keep my eyes open."

"I'll leave you to your slumber, then." Warne gave him one final glance, icy and assessing, before quitting the cabin.

Once he was alone, Ben stretched out on his berth. It was narrow, hardly capable of holding two people, and yet his arms ached to hold Alys. They had never had enough time together. Always, they had been interrupted by the creatures roused by his awakening magic.

Warne had been unsurprisingly chary in giving Ben any information regarding his markings or what they truly signified. If anyone knew what the markings meant, it would be Warne.

Now, though, Ben had another crucial task to undertake. Here, in the heart of the ship that had become his newest prison.

He closed his eyes, and fell asleep, praying his plan worked.

CHAPTER THIRTY-THREE

Exhaustion suddenly dragged on Alys with heavy rusted chains. Blearily, she looked up at Stasia, who was reviewing the chart with their intended course.

After they had fled the naval ship and its kraken, the *Sea Witch* had put in off the shore of a small cay, seeking a temporary landing place to avoid further encounters with the Royal Navy. Though she still sensed Ben within her, there had been no word from him. Anxiety had kept Alys from finding any comfort in the shelter of sleep.

Now, two days after she had seen him sail away from her, worry and weariness churned in her gut, a mix which seemed to suddenly catch up to her.

"Are you well?" her friend asked with a frown of concern. "You look as though your face is made of melting wax."

"Can't . . ." Alys blinked. Though she was tired, fatigue hit her all at once, with the force of a cudgel to the back of her head. "Eyes won't stay open. This your doing? You cast a sleepin' spell on me?"

Stasia gave her an unwavering stare. "I would never be so trite."

"Someone else in the crew, then. Susannah? Thérèse?"

"No one cast a sleeping spell on you," Stasia answered, exasperated. "Your weariness is likely due to the fact that you paced on the top deck all night."

THE SEA WITCH   391

"Did no such thing," Alys said. Or she tried to say, but her words came out in a jumble.

"The middle watch and morning watch told me," Stasia countered. "You bounded from stem to stern when nearly everyone else was asleep in their berths. And you didn't eat your supper."

"Whoever was in charge of last night's supper fed us boiled leather," Alys returned.

"We will find ourselves a new cook when the timing is more ideal. For now . . ." Stasia walked across Alys's quarters and took her by the wrist. She tugged Alys toward her berth.

"Sleep now," Stasia said with an astonishing amount of gentleness.

Alys could object, and force herself to stay awake. But she wasn't a child. So, she let her friend push her onto her berth and lay quietly as Stasia tugged a blanket over her.

"Wake me in thirty minutes," Alys insisted.

"An hour," her friend replied calmly.

Alys would have demanded she get her way, except her eyelids were leaden, and she could keep them open no longer. The last thing she saw before she surrendered was Stasia bending over her, her brow creased with worry.

There was nothing to be concerned about. Or so Alys wanted to say, but she wasn't able as slumber pulled her down.

She stood on a white beach, sapphire waves lapping at the sand and foaming around her bare ankles. Palm trees gently swayed as a soft warm breeze drifted across the water.

"Alys."

She turned at the familiar voice. Her heart leapt as Ben made his way toward her. He wore no shirt and loose pantaloons, and his markings danced across his sun-warmed skin. His unbound hair blew around his face and even from a distance his eyes were the same azure shade as the water that ringed the island.

She ran to him. His arms were around her instantly, and she pressed her face against his chest. Inhaling deeply, she caught his scent of seawater, wood, and leather.

"You're back," she murmured into the crook of his neck.

"I wish I was with you now." His hand cradled the back of her head, stroking her hair.

"You are," she insisted.

He pulled back slightly. "We dream together, Flame. At this moment, I'm asleep in my berth on board the *Jupiter*. See? Tea cakes generally don't fly in real life."

He pointed toward the sky, where a collection of small cakes sporting gull wings wheeled in circles, crying out to each other.

"Hell." She forced down the knot of disappointment stuck in her throat. "You're sound? Any harm come to you?"

"Sound, and no harm. Some hard questions were put to me, but I had answers for them. Strickland even complimented me on my resourcefulness and courage," Ben added bitterly. "It was all I could do to keep from running him through with his own cutlass."

"There'll come a time for vengeance." She stroked her hands along his chest and over his face. "Damn dreams. Why isn't this real?"

"It is, and it isn't." He gazed at her intently. "The *Jupiter* is currently heading toward Hispaniola, well away from the *Sea Witch*. With good fortune, neither ship should cross the other's path for a long while. That is what I came to tell you. With the *Jupiter* on its fool's errand, you are free to move on to the next step in search of the fail-safe."

"I've news as well. I saw a naval ship, not the *Jupiter*. It had a kraken."

"Hell."

"I watched it destroy a pirate's ship," she went on. "The sight's branded into my mind."

"It's happening, then. What Warne threatened is truly coming to pass."

"Your mission's done. No need to stay on the *Jupiter*."

THE SEA WITCH 393

"There's no way for me to flee the ship," he said with regret. "Not without having it give chase, and I'll never lead them to you. Trust me," he added, his gaze moving over her face, "I swear that when the opportunity presents itself, I will speed back to your side."

"It's good to have two navigators aboard the *Sea Witch*," she said. "We know twice as much about where we are."

His brow furrowed. "I must go. Even though I begged exhaustion, Strickland will not look kindly on his sailing master sleeping away daylight hours."

"Kiss me," she demanded, "before we wake."

He lowered his mouth to hers. His kiss was soft and reverent, tender and aching. The obstacles and distance between them fell away. She wove her fingers into his hair and opened her lips to him. He tasted exactly as she remembered, rich and deep, with the added flavor of yearning.

In the way of dreams, the more she held fast to him, the further away he seemed to get. He turned insubstantial, misty.

"Ben," she cried out. "Ben."

"I'll return to you," he answered, his voice growing distant. "I swear it."

She called out his name once more, but she was alone on the beach. The water stilled, and nothing moved, the entire world trapped in time, neither going backward nor moving forward.

Her eyes flew open and she was once again in her berth, staring at the planks overhead, the knots in wood she knew so well. She brought her fingers to her lips, yet there was no taste of Ben on her mouth. He was far away from her now.

SOMETHING JOSTLED HIM sharply. Was the ship under attack? Did the sea creatures bound to the mage's will suddenly revolt and turn against the *Jupiter*?

"Wake up, you bastard," Oliver barked.

394   EVA LEIGH

Ben tried to sit up, but strong binding held him down. He opened his eyes. A thick-armed sailor pinned him to his berth, as Strickland, Oliver, Gray, and Warne looked on.

They all wore hard, grim expressions.

"Explain this," Ben demanded.

"Traitor." Oliver nodded toward two more seamen standing by. One held a pair of manacles, and the other gripped shackles in his beefy hand. "Aligning yourself with that whore, that *witch*."

"Denial is impossible, Priestley," Captain Gray added when Ben was about to contradict the quartermaster. "We know."

Ben struggled against the man holding him down, but he was too large and brutish to be moved.

"I felt it." The mage sneered. "Your dreamwalking. To *her*. Everything you blathered to us earlier is utterly false."

Ben remained silent. There was nothing to be said, and he would tell them naught of Alys.

Warne bent down, placing his face close to Ben's.

"Without your dreamwalking, we'd have never known where to find her. There's a line, you see, drawn between your heart and hers." He placed his hand on Ben's chest, and though Ben struggled to shake him off, the mage dug his fingernails into him. "It has led us straight to her."

"In the opposite direction of where you pointed us," Oliver said disgustedly. "Turncoat. Betrayer."

"And we know that Tanner is after the fail-safe that Little George created," Warne went on, smiling.

"She'll take us to it," Strickland said with a tight nod.

"You've no use for the fail-safe," Ben threw back.

"Others do," Warne answered. "We find it, and destroy it. We'll add more creatures to our arsenal. Every ship in the fleet will have at least one monster as part of its weapons."

"This has to stop." Ben turned to Strickland. "This isn't what the navy is supposed to be."

THE SEA WITCH   395

"This is *precisely* the purpose of His Majesty's Navy," the admiral replied coldly. "To protect and advance the Crown is exactly our objective."

"Alys has nothing to do with any of this," Ben insisted. "She only wants to be left alone."

"She's a thorn," Warne returned. "We have to pluck her out of our paw."

"She'll be taken to England," Strickland said flatly. "Burned in London."

"A slow burning," Warne added. "Mages have unique ways of prolonging the agony. We use magic to keep the victim alive for as long as possible."

Ben thrashed wildly. He managed to throw off the sailor holding him, and when Warne backed up, Ben went straight for Strickland.

He slammed his fist into the admiral's face. Blood sprayed from Strickland's nose and coated Ben's fist.

"I know," Ben said through clenched teeth. "I know everything. *You* killed him. You and your piece of shit mage."

"What's this?" Captain Gray looked stunned.

"Stow it, Gray," Strickland snapped. "Unless you want to be *killed by pirates* as well."

White-faced, the captain kept silent.

Before Ben could land another punch, his arms were pinned behind him and he was thrown to the ground. As he lay on the floor, Strickland pressed his boot against the back of Ben's head.

"You never held much potential, Priestley," the admiral said with mock sadness. "I kept hoping you'd turn around, and, in the absence of your father, *I* could shape you into something worthwhile."

Strickland removed his boot and the seamen holding Ben hauled him to his feet and slapped the shackles and manacles onto him. Hot pain shot up his arms and spread across his chest.

Strickland walked to him and patted his cheek with far more force than a fond but judgmental parent.

"I had hoped you wouldn't be so disappointing," Strickland said.

The mage strode to Ben. He placed his hand on the center of Ben's chest, his fingers digging into Ben's skin.

"A turncoat cannot be trusted." The mage closed his eyes and his lips moved. Red light enveloped Warne's hand. It sank into Ben's skin.

Searing pain ripped through him, as though the mage tore his beating heart out. Yet Warne's hand remained on top of Ben's chest.

More agony shot through Ben, crackling into his veins and scouring every corner of his being. Alys's bright flame within him suddenly went out.

Warne pulled his hand away, and Ben sagged. Echoes of pain reverberated through him. Physical anguish, and something else. A hollow, devastating loneliness. An icy cold solitude that left his soul bleeding.

"No," he breathed.

Alys was gone. The connection between them had been severed.

His gaze met Warne's. The mage's pitiless eyes stared back.

She was gone from within him. All her heat and strength. Vanished.

There would be no way to contact her. No means to dream-walk again to warn her about what was to come. She might even believe him dead.

Strickland glanced at the sailors holding him. "Take him to the brig. I want a guard on him at all times."

"If he's ever left alone," Oliver added, "I will personally and with great gusto administer fifty lashes to whomever was supposed to be watching him."

"Aye, sir," the sailors gulped.

THE SEA WITCH

"The Redthorns are a dangerous—" Ben said.

Strickland's cheeks flushed. "Warne."

The mage stepped forward and made a pattern in the air with his fingers.

Everything around Ben went dark. When he next opened his eyes, he was lying on a cot in the brig. A guard impassively watched him from the other side of the glowing bars.

Ben sat up and put his head in his hands.

Alys and the crew of the *Sea Witch* were sailing to their deaths, and there was nothing he could do to stop it.

CHAPTER THIRTY-FOUR

A SHARP SEARING PAIN filled Alys as she reviewed a chart in her quarters. She clutched her chest, gasping.

"Are you ill?" Stasia demanded.

"I'll fetch Fatima." Luna ran for the door.

"Not illness," Alys ground out.

Luna paused, one hand on the doorknob.

"If not illness, what?" Stasia asked urgently.

"It's . . ." Alys rubbed at her heart. The pain began to recede, leaving emptiness in its place. Her soul rattled within the cage of her body. "Ben."

She dragged her gaze up to Stasia and Luna's alarmed faces.

"The link we shared." Alys drew in a sharp breath. "It's gone."

"He is . . ." Stasia cleared her throat.

"I don't know." Alys pushed herself upright, fighting the urge to curl in on herself. "He could be too far away for the connection between us to hold. Maybe it shattered. Or the spell that created it simply dissolved. Spells do that. They have a lifespan."

The navigator and quartermaster shared a skeptical look.

"He isn't dead." Alys's voice rang off bulkheads. "I would know it. I'd feel it."

"With the link between you vanished," Stasia said carefully, "how could you know or feel?"

THE SEA WITCH 399

"Because I would," Alys snapped. She dug her knuckles into her chest. "Forgive me, Stasia. But he can't be dead. He just can't."

Stasia's lips pressed into a slash. "It is, as you say, likely that the physical distance between you two is too great to support the magic that connected you. Only that."

"Yes." Alys squeezed her eyes shut, fighting to keep steady on her feet. "Yes, that's what it must be."

THE FOLLOWING MORNING, Alys stood on the forecastle deck, her spyglass trained on the island ahead of the *Sea Witch*. It was a small strip of land, only a mile across, with a thick green forest that lay just beyond the beach that ringed the island. It seemed vaguely familiar, but then, there were countless beaches across the Caribbean that looked alike. There were no columns of smoke from fires cooking breakfast.

"Is this what we seek?" Stasia asked beside her.

"The tides protect us if it isn't."

"Not especially noteworthy," her friend said flatly, "this island."

"But it's where the carving knife led us." Lowering her spyglass, Alys said, "Its insignificance gives me hope that this is the place we've been pursuing. Cunning as he's been throughout this hunt, Little George wouldn't pick anywhere obvious to hide his fail-safe."

"Hua says we should be able to drop anchor within minutes."

"We'll gather our landing party." Alys made her way back toward the main deck, trying to keep her thoughts on what lay ahead, how to prepare for what awaited them on the island, and not things beyond her control. Or the possibility that Ben was no longer alive.

If she let herself truly consider this, if she allowed herself to believe it . . .

She climbed down the companionway to the main deck and tried to ignore Stasia's look of sympathy, or as close to a sympathetic look as her friend could manage.

"He could be well," Stasia said. "The distance, I am sure."

Even as her friend spoke, Alys grasped for something that was surely hopeless.

She had to see Ben. She *would* see him. And when she did, she'd tell him . . . she didn't know what, exactly, she wanted to tell him. Only that her days had been endless and her nights lonely and that the ship was far too empty when he wasn't aboard it. She'd stopped herself several times from asking him to review a chart, or she poured two mugs of rum when she was alone in her quarters. But he wasn't there. And when she hoped to see him last night in her dreams, and he wasn't there, either . . . disappointment was a stone anchor heavy in her heart.

"Distance," Alys echoed.

"Surely that must be it," Stasia added.

Her friend's willingness to humor her made slivers of icy alarm dance across her skin.

She and Stasia reached the main deck, where the crew gathered.

"I want Stasia, Susannah, Inés, Dayanna, and Thérèse in the landing party," she announced. "Each one of you must take a brace of pistols, a cutlass, and a dagger, minimum. We don't know what's waiting for us, and if anyone gets themselves killed, I'll personally drag them back from the afterlife, and then make them pick oakum for a fortnight. Understood?"

"Aye, Cap'n," the crew assigned to the landing party answered.

"The rest will stay on the ship with Polly as acting captain."

Polly nodded and stood straighter, ready to assume the mantle of responsibility.

"We'll reconvene in five minutes," Alys added. "Dismissed."

As the group broke apart, Alys sped down to her quarters to arm herself. She tucked three primed pistols into her baldric, buckled on her cutlass, sheathed a dagger, and tucked several more knives into her boots. She grabbed the carving knife retrieved from Lambert's enclave, and placed it in a pouch tied to her belt.

THE SEA WITCH

She hesitated, then went to her desk. Unlocking the top drawer, she pulled out a shiny brass button. It had fallen off Ben's coat some weeks ago, and she'd snatched it up off the floor. At the time, she'd told herself she had taken it to keep her quarters tidy. She ran her thumb back and forth across the embossed design.

Closing her eyes, she pressed the button to her lips.

Before he had climbed aboard her ship, dripping wet and bristling with righteous anger, her life had followed its own rhythms. The *Sea Witch* found ships laden with gold and precious things, and raided those ships. When her ship would dock for shore leave and reprovisioning, she would find herself a lover, sate her body's needs, and then take to the sea again, unbound by the connections that could sour or lead to miserable heartache.

She cared for him.

Her eyes flew open. *Hell.* She'd done everything she could to keep this disaster from happening.

He *wasn't* Samuel, binding her to him with mouthed platitudes of love. What Samuel had professed wasn't love. It was the mask worn by a different demon: control.

Ben offered so much more than that. The treasure he'd given her . . . his true heart . . . She'd never had a prize like that from any ship she'd taken. To him, her freedom was celebrated, not held back.

Hellfire. She'd been mute when he'd left her. Never giving him what he needed. What she needed to say to him, not even the last time they'd dreamwalked. Regret was a shroud around her, weighted with stones, sinking her beneath the waves.

They might never see each other again. But if they did, what would she say? The only way to know would be to have him standing in front of her. And then . . .

She didn't know. But she'd make damned sure she and Ben had their *and then*. Whatever it brought.

She slipped the button into her pocket before striding from her quarters.

Back on the main deck, she watched as the ship dropped anchor a short distance away from the island's beach. Strange that so much relied upon a tiny strip of land, and yet everything to this point had led them here.

This was the end of their long search. It *had* to be.

The jolly boat was lowered to the water. A moment later, Eris swooped down, shrieking a loud alarm before landing on Stasia's shoulder. Her feathers were ruffled and she danced from foot to foot in agitation.

"The navy," Stasia exclaimed.

"Enemy approaching," Dorothea shouted from the crow's nest.

Everyone ran to the gunwale, and a collective gasp rose up.

The *Jupiter* raced toward them. *Three* massive sea creatures towed the flagship: the leviathan, the kraken, and a gigantic shark the size of a sloop. Hooks were embedded in the beasts' skin, and ropes were lashed from them to the man-o'-war. With three creatures towing the ship, it cut through the water at an impossible speed, foam flying into the air and waves parting as if cleaved by a gargantuan blade.

"How the hell did they find us?" Jane cried.

Stasia turned to Alys. "Did he . . . ?"

"He's no ally to the navy," Alys said at once. "It must mean—"

Her heart sank to the seafloor. She hadn't felt anything from Ben. Distance wasn't to blame.

He was dead.

At that moment, the crack of dozens of muskets rang out. Glowing bullets shot from the upper deck of the *Jupiter*. They sped across the water, propelled by mage-derived magic.

"Hit the deck!" Stasia roared.

The crew flattened against the wooden planks as bullets slammed into the masts and tore holes in the sails. Wooden

THE SEA WITCH

splinters rained down onto the company and Alys threw up a protective spell, sheltering the crew from the fragments.

Crouching, Alys and the company rose up just enough to look over the gunwale. The *Jupiter* had untethered itself from the sea creatures and aimed its heavy guns directly at the *Sea Witch*. Unlike Alys's ship, the naval vessel had two gundecks, along with several swivel guns mounted to the top deck. The *Jupiter* also boasted hundreds more crew members, including marines all armed with weapons charged with the mage's magic.

And the sea creatures were swimming straight for the *Sea Witch*.

Fear congealed in Alys's stomach. This would be a bloodbath. It would take the intervention of every goddess in the firmament for any of her crew to make it out alive.

"Raise the anchor," Alys bellowed.

The crew obeyed quickly to haul up the anchor.

"You and you," Alys said, pointing to two of her crew. "Keep the kraken at bay. Use whatever magic you can to push them back. And you two," she added to another pair of witches, "the same for the leviathan, and both of you," she continued to a third duo of witches, "on the shark."

"Aye, aye, Cap'n," the witches yelled.

They raced to the gunwale. Brows furrowed in concentration, they held up their hands as they threw spells toward the sea creatures. A whirlpool swirled around the kraken, sending it spinning. The sea surrounding the leviathan began to boil, and the beast roared as it swam backward, out of the heated water. The shark struggled to move closer as the witches churned the sea around it, creating massive waves.

"And you," Alys shouted to a cluster of witches. "Do what you can to keep the naval ship's barrage from hitting us. Fire back when you can."

The naval vessel's cannons boomed. At the same time, cracks rang out as marines fired long guns. Several witches gathered together, facing the *Jupiter*. As more magic-charged cannon fire and bullets raced toward the *Sea Witch*, a glowing spell shaped like a huge tortoise shell encircled the ship. The navy's ammunition slammed into the protective shell. The *Sea Witch* shuddered, yet the spell held, and the enemy's projectiles fell into the sea.

More witches fired magic toward the *Jupiter*. Spells began pouring from them: fiery rain, metal-shelled locusts, beetles that gnawed with red hot mandibles. Every conceivable defensive spell was launched at the naval vessel. The screams and cries of the seamen rose up above the din.

Stasia ran from crew member to crew member, to all the women who had no magic. The second-in-command charged their bullets and cannonballs with green glowing energy. Thus empowered, the crew fired back at the *Jupiter*. Bullets smashed into the naval ship's hull, some of them piercing the wood.

"The fucking mage is so arrogant," Alys muttered. "Didn't think we were enough of a threat to shield the ship."

That, at least, was in their favor. A moment later, a red net of energy encircled the flagship. The *Sea Witch*'s cannons and bullets ricocheted off the shield. Until Dorothea, Susannah, and Thérèse joined together to summon a counterspell, and the *Sea Witch*'s cannons and bullets reached the *Jupiter* again. But it wasn't enough.

Other crew worked the sails to keep the *Sea Witch* dancing in evasive maneuvers.

There was only one way to end this.

"Jane, Cecily, Cora," Alys shouted. When the three women raced up, Alys commanded, "Summon every wind you can to get us out of here. Hua," she added for the helmswoman, "set a course for open water."

The witches nodded and collected together, their eyes closed in focus. A moment later, the sails began to fill with strong gusts, and the ship lurched as it started to move out of the bay.

THE SEA WITCH 405

"Polly!" After the boatswain appeared at her side, Alys directed, "The landing party and I will make for the beach. You're to take this wind and get the *Sea Witch* out of here."

Though Polly looked concerned at leaving the ship's captain and crew behind, she answered, "Aye, Cap'n."

Alys pointed to the jolly boat. "Everyone in the landing party, we go now!"

Her crew obeyed at once, and as they clambered down the ladder, Alys cast a spell of impenetrable spiderwebs to protect them. Bullets lodged in the glowing silk.

"Take care of her," Alys said to Polly.

"This ship's my home," the first mate answered gravely. "The crew's my family."

Alys clasped Polly's wrist before she, too, climbed down the ladder. Once she was aboard the jolly boat, they pushed away from the *Sea Witch*. The oars were taken up as Stasia chanted lowly, summoning the force of the waves to speed the small vessel quickly toward the shore. Susannah added a spell-summoned fog to disguise them.

Riding in the rear of the jolly boat, Alys looked back toward the battle. The *Jupiter*'s cannons fired, sending up clouds of smoke. Cannonballs battered against the shielding spell. One smashed through the protection. It crashed into the hull, breaking apart the wood.

A second naval ship approached from the opposite direction. It was the same ship that had sunk the *Bold Fortune*. Beside it swam the ship's kraken, its long tentacles trailing in the water.

The *Sea Witch* veered around the second ship. As they passed, cannons and bullets fired from the naval ship.

The barrage hammered against her crew's magical shields. They smashed holes in the *Sea Witch*'s hull, splintered the masts, and ripped jagged tears in the sails.

Her ship disappeared around a spit of land moments before the second naval vessel fired again. The fusillade shot into empty air and the second ship was too slow to turn about. The *Sea Witch* was out to sea, her crew safe.

For now.

When the tides turned, Alys would get her revenge against the navy. For endangering her crew. For killing Ben.

But she had to survive what came next.

If there was such a thing as Lady Fortune, Alys prayed the goddess of luck wouldn't turn her back on the *Sea Witch*.

THE SOUNDS OF combat shook all around Ben. The *Jupiter*'s guns discharged in rapid succession, faster than he'd ever heard them fire before. And the flagship shuddered as a barrage of ammunition struck its hull.

Alys was in the middle of all of this.

Pulling on his manacles and shackles, they heated, searing his skin.

"Enough of that," the seaman guarding him snapped, jabbing him with a bayonet.

The ship shuddered around them. Men screamed. Yet for all the chaos aboard the *Jupiter*, it was nothing compared to what the *Sea Witch* was likely enduring. The naval muskets fired, and the cannons boomed. With Warne providing his magic to charge the ammunition, even the most skilled witch aboard Alys's ship wouldn't be able to offer enough protection to shield the vessel and crew from the barrage.

"Go above," Ben growled to his guard. "They have better use of you than minding one prisoner."

The seaman looked uncertain, but he stayed where he was. "Mr. Oliver promised a flogging if I desert my post."

"Hear how the marines' volleys are slowing? They're losing men. The witches will turn into ravens and board the *Jupiter*. You'll be dead if you remain here."

There had to be *something* he could do to help. Not while he was caged and chained like a beast, stuck in the brig on a lower deck with no porthole to offer him the merest glimpse of what was transpiring outside.

The ship convulsed and men cried out. There was a booming, and the hull of the brig exploded. The seaman guarding Ben shouted in alarm, leaping out of the way as shattered wood went everywhere. Ben raised his arms to shield himself from the flying debris.

Looking up, Ben could see the gun deck through the huge gap, which revealed a terrible scene. The *Sea Witch* was under assault, being hammered by gun and cannon fire from the *Jupiter*. Some shielding spells had been cast by the witches, yet they weren't enough to hold back all of the bombardment. Witches also cast spells to push a trio of sea creatures away. Yet the beasts fought against the magic and strained to get to the *Sea Witch*.

And sailing toward the island was the HMS *Fearless*. Yet it wasn't alone. Accompanying the ship was another enormous kraken. It was just as Alys had told him in their dream.

Its guns boomed as it fired on the *Sea Witch*.

Ben's blood chilled as the chains burned into him.

Then the *Sea Witch* turned. As winds filled its sails, the ship headed out of the bay. Yet a jolly boat sped toward the island slightly obscured by a fog. Even through the haze, Alys's bright hair was visible in the back of the boat. Ben's already icy blood froze solid with terror.

A naval cutter was close behind, full of nearly three dozen armed marines. Oliver was with them, his cutlass already drawn.

The sleet in his veins turned to fire as he pulled on the manacles. Agony coursed up his arms as the bands of iron glowed hotly and seared his flesh. His markings spread from the pain. They climbed up his wrists and the back of his hands the more he yanked on the chain linking his manacles.

"What the bloody hell?" The seaman gaped at him. "Them tattoos weren't on you afore. Here now, stop that. Leave them manacles alone." The guard jabbed him again with his bayonet.

Maddened by fury and fear, Ben pulled harder on his manacles. He smelled his own flesh searing.

With a snap, the chain broke apart, freeing his hands. Ben reached down for the chain between the shackles. He pulled, uncaring that his hands were charred by the magic-imbued metal. The chain broke with a gratifying snap.

The guard stared, his eyes wide and his face chalky. Ben's hand snapped out through the bars to grab the sailor's neckcloth. He slammed the guard against the iron of the cage and the sailor collapsed.

Gritting his teeth, groaning, Ben struggled to force the bars apart. Finally, they bent wide enough for him to shove his body through the opening.

Ben stepped over the unconscious guard before ripping at the hole in the hull. Wood splintered and dug into his skin. At last, the opening was big enough.

He pulled himself through the hole and dove into the water. The brine against the wounds on his wrists and hands burned like hellfire. He had to reach Alys, and if it meant destroying his body to do so, then so be it.

CHAPTER THIRTY-FIVE

Alys and her crew dragged the boat just onto the sand and charged onto the beach. Dense forest lay fifty feet beyond the beach.

"What is it we are looking for?" Stasia asked. Eris flapped on her shoulder.

"No idea," Alys replied. "Little George wouldn't have us dance such a merry jig, only to drop whatever it is we're hunting right in our laps."

"Whatever we are after," Susannah said tightly, her gaze fixed behind Alys, "they want it as well."

A cutter boat loaded with fully armed marines sped toward them, with an officer riding at the rear of the boat. He'd already drawn his cutlass, and even from a distance, she could see his eyes glitter with eagerness for the fight to come.

Alys quickly counted over thirty marines in the cutter, plus half a dozen seamen rowing, outnumbering her own forces six to one.

At least the *Sea Witch* had sailed away to safety.

"Are you ready, my beauties?" she cried to her crew as she pulled her cutlass from its sheath. She summoned a fiery magical shield on her free arm.

"Ready," her crew shouted back. Each woman bared her teeth and took a wide stance as they prepared themselves for the fight of their lives. They drew their blades, shimmering with magic, and summoned shields, while Stasia, Susannah, and Thérèse raised glowing hands.

As the cutter neared, a line of marines raised their long guns, pointing them at Alys and her crew.

"A wall of stone, now!" she shouted to the other witches.

They threw up a gleaming barrier, sturdy as granite. At the same time, the marines fired.

The bullets pinged off the wall.

"Now, a wave," Alys cried.

She joined the witches as they shoved against the water. It formed a wave that knocked sideways into the cutter with enormous force. A handful of marines fell overboard and disappeared beneath the surface.

The cutter drew closer and a second group of marines shouldered their guns, preparing to fire.

"The wall of stone again," Alys bellowed. The spell sprang up, a moment before the marines discharged their weapons. Bullets slammed into the magical barrier. The wall shuddered from the force, glowing cracks forming in the barrier's surface. Seconds later, the wall collapsed in a hail of sparks.

The cutter landed. Seamen leapt out to drag the boat onto the sand, and marines quickly alit to form ordered lines upon the beach. Their commander shouted orders. More of the armed men aimed their long guns.

Stasia slapped the sand, and it rolled up in a wave. It formed a thick berm five feet high, rising between Alys's crew and the marines.

The armed men fired. Clouds of smoke billowed from the detonating gunpowder. The bullets whizzed, and then lodged in the ridge of sand.

The infantrymen wasted no time in affixing bayonets to their guns.

"Charge!" their commander shouted.

THE SEA WITCH 411

The marines attacked in regimented lines, coats bright red beneath the blue sky. The first line ran toward the berm, with over two dozen men behind them.

"I'll heat the guns!" Thérèse yelled.

She aimed her magic toward the rifles' metal fittings. The iron and brass began to smolder, dully at first, and then they glowed red.

Screaming, the first line of marines dropped their weapons. They fell back and shook out their hands as they tried to cool their singed skin.

A second line of armed men charged with their bayonet-topped rifles.

"Hit them with sand flies," Alys shouted to her witches.

She and the others called forth black clouds of tiny but countless insects. The bugs swarmed around the marines, hazing their vision and stinging their skin. Crying out, swearing, the infantrymen swatted at the sand flies and shoved their faces into the crooks of their arms to avoid the insects' assault.

Yet the third line of marines advanced. With them was the naval officer Alys had seen in the cutter. He gritted his teeth and ploughed ahead, leading the final group of marines. The first line of armed men picked up their now cooled weapons, and joined their comrades in a frontal attack.

Inés and Dayanna waited until some of the marines were close enough. Then the women fired their braces of pistols in quick succession. Three men fell. And still, more rushed at them. Dayanna and Inés drew their cutlasses and launched into counterattacks against the infantrymen's bayonets.

Susannah and Thérèse raised their cutlasses. The metal blades glowed with magical energy. Both witches rushed toward the marines. Teeth bared, they fought against the men.

Facing off against two marines, Alys traded strikes and used a magical shield to block their blows. They pushed her up the beach with their attacks. She kept them at bay, and yet she couldn't get in a direct hit, always busy combating one of the men or the other without pause.

She kicked at the sand, and muttered a spell under her breath. The sand transformed into fire ants that landed on the men's faces and arms. They howled as innumerable red insects mindlessly bit their flesh.

No sooner had they retreated than an officer, a burly man with a cruel smile, took their place.

"The Tanner bitch," he sneered. He lunged with his cutlass.

"Tanner *witch*," she corrected, blocking his attack. "A bitch as well."

He was even more trained than the marines, and it was all she could do to defend herself as his attacks rained relentlessly down on her.

"Alys, back!" Stasia shouted.

Alys leapt away as lightning shot from Stasia's fingers.

The bolt of electricity glanced off the officer. It shot into the fringe trees at the edge of the beach, singeing leaves that sent curls of smoke into the sky.

With a smirk, the officer reached beneath the neck of his shirt. He pulled out a tiny metal octagon, suspended on a leather cord. Markings were stamped onto the metallic piece.

"Warne set me up, nice and proper." The officer tucked the medallion back under this clothing.

"Hellfire," Alys growled.

He attacked again. Alys parried his strike, but he kept on coming.

There were just too many of the marines. And no matter how Alys tried, she simply could not get the better of the officer. A venomous gleam shone in his eyes as he fought. Nothing, it seemed, gave him greater pleasure than fighting her.

"Get. The fuck. Away. From her."

Both Alys and the officer whirled to face the water.

Ben strode from the sea.

THE SEA WITCH 413

Water cascaded down from his hair and his clothing, and the waves churned at his boots as he stalked from the surf. His markings glowed on his body, and his eyes glittered with rage. Manacles with broken chains hung from each of his wrists, while the fragments of shackles remained on his booted ankles.

Relief that he was alive poured through her, and she nearly stumbled from the force of it.

For a moment, everyone froze, staring at him.

Ben was unarmed, but the marines' commander collected himself. He rushed at him. Ben kicked the man in the chest. As the commander went flying, Ben snatched his cutlass from the air. He slashed at another advancing marine, and the man crumpled.

"Traitor," the officer beside Alys shouted.

"I'm sending you to hell, Oliver," Ben gritted. He shouldered a path through the marines, and strode over the berm, until he faced the naval officer.

Oliver lunged at Ben, who parried the blade strike with his cutlass.

"Captain!" Stasia cried to Alys. When Alys ran to her friend, Stasia said, "We need a bulwark made of sand. It is not something I can do alone."

They both placed their hands upon the sand. Alys concentrated, summoning the constructive force of a mound-building termite. She and Stasia forced magic into the sand, pushing it with their combined power.

The sand jolted up in a long embankment. It rose fifteen feet high, with the *Sea Witch* crew, Ben, and Oliver at the top. The infantrymen below tried to slog through a trench of wet sand at the base of the bulwark, yet their feet kept sticking in the thick sludge.

Ben rammed his fist into Oliver's chest. The naval officer toppled down the bulwark. He landed in a stunned heap at the bottom, mired in the wet sand.

"Go, both of you," Stasia shouted to Alys and Ben. She jerked her head toward the forest. "Find the kataraménos thing we have nearly died for."

"I won't leave you," Alys yelled back.

"We will hold them off," Stasia answered as she launched a gale of wind down the bulwark, pushing the marines back. Susannah and Thérèse summoned stinging beetles to cascade onto the men as Inés and Dayanna fired their pistols, pausing long enough to reload, and fire again.

"Go, now!" Stasia urged.

Alys and Ben didn't wait. They sped into the forest.

As they ran, they reached for each other, and clasped hands as they sprinted toward the prize they had been seeking for so long. The stars only knew what would happen if they failed to find it.

BEN AND ALYS were only a dozen strides into the forest before he stopped and pulled Alys into his arms.

"Thank God," he breathed. "Thank God."

"Thank the goddesses," she shakily corrected him.

"I don't care who's responsible. All that signifies is that you're safe."

They held each other tightly for a moment, and he didn't know who was trembling, him, Alys, or both of them. Yet the sounds of battle raged just beyond the tree line behind them.

He and Alys stepped apart, and kept pushing through the woods.

"I believed you were dead," she said, ducking under a liana. "I couldn't feel you."

"Warne, the *Jupiter*'s mage. He severed our connection after you and I dreamwalked. There wasn't a damned thing I could do to warn you, and it bloody killed me."

"I didn't think I'd see you again."

THE SEA WITCH

He paused, and she did, too, long enough for him to stroke his fingers along her face. "I'll *always* return to you. Nothing in the whole of this cursed world can keep me away from you."

She gripped his wrist, and he couldn't stop the hiss of pain.

"Those chains aren't decorative." She looked down at the angry charred flesh of his wrists and sucked in a breath.

She placed her hands on the manacles and, closing her eyes, whispered words. With a snap, the manacles fell away from his wrists. She did the same to the shackles, which had burned through the leather of his boots.

As she did this, Ben explained, "Some adornments they gave me when they threw me in the brig. Unlike yours, theirs were charged with magic."

"I'll flay them and make a coat from their skin."

As they kept charging through the forest, Ben explained, "The navy has no plans to stop with using the creatures merely against pirates. They'll make the beasts their weapons in a global war. No ship, no country, will be safe. Not until the entire world is crushed beneath Britain's bootheel."

"By the tides." She stopped in her tracks and scowled. "I don't know what we're seeking."

"The carving knife might lead us there," he suggested.

She placed her hand on the blade, which she'd tucked into her belt. "I don't feel anything. But perhaps my magic can lead us to it."

She closed her eyes, and her brow creased. A moment later, she opened her eyes, and growled in frustration.

"I tore off my enchanted chains," he said. "Bent iron bars, and ripped a hole in the *Jupiter*'s hull. My magic . . . it's getting stronger. Use it."

"Without the thing connecting us, I don't know if it's possible."

"We'll bind ourselves to each other once more."

Voice firm, she said, "Before, we were robbed of choice. It happened, whether we wanted it or not."

"Do *you* want it?" he pressed.

"I do," she answered at once.

His hand cupped her cheek and she leaned into his touch.

"And I choose this as well," he murmured. "I choose you. I'll do so over and over again."

Her eyes shone. "There aren't texts showing how to create a bond without dreamwalking. I can only go where my heart tells me."

"I'll go with you," he answered.

She nodded once, then closed her eyes. He remained mute as silent words formed on her lips. As she spoke noiselessly, the space encircling them dimmed. It was as though the sun set quickly, shading the area surrounding them, first into afternoon, then dusk, and then full darkness.

The darkness grew blacker and more profound than any night. No light could be seen. Nothing was visible. Impossible to know what was where, his sense of direction set askew in this all-embracing shadow. He couldn't even tell which way was up.

"Now," Alys said, her voice coming from everywhere and nowhere, "find me."

Ben immediately reached out into the space directly in front of him. That was where she'd been, not moments ago.

His hand encountered nothingness.

He took a tentative step forward, and another, his hands outstretched, and yet all he felt was emptiness. The boundaries of the corporal world were gone. This dark void she had created with her magic didn't adhere to natural laws. It existed out of time and place. Even the sounds of fighting had disappeared and a limitless silence encircled him.

"Where are you?"

There was no answer.

THE SEA WITCH

Using logic and his skills as a navigator weren't possible, not here. Not when it came to following the call of her soul to his.

Drawing in a deep breath, he settled himself. He recalled the moment he first saw her at the top of the stairs at the tavern in St. Gertrude. The flash of her hair, the weapons she wore, and the fierce determination blazing in her eyes. How he'd chased her as though following a comet blazing across the sky, leading him to Alys Tanner.

Slowly, he began to walk. He didn't think, didn't try to use rationality. This was about what his heart demanded.

His steps lengthened and grew more confident. He didn't fear running into anything, or falling into an abyss. He feared nothing, not with her burning invisibly, bathing him with unseen heat. Without her sun, his world was barren and colorless.

Nothing stood between them.

All at once, his arms wrapped around her. He buried his face in her hair and inhaled, catching the scent of sea and sweat and sweetness that was all Alys.

The threads of her unfurled inside him. She was there again. The faint gleam of her essence grew more vivid, rising higher within him. His spirit shone into hers. They illuminated all the darkest corners of each other, glimmering brighter and brighter.

She was everywhere in him, as he was in her.

The world filled with light again. The darkness disappeared. They were once again in the forest on the island.

She drew in a breath. "Welcome home, Sailing Master."

"Safe harbor, Captain."

It happened quickly, two vines twining together. They rested their foreheads against each other. More radiance swirled around them, filling his veins with magic.

"I sense it out there." Her eyes glittered with energy. "The fail-safe's in this forest."

They ran deeper into the woods. Thick-trunked trees with twisting roots made the going slow. As they attempted to hurry, the sounds of combat grew fainter, yet did not disappear. They could still hear the wind conjured by Stasia, and pops of gunfire.

They continued, with Alys leading them as she followed the call of magic.

She drew up short when they reached a gap in the trees and bracken. Standing in the middle of the clearing was an unadorned small stone hut. It had four walls and a pitched roof made of rushes, a single window, and only an open space for the doorway. Plants climbed up the rocky walls on thick woody vines. There was no smoke coming from the miniscule brick chimney.

"This is it," Alys whispered. "We'll find what we're searching for here. So our magic says."

Cautiously, Ben and Alys approached the hut, weapons drawn. Every snapped twig beneath his boot made Ben sharply glance around in case they'd alerted some sentry, mortal or otherwise, of their presence. Yet nothing moved. Not even a startled bird took to the sky.

He stepped through the doorway first. Alys peered around him as they both examined the interior of the cottage. The floor was bare dirt, and once, long ago, someone had placed leaves and soft grasses on a section of it to make up a rudimentary bed, and the remains of a very old fire stained the brick-lined hearth. A piece of metal was bolted to the back of the hearth. There was a single battered cooking pot and a dented mug.

The only other object in the hut was a strongbox. It was made of metal that had darkened with the passage of time, with leather strapping and a thick steel lock.

If the fail-safe was going to be anywhere, surely it rested within the strongbox.

He approached the metal box, then went down on one knee. Taking a breath, he attempted to open it.

"Locked," he announced. He used the butt of his cutlass to slam against the latch, but it remained fastened.

THE SEA WITCH   419

Alys made a swirling gesture with her hands. "I'll summon the cunning of a rat to open it."

Golden light surrounded her fingers before shooting toward the strongbox. But the light ricocheted off the lock. They both crouched as it flew toward them, and then out the window.

"Well, hell," Alys muttered. "Another safeguard against magic."

She pulled the golden carving knife from a pouch. Yet when she inserted its point into the lock, nothing happened.

He cursed. "It would be too fortuitous to suppose a key was nearby."

She kicked through the bedding and lifted up the cooking pot, before running her fingers in the spaces between the stones in the walls. For good measure, they both searched the hut from the roof to the floor.

"Nothing, of course." Alys's jaw clenched. "The longer we're on this quest, the more I'm both respecting and hating Little George."

"I never supposed him capable of such guile," Ben admitted.

She knelt in front of the strongbox and pulled two daggers from her boot. Both of the knives she inserted into the lock. Frowning in concentration, she worked the two thin blades carefully.

"Like the lock on the church in Domingo," he said. "One of the skills you acquired as a pirate?"

"Norham, actually." She continued to focus on picking the lock. "When I was a child, my parents used to punish me and Ellen by locking our poppets into a chest."

"And you freed the poppets."

She froze, and her eyes went wide. "Did you feel that?"

"Rumbling." He widened his stance. "An earthquake."

"Not uncommon in these parts. I'd heard what happened to Port Royal."

The shaking stopped, and Alys bent back to her task. But

then the ground shook with even more force. The stones in the hut rattled with the strength of it.

Ben grabbed Alys's hand and hauled her out of the hut. The last place they wanted to be in an earthquake was inside a stone cottage of dubious stability.

The shaking continued, the stones jolting with more force. Yet the ground beneath Ben and Alys's feet was stable and unmoving.

Ben said, "What—"

The air filled with the sounds of stone rasping against stone. The hut verged on collapsing. And then the whole cottage shifted and groaned and lurched upright, the stones rearranging themselves.

Into the form of a giant human.

It stood about twelve feet tall, with wide shoulders and massive hands, and its face was made up of the smaller stones and bricks that had once been part of the hut. Large round pebbles were its eyes, and when it opened its mouth, it revealed rough teeth made of stone shards, which it gnashed at Ben and Alys.

"Jesus God," Ben exclaimed.

Ben and Alys dove in opposite directions as the creature swiped with its huge stone hands. It made a rumble of anger when Ben and Alys barely managed to avoid its next strike.

Ben rolled to standing. He struck at the giant's forearm with his cutlass, but the metal only bounced off the stone. When Ben thrust at the stone creature's leg, sparks flew as his blade glanced away.

Alys hurled a fiery spell at the giant. This, too, was deflected by the creature's rocky body.

"Fuck," she snarled from the other side of the clearing. "Nothing works against this thing."

"It has a weakness," he called back. "Everything does. Look closely. There must be something we can use against it."

THE SEA WITCH

They circled around the giant, evading its swinging arms and blows from its gargantuan stone hands. If one of its palms connected with their skulls, the bones would be pulverized into dust.

Alys gave a yelp.

Ben rushed to her side, yet she wasn't hurt. She pointed to a piece of metal on the back of its neck.

"That was part of the hearth," she said. "And look."

"There's a slot in it."

"Just the right size to fit this." She pulled out the gilded carving knife again. "The key."

He nodded. "I'll provide distraction."

Ben took up a position in front of the stone creature. He grabbed a rock and threw it at the giant's chest. The beast lunged for him, and Ben danced away. Again and again, he did this, narrowly missing the giant's stone hand breaking his bones.

Alys eased up behind the colossus.

Ben shouted at the giant, waving his arms and throwing more rocks at the beast. At the same time, Alys took a running leap.

She landed midway up the giant's back. The creature tried to shake her off, but she clung to the stones that comprised its body, even as her own body whipped this way and that. Ben attempted to keep the giant distracted with more yells and thrown rocks, yet it was too busy attempting to fling her off.

Gritting her teeth, digging her hands and feet into the gaps between the stones, Alys climbed up the creature's back. Until she was at the back of its neck.

She raised the carving knife high. Then she plunged it into the metal slot.

All at once, the giant stood straight and stilled. Its arms hung at its sides. And then the stones in the center of its chest shifted and opened.

A vial filled with shimmering blue liquid fell out. Before it could hit the ground, Ben dove and caught it. He sprinted away, putting distance between himself and the creature.

Alys leapt from the giant just as the stones of its body broke apart. Rocks fell and tumbled in every direction.

There was nothing left of the creature, or the hut. The strongbox remained, and as Ben watched, the lid popped open.

Slowly, he and Alys approached the strongbox. They peered inside.

A scrap of paper lay within. Alys picked it up so they both could read it. On it was written, *The storm will set them free.*

The paper went up in flames, and she waited until it burnt into ashes before scattering them in the dirt.

Ben held up the vial. Its contents shone sparking blue light onto their faces.

"Here's our prize," she said.

CHAPTER THIRTY-SIX

Cautiously, Alys plucked the vial from Ben's hand. The slim glass tube was faintly cool in her palm, and had no adornments. The liquid shimmered with the immensity of its potential and was contained by a simple cork stopper.

"The storm will set them free," Ben murmured.

She stared at the vial as she tried to unlock its secrets. Even as she did so, the sounds of combat could still be heard as distant pops of gunfire and booms from magically created lightning. Whatever way they were supposed to use this potion, they had to think of something quickly, or else her crew wouldn't survive.

What could it be? What was the next step?

"A storm has to be summoned," she realized. "With that, we can distribute the potion. But," she added, "on my own, I haven't enough power to perform such magic."

"Mine isn't nearly as developed as yours," Ben said, "yet it's yours to command, however you need."

"We can grow your power," she answered, "but there isn't time for that now. I need Stasia and the others. Between all of us, we should have enough magic to conjure the storm we need."

She and Ben left the clearing, stepping over the scattered stones that had once been the hut and then the creature. Alys tucked the vial into the pouch on her belt. As they sped through the forest, the sounds of combat grew louder and closer, including the angry shouts of women fighting marines on the beach. A pistol fired, followed by a man's yell of pain.

She and Ben emerged onto the sandy bulwark. Two dozen marines attempted to climb the barricade, no longer adhering to formations. Stasia, Susannah, and Thérèse threw lightning and jets of flame to hold them back, while Inés and Dayanna slashed with their cutlasses whenever an infantryman managed to reach the top of the bulwark. Yet the men kept coming. It was a stalemate.

"Hellfire." Alys pointed at the bay.

Two cutters full of marines headed toward the beach. Armed, fresh for combat, their superior numbers would overwhelm her crew.

"Damnation," Ben added. "Strickland and Warne, the mage, are on one of those cutters. And the *Fearless* is going to drop anchor at any moment."

"Look." Alys directed Ben's attention now beyond the bay.

The leviathan had broken away from the *Jupiter*, and swam toward the shore. It might not be able to leave the sea, but it could stretch out from the water to devour the *Sea Witch*'s crew on the shore. The kraken swam in the direction the *Sea Witch* had sailed.

Alys pulled out the vial. They had to use the fail-safe immediately, or else she, Ben, and her crew would all die on this beach, and the *Sea Witch* would be destroyed.

Oliver caught sight of the glowing tube in her hand. He scowled and, grabbing a marine by the back of the neck, shouted something into the infantryman's ear. The two men clambered up the bulwark. A shot of lightning, fired by Thérèse, singed across the marine's jaw. He tumbled down the sand, clutching at his burned face.

Oliver breached the top of the sandy fortification. He ran toward Alys, jabbing a bayonet-topped musket at her.

THE SEA WITCH 425

Ben leapt forward and knocked Oliver's attack aside with the guard of his cutlass. The two men struggled for control of the musket until Ben finally snatched it from Oliver's grip. Spinning the weapon around, Ben stabbed through Oliver's arm, just above the officer's bicep.

Snarling, enraged, the officer kept pushing forward. His expression set in fury, Ben plowed his cutlass's bell-shaped guard into Oliver's face. Blood spewed and Oliver collapsed, out cold. With his boot, Ben kicked Oliver down the bulwark, where he lay in an unconscious heap. One of the marines dragged Oliver toward the beached naval cutter.

Alys ran to her crew, and Ben joined them. "I need everyone's magic to end this. Ben, Dayanna, Inés, keep their men back."

Stasia placed her hands on Ben and the two women's swords, recharging them with fresh, glowing energy. He and the crew members positioned themselves at the top of the bulwark. Their swords flashed as they fought back surges of marines. Dayanna cried out when one of the infantrymen slashed across her shin, yet she kept fighting.

"What we need, my beauties, is a storm." Alys looked at each of the witches in turn. "The biggest, fiercest tempest any of us have ever summoned."

"Take hold of each other's hands," Stasia instructed. "Invite the largest squall you can. Gather the clouds. Implore the rain. Bring them all to us."

Alys held Stasia's hand, and she took hold of Thérèse's, and so on, until everyone was linked. Closing her eyes was an act of faith, when so much chaos and uncertainty surrounded Alys, but there was no choice. She reached toward the magic flowing through her and all the other women.

Their strands wove together in a bright living thing. Twining from many threads into a powerful braid of many colors.

With that braid, she cast out into the sky. She called upon the countless storms that swirled over the Caribbean, all the squalls and tempests and gales scattered over the sea. The water within her own body resounded with the force of so many storms, gathering them.

Wind buffeted her. She opened her eyes. Thick dark clouds raced across the sky toward the island as the leviathan continued to swim toward the shore. The clouds were heavy, shadowed with the promise of rain. The sky turned the color of soot.

Alys pulled the vial from the pouch on her belt. She unstoppered the cork and held the vial aloft, all the while summoning the upward flight of a seabird. Under her breath, she murmured coaxing words.

The potion within the vial rose up in a spiral. It wheeled and dipped through the air as it went higher and higher, until it disappeared into the gathering storm clouds.

The winds howled. The clouds shifted. Their color changed, from dark gray to a shimmering blue.

A streak of lightning pierced the air, followed by a crack of thunder. And then it rained. A blue glittering rain that fell on the island, the ships in the bay, the waves, and the massive creatures in the bay, including the leviathan twisting through the waves toward them.

Rain drenched everyone, dripping from their hair, and gleaming on their skin. Water soaked into the bulwark, and the sand beneath their feet shifted. The fortification buckled.

Fighting to stay on her feet, Alys stared out into the cove, watching, waiting. Hoping.

She pointed toward the creatures. "Their eyes."

The change was clear. The creatures' slitted pupils widened. The krakens, the leviathan, and the massive shark all shook themselves as if waking from a dream. For a moment, the creatures seemed disoriented, swimming in circles. Suddenly, they broke away and made for open water. The shark thrashed, breaking its ropes, and also swam free.

THE SEA WITCH 427

As one of the krakens passed the second naval ship, it lashed out with a tentacle, shattering the mainmast. The ship lost its mobility and drifted sideways.

Swimming past the *Jupiter*, the leviathan tore the hull with its claws, scoring long deep holes in the planks. Men shouted in the distance and the flagship listed to one side.

And then the creatures were gone. The storms abated, quieting, but the water containing the potion floated out to sea in shimmering blue eddies. It would spread across the Caribbean and other oceans, other seas, setting free all the creatures that had been forced to fight someone else's battles.

Alys's heart lifted, and her crew let out jubilant sounds. Ben didn't smile, but there was relief in his eyes.

A moment later, the cutters carrying more armed marines, as well as the naval admiral and mage, landed fifty feet down the beach. Men disembarked in regimented order as they prepared to attack. The infantrymen from the first assault kept advancing.

The battle was far from over.

Under Alys's feet, the bulwark continued to shift and disintegrate. She turned to her witches. "Bring it down!"

She, Stasia, Thérèse, and Susannah stamped their feet into the sand. The bulwark shuddered. Then it collapsed on top of the first group of marines.

Regaining her balance, Alys turned toward the next wave of armed men. There had to be at least two dozen of them. Their postures were upright, their steps assured as they marched up the beach to Alys and her crew. None of them were bent by battle fatigue, as she and her crew were. Holding out against them, defeating them, wasn't possible.

Alys and her crew had used the fail-safe, but they wouldn't leave this beach alive.

A thunderous roar shook the skies as cannons bellowed. Streaks of blue and purple and green energy arced across the water. Magically charged cannon balls crashed into the new group of marines and exploded in a deafening boom. All that was left of the men was smoldering sand.

The *Sea Witch* sailed back into the bay. Smoke plumed from its cannons.

At the sight of their ship's return, Alys and her crew shouted in relieved welcome.

Witches gathered at the ship's gunwale. A golden glow collected around them, then shot across the water. As the magic sped over the sea, it pushed the water into a massive wave that headed toward the beach.

Thundering, the wave crashed over another group of marines. Men were carried out into the bay, leaving behind boots and dropped long guns.

The enemy's numbers thinned. Yet there was still close to a score of marines left on the beach.

Eyes blazing, hair flying around her head in a dark halo, Susannah lifted up, hovering five feet off the ground. Winds buoyed her as she flew over to Inés and Dayanna. More gusts of wind arose to surround the three women. Dayanna and Inés lifted high, joining Susannah. Using her hands to control the wind, Susannah guided them over the advancing men.

Inés's and Dayanna's cutlasses gleamed as they slashed down at the men. Terrified, the marines cowered or ran despite the bellowed commands of their officers.

Stasia threw jets of fire at the marines' powder horns. The gunpowder heated and exploded, and screams followed. As the men fell, Thérèse charged into the fray with her glowing cutlass whirling in a frenzy of attacks.

The admiral and mage strode toward Alys and Ben.

Ben went straight for Strickland. The two faced each other, circling briefly before launching into a clash of cutlass against cutlass. Contempt twisted the admiral's face, while Ben's eyes were cold with fury as he struck and parried skillfully. His jaw was set and hard.

Nearby, Alys hesitated. Should she go to help? Would she only be in the way?

The mage marched toward the action, pulling a small bottle from his pocket and raising it to his lips. Dragon's blood potion. If the mage drank it, his power would be nearly unstoppable. Alys's own magic already frayed around the edges. She needed balancing to restore her full ability, yet there wasn't time for that.

Alys sprinted toward the mage. She rammed her elbow into his hand. The bottle of dragon's blood flew through the air before spilling in the sand.

"Bitch," the mage snarled. He drew his cutlass.

"It's *witch*."

CHAPTER THIRTY-SEVEN

"Traitors deserve no trial," Strickland snarled as he charged at Ben.

"Betrayers deserve no mercy." Ben widened his stance as his former commanding officer attacked. Sword pointed at Ben's heart, Strickland sprang forward. The admiral's posture was perfect, his technique straight from the most respected fencing manual.

Ben parried Strickland's blow, knocking it to the side. He dove down, rolling across the sand in a way that wouldn't be found in any sword-fighting book.

Stunned by Ben's unsanctioned technique, Strickland drew up short. He shouted in pain as Ben's blade cut just above the admiral's knee. Blood darkened the fabric of his breeches with crimson. Hobbling, Strickland spun around.

Ben was on his feet when the admiral attacked again with a textbook combination. Ben parried, then slashed across Strickland's torso. There was a crunching sound as Ben struck hard enough to crack ribs.

Strickland stumbled back and looked down at himself, his expression disbelieving and twisted in pain. He gazed up at Ben, who strode toward Strickland.

A wall of fire sprang between them, its blistering heat forcing

THE SEA WITCH   431

them apart. The admiral's arrogant face sneered at Ben from the other side of the flames.

"Warne's protecting me," Strickland jeered. "What can your witch whore do for you?"

"She can fight," Ben answered, watching Alys bear down on Warne. "And kill your fucking mage."

"An ignorant witch is no match for an educated mage."

Ben drew himself up, his sword ready. "Underestimating women sends you straight to hell."

ALYS TRUDGED THROUGH the sand, toward the mage. He turned, just in time for her to kick him in the stomach. Retching, he bent over. Yet the wall of fire continued to blaze between Ben and Strickland.

She summoned a wave. The water crashed over the flames, and they sputtered out. With the fiery barrier gone, Ben moved in quick purposeful assaults as his commanding officer struggled to keep up. Yet Strickland managed to get one blow in, his sword stabbing into Ben's shoulder.

She cried out in pain as thousands of invisible thorns pierced her skin. Pinpricks of blood dotted her visible flesh, blossoming red beside her freckles. It was as though she was being flayed alive. The mage's hands formed complex shapes in the air, casting more spells.

Forcing herself upright, Alys slogged toward him. She faked an attack, and he moved to deflect. He spun in one direction and she lunged with her cutlass raised.

She brought her sword down.

The mage screamed as his severed right hand fell to the sand. Blood streamed from the wound in a red cascade.

The thorny pain stopped. Replaced by a vibration traveling up her sword arm. It surged, and a ferocious ringing sound stabbed through her head. She was almost blind with agony.

The ringing . . . it came from her cutlass. All along the blade, the mage's blood congealed into patterns and figures.

She dropped her sword. Yet the ringing continued, filling her head with white-hot misery.

The mage chuckled through his grimace of pain.

"Stupid witch . . . you haven't stopped it . . ." the mage gasped as he sank to his knees. "This is . . . but one battle . . . the war . . . the war is coming."

"What war?" Alys demanded, grabbing the mage's hair.

But the mage only smiled. "A war . . . you'll never win."

Still in agony, Alys threw the mage forward, and he sprawled in the sand.

"We've heard enough from you," she rasped.

Mustering her last scraps of magic, her hands clenched around all the air within the mage. She pulled it from his lungs, dragged it from his mouth, stole it from every corner of his body.

His eyes bulged and his mouth gaped wide. He clawed at his throat in a desperate attempt to breathe. Yet he couldn't. He writhed in the sand, making awful smothered sounds. Hand shaking, he reached for her. He thrashed, and then . . . stilled.

At once, the ringing in her head stopped. She gasped, released from agony.

Alys turned at the sound of steel against steel. Ben and Strickland battled their way up the beach. They fought on, despite their wounds.

She hadn't enough power left in her to take the air from the admiral's body. Her arm shook with exhaustion as she tried to pick up her sword. There was nothing she could do to help Ben. All she could do was watch. And hope.

BEN HAD HEARD Alys's cry of pain. The sound had torn him into bleeding shreds, more than the wound in his shoulder. At once, he'd spun to go to her aid, but Strickland had blocked his path. Limping, the admiral had struck with surprising

THE SEA WITCH   433

speed, and Ben had been forced back to parry Strickland's offense.

Now, Warne's twisted body lay in the sand. Alys stood near the mage's corpse, her skin covered with flecks of blood, her face drawn and weary as her wet hair hung in tangles around her, and she struggled to grab her cutlass. But she was alive.

Ben turned back to Strickland. The admiral had one hand pressed against his side, red dripping through his fingers, and he kept weight off his wounded leg. Yet Strickland's mouth twisted in disgust as he glared at Ben, the length of their swords between them.

"A failure," the admiral jeered. "That's what you were to him. What you are now. Disgraced in the navy, whoring yourself with that witch pirate. A disappointment to him, that's all you'll ever be."

Ben's jaw firmed. "His approval isn't necessary. Neither is yours. Killing you is for myself."

Strickland spat onto the sand. "When this is done, I'll personally take Tanner to London and light the torch on her bonfire."

Sword first, the admiral pounced.

Ben rammed his fist into Strickland's face before knocking the blade out of the stunned admiral's grip. The sword fell to the sand.

Strickland's eyes widened.

"I'm unarmed," Strickland said, desperation in his voice. "An honorable man wouldn't slay an unarmed man."

"*Honor.* That word doesn't belong in your mouth. You showed no honor murdering my father. I don't give a fuck about killing you."

Ben stabbed the tip of his cutlass straight into Strickland's heart.

The admiral looked down at the weapon plunged in his chest, then back up at Ben. He opened his mouth to speak. Nothing came out but a trickle of blood.

Ben pulled his blade from Strickland's heart.

Strickland sank to his knees. Ben knocked him over with the heel of his boot, and the admiral splayed in the sand, motionless. A wave washed over him. When the water ebbed, it was pink with Strickland's blood.

Shouts arose from the remaining marines, still fighting the witches. Seeing their admiral and mage lying dead on the beach, they fled for the cutters.

"Ben." Alys ran to him, wrapping one arm around his waist and he pulled her close.

They stared down at Strickland's body. It seemed much smaller now.

More bodies littered the beach, and marines and seamen piloted their cutters back to the broken naval ships listing in the bay.

Ben waited for a sense of relief, of victory. He stared up at the cloudy sky. "It's over. It's all over."

To his own ears, his voice sounded hollow, as if he was deep in a cave.

Alys cupped her hand against his jaw and angled his face toward her. He stared into the hazel of her eyes, all the greens and browns and golds. Smudges of exhaustion ringed beneath her eyes and she was filthy and bedraggled and beautiful.

"They've taken so much from you," she said gently. "Don't let them take your heart."

She lifted onto her toes and kissed him. The touch of her lips to his roused something within him, the pain and sorrow and fury and feeling awakening at once. He gasped into her mouth.

"There you are," she murmured. "Don't worry, Sailing Master. I've got you."

He held tightly to her as shudders wracked his body. And she held him. And there would always be pain, but that was all right, so long as he had her.

"Ben . . ." There was worry in Alys's voice.

THE SEA WITCH   435

"We've won the day, Flame," he said. "There's naught—"

"Look." She pointed toward Warne's severed hand.

It was moving.

The hand continued to twitch. Yet they weren't the last spasms of a dying creature. It formed complex shapes and forms in the air.

"It's finishing the spell Warne began," Alys said in alarm.

Alys ran and stabbed the hand with her cutlass, and it went still.

Then . . . screams went up. Three of the fleeing sailors dropped to the sand, curling in on themselves. They shook and shouted, and tore at their clothing. Their bodies twisted, their muscles stretching horribly. Markings appeared on their flesh. Markings that Ben knew all too well.

Torment tore through him. Something . . . something lived in the husk of his body. It pushed against the inside of his skin. The thing inside him fought to break free. He doubled over as his vision dimmed.

"BEN," ALYS SHOUTED. She moved toward him, but he pushed her back.

"Stay . . . away." His voice had changed, becoming raspier, deeper.

She gasped as his clothing tore. His shoulders grew impossibly wide. The breadth of his arms split the seams of his coat. His feet lengthened, as did his now black-clawed hands. His skin shivered and peeled. Gray blue scales emerged from beneath his flesh. His rangy form knotted into thick muscles. Piece by piece, his clothing fell away as he continued to change. Inch-long spikes emerged from the skin along his arms and down his back.

"Run," he grated.

But she couldn't. She stared as he rose up, stretching and lengthening to ten feet tall. His hair hung limply around a face that was and wasn't Ben. His mouth widened.

He tried to speak. But his teeth were now jagged and sharp. Gills erupted along his throat.

She gazed into his azure eyes, seeking *Ben*. For a moment, there was terror and awareness, and heartbreak. And then a gray film covered his eyes. Her connection to him was clouded by animal ferocity. *Ben* disappeared.

"My love," she whispered.

The creature in front of her stood still for a moment. They stared at each other. There was something familiar about it . . .

She could reach him, somehow. Use the threads that wove them together to—

Roaring, claws out, the creature dove for her.

Alys hit the sand as Stasia threw her down. She barely understood what was happening, only that her friend dragged her across the beach.

"Cease fighting me," Stasia growled.

Alys couldn't stop. "They did this to him."

"Him and the other sailors. No end to the Royal Navy's treachery. Cursing their own men."

"I have to get to Ben," Alys insisted. "Have to help."

"There is no help for him," Stasia answered grimly.

"But—" Alys grunted as Stasia threw her against the prow of the jolly boat.

The three other sailors who had transformed were also charging toward them. They were smaller than Ben, their skin a greenish color, but they had the same scales, the same claws.

Dimly, Alys was aware that the landing party was lifting her into the jolly boat as they hurried out into the water. Inés and Dayanna took up the oars, and Susannah and Thérèse cast a spell to speed them along the top of the waves.

Alys clambered to the stern, facing the island. Four monsters now dotted the beach, and the creature that had once been Ben was the largest of them all. He charged into the waves in pursuit.

Stasia muttered something under her breath.

THE SEA WITCH   437

Suddenly, Ben stopped, and he roared in what sounded like frustration. Seaweed wove up from the shallow water and wrapped itself up his legs.

"I am sorry, fili mou," Stasia said to Alys. "He is lost now."

"I saw this." Alys's words were hoarse. "The beach. The creature. The first time I dreamwalked with him. I saw this."

"It was fated."

The boat sped toward the waiting *Sea Witch*. The *Jupiter* listed, cutting a weak circle in the water. The *Fearless* could only limp with its broken sails. Both ships let them pass, each deeply damaged by the liberated sea creatures.

Alys pressed a hand to her aching chest. Her heart split apart. Hot tears gathered in her eyes and she blinked them back, yet a few ran down her cheeks and into the hollow of her throat. She reached for him along the threads that wove between them. All she felt was chaos and brutality.

He was in there, somewhere. He had to be.

Tearing through the seaweed that bound him, the thing that had been Ben tried to pursue, but the jolly boat was too far away. The creature grew smaller as the boat neared the *Sea Witch*.

"Fate?" Alys's gaze never left him. "Doesn't exist. There's only the fight."

★ ★ ★ ★ ★

ACKNOWLEDGMENTS

The Sea Witch has sailed on a long and, at times, arduous voyage. It would never have made it into your hands, dear reader, without the support and guidance of a whole pirate ship's crew of incredible people.

To my agent, Deidre Knight, thank you for supporting and championing my new direction, and for being in my corner. To my editor, Cat Clyne, thank you for being so excited about my ship of pirate witches, and helping bring them into the world.

To my husband, Zack, there are literally not enough words in the entirety of language that can express my gratitude for everything you have done to support me and *The Sea Witch*. You've been there from the very beginnings of this book, helping get it to market, plotting, choreographing fight sequences, wiping away my (copious) tears, celebrating my victories, reading *so many* iterations of this book and offering expert guidance. You truly are an IRL romance hero.

To Echo Molina, Jen DeLuca, Leah Findler, KB Alan, Joanna Shupe, Diana Quincy, Nicky Silber, Lauren Dane, Megan Hart, Adriana Herrera, and Dawn LeFever, thank you for encouraging me, listening when I struggled through this journey, and cheering me on.

To C. Morgan Kennedy, thank you for your thoughtful sensitivity read. You truly helped make the world of *The Sea Witch* a richer place.

To Franziska Stern, the artist who created the book's cover, and Elita Sidiropoulou, who provided the art direction, thank you for the cover of my dreams. You couldn't have been more perfect. And thank you to Ambur Hostyn, marketing manager for Canary Street Press/ Harlequin Trade Publishing, for helping to get readers eager for this book.

And to you, dear reader, thank you. This is a *difficult* timeline, and the fact that you've chosen to spend a few hours finding adventure and romance with me and my crew of pirate witches means so much to me. I hope that we can find a way to fight back, chase joy, and celebrate each other, together.